DO NOT REMOVE
CARDS FROM POCKET

ALSO BY CONALL RYAN

Black Gravity

HOUSE *of* CARDS

Conall Ryan

♥ ♣ ♠ ♦

HOUSE

of

CARDS

ALFRED A. KNOPF   NEW YORK   1989

THIS IS A BORZOI BOOK

PUBLISHED BY ALFRED A. KNOPF, INC.

Copyright © 1989 by Conall Ryan
All rights reserved under International and Pan-
American Copyright Conventions. Published in the
United States by Alfred A. Knopf, Inc., New York,
and simultaneously in Canada by Random House of
Canada Limited, Toronto. Distributed by Random
House, Inc., New York.

A portion of this work was originally
published in *Playboy.*

Library of Congress Cataloging-in-Publication Data
Ryan, Conall, [*date*]
House of cards / Conall Ryan. — 1st ed.
p.   cm.
ISBN 0-394-57214-9
I. Title.
PS3568.Y27H6   1989
813'.54—dc19   88-45819   CIP

Manufactured in the United States of America
First Edition

To

Lynda Truman Ryan,

with love

Acknowledgments

Enthusiasm starts a book. Endurance finishes it. I am extremely thankful for the guidance and encouragement I received from the following people while writing this book: Elisabeth Sifton, Anne Freedgood, Mary Ann Eckels, Jed Mattes, Robert C. Ryan, and, most of all, Lyn, who endures me still.

Contents

HOUSE *of* CARDS

1

Openers

Poker is a game for blood." Martin Oakes's face could look inspired and wrung out at the same time, or like nothing at all. He turned from the blackboard, shoulders shrugged forward, and stared at his pupils. There were seven of them, spaced evenly around the oval-shaped table, and his stare could make them all feel cold as nails. "Show nothing," he said. "A little swallow, too much blinking, the slightest curl of a smile or frown, and you're done." Their schoolbooks stood next to the door, pyramids of math and history and science, topped by *Scarne on Cards*, "the newest revised edition of the cardplayer's bible, by John Scarne, the world's foremost card authority." Martin Oakes never let them use the book in class. "The only things you bring to a poker table are your money, your brains, and your guts," he was fond of saying, and as things stood, he let them bring only two of those. "What is poker?" he asked.

"A game for blood," they said in unison. Carl Rice's voice cracked.

"I didn't hear you."

"A GAME FOR BLOOD!"

Martin Oakes scratched the stubble on his cheeks. He hadn't slept. Coming home agitated after a game in Concord with two stockbrokers, an architect, and a surgeon, he'd played Chopin Nocturnes, smoked cigarettes, watched the sun come up, and finally run a mile. It took Martin Oakes hours to work a poker game out of his system. The stockbrokers had known the odds, played sound poker, and drunk Scotch. Martin Oakes had waited. When the Scotch kicked in, they became undisciplined and careless. The architect couldn't resist spreading his hand on the table after a successful bluff. That cost him later. And if the surgeon operated on patients the way he played cards, Martin Oakes feared for their lives. He'd lost a night's sleep and won twelve hundred dollars.

In consequence of the effort, his head ached and now his students grated on him even more than usual. He circled the table, pausing to rearrange their hands, throwing chips into the pot when the bets were too low, pulling them out when the bets were too high.

At the end of a hand, wanting a cigarette but determined to set a good example, he said, "Mr. Vitagliano, who opened that hand, please?"

"Penny." James Vitagliano—or, as he preferred to be known, Jimmy V—still harbored bitterness over Martin Oakes's decision not to let him wear a visor to class. He shrugged his shoulders under his new shirt, an extra-large Hawaiian print, which covered his small frame like a sail waiting to be raised. Pure silk.

"So we can assume she held jacks or better," Martin Oakes said, shaking a cigarette loose from the pack and sliding it into the hollow of his palm. "How much did she bet?"

"Hold it. . . . Twenty?"

"Twenty-five. Whereupon Mr. Collins, who seems more intent on watching the birds than playing poker, folded. Mr. Simon, however, saw her bet and bumped her the limit, making it seventy-five to you. What were you holding?"

"Four spades. Ace, jack, ten, four."

"And the seven of hearts."

"Right."

"What did you do?"

"I called."

"You certainly did. Could you explain to me why you thought you had any business doing so?"

"Well, it's like you say, Mr. Oakes, you've got to pay to look."

It angered him when they took his remarks out of context. "If you're too blind to see how dim your own prospects are, seeing the other hands isn't going to help you."

"I had a hunch I was going to get that fifth spade."

"You drew the jack of diamonds."

"Bad hunch."

"I hope you don't think I'm picking on you, Mr. Vita-gliano."

"Oh, no." Jimmy V had broken his nose three times and dressed, according to his mother, like a pimp. She didn't understand fashion, was her problem.

"What is the rule?" Martin Oakes demanded. "Under what circumstances do you stay in with a four-card flush? Under what circumstances do you fold?"

"Well, the odds of drawing the fifth spade are five to one," Jimmy V offered lamely.

"Five-point-two to one, to be precise," Martin Oakes said. "Which means the pot must contain at least five times the cost of your card for you to stay in and draw."

Jimmy V calculated for a moment. "Only two hundred in the pot with Aaron's raise. Guess I made the wrong decision."

"You weren't even close," Martin Oakes agreed. He reached for his tea. Instead of drinking it, he held the cup beneath his nose and inhaled the thick camomile mist. "So you were in the pot for a hundred. Miss Gunn and Mr. Simon each drew two cards. What did that tell you about their hands? That is, if this premonition of yours left you any time to speculate about what they might be holding."

"I figured from only betting twenty-five, Penny had a pair with a kicker."

"Two queens and an ace," Penelope Gunn confirmed without taking her eyes from Aaron Simon. Knowing she had him beaten two hands earlier even though he kept calling and raising her, she'd wanted to say, *Aaron, you dope, I've got four eights and I'm wild about you.*

"Miss Gunn," Martin Oakes said, disappointed, "if you hold on to a kicker you must make a stiffer opening bet."

"I paired up the ace on the draw."

"I couldn't be happier for you." He turned back to Jimmy V. "What about Mr. Simon?"

"Maybe three of a kind," Jimmy V said. "But you know Aaron. He loves to pull a bluff."

"Three tens," Aaron Simon said. "Read 'em and weep, *paisan.*" He liked sitting across the table from Penelope Gunn, unattractive as she was. But those four eights still bothered him. He'd only seen three reflected in her thick glasses. He suspected it had something to do with the track lighting.

Martin Oakes decided to hell with it and lit his cigarette. "How many times do I have to tell you? There is no sixth sense. There are only five, and it is how you combine them that gives you the winning margin. That means your eyes are open, always. Your ears are tuned to all frequencies. Your nose is a magnet to every smell in the room. Taste —you must taste the pot. That is your food in the middle of the table. Develop an appetite for it. And last of all, feel. Feel nothing. Nothing but the texture of the cards and the grooves in the chips. Pick up your cards, bet, draw, bet again, play them or fold up, win or lose, but leave the hunches and premonitions to the other players. Concentrate on feeling what they're feeling and you'll know how to break them."

He cut a deck of cards with his left hand, strong and limber from playing the piano. He discouraged flamboyance as a rule, but the one-handed cut got their attention. The cards rose and fell in a single, even wave. He tried to ignore the sharp pain in his temples.

"There will be a Test today," he said.

A Test. An Exam meant everybody. A Test meant one. The students stared at their cards or stacked their chips, wondering which of them Martin Oakes planned to run out of class. SHOW NOTHING! a sign on the wall warned. Beside it, another: THINK! ACT! WIN! Testimonials from parents filled the cork announcement board, giving Martin Oakes credit for their children's better grades, cleaner rooms, improved personal hygiene, and newfound problem-solving ability. Poker lessons, one father wrote, had given his son the confidence to fix a decrepit lawn mower and build his dog a house with real shingles. "Thanks to you, Mr. Oakes," his letter concluded, "Keith is now simply a nicer person to be around." Some of the letters were from former students who had gone on to more significant accomplishments, among them a dancer who was now serving her apprenticeship with a ballet company and a boy who had put off entering college to start his own electronics business. Not every letter he had received spoke of success, but all credited Martin Oakes with instilling in his students a unique blend of purpose and tenacity. He didn't post the negative letters. Beneath a poster of Nadia Comeneci frozen on the balance beam, he had pasted the word CONCENTRATION. A fire burned in the potbellied stove, smoke curling up its metal stovepipe to the peak of the A-framed studio. Behind the piano, a sliding glass door led to a porch; the porch jutted into the woods. Birds fought over suet in the autumn twilight and swooped through the trees trailing chimney smoke.

A Test. Finn Collins and Jimmy V exchanged a bland look, each confident the other was about to be humiliated.

Carl Rice tossed his cards bottom down across the table to Brian Willoughby and said, "Here, Willow. No sense in me betting them up when you've already snuck a look at them."

"You can be beat, Carl," Brian Willoughby said. "Just because you win most of the time doesn't mean you can't lose." Brian Willoughby usually gave away good hands by forgetting to breathe. The effect of a full house on his face was immediate: already deep brown, it would turn the color of a roasted chestnut. Carl Rice had speculated aloud that four of a kind might kill him.

"Losing's got nothing to do with it," Carl Rice said. He hardly ever lost.

"Every time you lose, you say someone looked at your cards or held out an ace."

"There you go, Willow, heating up."

"I'm not heating up."

"It looks to me like you're heating up. It looks to me like your eyes are going to pop right out of your head."

"Just deal the cards," Brian said, smiling to control his anger.

"Enough," Martin Oakes commanded. "Put the cards away." The cards on the table were quickly collected and trimmed into two neat decks. The students counted their chips and entered the totals on a scorepad. Then they slotted the chips into a cracked mahogany box. Jimmy V managed to brush his fingers across the lid, but before he could run his thumbnail along the felt lining, Martin Oakes pulled the box off the table and snapped the lid shut. "Two minutes. No talking. No thinking. When something comes into your head, just let it slip away. Picture your mind as a house with all the doors and windows open, your thoughts as the wind that blows through the house. With all the doors and windows open, you can't keep the wind inside." Martin Oakes frequently kept the cards and chips out of their hands as a reminder that they weren't really worthy of them. Playing in pantomime improved their concentration. Breathing exercises lengthened their attention spans. "Slowly, slowly. Not in the chest. Pull each breath down as far as you can."

A Test.

"Relax," Martin Oakes said. Two minutes passed. He clapped three times and they opened their eyes, relaxed as a pen of rabbits who could smell grease spitting in the pan. "I assume you've memorized Scarne's rules," he said, drumming his fingers on the book. "What is the first, Mr. Simon?"

"When you have nothing, get out," Aaron Simon said, thinking, *Not me, Oakes, not me.*

"Mr. Collins. Rule two."

I didn't show anything, Finn thought. *I'm safe.*

"Mr. Collins, we're waiting."

"When you're beaten, get out."

"Please sit up in your chair, Finn. You're going to get curvature of the spine. Rule three, Miss Jaagstrom."

Erika Jaagstrom did her best to smile. "When you have the best hand, make them pay." *Choose me and I'm dead.*

They were the rules Martin Oakes lived by, three simple commandments delivered to John Scarne beneath the burning marquees of the Las Vegas Strip. He wrote them on the blackboard:

When you have nothing, get out.
When you're beaten, get out.
When you have the best hand, make them pay.

"It all boils down to discipline," Martin Oakes said. A TEST.

They remembered Billy Riordon after his Test, broken and sobbing. Aaron Simon, who went to the same school Billy went to, couldn't look at Billy when he passed him now in the halls. Billy carried a deck of cards backed with fifty-two different Playboy Bunnies and talked about only two things: how Martin Oakes was a fraud and how he, Billy Riordon, could beat anyone in the class in a square game of poker, ten dollars, winner take all. But no one would play him. "You shouldn't be carrying those cards, Billy," Aaron warned him.

"Billy Riordon carries what he wants." Billy had the annoying habit of talking about himself in the third person, as if he were a sportswriter describing the second coming of Babe Ruth.

"They don't let doctors practice medicine without a degree, right?" Aaron said. "They don't let lawyers inside the courtroom unless they know the law. You don't know poker, Billy. You should put those cards away before someone takes them away."

Aaron wouldn't have minded playing Billy, who by any measure was an atrocious poker player. But he feared word might get back to Martin Oakes. Students in the poker class were forbidden to gamble, and if caught doing so were subject to expulsion without a Test. Martin Oakes became particularly ill-humored when detractors—especially parents whose children had been turned down or put on the waiting list—questioned his policy, the gist of their complaints being that it was like teaching the student to shoot a gun and denying him bullets. "Your children can live with contradictions," he told them. "If you can't, sign them up for music lessons."

Many parents took his advice. But the contradiction didn't bother Aaron Simon. Mostly because Billy Riordon didn't have ten dollars to lose.

All agreed on one point: Martin Oakes tried to recruit the best. When a student didn't measure up and had to be tested, mercy was, naturally, out of the question. But Martin Oakes did not tolerate ridicule. "I choose extraordinary children—extraordinary by my standards, not their parents' —and I expect them to perform," he'd said the night before, to take the surgeon's mind off all the money he was losing. "My kids are workers. When there's a student who can no longer contribute to the class, they must kick him out. There's nothing vindictive about it. It's just something that has to be done."

The surgeon, who counted an elderly man's ruptured spleen and an eleven-year-old girl's tonsils among his less successful operations, tried to point out that results weren't everything. "I hope you give them a chance to learn from their mistakes."

"I give them as many chances as the others will let me." Martin Oakes regretted having once demonstrated the finger exercises he taught his students to the surgeon, whose hands had lost most of their suppleness and were unable to imitate the movements. The doctor had since taken to staring at Martin Oakes's hands with a surgical gleam in his eye for long periods of time during their games. "Once you've lost your dexterity, you can't win it back," Martin Oakes would say, performing a one-handed cut and thinking of the poker match between Smooth Jake Warner and the retired concert pianist Ivan Smid. Smid hadn't played a note in five years.

Martin Oakes was already well known in New England for his showdown with Smooth Jake when an article about his poker class appeared in the *Wall Street Journal* as part of a series on competition and American culture. The article caused a brief public furor, followed by a considerable and sustained increase in the number of applications to the class. Faced with formalizing his admissions procedures, Martin Oakes wished he had never let the reporter in the studio door. The outcome of the game with Smooth Jake was still unknown because neither participant would talk about it, and the mystery only made the story more appealing to the press. Ignoring Martin Oakes's objections, the reporter from the *Journal* eventually speculated that the game had ended in a draw, that Oakes and Smooth Jake had reached the agreed-upon time limit before either could wipe the other out. He neglected to add that he had been unable to persuade Martin Oakes to confirm or refute this suspicion:

Martin Oakes hovers above his young students during a simulated game, perpetually shuffling and reshuffling a spare deck of cards in his huge left hand. His right hand, meanwhile, grabs chips, rearranges cards, corrects posture, and—when a student succeeds in combining guile and enterprise to win a large pot—ruffles hair and administers pats on the back. In the midst of this nonstop, unpredictable pressure, his students appear calm, but the room vibrates with an almost audible hum.

Enrollment is small. Martin Oakes admits only seven students at a time. Of that number, he says, four or five will complete the entire course. Others will drop out along the way. Mr. Oakes will not say whether dropping out is voluntary or forced. Behind him, the buzz of young students reciting the odds of bettering pairs and four-card straights suggests that this is an environment where drones don't last and the unmotivated need not apply.

The beehive theory never worked on Martin Oakes's wife, Jennifer, however. "That class isn't a beehive," she said when he told her he was going to give another Test. "It's a shark tank. You saw what they did to Billy Riordon. Admit it, Martin. They enjoyed it when he broke down. They may have looked placid on the outside. They're good at that. But inside they were ripping him to pieces. Don't you ever worry about what you're teaching them?"

"It's important for them to come together when someone is being expelled," he said. He'd taken down the SMELL BLOOD poster when parents objected, but nonetheless he managed to communicate it as a principle. "I can always tell when it's time," he said. "Their eyes dance."

"Feeding time," she said. "They're vicious."

"It comes naturally to them."

"You say that as if it's a source of pride."

"Even viciousness can be channeled constructively." The victims selected themselves. That part was easy. But the others had to be controlled. Martin Oakes had never planned on giving the Tests, but experience had taught him it was either that or let the students administer their own tests. So he had established an orderly way of going about it. When one of them failed, the rest had to share the disappointment and responsibility for that student's failure.

His wife remained unconvinced. "Just want them to realize their full potential, is that it?"

"All I know is I can build on a kid's natural aggressiveness. But I can't restore an adult's lost nerve."

"That again. You know, they can sense your disdain for their parents. You're the only man I know who can yawn without opening his mouth. But this paralyzing cautiousness you're always accusing parents of is nothing of the sort. It's growing up. Just growing up. Does everyone have to be prepared to lose it all at any moment?" *It's easier to gamble when you don't have kids of your own,* she thought, but she couldn't bring herself to say it.

"Darling, we've already had this discussion."

"Why do you only call me darling when you're trying to avoid the issue?"

"I'm not trying to avoid the issue."

"Then tell me. What are you teaching them?"

"What's the point? You're just going to heat up."

"I'm already heated up. You never talk to me. Our phone rings every night at 3 a.m. and the caller never talks to me. What's going on around here? I live with a man who doesn't talk and a prank phone caller who as far as I can tell doesn't breathe. Or sleep, for that matter. But then, three o'clock in the morning is prime time for poker players, isn't it?"

"We can't be certain it's one of them."

"It's one of them."

They had got a call every night for two months and Jennifer Oakes was convinced only a trained poker player could go that long without saying anything. "From now on

—darling—you answer the phone. The two of you will get on splendidly not talking to each other." He always went right back to sleep after the phone calls, but it took her at least an hour. The ringing had become a sharp point on her loneliness. She no longer tried to answer the phone. The silent caller couldn't be captured. So she lay in bed and counted the rings, and when the line finally went dead she clutched her pillow and kneaded the blankets, treading water, afraid to let herself slip into the sleep that lurked beneath her in a vast night ocean so silent and barren she could barely imagine the day.

MARTIN OAKES had met Jennifer in a Saint-Emilion wine garden. He was with two other sailors, on leave from their ship anchored off Villefranche-sur-Mer. She was alone, sitting with her arms crossed in the southern corner of the garden. Behind her, ivy crawled up a thirty-foot stone wall worn smooth by centuries of rain. There were eight glasses on her table, each filled with pink champagne. A half-full bottle stood in the middle of them. Seven empty chairs ringed the table, which was big enough for only four. Martin Oakes watched her for twenty minutes. No one came to sit in the chairs or drink the champagne. After an interval, she drew a cigarette out of her purse and smoked it. He noticed that under the table her legs were crossed. They were very fine legs. She wore high-heeled sandals, and he could see red nail polish through her stockings. It matched her lipstick. Her face was calm and blank as the wall behind her. Around her, soldiers and tourists drank the local wine. It was a noisy place, but Martin Oakes, intent on this girl with the perfect poker face, thought he could almost hear the bubbles fizzing in the glasses on her table. He wondered where her friends had gone. It was possible she'd simply sat down for a rest, that the champagne drinkers were strangers. But the glasses were full, and Martin Oakes had never known that many people who could leave that much champagne untouched. It was an exciting moment. Fortified with several glasses of the house red, he finally approached her and without introducing himself recited Hugo's "Demain dès l'Aube" in faltering French.

When he finished, she said, "That's pretty good French for an enlisted man."

"Drafted," he said.

"But there's no war."

"There was one."

"And now?"

"Now I'm waiting."

"For another war?"

"For direction."

"Might be difficult, some officer always telling you what to do."

"The orders you get used to. The canned food, though —never."

"Canned food," she said, her voice indicating nothing either way.

"You're American?"

She nodded.

"From where?"

"We've lived all over."

"Don't like to give much away, do you?"

"I'm sure I don't know what you're talking about."

And their romance began. She married him without ever explaining the pink champagne or the missing revelers. They took their honeymoon in Lauterbrunnen, nestled in the Swiss Alps beneath the Jungfrau and dominated by a thousand-foot waterfall. She could hear the waterfall cascading down into the village as Martin Oakes opened the door to their train compartment, and remembered thinking as she stood looking up at it from the platform that it was as if he had opened the door to a whole new life, a life that would be cool and strong and constant.

They returned to Massachusetts and moved into a Belmont apartment that had once been the professional dancers' quarters for a ballroom. The apartment building sat on a hill overlooking Boston. The ballroom was still attached, but it had been turned into a basketball court. They stole down one night and waltzed in their socks around the parquet floor, bowing elaborately in the dark, pretending not to know each other.

Martin Oakes bought a mattress and slung it on the floor of their bedroom. Cardboard boxes served as their dresser drawers, clothes hampers, and filing cabinets. The other rooms were empty. Jennifer often stayed awake at night waiting for him to reveal the names of past girlfriends in his sleep. But he didn't talk. She watched closely for body movements. He didn't move. He got by on very little sleep and he didn't waste any of it recounting past adventures. Feeling a night current of uncertainty, she would lean over and wait for her hair to rock gently in front of his nose to confirm that he was breathing.

Months went by. He said he would get a job but he never got around to it. They spent the days drinking tea and smoking cigarettes and reading the newspapers and testing each other with pleasant deceptions. She grew used to hearing cards riffling on the various surfaces of the house, a waterfall of polished paper. Toward night, he would go out to find a game. Usually he came home with money, but people sometimes paid him off with products and services:

watches, china, furniture, silverware, box springs, home
appliances, wallpaper, plumbing, and paint. The items he
had acquired with pure skill left the unsettling but accurate
impression that the apartment had been decorated entirely
by chance.

For Jennifer, it was like living in a ghost town that all
the previous tenants had fled from, leaving behind their
most precious belongings. "Nothing goes together," she
would complain.

"It all makes sense to me," he would reply, seeing a
consistent pattern of victory in his surroundings.

During the days, he often studied the photographs she
kept bound with a hair ribbon on her nightstand. He was
particularly intrigued by a faded color snapshot dated 11-73
that showed her leaving a football game trailed by two boys
who appeared not to be getting along with each other. She
peered out from the photo without expression, challenging
him to place her location. Her unbuttoned, ankle-length
quilted coat had risen behind her like a cape in the autumn
breeze. "Where were you in this one?" he asked her one day
over lunch.

"At a football game," she said.

"I can see that." *Smooth. Oh, yes. She's almost perfect.*
"But where?"

"I'm not sure I remember."

"There must be something important that's made you
keep it all these years."

She glanced over his shoulder at the photograph. "I
was very fond of that coat."

"That's all?"

"All I can think of."

Behind her in the photo, the teams were still playing.
The scoreboard indicated that the game was only in the third
quarter. A sign in the stands said GO, 'JACKETS! He took the

photograph to his tiny study overlooking the parking lot. Using a magnifying glass, he connected the bottle of ginger ale she held in her hand to a soft-drink company that was now expanding nationwide but had incorporated in the Midwest.

He never asked her who the boys were, or what teams were playing. He wanted to solve the football photograph by himself. All of the clues were there. It took him only a week to piece them together. Mixed in with the piles of leaves, dotting the playing field, flying from the hands of exuberant spectators, so obvious that they had escaped his notice: hundreds, thousands of horse chestnuts. Buckeyes everywhere. The freckles of Ohio. All the more intriguing since to his knowledge she had never lived there. There was one other photo of her in the coat, leaning against the passenger door of a '70 Plymouth Satellite with a Michigan plate, her head partially blocking a sign that said LEDO—50. He checked the date—11-73—then found Toledo on the map and drew a fifty-mile radius around it. She was cunning. She was elusive. But he had her surrounded.

Meanwhile, she kept waiting for him to cry out from his slumber, aware that he now practiced his breathing exercises when he first climbed into bed in an effort to convince her he was asleep. "You were humming that difficult passage from the Bach again last night," she informed him one morning, without a hint of triumph in her voice. "You always seem to stop at the part where your hands get tangled up crossing over."

When she left the house to return a pile of books to the library, he stood at his study window to see which car she would choose, then went straight to the piano and practiced the passage until he could play it flawlessly.

By this point in their marriage, he had won five cars in poker games. All were used, and all were worth less than

the cash stake he'd granted his opponents in exchange for
them. But it was fun to drive away in his winnings. He
thought of the cars as giant metal chips. You were taking
more than a man's money when you drove away in his car.
You were taking his mobility. One month, Martin Oakes
paid the rent with a rusted-out Blazer just to make more
room in the driveway, but he and Jennifer still had key
chains worthy of security guards. Every time Jennifer went
out alone, she pulled the chain from her purse without
looking and drove the car that matched the random key
she'd selected. As long as he was looking for patterns, she
was determined not to establish any.

Having completed his analysis of the football photograph, he decided to announce his findings in bed. "Defiance, Ohio," he said casually, chin tucked under the covers,
eyes closed.

She put her book down. "So you've finally figured it
out."

He told her about the ginger ale, and the scoreboard,
and the decals on the football helmets, and the buckeyes,
and how he had drawn the radius around Toledo based on
the sign in the other picture, and how he had pulled the
noose tight to the southwest.

"You're right," she said. "I could have told you it was
Defiance."

He opened his eyes and sat up in bed. "But I thought
you said you didn't remember where the picture was taken."
This was no time to change the rules.

"I remember it now," she said, leaning against the
maple headboard he'd recently attached to the bed. "Jeff
Tingley is the boy on the left. I'm pretty sure he went on
to become a game warden or a vet or a taxidermist; anyway,
something to do with animals. The other boy is Aubrey

Botsford. He and I dated for three weeks, until he left me for the girl who was helping him cram for his engineering midterms. Want more?"

He couldn't understand why she wanted to ruin all of the fine work he had done. "Look at this," he said quickly, reaching into his pocket and pulling out a yellowed newspaper clipping. The headline, from a paper called the *Crescent News,* read: " 'JACKETS STING REDMEN WITH FIELD GOAL IN FINAL SECONDS, 31–30." "I thought after all this time you might want to know how the game turned out."

"Why did you go to all this trouble?" she asked, showing no interest in the clipping.

"It was no trouble."

She handed the clipping back to him. "You're making me wish I still had that coat." She opened her book again and peeked out over its spine. "By the way, the Torino needs an oil change."

"Why don't you just drive one of the other cars?" *She knows how much I hate bothering with these things.*

"Because the Torino's my favorite. An old man almost broadsided me today as I was pulling out of the library parking lot."

"You didn't tell me about that."

"I'm telling you now, aren't I? I hit the gas and just managed to avoid him. Thank God for eight-cylinder engines. It was a lucky thing I was in the Torino."

"Lucky?" he asked, fully mortified now.

"Yes, Martin," she said. "Don't you believe in luck?"

As his appearances at home became less frequent, she began to think of him as invisible, unaware that he often watched her from the gallery at the club while she swam laps in the pool beneath him. Her legs were still very fine.

◆   ◆   ◆

SHE WATCHED HIM now through the kitchen window that bordered the back porch and looked in on the poker studio's sliding glass door, hands absentmindedly doing the dishes in scalding water. Whistling softly, more air than notes, and wondering if her husband's next victim would take a Test as badly as Billy Riordon.

2

The Proposition

The twisted idea of teaching poker to kids had begun with a bet.

"That's it for me, Oakes," Ward Jenks had said, staring down at the card table. His cigar was half-lit and his disposable lighter was almost out of fuel. After shaking it several times, he finally managed to scrape a flame out of the lighter, but by that time the tip of his cigar had turned black and become unsmokable. A slim pile of ten-dollar bills stared up at him. No hundreds or fifties left. Not even a twenty. Just forty or fifty dollars in tens. Without counting it, he pushed his remaining money into the pot and winced when Martin Oakes matched the bet and spread his hand. Full boat. Tens over threes. Better than Jenks's three sevens. Sweating steadily, Jenks folded his cards shut along his brow. "What I mean is, that's it for me permanently. No more Martin Oakes Fund. From now on, I'm in a charitable mood I'll contribute to public television or celebrity golf.

Which is where I tell my wife it's going now." Jenks drew
salaries from three different state agencies, but spent most
of his days at the Kensington Country Club winning small
amounts of money from truant bankers and ex-Boston
Bruins. Lately, the phlebitis in his right leg had been acting
up again and he had taken to sitting in the clubhouse, poised
over a backgammon board, reading magazines and patiently
rattling dice in an empty water glass. Sooner or later, someone would wander in off the eighteenth green, order a beer,
hear the dice, and ask to roll a few games.

"Jenks is right," their host, Sam Kim, said. Kim, who
had tapped out his thousand-dollar stake several hands earlier, ate beef from a long fondue fork and sipped a daiquiri,
smiling to show Martin Oakes it was nothing personal.
"With what you've been taking off me every month," he
said, smile hardening, "I could be putting you through
college."

"Careful, Sam," Jenks said.

"Well," Kim answered, "it's conceivable that at some
point he might decide to go."

Martin Oakes sat quietly, features smooth as liquid,
looking at the four thousand dollars he had just won. An
oscillating fan sent ripples of air across his face as it swung
back and forth on a nearby table. "What is it you think I
still have to learn, Sam?" he asked mildly.

Sam Kim leaned forward. "Nothing, Martin. In your
case, I suppose poker's enough." The daiquiri had left a
trace of green along his upper lip. Behind him, the fondue
pot gurgled on its chopping-block base. The meat was arranged in semicircles on a large platter, the edge of each
piece slightly overlapping the next to mirror the fanned-
open decks of cards that lined the perimeter of the main
table. Next to the fondue pot, there was an ice chest with

beer and a pewter serving dish piled high with cookies. The cookies were stale and nobody was eating them. Scattered around the room were bowls of cold peanut noodles, raw shrimp, pickled cabbage, batter-fried chicken, rice crackers, shredded carrots, dumplings bound together with scallions, and a variety of dipping sauces. Sam Kim turned to the others. "What's the matter with you guys? This meat marinated for twelve hours." There were two more thousand-dollar losers: Gibbs, the mathematics professor who had searched in vain for months to find the algorithm that would solve Martin Oakes; and Valovcin, the college-wrestler-turned-trial-lawyer who in his more profitable moments would smile and wink at you and chuckle quietly, saying, "I live to litigate."

"You always lay out a nice spread, Sam," Valovcin said. "But you play a lousy hand of poker."

"It's my entertainment," Kim said, still looking at Martin Oakes, "not my living." Sam Kim had got rich by importing clothing from Korea. Recently, he had begun purchasing a variety of businesses around Boston, including a lumber store in Cambridge, a cookie factory in Somerville, and a two-screen cinema in Quincy. He paid the theater's projectionist a generous retainer so he could spend afternoons alone in one of the theaters watching movies. The movies were seldom memorable, but Sam Kim found that an empty theater was a good place to reflect on his success. Sam Kim had momentum. He could sit in the dark with his feet up and his eyes closed and a bucket of popcorn on his lap and still make money.

Martin Oakes shrugged. The prospect of ending another lucrative weekly game filled him with the wistfulness of an experienced fisherman who suspects he's pulled the last trout out of his favorite stream but can't resist the urge to cast into the empty waters one last time. "Apparently, I don't have an education and I don't have a real job. But I have your thousand, don't I, Sam?" As he spoke, he consolidated the bills in front of him. "Of course, dropping a little hard-earned money is no reason to let yourself get maudlin in front of everybody." There was a small knot of anger in his voice. He smiled to diffuse it.

"Don't flatter yourself," Sam Kim said. "For what that money means to me, we could be playing Monopoly."

"Then perhaps I could interest you in a somewhat larger wager," Martin Oakes said. "Give you the opportunity to win back your tuition money."

"What's the bet?" Sam Kim asked.

"We both put up five thousand dollars. A month from tonight, you play your son for an imaginary stake of the same amount. He beats you."

Sam Kim waved his glass dismissively. "You obviously don't know my son. If you did, you wouldn't risk it."

"Give me a month with him," Martin Oakes said. "Two afternoons a week. I teach him how to play poker. Then he teaches you."

"I wouldn't mind some of this action," Gibbs said. "I've got a couple of daughters. With five grand you'd still have trouble getting either of them out of bed before noon on a school day."

"The bet extends to all of you," Martin Oakes said, baiting the hook a little more. They all had teenaged children—all but him. "Five grand to play your kids. But first they spend a month with me."

"Only five thousand?" Sam Kim asked.

Martin Oakes considered for a moment. He'd cast and felt the line pull tight, but now he was momentarily uncertain of what he had caught. It didn't really matter if he had snapped at the bait of his own anger. There was nothing to do now but reel the line in, even if he found himself attached to the other end of it. "Name your figure," he said.

"Ten thousand," Sam Kim said, "for you." He stabbed another piece of meat and dunked it in the hot oil. "If I win, you work at my theater for a week. I'm sure you'd agree that ten thousand dollars is adequate compensation for a week's work."

"What will I be doing?"

"Ushering people to their seats. I have a nice red uniform you can wear."

Martin Oakes had no intention of ever wearing a uniform again. He wondered how Sam Kim could have such an accurate insight about an opponent's fear and still play poker so poorly. Maybe it was the daiquiris. Or maybe the game was just an elaborate form of Monopoly to him, not important enough to concentrate on. "I'm willing to raise the bet to ten," he said. "But it would take a lot more than that to get me to work for you."

"We can talk about that after the game," Sam Kim said, certain that he had finally outwitted Martin Oakes. Sam knew nothing about fishing. What was under the water could stay there as far as he was concerned. Sam Kim liked his problems visible. Once he found a weakness in someone, he worked on it with the careful precision of a boxer who has opened a cut over his opponent's eye.

"We can talk all you want," Martin Oakes said, "right after you pay me."

TOM KIM, a slender boy of fifteen with a high forehead and carelessly combed black hair, arrived at Martin Oakes's apartment for his first lesson an hour late. His shoulders already had grown to their adult width; it wasn't clear yet how the rest of him would fill out. They didn't introduce themselves. The boy hadn't wanted to come but his father had made him. Martin Oakes took him to the kitchen table, sat him down, and gave him a pencil and paper. "Write a one-line description of your father."

"This place looks like a museum," Tom said. Gold and silver music boxes competed for space on the kitchen counter. A carved wooden statue of a Scottish clansman in full battle cry stood in the corner near the hallway. The Oakeses had draped a cooking apron around the clansman's neck and covered his hands with oven gloves. "Where did all this stuff come from?"

"I won most of it. Start writing."

"You're kidding me, right?"

"No. I'm not kidding you."

Tom tapped the end of his pencil on the kitchen table for a full minute, doing his best to convey indifference, then wrote something down.

Martin Oakes read as far as "My father is a respected member of" and threw the piece of paper back at him. "Don't try to get him a job. Describe what he's like."

"Oh," Tom responded, "I get it," but it took him five more tries before Martin Oakes thought they had something they could work with:

> *My father has worked hard and he wants everyone to know it.*

"Okay," he said. "Tell me what that means."

"Well . . ." Tom began.

"Write it down," Martin Oakes said. Tom spent an hour expanding his theme into a paragraph. They argued over every word. Martin Oakes prepared some camomile tea and told the boy it would calm his stomach. Tom said his stomach felt just fine, it was his mind that was aching. After three complete rewrites, Martin Oakes dismissed him for the day.

Tom came back later that same week, this time arriving only half an hour late. Martin Oakes shook a cigarette loose from his pack and tossed it across the kitchen table. "Go ahead. Smoke it."

"I don't smoke."

"Your father does."

"So what?"

"So smoke it the way your father smokes."

"Why?"

"So I can see how observant you are."

"It's not his brand."

"That's a start." Martin Oakes pulled Tom over to the full-length kitchen mirror, above which the thousand-foot waterfall of Lauterbrunnen cascaded around Jennifer Oakes down to the borders of the 8½-by-11-inch photograph.

"What's that?" Tom asked.

"What does it look like?" Martin Oakes asked, averting his eyes from the mirror. In the beginning, right after receiving his discharge from the Navy, he had practiced for hours in front of a full-length mirror, smoothing out every feature, refining the movements of his hands until they were almost imperceptible, turning his clothes into different patterns of diversions. But he never looked at a mirror now. A mirror might bring back the details of himself that had taken so much time to blend, hide, and forget.

"A woman and a waterfall."

"See, you're a natural at this," Martin Oakes said. Jenny had walked into their room one day and found him standing in front of the mirror, shuffling, transfixed. The

cards felt like perfect extensions of his hands. He couldn't
stop to acknowledge her. It was difficult to tell if she was
really there. She waited by the door until she realized he
wasn't going to stop, then left without saying anything. An
hour later, as the other details of their bedroom began to
poke through the holes in his concentration, he realized
what he had done, and became frightened that in the course
of learning the secrets of his trade he would someday slip
out of sight without even leaving their room. He lit a match
and held it out to Tom. "Smoke."

"Your wife?"

"Yes. Forget her. Watch yourself in the mirror."

Tom took a shallow drag off the cigarette and exhaled
self-consciously. "She almost looks as if she's in the waterfall."

When Martin Oakes thought of Lauterbrunnen now,
before he saw anything he heard the waterfall. The whole
village, all the once-hidden magic of Jenny, was captured in
that steady, inexplicable rush of water.

Once he got started, Tom did a much better job of
imitating his father than Martin Oakes had expected him to:
ignoring the mirror, he sat down in a chair, patting an
imaginary paunch as if he had just consumed a satisfying
meal. Then he took a long draw on the cigarette, scowling
as he took the smoke in, coughing only slightly, letting his
eyes roll up under their lids for a moment before blowing
the smoke out in two thin plumes through his nose. Between
drags, he rolled the filter back and forth between his thumb
and middle finger, worrying fresh tobacco out of the wrapper, chin inclined to his chest in a posture of studied contem-
plation.

"Good performance," Martin Oakes said. "Your father
seems to work hard at smoking."

"My father works hard at everything."

"Sometimes the best thing to do with force is get out of its way," Martin Oakes said.

"Oh Christ," Tom said, "don't get Oriental on me." He had smelled something familiar when he arrived. The cigarette had erased the scent, but now that he was through smoking, he recognized it as the marinated beef his father prepared with such care for special occasions.

Martin Oakes was already on his way to the oven, swiping an insulated mitt from the clansman, then removing the pieces of beef from a cookie sheet with a spatula and putting them on a plate. He put the plate on the table in front of Tom and said, "Eat."

"I wouldn't figure you for a cook."

"I wouldn't either."

Tom looked at the meat. "No fondue fork?"

"In my experience, your father eats the first piece with a fork and all the others with his hands."

"Of course," Tom said. He picked up a piece of meat and stared with distaste at Martin Oakes's oven. "You probably dried it out."

"Try to make do."

Tom took a small bite and said, "This is almost like Dad's."

"That is Dad's," Martin Oakes said. "I brought it home with me the other night."

"In what?"

"The plastic bag your father gave me."

"Not bad. A little dry."

"Eat as your father eats."

Tom ate two pieces in silence, then pushed his plate away. "You know what this is like? This is like stealing a lock of hair from someone you don't like so you can paste it on a doll and stick pins in it." He stood up. "I don't have an appetite for that and"—nodding toward the meat—"I don't have an appetite for this."

"I didn't steal it. He gave it to me. And I've got nothing personal against him," Martin Oakes said. "To me, it's just a bet."

"You expect me to believe you'd go to all this trouble for a simple bet?"

"Ten thousand dollars is worth a little trouble."

"Well, it's a dumb bet to begin with, and you know it. Why should I win you ten grand when I can just lose and give your ten to him, make him happy?"

"I wouldn't be surprised if that's exactly what he expects you to do." Martin Oakes ate a piece of the meat. It was almost too dry to chew. "He warned me that you were unmotivated."

"My father sees everything simple. If you're not dying to become a business mogul, you're a lazy bum."

"Then if you lose the game, he'll probably just figure you for a loser. Go ahead and think you're giving my money to him as a gift. But he'll still think he's won it."

"My grandfather taught Okinawan karate. I asked my father if I could study it last year, and he went out of his mind. 'This is America,' he says. 'If you want to learn how to defend yourself, you are going to need a gun.' That is what passes for wisdom with him." Tom lifted his legs and crossed them on top of the kitchen table. The laces to his sneakers were untied. Martin Oakes stared at him without emotion. "He's ashamed that his father practiced a Japanese martial art. My father doesn't believe in empty hands. He thinks hands should be full of money, not calluses."

Without any warning, Martin Oakes swung with his open right hand and knocked Tom's feet off the table.

"You're probably not quick enough for karate," he said. "You ought to tie those laces. You're liable to trip over them."

"For my father," Tom said, without acknowledging what had just happened, "anything that doesn't make money is worthless."

"Well," Martin Oakes said, "here's your chance to make some money at his expense."

Tom laughed bitterly. "Sure. For you."

Martin Oakes took the plate off the table and scraped the meat into the trash can. "We've done enough for today," he said. "It's up to you. I don't deny that I would like the opportunity to teach your father a lesson. He has a rather simple view of me that I would like to correct. But it's still only a bet, and I've lost a lot of bets before. Unless you're as interested in teaching him a lesson as I am, don't bother coming Thursday."

Thursday came and went. So did Friday. On Saturday morning, Tom called Martin Oakes and said, "All right. I'll play. Just don't tell me it's nothing personal."

"Between your father and me?"

Tom shook his head on the other end of the line, and tapped his knuckles on the mahogany desktop in Sam Kim's private office. Though he wasn't aware of it, his mannerisms were remarkably like his father's. "Between all of us."

For his third lesson, Tom showed up in one of his father's business suits. To compensate for its bagginess, he had pinned two tucks in the jacket and gathered three of the pants' belt loops together at the back. When Martin Oakes opened the door, Tom smiled and said, "Excuse me, Mr. Oakes, but have you seen my son?" He was disappointed that after all the trouble he had gone to, Martin Oakes hadn't planned any pantomime. An unopened deck of play-

ing cards sat on the kitchen table. Jennifer Oakes's swimming cap dripped over the back of a chair. "What does your
wife think about your gambling?"

"I doubt she spends much time thinking about it at
all." That was a lie, but it beat telling the kid a long,
complicated story. Besides, he wasn't sure the story would
be any more true.

Tom nodded, carrying the suit well in the shoulders.
The possibility that Martin Oakes's wife disapproved of
poker made him feel as if he and Martin Oakes had more
in common. "Why don't you have any kids of your own?"

"My father was in the Navy. Every year, sometimes
every few months, we would move. I remember hating it.
But it taught me how to blend in. And then I joined the
Navy, too. By that time," he said, looking at Jennifer's
swimming cap, "I guess I had gotten more used to water
than land. It really didn't matter to me where I was living."

"Are you like your father?"

Looking at Tom pinned together in his business suit,
Martin Oakes couldn't suppress a laugh. "Well," he said,
rearranging his face into the bland mask he favored, "I
decided not to drag around any kids with me. And I wound
up hating the Navy. Maybe he hated it, too. He never told
me."

Jennifer Oakes came to retrieve her cap, entering the
kitchen with a fluidity Tom hadn't seen since his late grandfather demonstrated kata for him. She brushed a hand
across Martin Oakes's shoulders on her way to the refrigerator, then took out a carton of milk and poured herself a
glass. It reminded Tom of the photograph over the mirror.
Everything about her flowed, even when she was standing
still.

"This is Tom Kim," Martin Oakes said. "Mrs. Oakes."

"Jenny. Nice to meet you, Tom," she said.

Tom held out his hand. The cuff from his father's suit jacket extended almost to his knuckles.

She shook his hand without mentioning the suit. From her eyes, Tom couldn't tell if she had even noticed it. "I hope you win your game," she said. "Martin has great confidence in you." She squeezed her husband's shoulder and looked for signs of intelligence in the boy. "I wish I shared it."

"I wish I did, too," Tom said.

"Tom just might have some talent," Martin Oakes said.

"Does that mean I should continue to pack?" she asked, nodding toward the columns of boxes in the hallway.

"Well," Martin Oakes replied, "we have to leave here at the end of the month in any case, so I suppose you might as well." His face flashed brighter for an instant. She responded with half a smile, the substance of which seemed to be that she would continue to endure him even though he was hopeless.

Tom could see there was tension behind the affection they shared. "She doesn't like it at all, does she?" he said when she was gone.

"We just put a down payment on a house in Lexington," Martin Oakes said, uncomfortable that he had already revealed to Tom his fear of finally settling down. She hadn't made Martin Oakes coax the emotional card out of her. Told him flat out she wanted a house. That was fine. He'd get her a house. Might lose it later, but that's what she gets for marrying a gambler. By now it probably didn't surprise her that he was betting their immediate future on a fifteen-year-old kid in an oversized suit and sneakers. "We'll be moving in at the end of the month."

"It's not really fair, you know, making me responsible for whether you get to keep it," Tom said.

"It's not your responsibility."

"Like hell. Did you see the way she looked at me? My father's right. You're not nearly as smart as you think you are. This isn't just another bet. If you go to the track and bet on a loser, you can't blame the horse. But this is different. I'm not a horse. Who cares if you blame me or if I end up blaming myself?"

"We'll hang on to the house, if that's what you're worried about. This game isn't the only thing I've got going."

"Is playing poker really the only thing you do?"

"I wouldn't call it *playing.*"

"It must drive her crazy."

"It didn't used to."

Tom shook his head and started to open the deck of cards, but Martin Oakes took it from him. "Let's talk."

"Talk, talk," Tom complained. "He's not about to let me talk him out of ten thousand dollars."

"When you're playing your father, and he wins a few hands in a row, you'll feel a tremendous energy coming at you. I've felt this energy myself. Your father is accustomed to power. When he's winning, he can be very intimidating."

"You don't think I know my own father?"

"It's interesting," Martin Oakes said, "that you think you know each other so well. I suppose we'll find out. The one who understands the other better will win. Just remember that while you're on opposite sides of the table, you'll be opponents, not father and son. The discipline he can exert over you elsewhere should have no relevance at that table. That's why the first victory you must try to win is a victory over his personality. Wait for the moment when he begins to act like a father. Encourage his forcefulness. But when it comes, get out of its way. Force dissipates very quickly when it encounters no resistance."

"He doesn't scare me."

"Of course he does. But you can turn that to your advantage."

Tom couldn't shake the thought of Jennifer Oakes's speculative look at him as she had left the kitchen. "I don't have a chance," he said. "You've got a way to win. But either way, I lose."

"Listen carefully," Martin Oakes said, "and you won't be afraid of him anymore, whether or not you win."

"I've been listening for more than a week," Tom said impatiently, "and we haven't even opened a pack of cards. When are we going to start learning about poker?"

"We've started."

Martin Oakes didn't bother trying to drill complicated probabilities into Tom's mind. There wasn't nearly enough time for that. Instead, after he had taught him how to rank the hands, he concentrated on getting him to memorize Scarne's three rules. During the fourth class, he dealt two hundred simulated games. Tom had the natural inclination to keep playing his hands with the expectation that bad cards could only get better the longer he held on to them. Martin Oakes did everything he could to discourage this habit. "When you have nothing, get out right away. Don't wait. When you're beaten, admit it and fold."

"I don't understand," Tom said at the end of an hour, frustrated. "How can I win when I'm quitting all the time?"

"By holding on to your money instead of giving it away. It doesn't matter who wins the most hands. In my games with your father, he's won more hands just about every time. But he's never won any money from me."

"Yeah, well, your record's about to come to an end."

"You're doing fine. Don't give up. We'll get you there."

"When I come home now, he slaps me on the back and asks me if I want to play a few practice hands—make sure we give everybody a good show."

Martin Oakes had warned Tom not to play or even talk about poker with his father until the night of their game. "He's getting worried."

"No, he's not. He can hardly wait. They're all going to be there. Gibbs. Jenks. Valovcin. Maybe even some of his business associates. He's planning to make a real circus out of it."

"If you don't concentrate now, you won't be able to concentrate then. Let's work on your face."

"I can't win by staring at him."

"Staring at him without showing him anything is going to be a big part of it." Martin Oakes laughed at his student's uncertain frown. "I'm going to teach you a trick." Tom had had a miserable time trying to reshape his face into a mask. Almost every hand was new to him, and his expressions mirrored his cards so clearly that Martin Oakes could sit across the table and tell him what he held with astonishing accuracy. Martin Oakes dealt him a fresh hand and told him to pick up the cards but wait before fanning them out. "Okay," he said when Tom had the cards in front of his face. "You have four aces."

"Not even you can know that!" Tom said.

"Look at the cards slowly," Martin Oakes said.

Tom fanned them open. "King high," he said, shrugging.

"Close up your hand. And whatever you do, don't shrug. All right. Look at them again now. And remember. You have four aces."

"Still looks like a king high to me." Martin Oakes shook his head. Tom began to smile. "No. You're right. I have four aces."

"You are going to have four aces on every hand," Martin Oakes told him. "You are going to pick up your cards the same way, with only one card showing at first. That card will always be an ace. Until you can see that ace very clearly, don't look at the rest of your cards. When you see the ace, fan open the rest of your hand, one card at a time. The first four cards will always be aces. Concentrate on seeing the aces. What do you do when you see four aces?"

Tom smiled broadly.

"That's right. You smile. Because you can't believe how lucky you are. You can't believe you could draw four aces every time, but that's what you're doing. Before you even bet, you know how the game is going to turn out."

"What do I do when I go back to seeing the king high?"

"You fold, of course. Because any particular hand is unimportant. The important thing is that you know how the game is going to turn out."

"I'm going to win."

"That's the idea."

For the rest of the afternoon, Martin Oakes dealt and Tom practiced picking up his cards and looking at them. Whenever his motions deviated from the economical movements he had been taught, they started over. Visualizing the four aces had to start as soon the cards flew off the deck. By the end of the day, Tom had smiled so much his face hurt. When he asked if they could quit, Martin Oakes said, "Yes, in five more hands." On the third hand, when Tom picked up his cards, there really *was* an ace staring back at him. He squeezed the next card into view. Another ace. Then another. And another. He beamed across the table at Martin Oakes.

Martin Oakes looked at him and saw no difference in the way he had reacted to the other hands.

"I'm beginning to like this game," Tom said.

THEY HAD one more class to get ready. Tom complained that it wasn't nearly enough. He could rank the hands, apply Scarne's rules, and manipulate his cards as cleanly as a Marine performing a rifle drill. He had also learned how to read a magazine by looking only at the pictures. "Photographers are more honest than writers, as a general rule," Martin Oakes told him.

"Great," Tom would say, looking at an Afghan refugee without arms or a television evangelist with blow-dried hair and stretch pants. "So the world's a mess."

"Keep smiling."

"Let me know when you make up your mind whether you want me to see things or not see them."

"You'll have to make up your own mind about that."

With his eyes closed, Tom could now accurately identify any of a dozen different balls when Martin Oakes dropped them on the linoleum kitchen floor, sometimes even two at a time. It had taken him a while to separate the sounds of the racquet ball and the tennis ball, but once he did, he couldn't imagine how he had ever thought of them as alike. "If we just had a little more time," he said now, without confidence.

"I've been saving a few things for the end," Martin Oakes said. "Today I am going to be your father."

◆　◆　◆

"Do me a favor, will you, Tom, and turn off the smile," Sam Kim said. "It makes you look retarded." He was already down fifteen hundred dollars, but he was sure anyone would agree there wasn't much he could have done with the kind of cards he'd been getting.

Tom responded to his father's request by pushing two crisp orange five-hundred-dollar bills into the middle of the table. Monopoly money. Courtesy of Martin Oakes. "Thousand to you."

"I think you're bluffing me," Sam Kim said, raising the bet another five hundred. It infuriated him that his son had refused to talk to him during the game. No one was eating the food he had taken so much time to have prepared, either.

Tom matched the raise and said tonelessly, "Call."

"Eights and fours."

"Straight." Tom smiled across the table, eyes unblinking. He could hear the whir of the fan, feel the cool air sweep back and forth across his face. The uneaten food produced a confusion of scents, but his sharpened sense of smell placed each dish in its correct location. It still felt strange to him to be so thoroughly alert. Martin Oakes had been right. When Sam Kim had exceptional cards, he squeezed them so hard his knuckles turned almost white. But his hand had stayed slack during the last hand, even after the draw, so his son had decided that his straight was safe.

In a corner of the room, Valovcin, the wrestling lawyer, nearly choked on his beer. "My God," he whispered to Jenks, whose massive head floated in and out of view beneath a cloud of cigar smoke. "Oakes has turned the little bastard into a machine."

Jenks, who had laid a thousand-dollar side bet on Sam Kim with Martin Oakes, said, "Machines don't smile like that. It's still early. The kid'll break down."

In the course of the next hour, Sam Kim's luck
changed, but his paper fortune continued to diminish. He
dealt himself four threes, but Tom folded before he had
any chance to enjoy it. On the very next hand, Tom dealt
him a pat hand—three jacks and a pair of tens—stayed in
for two small bets, and folded again. In the ten hands they
played that hour, Sam Kim won eight of them and still lost
money. In the pivotal game, he held a flush, but with his
son betting the limit in every round, he wasn't sure it
would be enough. He stayed in anyway, letting Tom drag
him along.

On the other side of the table, Tom, who held four
fives, concentrated on his father's right hand and saw it
squeeze and slacken, squeeze and slacken; a good hand,
certainly, but not four of a kind. Every time it was his turn,
he bet the maximum without mercy, and marveled that as
his father's confidence decreased (toward the end, the
knuckles were no longer white), his willingness to see his
hand through strengthened. When Tom spread his winning
hand, his father looked across the table and saw a smaller,
even more ruthless version of himself, a hungry youth who
would never be satisfied with owning stores and watching
movies alone in the dark.

Gibbs, the mathematician, inclined his shaggy head
toward Jenks and muttered, "Your thousand's gone, Ward.
Look at him. His concentration's completely shot. The kid
has gotten inside his head."

By the time Tom took the last of his father's Monopoly
money, they had all accepted the fact that he would win.
What surprised them was the grace Tom demonstrated in
victory. There was no celebration. As soon as the game was
over, his smile disappeared, and his eyes stared down at the
table, as if he were ashamed to look at his opponent and
recognize him as his father again.

"Well, Martin," Sam Kim said finally, "I suppose I should congratulate you."

From a corner of the room, Martin Oakes inclined his head politely, but said nothing.

"You ought to congratulate your son first, Sam," Jenks said with a laugh, exhaling a column of smoke and holding his hand out to Tom.

"Please," Tom insisted, taking Jenks's hand but not shaking it. Jenks was surprised by the strength of his grip. "I get your point, but there's no reason to talk to him like that. Remember you're a guest here."

"He was a good student," Martin Oakes said to Sam Kim, looking around the room for his jacket. "You ought to ask him about your knuckles sometime." He ignored Tom, who frowned at the latter remark.

It was Tom who saw them all to the door, and wished them a pleasant evening, and thanked them for coming. Sam Kim still hadn't risen from the card table. When Jenks and Valovcin and Gibbs were gone, Martin Oakes turned at the door and said, "You made a few mistakes, but overall you played pretty well."

"Thank you, Mr. Oakes," Tom said, still frowning slightly and blocking Martin Oakes's view of his father. "I wish you had told me about his knuckles earlier. It would have saved us a lot of time."

"Probably not," Martin Oakes said.

"I almost told him about his habit before the game. I guess I thought it was unfair, somehow. But I couldn't tell him. I don't know why." He smiled. "Well, at least now I can make some money at school."

"That was hardly the point—" Martin Oakes began.

"Mr. Oakes," Tom interrupted, "can't you tell I'm kidding?"

Martin Oakes looked at him and was filled with doubt.

◆ ◆ ◆

SAM KIM called Martin Oakes's unlisted number in Lexington a month later. "He's changed."

"He's a lot like you," Martin Oakes said. "Maybe you just didn't recognize his potential. How did you get my number?"

"I've changed, too," Sam Kim said quietly. "This is difficult for me, Martin. But I'm afraid it's my duty to thank you." When Martin Oakes didn't respond, Sam Kim continued, "Have you ever heard it said that deep down, every gambler wants to lose?"

"Yes. I don't believe it."

"I can't imagine how you could. In your case, perhaps it's not true. You see, what I'm calling about—"

"Tom hasn't decided to become a gambler?"

"No. Tom has decided to study karate. And I have decided to let him. His instructor is Armenian. Runs a very strict dojo. But privately he has confided in me that Tom has superior potential." Sam Kim cleared his throat. "Anyway, that isn't the point."

"Are you all right, Sam?" Martin Oakes asked.

"Yes. I'm more than all right. I'm going to tell you this fast and hang up before I embarrass myself any further. Martin, you helped me win him back just when I was in danger of losing him."

"I think you're putting more into this than you should," Martin Oakes said.

"For Christ's sake, Oakes, I'm not talking about poker. I'm talking about honor."

"He already had that, Sam. He might even have inherited it."

"Yes, but it was you who brought it out in him. He

leapt forward in that month before our game. He became
. . . maybe not mature, but focused. He carries himself
differently now. But the main thing is, he listens. Do you
have any idea how much parents would be willing to pay you
to get their kids to listen? You wouldn't believe how much
better Tom's doing in school."

"Well, as long as we're admitting things to each
other," Martin Oakes said, realizing he almost never
thought about the ten thousand dollars he had won but still
remembered every one of the poker lessons, "I will say that
contrary to all my expectations, it was a pleasure to teach
him. Now tell me, who gave you my telephone number?"

"You know more than you think you do," Sam Kim
said. "You should consider teaching other kids."

"I don't think so."

"I'll put up the money. Kids need discipline."

"I'll leave it to their parents to provide it. Sam, in a
year or so Tom's going to take out your favorite car and
crack it up and come home after midnight with flimsy excuses and beer on his breath. I don't want you calling me
then."

"If he learns that sort of behavior, it won't be from you.
I'm hoping your lessons stick. I've said some disparaging
things about your way of life, Martin. I'm not naïve enough
to believe that I can take those things back. But my view-
point has changed, and I wanted you to know that I feel
indebted to you."

"Okay."

"Do you think you'll ever get a call from Smooth Jake
Warner?"

"I don't know. I know *he* has my number, because I
sent it to him. Maybe he'll retire first. He's been ducking
me, letting me sweat, but sooner or later I imagine he'll

decide he has to give me a game. I've beaten everyone else."

"What do you think you'll do after he beats you?"

Martin Oakes laughed. "Now that sounds like the old Sam Kim."

"I'll keep that usher's uniform cleaned and pressed."

"I'm afraid it wouldn't fit," Martin Oakes said.

"Oh, one other thing," Sam Kim said, with just a touch of pride in his voice. "My knuckles don't go white anymore. I've been killing Jenks and Valovcin. Maybe we can get a game of our own together again sometime."

"Did I ever tell you about your eyebrows?" Martin Oakes asked.

3

Scarface

Every class started the same way. The students arrived punctually at four, dropped their books, hung up their coats, found their place cards, sat down, and awaited the smell of camomile tea that preceded Martin Oakes's entrance at 4:05 through the French doors connecting the poker studio to the dining room. Martin Oakes didn't care which of the many towns around Boston they came from. It didn't matter whether they walked, hitched a ride with their insufferable parents, rode a bike, or took a broken-down bus. There were no excuses for being late. No excuses for spoiling his spectral entrance. His tea tray held a Jena glass pot and cup, a ceramic pot of honey with a wooden honey drizzler, a plate of biscuits, two sealed decks of Bicycle playing cards, two notebooks, and an antique mahogany box of poker chips, ingrained with coal dust and gun grease, that Martin Oakes called the Coffin, in deference to Wyoming at the turn of the century, "when the stakes were life and death." After putting a deck of cards and a notebook for class minutes on the table, Martin Oakes prepared himself a cup of tea, then opened the Coffin lid and gave each player the equivalent of five hundred points in chips. Scores for the previous week and cumulative scores for the year were posted next to the blackboard. After twelve weeks, the high cumulative score was $+23,550$, the low $-19,350$.

There was going to be a Test.

"Our deal is simple," Martin Oakes said. Students faced with the prospect of expulsion often seemed louder to him when they weren't saying anything. He could stop the game, but he couldn't quiet the hum. "You are here to learn," he said, fanning his colorless eyes across the room, letting them all feel the chill. "Being gifted isn't enough. You have to work at it. I can tolerate family problems and raging hormones. I can even put up with bad manners. But laziness and dishonesty is where I draw the line." They were doing their best to look indifferent. It almost made him laugh. He had seen it before. It was all part of the ritual of bringing them together before cutting one of them off. "Your parents are convinced I'm channeling your rebellion," he continued, "but we know better, don't we? Look at you. Same jeans. Same television shows. Same pimple-cream rock 'n' roll stations. Same soft drinks. I'll bet you can hardly wait to drive the same cars."

"That's not true," Penelope Gunn snapped. She could have used a drink. "My mother's the one who buys the designer jeans and disposable jogging gear. I get it from her all the time about not belonging. She says it's unhealthy I like Wagner. What's unhealthy about Wagner? Hitler liked him. Hitler liked beer, too. Does that mean everybody should stop drinking it? Who cares what other people think?" It certainly felt fine, however, sitting across the table from Aaron Simon and having him look her in the eye. "The only thing I belong to is this class."

"Not if it's your Test," Jimmy V said. *A tan,* he thought to himself, *is what I need. A tan would go well with the Hawaiian shirt.*

"Or yours," Brian Willoughby whispered, nudging him. Brian never had to count his chips. He could tell how many he had by simply weighing them in his hand. "Maybe he found out about the football cards."

Jimmy V sold football cards at school and split the proceeds with his older brother Salvatore, who drove a BMW and collected unemployment. After doing a little time, Salvatore had come out of prison looking even more fearsome than when he had gone in, but without the swagger. Calm, not bitter.

"I don't believe it," Jimmy V had said. "BMW. Lots of time, do what you want. And Carol Banetti. For God's sake, Sally, Carol Banetti! You've actually touched the Holy Grail!" Salvatore said nothing. According to his mother, his heavy-lidded eyes would lull you to sleep, you wouldn't even know what hit you. Jimmy V said, "You know something? You've gotten all quiet, Sally. Sometimes it scares me, how quiet you are, driving around in your quiet car no one knows where it came from. I just want to know one simple thing. How did you get your ugly hands on Carol Banetti?"

Salvatore had spent his sentence in a medium-security Boston Harbor prison, exercising, swapping criminal gossip, watching planes take off and land at Logan International Airport, placing bets on the greyhounds that ran at nearby Wonderland, and adjusting his nose to the honest gas of the waste-treatment facility that shared the prison's tree-bare, pockmarked island. It wasn't easy time, but there was a placid quality about it that hadn't escaped him. Carol

Banetti visited every Saturday. "What, Jimmy, you want to know how it works?"

"I know how it works, Sally, for Christ's sake. Remember the girl I told you about—Erika? I'm just asking, how do you do it?"

It was a question Jimmy V asked often. Salvatore always answered it the same way: "Just try not to be an asshole, Jimmy."

Jimmy V owned more clothes than the other six students combined. Not that many of them fit him. He stole without bias from laundromats throughout Greater Boston. He'd picked up the Hawaiian print in Kenmore Square on the way home from a Red Sox game. Big fat guy had his nose stuck in a *People* magazine, didn't see a thing. Jimmy V liked to size up his victims beforehand—save himself a trip to the Goodwill bin—but usually there wasn't time. "Salvatore," he said, "I just can't get over how little attention people pay to their clothes." Jimmy V counted among his collection an Air Force sweater from Lexington; L. L. Bean double-seated trail pants from Belmont; a medley of silk disco shirts from Newton; a wool knit jacket from Guatemala via Cambridge; T-shirts of every size, shape, and slogan; and enough jogging equipment (he liked to brag) "to become an official sponsor of the Boston Marathon."

Of course, he avoided the laundromats in his own neighborhood. "Wouldn't do, would it, Jimmy," Salvatore asked, "get caught strolling down Mass. Ave. in one of Father Domenic's new golf shirts?" Father Domenic was a gregarious priest who had a reputation for taking confessions during the spin cycle. "Doesn't dole out the Hail Marys or nothing," said Salvatore. "Just gives advice, you know, the kind of stuff you can use." Having heard that advice on more than one occasion, Jimmy V couldn't help marveling at how similar it was to Salvatore's outlook on life.

"Who's rebelling, Mr. Oakes?" Erika Jaagstrom asked, using the voice she'd cultivated especially for class. She smoothed back the loose strands of hair that had fallen in front of her ears. "It seems to me we're all pretty well under control here." Fingering the string of pearls her grandmother had given her, she looked at Penny and Jimmy V. "And we certainly aren't wearing the same clothes." Erika had a recurring dream about a casino. Martin Oakes was playing five-card stud. She wore a silver dress hugging curves her body hadn't developed yet. Her hand, nails painted a metallic-Corvette color, rested on his shoulder. A cigarette hung out of the corner of his mouth, giving off a thin ribbon of smoke but never burning down. When she removed her hand, he turned and said, "Not yet, darling. You're my good luck." What he liked about her in the dream was what she liked about herself. She was always under control.

The autumn wind howled outside the poker studio as the sun shrank farther down on the horizon. Martin Oakes cut the deck without saying a word. There was a fluidity and snugness in the way he manipulated the cards that made it difficult to tell where his hand left off and the cards began; rising and falling, his hand described the cards the way water describes a coastline. There was tension in the room. He enjoyed it. His students would have to learn to live with it.

"We're different, or we wouldn't be here," said Finn Collins. Slender, with tousled hair, Finn had already conceded his forehead to acne blemishes; they continued to march toward his chin. He looked at Erika for approval, but her eyes were fixed on Martin Oakes.

Like every boy in the class, Finn longed to kiss Erika's neck and twist his fingers in the thick braid of snow-blond hair that hung down to her waist. During Aaron Simon's party that summer, when all the girls met out at the garage for a cry, Finn had followed, hiding outside the garage door while the girls worked themselves from sniffles to steady weeping. It didn't take long. But after everyone else was cried out, consoled, and rejuvenated, Erika kept right on crying, the ache she'd opened up widening instead of closing, sobs turning to shrieks, shrieks giving way only to breathlessness. Some of the girls became frightened. Others hardened with embarrassment. Each had begun to wonder if crying together was such a great idea after all. "Thank *God!*" one whispered when Erika told them to leave her alone, she would be all right. Finn crept around to an open window as the girls filed past him in the darkness to the house. Stars winked in the hot night. Someone in the house put on "My Cherie Amour," a hit before any of them was born. Finn could hear Erika's tears splatting against an empty gas can in the garage and believed she was the most sublime creature the world had ever known.

The crisp autumn light cut through the poker studio and brought out the deep red in Erika's cheeks, making her seem to Finn as fragile and alluring as a leaf at the peak of its beauty. She would stay young as she grew old. Erika the cool red autumn leaf. Finn wondered how far she'd go to keep him from telling Martin Oakes she was an uncontrollable crier.

"Tell us who it is," Aaron Simon demanded. "Tell us who you're going to test." Aaron could feel the muscles in his stomach knotting, and had to concentrate to avoid tapping his feet. He looked around the room for something to break if his name was announced. Breaking something would help prepare him for the hell he would surely catch from his father if Martin Oakes ran him out of class. "Look at you," his father would say in his most miserable, do-I-deserve-this tone. "You're another Billy Riordon." Even now he liked to say, "Watch out, Aaron, or you'll become another Billy Riordon." Poor Billy. Since Martin Oakes had started his poker class, the failures had become as well known as the successes. When his eyes lit on the Coffin, Aaron imagined himself turning it upside down over the piano, the chips clattering on the keys and banging the piano wires. Every time Martin Oakes played a note from then on, the chips would buzz and spin in the piano's wooden belly, mocking him.

Carl Rice said, in his reedy little voice, "Can't you see, Aaron? He's just trying to get you to react." The son of two psychologists, Carl had taken up the violin at three, computer programming at eight, and downhill racing at nine. He was convinced his parents had plans for him, but he still wasn't sure what they were. When he was quiet, they brought up childhood: "Carl, your frustrated nonverbal phase was unusually long. Violin released the demons pent up inside of you." "I'm quiet," he always shot back. "Quiet is quiet." No use telling them they hadn't shut up long enough for him to get a word in edgewise. No use telling them the demons were still alive and well. When he was angry and ate, they chuckled in their nervous way: "Carl, there is some concern among us that food is becoming a dangerous transitional affection object for you." "Transition to what?" he complained. "Fat?" though nothing seemed to put meat on his bones. Carl had wispy yellow hair and brittle knees that clicked as he walked. He enjoyed seeing other poker players break down. He would prolong games, keeping his opponents barely solvent while he savored their last chips. Martin Oakes warned him it was a weakness. Carl didn't care. He was the finest player in the class.

A bird ricocheted off the sliding glass door, collected himself on the back porch for a moment, and flew off again. The spill failed to dislodge the large piece of suet he held in his beak. Something about Martin Oakes's house inspired tenacity. Carl Rice turned from watching the bird to look at Aaron Simon squirming in his chair across the table, and said, "Of course, in your case, Aaron, you have good reason to be worried."

"You miserable little slime," Aaron said.

Martin Oakes raised his hand for quiet. He looked them over, smiling tightly, letting the silence sink in. Hopeless. All of them hopeless. Sometimes he wondered why he bothered. Maybe he should just go back to taking Sam Kim's money.

"When I was stationed down in Panama," he said, putting his deck of cards gently on the table, "there was this Kentucky Fried Chicken place everyone went to on weekend leave, just like the ones in the States. Panama is a strange country. There are rich people and poor people. Nothing in between. It may sound odd to you, but the Kentucky Fried Chicken was considered a very fashionable place to be seen. So the rich people would go inside and eat, and the poor people would hang around outside and beg for scraps. Mostly women and children so thin you could see through them if they weren't so filthy. Now, the rich people and the soldiers had one thing in common, which is we didn't want the poor people grubbing up our nice clothes and uniforms. God knows, it's difficult enough keeping the Colonel's chicken grease and that lumpy gravy off while you're eating. So we had this trick. We'd put all our trash together in one big bag and throw it to them as we were leaving, figuring

by the time they foraged through all that paper and plastic
and found the Styrofoam container with the mashed
potatoes in it, we'd be long gone. The only problem was,
some of the young boys were smarter than we thought.
They'd follow us, knowing that one tug on the sleeve of our
dress whites was going to get them a coin or a fist, but willing
to take the chance. One night, this friend of mine had an
idea: why not get them to run a race? First prize would be
the largest bucket of chicken the Colonel sold. The way this
friend saw it, even these little boys had some dignity.
Wouldn't they appreciate a handout better if they felt they'd
earned it? So we took these boys—there were about ten of
them—across the street to the parking lot, and lined them
up, and my friend fired a real bullet to start the race, and
off they went, dirty and frail beyond anything you can imagine, most of them in bare feet, running like hell over the
broken glass and pitted pavement, their mothers screaming,
because by now everyone knows the prize is the Colonel's
largest bucket of chicken—my friend's already bought it
and it's sitting there with steam rising up through the cardboard lid—and in no time here they come, jostling elbows,
all bones and grimaces, black hair pasted back against their
foreheads, and then one breaks free of the pack—we called
him Scarface later because he had a long scar down his
cheek—legs churning, chin buried in his chest, pulling
away until it's obvious he's going to win. Well, my friend,
who's very pleased with this spectacle, is waiting at the
finish line with a poncho he's pulled off one of the women,
which he intends to use as a checkered flag. But Scarface
surprises him. As soon as he crosses the finish line, he
scoops up the bucket of chicken and simply keeps on running, bare feet raw as hamburger, keeps on running right
down the street into an alley, followed by the other boys and

their mothers and sisters, all of them meaning to have a taste of the Colonel's famous recipe."

Martin Oakes closed his eyes, smelling the chicken and sweat from that night in Panama. The world had been in sharper focus then. The students squinted at him. So? "Mr. Willoughby," he said, his voice coming to them from a southern hemisphere, "what is the moral of this story?"

"Doesn't sound like it has any moral."

"Think."

"I'm not sure hungry people really care about morals, Mr. Oakes," Brian Willoughby said.

Martin Oakes was about to ask Brian another question when Jimmy V interrupted: "What, your friend figure Scarface's going to hang around and express his gratitude or something, maybe eat with a knife and fork?"

"Mr. Vitagliano, you have the makings of an idea. Develop it."

"Well," Jimmy V said, looking around the room nervously, "I guess it's about rules. He thought they were going to play by his rules, but they didn't." Rules. Jimmy V smiled. Of course. Everything in this goddamn class is about rules. "You saying one of us is trying to pull a Scarface on you?"

"Whether you're playing a game or working at a job, you must always recognize the stakes," Martin Oakes said. "To recognize those stakes is to control them." It was sad in a way. Sad that one of them had to go. "None of you is unintelligent, or unwanted, or bad. One of you, however, has forgotten the main thing you're gambling for: the right to be in this class. I'm sure each of you can think of reasons why you should be singled out. Remember them, and correct them, even if you aren't tested today."

With that, Oakes announced the student's name.

Through the sliding glass door, across the back porch, he could see Jenny pinching leaves from a spider plant in the kitchen window, feel the rumble of the pipe in the basement as she turned on the faucet to water it. In a house big enough for six, they could never seem to lose sight of each other. The water coursing through the pipe beneath his feet reminded him of her remark about the shark tank. He could see the water silently rushing out of the faucet in the dusk-framed kitchen window, and he laughed inwardly at the thought of her trying to drain the poker studio. Take away their water and the dangerous little sharks couldn't swim or bite. Well (it appeared to him that she had drowned the plant), it was no use. He had no choice but to conduct a Test. He looked away from Jenny and said the student's name again, this time concentrating on the reactions of the others. Unable to suppress relief, they exhaled quietly so that for a moment the room itself sighed. Then they hardened to poker masks again, eyes dull beneath the track lights.

The accused student stood up and said carefully, so that everyone could hear, "I won't take it."

"Of course you will. Sit down," Martin Oakes said. The student sat down. Oakes felt the pulse in his temple. Checked his watch: five on the button. "Our subject today is deceit," he said. "Specifically, the deceptions perpetrated by one member of this class on the remaining six of you. It is my belief that deceit has no place in this class. But I will present the evidence to you and let you decide."

"I don't know what you're talking about," the accused student said, without meeting Martin Oakes's eyes.

"Oh, it's really very simple," Martin Oakes replied. "I'm saying you are a cheater."

4

Aaron

O f all the stacks of books by the studio door, Aaron Simon's stood tallest. He was an incessant reader. His stack included Will Durant's *Our Oriental Heritage* (where he got all his facts about samurai), Erika's math text (from which he intended to copy all the notes), the most recent issues of *Ellery Queen's Mystery Magazine, Newsweek,* and *Sports Illustrated,* and a six-month-old English essay for which he had received a D and a visit from the guidance counselor at his school in Lexington. "Aaron," the guidance counselor had said after he turned the paper in, "I think we might have a problem here."

I Want to Kill My Father
By Aaron Simon

First, you have to understand, he's already half dead. So I'd only be half killing him. He drives a silver and black Sleazemobile. The back seat is a couch. You could bring cattle to market in the front seat. Or in my father's case, a pig. One of the strange things about my father Stanley Simon is that he is fat as a pig but he never sweats. Never. I'm telling you, he is one of those people nothing bothers. That's because he never pays attention.

My mother likes to shop. My father likes to drive. But he refuses to drive my mother to shop because she goes to malls where they "play crinkle-fenders" in the parking lot. My father has a million sayings like "crinkle-fenders" and "strip-mine cinch" and "ocean excavating" and "rummage racket." My mother calls them Stanley Simonisms. Most Stanley Simonisms are designed to keep him from doing the two things he hates the most: getting up and moving. One day traffic was all snarled in front of us and I said, "Watch out, Dad, they're really playing crinkle-fenders up there." I could've killed myself.

Point is, anyone so much as scratches my father's car he probably just digs a hole and crawls in.

You want features? His boat's got power steering, power windows, power locks, power trunk, and power brakes. Also cruise control, an electric rear-window defogger, air-conditioning, AM/FM, a four-position adjustable-tilt steering wheel, four-speed windshield wipers, interior lights that stay on for one full minute after you get out of the car, and get this: a computerized voice that badgers you to buckle your seat belts and says things like "All monitored systems are functioning properly." Like my father doesn't do enough talking for one car, right?

The most annoying feature though, you ask me, is this little toggle switch that controls the driver's seat. When we drive to New York for the holidays I have to sit in the back and listen to Muzak—which he turns way down low so it annoys you gradually—while he sits there with the toggle switch moving his seat up, down, forward, back-ward, and tilted. The way it works is the longer we drive, the further he slumps down in his seat, until his belly's pushing up against the wheel. Then he tilts the wheel out of the way and jacks the seat up another notch. Up goes his belly, like a cake baking. Four and a half hours of that can ruin you. Take my word.

One thing my mother says to him the other day really gets me. "Stanley," she says, "you know comfort's every nuance." He just smiles. You know my father's smiling when the corners of his mouth disappear into his cheeks (another way to tell is he taps his toes). Then she goes off shopping in her Toyota and I make a crack about his favorite radio station which he doesn't like, something about it being the only music you can dance to in an open casket, adding some details which I think are pretty humorous, but would you believe he actually gets mad for a change, even though he really can't keep it going. Tells me I can damn well walk if I don't like the transportation. I don't really mind Muzak. I just don't think it's too realistic. I don't care what anybody says, five hundred violins and a chorus of Mormons is not what Lennon and McCartney had in mind when they wrote "Hey Jude."

The news on those stations is a joke, too. The guy'll say, "This afternoon, Israeli troops unleashed a savage rocket attack on renegade Druse militiamen in the Shufe Mountains above Beirut," but his tone of voice is "Relax, Stanley boy, Beirut's a world away, and we don't really give a wink about those people anyway, do we?" This is his station's slogan: "At home, at work, or in your car, relax with JIB, W-J-I-B." What's so important about relaxing?

Let me tell you about my father. I actually heard him say to my mother that he always keeps a five and five singles in his wallet in case his boss ever needs change for a ten. This is the man who gave me my genes!

Try to picture this man. He drives in the breakdown

lane on the highway, not just during rush hour, but any time the traffic's thick. So I ask him once don't cars ever break down and what are all those other drivers giving him nasty looks for and he says when you have a competitive nature and a tight schedule you can't be bothered by such things. Says it like Clint Eastwood in a corner out of bullets. Well in the first place, we're driving to see my aunt and uncle, who my father happens to hate. So you can forget the tight schedule part. And as far as competitive nature goes, the only thing I've ever seen him get competitive about is second helpings at the dinner table. Good luck to you, you think you're going to get the last latke when Stanley Simon's got his eyes on it.

Naturally, he parks in the handicapped spaces at the supermarket because they're convenient and nearly always unoccupied. Claims the ratio of parking spaces to actual cripples is way out of whack. The way it works, I guess he figures by the time he picks up his *Wild Turkey* and Rolaids and barges through a couple of checkout lines, the cops won't have had time to write him up. My father will only drive to the supermarket to buy food his doctor doesn't allow and booze my mother refuses to buy. Also Turtle Wax. He is very big on Turtle Wax. Forget my basketball games, even the one for the city championship. That car's got to shine.

My father's job is maybe the biggest laugh of them all. He's in Human Resources. Understand, now, my father Stanley Simon is a human who doesn't have any resources. So naturally, he works at it, right? What he does, he interviews candidates for positions with his company. He also plans picnics at Plymouth Rock and trips to the Symphony and employee incentive programs that his boss always shoots down. But his main job is recruiting. "Aaron," he tells me, "anyone's qualifications can be in order. I'm paid to judge character." Can you imagine?

Maybe it's drastic, me wanting him to disappear into his radio or drive his sled off a cliff. I've been thinking about it, and I realize I want to be a judge of character, too. Maybe it runs in the family or something. Thing is, the only one I want to pass sentence on is him. And I say guilty. Guilty, guilty, guilty! The truth is I really couldn't give a nod. But facts are facts. The man has got to go.

"Your teachers tell me this is only the most recent example of your negative attitude," said the guidance counselor, Mr. Spriggs. A fly hovered near the ashtray on the corner of the table. Mr. Spriggs flicked at it with Aaron's paper. He chain-smoked Gauloises, which made him popular with the ninth-grade girls, and wore a beret, which made the other teachers snicker.

"My father and I don't get along," Aaron said, staring at Mr. Spriggs's favorite print hanging on the opposite wall: two leggy women sipping pastis and sharing a wedge of cheese in a café on the Rue Mouffetard. The cheese looked as if it were turning to liquid under the sun.

"That's unfortunate, Aaron," Mr. Spriggs said, also looking at the print. For reasons he didn't fully understand, the print seemed to make people talk more freely. "However," he continued, waving the rolled-up paper again, "this hardly qualifies as an essay on hubris."

"Overbearing pride or presumption," said Aaron, who'd come prepared. "Right? Insolence. Arrogance. Sounds like Dad to me."

"Wouldn't you agree there's a little bit more to hubris than that?"

"You mean like thinking you can trick the gods?"

"Yes," Mr. Spriggs said. "Or become one."

"I don't know anyone wants to be a god these days,

except maybe Jimmy V, who's interested in fixing football games. The way I see hubris, Mr. Spriggs, what it comes down to is thinking you can get away with it."

"With what?"

"Whatever it is you shouldn't be doing. Like cheating on your taxes. Or riding in the breakdown lane. Or parking in the handicapped spots. My father's whole life is getting away with it."

"You've left out the most important part. People with hubris overreach themselves and get punished for it."

"You want me to call the IRS?"

Mr. Spriggs used his stub to light another cigarette. "It's easy to find fault in people, especially in those closest to us. I'm sure if you took a more objective look at your father, you'd see admirable qualities as well."

Aaron shook his head. "Ocean excavating."

"Excuse me?"

"It's one of his Stanley Simonisms."

"What does it mean?"

"It means if you're looking for his good qualities, you should get a shovel and a pail and go to the beach and start digging."

"In the sand?"

"The water." Aaron looked at the two women and the runny cheese and wondered what it sounded like to tell secrets in French. "You know, I just thought of something. Human Resources. That's more or less your line of work, too, isn't it, Mr. Spriggs? Except instead of hiring people, you just want them to get along?"

For all its disappointments and uncertainties, Mr. Spriggs loved his job. "You're right," he said. "I do believe it's important for people to get along. Which is why I'm going to call your father."

"No!"

"Don't you think he deserves to know that his life is in danger?"

"His doctor's already warned him. Come on. You know I'm not serious."

"I'm told you seldom are. I'm told that you neglect your studies even though you are capable of being an exemplary student, that you gamble, that you have been known to threaten other students with violence."

"I've quit fighting. I am officially retired."

"Not according to my information."

"Look, didn't you ever fight when you were in school?"

"No. I ran."

"Then I'll tell you how it works, help you do your job better. If you get in a fight and win, not much time goes by before someone else challenges you."

"So avoid the first fight."

"And get beat on? I'm sorry, Mr. Spriggs, someone whacks you, you either whack him back or smile through the tears. I mean, you forgive and forget, but first you rip his head off."

"I take it you like to fight."

"You don't always want to. Sometimes you just have to. The other kids make you."

"How is it, then, that you managed to retire?"

"There's no one left."

"Someone will come along."

Someone already had, but Aaron wasn't prepared to talk about it. "Yeah, I suppose you're right. Someone always does."

"Billy Riordon's about your size."

"Mr. Poker?" Aaron smiled. "Oh, no. Not old Billy. He doesn't like to mix it up at all. Says he's worried about hurting his hands. Of course what he's really worried about is someone hurting the rest of him." Billy looked old for his age, and he was starting to attract some of Mr. Spriggs's ninth-grade admirers away with his slicked-back hair and one-handed cut. Aaron was a little jealous of Billy's increasing popularity, but it amused him to think that Mr. Spriggs might also consider Billy a rival. "Look, Spriggs," he said, enjoying the guidance counselor's frown, "Billy trots up Mass. Ave. to some guy's house to play poker once a week and spends a lot of time bouncing tennis balls behind his back and posing in front of mirrors pretending he's a Secret Service agent." Aaron had seen Billy demonstrating his audio acuity to Erika Jaagstrom the previous week and had wondered aloud if Billy could tell the difference between golf and tennis balls while they were bouncing off his head; but Billy and Erika had both ignored him. "He's a joke."

"He seems to be pretty popular with the girls."

"So do you, Spriggs. And you've already admitted to being a runner."

"I want you to write another essay, Aaron," Mr. Spriggs said hurriedly. "Same topic. But pick another subject. Someone who's not just proud. Someone's who's overreached and been punished for it."

Aaron thought a moment, looking up at the women whispering their secrets in French. "I want to kill my father," the blonde said, licking a piece of cheese off her dark red fingernail. "Poison," the brunette suggested, taking a sip of pastis and hitching up her skirt to show a little more leg to the street. "Poison is the way to go. Slip a few capsules into his nightcap and he'll drown in the bath."

"Aaron?" Mr. Spriggs said.

"I think I know just the guy," Aaron said.

The next essay earned him a three-day suspension, and

brought him closer to Martin Oakes's poker studio, where, it was said, miracles in juvenile rehabilitation were being performed.

THE RAINBOW KING
By Aaron Simon

This story is about Cola, the greatest pisser I have ever known. Cola is what you might call a child prodigy. At this school, they teach us to adjust our bladders to the period bells. There is, we are told, a time to live and a time to die, a time to reap and a time to sow, a time for math and history and science, and a time to piss. You ask me, it's oppression. They figure if they can tell you when to piss, they can get away with anything. Each day after second period, Mr. Lyons marches us down to the bathroom double-file. He never comes in, but that figures. It is generally acknowledged that Mr. Lyons isn't human.

We make a sport out of pissing. We call it "doing rainbows." The idea is to back up from the urinal as far as possible and still be pissing in it.

Cola is the king. He is a little guy, under five feet easy, but what a pisser! Somewhere inside that Hobbit's frame lurks the water pressure of a hook-and-ladder truck. The bathroom tiles take a regular dousing from the rest of us, but never from Cola. His rainbows always find their pot of porcelain. And he isn't only good for distance. He can really make it last. One morning, he backs up all the way to the sinks on the opposite wall, a feat never before achieved. After that, he's famous. We call him Pissing Paul Bunyan because it seems like he can cross state lines with it. When our basketball team plays a school from across town, the first thing the other team wants to see after the game is our fourth-string guard take a leak. Teachers —most of whom are considered inhuman and therefore out of the running for live performances—speculate about

Cola's prowess during kickball games at recess. Janitors complain that pretenders to his throne are turning the boys' bathroom on the second floor into a small lake (which goes to show you don't have to have feet the size of Paul Bunyan's to create one).

Now, Cola doesn't confirm the rumor that he only pisses once a day, but he doesn't deny it, either. There are seven urinals side by side in the bathroom, and it isn't long before Cola is routinely performing "the Seven Gables." If you have your lunch money on you, Cola will offer to trapshoot an empty milk carton and let you throw it. But his greatest trick of all is "the Firing Squad," the only trick in which he doesn't back up from the urinals, but unzips at the sinks, waits until the pressure inside him builds up to an almost intolerable degree, then lets fly.

I've never seen him miss.

It all begins to go downhill the day Cola falls in love. Her name is Patty Lebow. First he sells her a bag of oregano for twenty dollars. Then he falls in love with her. Now he naturally wants to show her what he does best. The morning we smuggle her in, Cola confesses to me that he's drunk so much water it's a miracle he can still walk.

"Cola," I say, "this is risky, bringing in a girl. Anyway, do you think she'll really appreciate it?"

"Her hair," he says, all dreamy and blind with passion. "I love her hair," he says.

"Is that enough?" I ask him.

"Have you ever seen hair that thick?" he asks me.

"No," I say. It's true. Patty Lebow has piles of it.

"I could dive right into that hair," Cola says. "Like a cloud."

"Well, I'll tell you something, Cola," I tell him. "You know the reason her hair's so long and thick? Because she's got nothing but fertilizer for a brain. That's all her head does, is grow hair." I mean, do you know anyone

else who would buy a bag of oregano for twenty bucks? And swear she got high?

But he insists. *What can we do? We smuggle her in. Patty Lebow's hair is like a cloud. She walks, you think her feet are going to leave the ground.*

So there we are, about twenty of us, squished into the lav and it's quiet as death. Cola begins his performance with a Firing Squad and has so much left over that he decides to do a Seven Gables, too. He's on gable number three when the principal, old Mr. Fleming, barges in. You can't blame the rest of us for not spotting him. Cola has never done a Firing Squad and a Seven Gables at the same time before. It is quite a spectacle, enhanced by Patty Lebow, who is making a sound like a knock-off whistle.

We call Mr. Fleming "The Phlegm" because he has a way of clearing his throat when you are thumbed down to his office that makes you feel like you just bombed Pearl Harbor or something and are doomed to a life of infamy. When he sees Cola—well on his way to gable number four —his face looks like a cherry bomb approaching detonation. When Cola sees The Phlegm, his piss just dies on him. But he's too petrified to move. His whole body is frozen with fear. The piss jumps out of the bowl and recedes across the floor toward his pants. Patty Lebow begins to cry. Finally, Cola makes a try for the urinal, but The Phlegm is in his way. I will never forget the look on The Phlegm's face as Cola accidentally pisses all over his shiny black shoes.

"This is the saddest day of my life," Cola tells me later, and when all I can think of is The Phlegm's shoes and Patty Lebow raining tears and Mr. Lyons out in the corridor clapping thunder, I have to agree the situation is dark.

I hear Cola has to go all the time now. He raises his hand and leaves in the middle of class. Maybe he's prac-

ticing, trying to see if he's still got it. Maybe if he'd said to hell with The Phlegm and finished all seven gables, neat as can be like always, he'd be okay now. I don't know. Cola is very quiet and keeps to himself like those people who wind up murdering their families with an ax. I'm not saying he will do anything like that, but after seeing him be everybody's hero, and put his hands in Patty Lebow's hair, it kills me to see how he mopes around now. I suppose that's what happens when you grow up to be Pissing Paul Bunyan only to be chopped down by chance.

Time certainly does strip us of our dignity.

5

Erika

Erika Jaagstrom considered herself slighted for not having been born in time to ripen during the Beatles' era. Left alone in her house in Lexington, an odd Victorian bounded on three sides by a wide porch and topped by a cupola under constant attack by pigeons, she would play a tape of the Hollywood Bowl concert at earsplitting volume, shaking her head, raising her arms until her shoulders felt ready to dislocate, throwing herself down the bannister, sock-skating across the porch her mother kept slick as a bowling alley, twisting and shouting just like the girls she'd seen in the TV documentaries. She was dying to catch whatever they had, but somehow it always eluded her.

Erika's father, a software engineer, had designed one of the internal tracking systems for the MX missile. Despite pressure from his colleagues, he refused to call the missile Peacekeeper. "Let's face it, a bomb is a bomb," he had told Erika casually over lunch in the company cafeteria. At his invitation, she had taken the day off from school. A contingent of visiting Air Force officers sat at the next table. The company Jaagstrom worked for passed out illustrated lists of Air Force and Navy rankings, but he had never got around to committing them to memory. A sign on the cafeteria wall advised employees to APPROACH CORNERS CAREFULLY. BE SECURE. REPORT ALL UNAUTHORIZED CONVERSATIONS. The message was polite but pointed: in a need-to-know environment, snitching on someone could actually make you feel good. "We talk about strategic defense and peacekeeping and human ordnance," he told Erika, speaking loudly enough to be heard by the fly-boys huddled nearby. "And we pretend to be obsessed with all the abilities: vulnerability, survivability, maintainability, reliability. It's all a lot of sad smoke, though. What we are really talking about, Erika, is putting metal to the target. What we're really talking about is maximum bang for the buck. We should give the damn bomb a name that describes what happens *after* it goes off. Certainly not the kind of peace I'm interested in keeping —how about you?" He pulled the photo ID badge off his shirt and clipped it to her lunch tray.

"It's a nice picture of you," she said. "What does the green dot mean?"

"It means I get to read horrid documents that the yellow dots can only speculate about." Jaagstrom had built his little pieces of things over the years: mostly defense systems software, every now and then a diagnostic program specification or some software quality metrics tools. Only recently had it occurred to him that none of the pieces fit together. Everyone who knew him, from his wife to the Defense Investigative Agency man who periodically tapped his phone, agreed that this revelation had produced in him a rather shocking bluntness.

"My friends call you Dr. Bomb," Erika reported matter-of-factly.

"Why *Doctor?*"

"I don't know. I guess they think you're sort of taking care of it."

"Responsibility crept up on me," he replied, angry at the meaningless words he used every day, stirring the contents of his thermos carefully because he believed what they said about the ice cubes bruising the gin. "I don't want it to sneak up on you."

"Do you remember the Beatles?" she asked him.

"You've got to be careful, Erika," he said. She wasn't sure whether or not he'd heard her question. He seemed preoccupied with the Air Force officers. "They can turn you into something you don't want to be."

Erika danced on into winter, the season with which she shared a solemn affinity. It was a dull, hard edition that year, short on snow but bitterly cold. Then came the news that her grandmother had gone into the hospital for another operation. By now, it was difficult to say what was holding the old girl together.

"She's a tough old crone," Erika's father said.

"That's no way to talk about your mother," said his wife.

"You watch," he said, voice edged with admiration, "she'll beat this one, too. She's so full of vinegar and preservatives nothing can kill her."

He was braced for his wife's next question. He'd been meaning to ask it himself for two years. But he couldn't. She had to. Even Erika understood that. "Isn't it time your mother moved in with us?" she asked. Later that same night, she came into Erika's room to confirm the arrangement. "Grandma is coming here to rest."

But Erika knew that wasn't true; she was coming to die. "Please don't bring her here."

"We have to do what we can, Erika honey. We're responsible for each other."

Erika, who returned from school to an empty house every day, said bitterly, "You can't even leave me alone."

"I'm taking some time off from work," her mother said, "so I can look after her. But I'd appreciate your help."

My house, Erika thought. *It's my house.*

It frightened them all when she arrived, pale, fifty pounds lighter than they'd ever seen her, the breathing in her chest hollow as a rattle. They took her to her room on the third floor. Erika didn't see her for six days. Her food went up on a tray. Her coughs floated down the back stairs. They bought her an AM radio so she could listen to the talk shows. Erika's mother cleaned the family silver for the first time in years. No corner of the Jaagstroms' old Victorian house went unvacuumed. The floor glistened brighter than ever with polish. The dog got brushed. Erika's father fixed the cupola windows, damaged by a branch torn off during a spring storm. The pigeons hovered in the tree the branch had come from, looking for another way in.

Believing her grandmother deaf, trying to believe she wasn't there at all, Erika still played her Beatles records after school, though perhaps not quite so loudly. Despite all her mother's cleaning, there was a different smell in the house now, like a heavy black coat taken from a footlocker. It hung about her grandmother when, on the seventh day, Erika finally bumped into her on the back stairs.

"Those Beatles," she said, fixing Erika with a stare. "They were really something." She was wearing a corduroy bathrobe. Her coarse gray hair was pinned back in a bun.

Her feet, bare on top of a pair of her son's flip-flop sandals, looked gray blue.

"Where are you going?" Erika asked.

"Get a cookie. You mind?"

"No. Why should I mind?"

"You're right," she said, and started down the last flight of stairs, clutching the bannister, "why should you?"

Erika wondered if she should reach out and take her elbow. The smell was cancer, eating away her grandmother from the inside out. The old girl was diabetic and half-blind and brittle as a breadstick, but not, it turned out, so deaf as all that. "Want some help?" Erika offered.

Her grandmother turned, frowning slightly. "You mean, getting a cookie? That I think I can manage, thank you."

"This kid I know, Carl Rice, he calls them oral gratifiers."

"Sounds like a fun kid."

The next day, Erika put five cookies on a plate and took them upstairs to her grandmother with a glass of milk. An hour later, she could hear the slap of flip-flops and raspy breathing on the back stairs. Before she could ask, her grandmother said, "Got to wash the plate."

"I'll wash it."

"I need the exercise. Never know when Larry Bird will pull up with an injury."

"Grandma!"

"You're right. Bird's pretty durable. Maybe I'll have a whiskey."

"Can I have one, too?"

"Depends. What's your excuse?"

"Never had one."

"Best not to start. You wish I weren't here, don't you?"

"Don't say that."

"Well, don't think I like being here."

Visitors came, and Erika's mother fussed over the footprints they left in the hall. After a few days, the footprints disappeared, the flowers wilted, the telephone calls from well-wishers dwindled, and the waiting began in earnest. Waiting on the brittle old girl who wouldn't use her cane and always seemed to be looking for a cookie or a book or the blessed radio listings—any excuse to stay out of bed. Waiting for her to die. Finding her slumped on the living-room couch, momentarily breathless, Erika said, "Why don't you ever ask me for anything?"

"I can't think of anything in particular I need."

"Something to eat. Something to drink. A sweater."

"Oh, I've given all that up. I've been thinking it might be nice to have a new body, but you know what? I'd probably just sit in the sun until that one shriveled up, too, probably just eat until my ankles got all fat and swollen. No, I don't imagine a new body'd be of much use, either. I've grown accustomed to being ill." She ruffled the neatly arranged fan of magazines on the glass tea table. "Your mother seems to have an unusual penchant for cleaning."

"I'm afraid to touch anything."

"You should come up and visit me sometime. She seems to run out of gas when she hits the third floor. Still does the vacuuming and dusting. Can't get the floors polished to a blind, though. And my room is a mess. She walked in last night, took a look at my dirty socks and the pretzels on the radio stand—I think it about killed her. But she didn't say anything. I don't mind cleanliness, but does she have to be polite, too?" She pulled herself up into a sitting position. "Another window fell out of the cupola."

"I know. Dad says it's a sign. Mom says he just forgot

to dust the frames before he slapped in the putty. They quarrel a lot, lately."

"It's me."

"Wasn't you, it'd be something else."

"Erika, dear, I want to tell you something. Only the very old and the very young know what they're doing." Leaning forward now, half smiling: "The rest of us just muddle along." She patted Erika's knee, her mottled hand shaking slightly. "Don't tell your mother, but I like hearing those pigeons coo and flap around up there."

Erika couldn't understand why free birds, even dirty birds like pigeons, would make such a concerted effort to be cooped up. "Grandma, are we making you comfortable?" Erika was the first to ask that question and her grandmother didn't know how to answer it. "I mean, if you need anything, I wish you'd ask me."

"Your father keeps bringing me things. First flowers. Then that radio. Then a book on gardening. Tell me, do I look like a gardener?" Erika didn't say anything. They both knew she looked like hell, and neither of them could think of a way to make a joke out of it. "I'd be happy if he just sat down for five minutes. But he's already heard all my stories. He thinks I should grow tomatoes."

"I don't think he knows what to do," Erika said, thinking: *Neither do I, come to that.*

"Tell you what I could really use, is someone to prep my finger clicker and read my chem strips after I've smeared them, maybe even help me load the right amount of insulin into the syringe. Think you could manage that?"

"I'll try."

"That's fine."

"Does the needle hurt?"

"Not as much as going without cookies."

"Mom says we have to make you comfortable."

Her grandmother chuckled. "You know, I think she's more scared of this than I am," she lied.

"But Dad says you're a tough old crone."

"So I am," she said, putting her hand to her mouth, her lips dry as clay. "So I am."

Erika did not feel sad about her grandmother. She feared she never would. The mystery of death left her heart barren. At night, she lay in bed feeling her body all over for lumps. She worried her blanket in the dark until the fringe was threadbare, waiting for the pain to come. But during the day, she concentrated on her grandmother's problems. When the old girl was thirsty, Erika appeared with a drink. When it was time for a blood test, Erika swept into the room and handled the needles and chem strips with the efficiency of a registered nurse. Her grandmother asked, if it wasn't too much trouble, would she mind looking for a particular Aretha Franklin record? Erika returned with it two hours later. They were home alone. They put the record on. "The Beatles were good," Erika's grandmother said, whapping the bedpost with her cane, "but Aretha Franklin is forever."

Winter softened unexpectedly during February, bringing warmer temperatures and occasional dustings of snow. Erika and her grandmother drank tea in the afternoon and made fun of the people on the radio talk shows. Erika almost forgot her grandmother was going to die soon. Such was Erika's calming effect on her that she practically forgot it herself. But there it was, between them, solid as the unforgiving rock of ages, nestled in amongst their loneliness on those long, dark afternoons. It was sleeting the day Erika's grandmother rolled back the sleeve of her nightgown and held out the inside part of her forearm for Erika to see. There were six numbers stamped on her wrinkled skin, stamped on as neatly as typewriter keys hit a page. "Remember this?"

"Of course I do," Erika said.

"Know how I got it?"

"Yes." *Dad says you couldn't shut your mouth,* she thought. *Why couldn't you? Why couldn't you have shut your mouth and run?*

"When you were two years old," her grandmother said, "just learning to count, I remember sitting like this, drinking tea with your mother. I held you in my lap. It was a beautiful spring day. The air was bursting with familiar scents—flowers, tree buds, the breath of freshly mulched gardens. And it was just hot enough so that as your mother made the tea, she needed to dab at her forehead with a handkerchief. I remember all the details of that day because of you. Two years old. Just learning to count. As your mother and I talked, I kissed you on the hair and helped you when you couldn't remember a number. You had the most delicate little fingers. As you counted, you touched my neck, my arms, my stomach. Several times, you forgot which number you were on and skipped back and forth: 1-2-7-6. I told you no, let's start from one and see if we can count all the way up to ten without missing any. You just laughed and said it again: 1-2-7-6. It was then I felt your finger on my arm, saw you pointing. You see, you were saying the numbers on my arm.

"At that moment, I pleaded with God: Never let her know, never let her be touched by this. You, so giggling and happy on that beautiful day, just a pretty little girl learning to count. And at the stove, your mother smiling as she dabbed the sweat off her forehead and poured the tea. I felt such love for you both then, such joy that those familiar scents come back in the spring." She ran her finger over the

number. Just a scar now. One in a series. "I love you,
Erika."

"Don't say that."

"Why not? I love you. I love you."

"Stop it!"

"What are you so afraid of? It's pretty natural, you
know."

"I don't care. Just don't start with that."

"I want to tell you, Erika, I was wrong to plead with
God that day. First, He never listens to me. And even if He
did, what I asked for cannot be. The thing you must realize
is, circumstances will mark you whether you like it or not.
So there's no sense in marking yourself. Please realize this,
Erika. I'm just a foolish old lady, but I'm telling you it's not
the pain, it's the getting over it that counts."

Show nothing, Erika thought.

"I'm over all my pain now," her grandmother said.

Two more weeks passed. The coughing got worse.
Erika's father said it sounded like the old girl was mixing
cement up there. His wife's agenda for improving the quality
of their home included new wallpaper for the living room,
new carpets for the hall and vestibule, and new blacktop for
the driveway. He objected to having his weekends booked
six months in advance. She, in turn, objected to living in a
hovel. It seemed there was no middle ground. Erika
knocked on the door to her grandmother's room. "Want to
go for a walk?"

"On these legs?"

"Borrow Dad's. He never uses them."

"It's snowing."

"I thought you were sick of the house."

"Oh, all right."

They got as far as Lexington Green. That was when the

old girl's legs quit on her. Erika helped her to a bench. "I'll go call home. One of them can drive down and pick us up."

"It's snowing," her grandmother said, cold not because it was winter but because she wasn't going to see the spring.

Erika went running off to find a phone, cursing the snow, which was already collecting nicely around the Minuteman statue's shoulders and musket. No one was using the library phone. She dug in her pockets. No money. She ran into the library, past the periodicals. Who should be standing by the card catalogue but Aaron Simon. Studying for a change. Amazing. "Aaron, give me a dime."

"Great news, Erika. Did you hear I got into Oakes's class?"

"Congratulations." The story was going around at school about a gambler from Lexington who had turned part of his large Colonial-style home into a poker studio, but Erika had no idea why Billy Riordon and Aaron Simon would pay to learn the game, or why the gambler would bother to teach them. "Do you have a dime?"

"It's really snowing like hell out there."

"Aaron, will you shut up and give me the goddamn dime!"

She made her call and hurried back to the Green. The Minuteman's tricorne hat was covered with snow. Her grandmother sat on the icy bench, hands folded in her lap, eyes unblinking, the entire line of her jaw gone gray. Erika would remember her like this, back straight, knees together primly, the look of determination on her face twice that of the Minuteman—in her frailty, somehow, a sturdier monument. "They're coming," Erika said, brushing the snow from her coat, then putting her arms around her. "Don't worry. They're coming."

◆   ◆   ◆

THE FUNERAL WENT WELL. Erika's mother was pleased. Erika made it through fine. At home, she listened to the radio talk shows and the Aretha Franklin record. She was fine.

Fine until Aaron Simon's party that summer, when Melanie Bradley, who could turn the tears on and off at will, suggested they all go out to the garage for a cry.

6

Carl

Three months before applying to Martin Oakes's class, Carl Rice celebrated his thirteenth birthday by hiding in the trunk of his parents' Buick Skylark. It was Saturday. When he woke up, he stayed in bed, practicing different kinds of smiles. Teenaged smiles. Wiggling his toes as if he were a swimmer poised to leap from his starting block into the water, even though he couldn't see the other end of the pool. Stroking the hair in his armpit, a man now. Thirteen. Sweet thirteen. Carl turned the idea of adulthood over in his mind, and decided it suited him.

This year, he expected a different kind of present from his parents. A grown-up present. No more remote-control planes. No more attempts to redecorate his room. No more trips to the circus, which they ruined by analyzing every-thing except the elephant dung. Give them time, they'd find something significant in that, too.

No, thirteen was special. Carl had his hopes pinned on

a ten-speed bike with some real racing gear: the skintight knee-length shorts, the special shoes and gloves, a Team USA shirt and cap.

Carl had never been athletic. But this summer they'd been in Nice when the Tour de France came ripping through. His parents couldn't have been less interested. They rolled out their wicker mats on the pebbles at Ruhl Plage and read, squinting up into the sun, each pale as a flounder's belly. A girl with shorts hitched halfway up her buttocks and a stack of papers under her arm picked her way between the sunbathers: *"Nice-Matin. Demandez Nice-Matin."* An Algerian hawked drinks: *"Bira. Ginni.* Schweppesssss. Seven-Up-up-up, C-c-cola-ooo." As the bicyclists approached, they pushed a wave of noise out in front of them, quiet at first, gathering force as they swept through the old town, then crashing onto the Promenade des Anglais as they emerged from the shade and cobblestones and poured across the sun-bleached road above the Mediterranean. Their caps and shirts washed together in a blur of speed, but each color remained distinct; the riders flowed past like liquids that wouldn't mix. Carl scrambled up the steps from the beach in time to see the determination that shone in the eyes of the leader, Vachon, as he sped down the Promenade des Anglais. Vachon, getting old now, but so placid in motion he could seem arrogant even at the brink of exhaustion. By the time the next rider arrived, Vachon had already made the Negresco. An Air Inter jet let down its flaps above the airport at the outskirts of town as Vachon disappeared around the bend of the Promenade. Carl smiled, feeling the skin pull tight across his face. In his heart, he knew he was just as determined as Vachon, just as ready to leave the others behind. He floated on his back an hour later, ears beneath the water, listening to the pebbles softly click together as they washed back from the beach, determined. He swam in and hobbled across the pebbles to his parents. "I want a ten-speed."

"Didn't I tell you?" his father said to his mother, both of them burning quite nicely now. "Didn't I?"

"Carl," his mother said. "Really. You are so impressionable." She wasn't wearing her bikini top. Carl picked up a handful of pebbles to avoid looking at her breasts.

"It's almost predictable," his father said.

"Listen," Carl said. "I'm serious. I want a bike. For my birthday. I think I might like to race."

"With your knees?" his father asked.

"My knees are fine," Carl said. He cracked his knees as absentmindedly as other people cracked their knuckles. When he walked, they made a dry clicking sound. "They'll hold up on a bike."

"Those racers are serious," his mother said.

Carl knew she didn't really take them seriously. She believed athletics were generally for people who couldn't read. When she had insisted that he try downhill skiing, he understood her motives were social, not sporting. She cheerfully forced him out onto the slopes until his knees resembled swollen grapefruit. Her first question when he limped back into the lodge was always "Did you meet any nice people?" As if lifetime friendships were just waiting to be had in all the lift lines. During the awards ceremony for a slalom race in which he'd finished third, she leaned over and whispered, "You know, Carl, you could try a little bit harder to make them like you." He laughed at her. He wasn't after affection. He got enough of that at home. "I love you" was his mother's favorite way of building up to something she wanted him to do for her.

"I read an article in the *Trib* this morning about blood

boosting," Carl's father said, shielding his eyes from the sun with his freckled arm. "Apparently, it's the latest thing with these Tour racers. Six weeks before a race, the cyclist has two pints of blood drawn. That gives his body enough time to replenish its normal supply. When the race is just days away, his trainers reinject him with the old blood, which they keep frozen. Sounds a bit vampirish, doesn't it? The theory is boosting gives the cyclist more red blood cells, carries more oxygen to his legs." He poked Carl in the leg with his magazine. "Next thing you know, these guys'll be sleeping in coffins and holding the Tour de France at night."

"I wonder how many of those trainers have actually earned a medical degree," Carl's mother said. He wished she would put on a shirt. "If my son has to take up a sport that involves sweat," she said, as if he weren't there, "I hope it's tennis. Tennis might do him some good."

"I despise tennis," Carl said.

"Golf, then. But I rather doubt you'd be willing to boost your blood to get a competitive racing edge, Carl."

"You'd be surprised by what I'd do to win."

His mother poked the skin on her shoulder, watched the color go from red to white to red again. "All right, Carl. You want a bike? We'll get you a bike."

So now he lay in bed, ready to get up and become a man, ready to put on his new racing suit and take a spin around the Lexington Green. His mother came into his room. "Are you still in bed?"

"What does it look like, Mom?"

"Look, you want to stay in bed, stay in bed. Your father and I have decided to take the day off. We're going for a drive."

Carl was enjoying this. "Oh? Where?"

She paused for a moment. "Well, wherever we end up.

Somewhere in New Hampshire, probably." She made a dismissive gesture with her hand. "We plan to just go and see where the road takes us."

"Well, have fun."

"Carl, is something wrong? You have that funny look on your face again."

"What funny look?" *It's true,* he thought. *I have changed.*

"The look you get when you're scheming."

"I just think it's kind of strange, getting in the car for a drive, you don't even know where you're going."

"Well, we'll call to check up on you," she said, her thoughts obviously elsewhere, even though it took her several strides to reach the door.

As soon as the door shut, Carl leaped out of bed. He wondered if she thought he'd believed her pathetic excuse for going to pick up the bike. So they were planning to surprise him. He went downstairs. His father was packing sandwiches and beer in a cooler. Playing it through all the way.

"Morning, Dad. Getting ready for your little drive to nowhere?"

"I see you woke up on the sarcastic side of the bed today."

Carl went out through the garage, past the Mercedes they never drove, barefoot, with no particular plan in mind, thinking vaguely of the pebbles that softly clicked together beneath the water in Nice, old and smooth and impervious to earthbound events. All his ailing joints needed was a little lubrication. The trunk of the Skylark was open. So his parents were planning to surprise him. Maybe he would surprise them first. He climbed into the trunk and pulled it shut after him.

His father walked out with the cooler, swore under his breath at the closed trunk, and put the cooler down on the roof. "Keys, Rice," he mumbled to himself. "It would help to remember keys." His voice faded as he started back toward the house.

"Better remember your cash, too, Dad," Carl whispered, hoping he wouldn't be discovered.

His mother came outside. She had a distinctive scuff-walk; without seeing her, Carl could identify the sound her shoes made as they kicked up gravel in the driveway. Ear pressed to the panel that separated the trunk from the car's interior, he listened as she opened the back door, dragged the cooler across the roof, and dropped it on the back seat.

Carl's father returned with the keys. "Where's the cooler?" he asked.

"Back seat," Carl's mother replied. "Come on, honey, let's go."

There was very little traffic. In motion, the car assumed the character of Carl's father: steady, cautious, no sudden starts or stops. A half hour passed with his parents barely exchanging a word, and then only about current patients. From what little they did say Carl concluded the patients were hopeless but could afford not knowing it. One of the women who visited his mother had the habit of sticking her hands into a toaster.

Carl felt extremely clever. He had thought for some time that he might have a future in clandestine operations. Pulling off the trunk caper confirmed his talent. Navigating in the darkness, he pieced together his parents' conversational clues and decided they'd driven out to Route 128 and were now heading north on 93.

There was a pop. "What are you doing?" he heard his father ask.

"What does it look like I'm doing?" his mother replied. "I'm opening a beer."

"Don't you think that's maybe a little—"

"Irresponsible? Certainly. This is our day off, remember?"

Carl wondered when they were going to get to the bike shop.

"Well," he heard his father say, "if you're going to get me arrested, I don't see any reason why I shouldn't have one, too."

There was another pop as she opened him a beer. Unaware that Carl lay hidden in the trunk, his parents laughed in their nervous way as they crossed the border into Salem, New Hampshire. Carl's father spent the next several minutes trying to pronounce *bienvenu*. Four pops later, the car stopped and Carl's heart soared.

"Got to take a leak," his father said.

When he got back in the car, Carl heard his mother say, "I have a surprise for you." Her voice had got thick.

"What is it?"

"Listen."

Carl heard her fumbling with the cassette deck. There was a brief hiss on the speakers mounted above his head. Then the music started. It was a "Sesame Street" tape. Linda Ronstadt began to sing "I Want a Horse."

"Honey," Carl's father complained, "that's for kids."

She turned the volume up. "And what is it you think you are, dear?"

They laughed again, looser now, Carl's mother thumping the dashboard in time with the music. The Doobie Brothers sang "Winkin, Blinkin, and Nod." James Taylor sang "Jelly Man Kelly."

"I remember when we got this tape," Carl's father said. "Carl was what, three?"

"Four."

"He smiled then."

"He smiles now. You just don't like it that he smiles at us."

"Sometimes I think he's evil."

She laughed. "He can be a little demon at times."

"Do you think he hates us?" his father asked.

"It's just hormones. We ought to put the television in the basement and make him practice the violin more."

Arms hugging his shins, Carl listened to the brittle whisper of his knees.

When Ernie and Bert started belting out "The Sharing Song," Carl's father declared, "Jesus Christ, this music is too good for kids!"

Carl wanted to scream then, but the pain in his knees and the Vachon in his heart wouldn't allow it. No use starting. Might never stop. Might end up like the toaster lady. Instead, he banged rhythmically against the backs of the speakers. After he had banged for a while, they stopped the car and opened the trunk.

His mother said, "What in God's name are you *doing* in there?"

"Seeing if I can live without light." Uncurling slowly, he fixed his father with a terrible smile. "I should have known you really were going nowhere, Dad. It's your favorite place, isn't it?"

"You stop that," his mother said. "You stop that this instant!"

Smiling fiercely, Carl watched his father get back into the car and grip the wheel with enough force to rip it free. A weak man with a strong grip. Couldn't even look his own son in the eye. A half-empty beer sat on the dashboard. Cheerful music roared up from the open trunk.

"Mom, it's my birthday. Remember? It's my birthday." A noticeable shudder ran down Carl's shoulders to his fingers. But his voice stayed even. His knees were swollen from being curled up in the trunk for so long. He held on to the car's bumper, unable to bring himself up to his full height. "Why couldn't you remember? Why couldn't you?"

That night, his parents asleep, Carl returned to the car and carefully pulled out every last inch of the "Sesame Street" tape.

THE RICES PICKED their way through a fleet of ill-matched automobiles and waited outside the poker studio for fifteen minutes before Carl's interview with Martin Oakes. The class had run over. Carl turned the bill of his bicycle cap backward and peeked through the tiny windows by the studio door while his parents fidgeted on the porch and checked their watches. He could see a few of the students' backs, but it was difficult to get an angle on what was going on around the table. When class adjourned, the students filed out one at a time, silent and stony-faced, eyes projecting the mock toughness of new recruits. Erika Jaagstrom descended the stairs and cut between his parents as if they had no more significance than the shadows from the pine trees in the front yard. They had stood in her path, poised to make the normal human transactions, to exchange a glance for a smile, a wave for a nod, but she ignored them completely. Carl knew that the other students—to use a common but in this case quite appropriate expression— would almost certainly follow suit. He lurked nearby, observing them as they left.

"They all look so confident," Carl's father said approvingly.

"To you, maybe," Carl said. He had already got a line

on what made each of them tick. The girl with the braid was an attractive example. Carl believed he had a built-in radar screen, and there was no denying that Erika had registered a significant blip on it. Not like the love she probably inspired in others, but significant nonetheless; a blip of curiosity that made him want to know what was swimming around under the brilliant, icy surface of her features. It was clear to Carl that she had rubber bands in more places than her hair. He thought it might be interesting to find out where the other rubber bands were holding things together. It might be fun to pull them, snap them, tear them loose, and watch all her secrets come tumbling free.

"Please accept my apologies for the delay," Martin Oakes said when they were safely inside. "Some of my students find it difficult to understand why pairing up a hole card is so much more valuable than pairing up an up card."

Carl's father seemed ready to say something, but swallowed the remark instead and turned to his wife in an effort to steer Martin Oakes's attention away from him.

"Perhaps it would be helpful if I summarized Carl's accomplishments," Carl's mother said, frowning at her husband.

Martin Oakes waved his cigarette. "I don't think that will be necessary." She had assembled a portfolio of Carl's certificates, science awards, slalom-racing ribbons, freehand drawings, school essays, and recital programs. Martin Oakes now held the package in his lap. He had already dropped some ashes on the cover. "It feels impressive, anyway," he said.

"Well," Carl's father interjected uncertainly, "as you can see, he's been a very successful boy." He was standing by the door, still waiting for an invitation to take off his coat.

Martin Oakes hadn't opened the portfolio yet. "Why

don't you wait outside," he suggested to Carl's parents. "I think I would prefer to talk to Carl alone."

"Oh, uh, yes," Carl's father stammered, retreating to a position behind his wife. "Certainly."

Carl remained standing by the door. His mother left first. When his father was gone, he said, "He's scared of me, too."

"Oh?" Martin Oakes said. "And what is it about you that inspires fear?"

"I don't know," Carl said. His tone was flat, not boastful. "But for some reason, he's terrified." It seemed to him the simplest, most precise way to explain why his parents had brought him to this place.

Martin Oakes sat peacefully looking at his next student. There really wasn't much to say. Carl had come to the place where he belonged.

Carl finally spoke. "What is it?"

"Have you ever played poker before?" Martin Oakes asked. For surely this kid was a born cardplayer, a true natural talent, just waiting to be shaped. There was some Smooth Jake in him. Some Ace Roldan. And some unique qualities, too. Did he know it himself?

"No," Carl replied.

Martin Oakes had often wondered if he would have the opportunity to teach the game to someone who might ultimately choose it as his profession. Until now, he had thought the odds were against it. But here was a kid with obvious focus and detachment, the two most important qualities in a successful gambling career, excluding guts. It was possible that his hands wouldn't be quite dexterous enough at first, that his motives would have to be molded from hate into a tool kit of less pure emotions. But Martin Oakes could see the boy had promise. His mind was already refined, and wouldn't wander. His nerve only required sharpening. Here was someone who didn't particularly mind being transparent—who recognized it as an advantage, an adventure that could be full of possibilities.

"Sit down, Mr. Rice."

Carl sat down on the other side of the poker table. "I don't want to be in this class. You can't do anything for me."

"Maybe not," Martin Oakes agreed. He flipped through the portfolio. Carl had played the Bach E Major Partita at twelve. According to his typeset biography, he was now studying physics. "Do they occasionally let you sleep?"

"They let me do whatever I want."

"Your father seemed nervous."

"He's a shrink. So's my mother. They're paid to be calm, so they tend to go a little bit berserk during their off hours."

"Give me an example."

"Well, when kids get up in the morning, normal parents say 'Good morning' and maybe ask what kind of cereal they'd like for breakfast, right? When I wake up, mine come into my room and ask me to tell them about my dreams. I've had a lot of weird ones lately. But I tell them I can't remember anything. You'd think my dreams were a play you couldn't get tickets to."

Martin Oakes slid the portfolio across the table to him. "Did you really want to do all of these things?"

"I don't know. I guess so. My mother has this weird thing about not wasting any time. I think she figures if you don't keep busy, you start putting your hands in toasters and hearing voices and having dreams that can be turned into groundbreaking books."

"And poker?"

"What about it?"

"Your idea or theirs?"

"Theirs, of course." His voice never rose above a name-rank-and-serial-number formality. "You see, Mr. Oakes, I'm not their kid. I'm their experiment. They talk to their friends about this class as if I'm already one of the students. Your results are impressive, my father likes to say, even if your methods are unorthodox. They've *studied* you, Mr. Oakes. They know all about that ballerina, and the kid who took ten thousand dollars off his father, and the electronics wizard, and the kid from Needham the *Phoenix* did a piece on who claims you're the reason he aced the SATs. 'I wonder what he could do with Carl,' they say."

"Your parents seem to have high hopes for you."

"Not really. They just think no experiment is complete without me in it."

"My class is not an experiment, Mr. Rice." Sam Kim hadn't put up any money when Martin Oakes returned from his game with Smooth Jake and finally decided to start the class. But Martin Oakes wondered sometimes if Kim—unsuccessful at getting him into an usher's uniform—had instead skillfully maneuvered him into a peculiar form of civic duty. The thought of Carl Rice's father analyzing the relative merits of his class at a cocktail party as if it were the latest fad disturbed him. Or worse: was his class already in danger of becoming an institution? He could picture Sam Kim alone in his Quincy theater, munching popcorn and being entertained by this new, civic-minded Martin Oakes up on the screen, telling children the secrets of poker and actually getting satisfaction from teaching them what he knew. A black-and-white movie with a homespun sound track. From his position in the darkness, Sam Kim would smile at Martin Oakes's screen-sized pride and recognize it as a weakness.

Carl allowed himself to study the poker studio carefully for the first time. His eyes were immediately drawn to the antique box of chips. "Then what is it, a museum?"

"Just a class, Mr. Rice," Martin Oakes said. "A place to learn."

"What's the point of learning poker?"

"I don't know," Martin Oakes responded calmly. "What's the point of learning history, or music, or physics, or downhill skiing?"

"I like to win things," Carl said.

"I don't offer any certificates," Martin Oakes said. "There will be nothing to add to your portfolio. And I don't offer any sympathy. There are a few things I can teach you. But it will be up to you to apply the lessons." He held up the portfolio. "They could turn out to be useful no matter what you decide to become."

"It won't be any of those things," Carl said.

"You still have plenty of time to choose."

"Oh, I've already chosen." His voice changed registers for the first time, becoming quieter and taking on a slight edge. "I plan to become a spy," he said.

"Really?" Martin Oakes smiled. So he was a kid after all. "And why is that?"

"To find out things I'm not supposed to know. Keep from getting bored."

"Poker players are spies, too. At least the good ones are. And they're seldom bored. Might be good training for you."

"Are you saying I'm in?"

"Yes."

"Well, I'm serious about being a spy."

"I believe you. Is that why you hid in the trunk?"

7

Willow

Good morning, ma'am," Brian Willoughby said to the woman as she pushed her cart through the "in" door to the supermarket. He carried a clipboard under his arm and tapped the side of his leg with a pencil.

"Hello," the woman said. Tall and blonde. Nice clothes. Wary, but not rattled. Brian could spot a mark before she put the first item in her cart. This one was a supple thirty-five or -six, little crow's-feet at the corners of her eyes, but otherwise very smooth. Tennis legs and a tan.

"Welcome to Heartland Food Warehouse," Brian said. Shoulders squared, skin a clear brown, he was tall enough to look her in the eye. He smiled easily, but his manner was professional. His head rose well above his shoulders, and his chin remained tucked, as if he were a soldier. "You got a proud neck," his father often told him. "I didn't know better, I'd think you had something to be proud about."

The door opened into Produceland, by itself bigger

than most supermarkets. The woman stopped her cart next to a bin of artichokes and surveyed the place. To leave now, she'd have to walk all the way around the store. A family of Cambodians with five shopping carts wheeled past her to inspect a crate of scallions. "You work here?"

"Work here? I practically live here," Brian said, winking. Winking always put them off their guard. "I'm a food service manager." A title didn't hurt, either. Gain their respect.

"I'm afraid I don't follow."

"I work for myself." The Cambodians tossed out the bunches of scallions they didn't like and loaded the crate into one of their carts; had to be restaurant people. "For you, you want."

Now she was really confused. That was the problem with first-timers. They came prepared to shop. Heartland veterans came prepared to do battle. A man with a cut-off jean jacket shoved her cart aside and hoisted a bag of oranges over his shoulder. His back was soaked with sweat. Brian smelled the unmistakable combination of bad hygiene and hot vinyl, and guessed he was a truck driver.

Using her cart as a shield, the woman pressed closer to the produce bins, then turned to see if anyone else was threatening to career into her. "This place is a madhouse."

"Yeah," Brian said appreciatively, his laugh genuine as she wrinkled her nose at the truck driver's odor. "Say," pulling the clipboard out from under his arm now, "how much do you spend on a week's groceries?" Smiling. "If you don't mind my asking."

"About a hundred thirty."

"Three kids?"

"Two."

"You must grow them big," Brian said, tapping the

pencil on the clipboard and biting his lower lip as he did the calculation in his head. "Tell you what. I'm going to save you forty dollars."

"Aren't you a little young to be accosting strangers?" she said mildly. "And if you don't mind my asking, what are you doing at the supermarket in the middle of a school day?"

He raised his neck to its full height. "If I could just look at your list for a moment." She clutched it to her blouse. "Come on," Brian said, hand open, wiggling his fingers, "I won't tell anyone what you eat." She had to smile at that. "Just let me see it for a minute." She handed the list to him. He put on a scowl while he looked at it. You could come on with the charm only so long before they expected some professionalism. "Ah," he said when he came to the dog food. "A dog. That explains it." He carefully examined the rest of the list. "Yes," he said finally. "I'd say we can get all this for ninety dollars. Ninety-five, tops."

"We?" she asked. A speculative glance had replaced the smile. She was embarrassed to be shopping with the blue collars and the immigrants. But she was practical.

"You have coupons?" She shook her head. "No problem," he said, and riffled the pages on his clipboard. "I've got most of these items covered."

"What do you want?" she asked flatly.

"Ten dollars," he said. "I help you shop. You're in and out in forty-five minutes. I show you where things are. Spot you my coupons. Take you to the fastest checkout line. Roll the cart out to your car"—he was willing to bet that she and her husband drove a Volvo, another practical decision—"and load the groceries into your trunk. You pay me and still save thirty dollars. Sound like a good deal?"

"How do I know I can't save forty dollars myself?"
"You can. Next time. That's the best part. Next time
you know how." Nearby, a woman in a thick corduroy
smock was loading cantaloupes onto a bed of plastic grass.
"Hey, Jill," Brian hailed her. Jill had bluish hair and the
thickly veined legs of a career waitress. Brian took the
blonde's arm. "This woman wants to know if I'm worth ten
dollars."

"How much he promise to save you?" Jill asked, cra-
dling a melon in her palm as if she were preparing to roll
a frame at Sammy White's Brighton Bowl, where she spent
every Thursday night candlepin bowling with friends she'd
known since parochial school. Her average was ninety-five,
up four pins from last year, and almost good enough to get
her on "Candlepin Jackpot." Channel 5 taped the show at
Sammy White's during the week and aired it on Saturday.

"Forty dollars," the blonde woman replied, "minus his
fee."

Jill sighted the woman like a headpin. "Well, it was
me, I'd hire him. He knows the store better'n anybody
works here. Plus he's got a calculator in his head. Gets you
the best buys, and keeps track of your bill as you go along."
TV, she thought, and though it was only a melon she was
holding, she could smell the extra polish they slicked on the
lanes at Sammy White's and the deodorant they sprayed into
the rented bowling shoes. TV would be a kick, she thought,
if I could bowl three strings before the bursitis put a grip
on my shoulder, if the glare the lights threw off the oil didn't
spoil my aim, if I had this blonde's legs. If, if, if. What's
the use? "You still save thirty dollars," she told the blonde
woman, eyeing her slim, tanned legs. "Only drawback is you
got to listen to him talk." Brian winked at her and she
smiled. A good kid, she thought, and so well groomed.

Looked a little bit like Sidney Poitier. Had the same proud
neck.

"All right," the blonde woman said to Brian. "Let's
give it a try. My name is Winter. Like the season."

"My name is Brian Willoughby," he said, "but people
call me Willow. Like the tree."

"Well, Brian," she said, checking her watch, "it is now
exactly ten-twenty. Let's see if you can get me out of here
by eleven. I assume your service is guaranteed?"

"Ten dollars if I bring you in at ninety," Brian said.
"Five dollars if I bring you in under ninety-five. No charge
if your groceries cost more than ninety-five." When
she nodded, he removed several pieces of paper from
the clipboard and held them out to her. "These are for
you."

"Maps?"

"Copies of the floor plan. Put them in your purse. Use
one each time you shop. I'll show you how." Brian reached
into his coat pocket and pulled out a pair of scissors and a
glue stick. Then he smoothed out a copy of the floor plan
on the counter. A small box with an X inside had the caption
"You are here." There were boxes next to every section of
the store. Brian began to cut up the shopping list. "First
thing we do, Mrs. Winter, is get organized." When he was
through cutting, he took the cap off the glue stick and pasted
the pieces into the boxes on the floor plan. Then he asked
her to hold out her hands, and dealt her the coupons that
matched items on her list. "Now," he said, "we're ready to
shop."

"What's this about you having a calculator in your
head?" Mrs. Winter asked.

"Oh, I'm just fast with numbers," Brian said. "My
mother says it's a gift."

◆ ◆ ◆

"A GIFT?" Terence Willoughby asked his wife a few miles away, unconvinced. His voice wasn't any louder than usual, but it had the edge he'd learned to substitute for shouting. He rattled the ice in his mug and glared at the four men who were supposed to be laying concrete in the bottom of the pool. One of the men pawed at some wet cement with a rake in the deep end. One was busy rolling himself a cigarette. The other two were rubbing sunscreen lotion on the backs of their necks. "What good is it going to do him, with his attitude? I don't care about his gifts, Connie. Far as I'm concerned, he's had too many for his own good. What he needs is a good kick in the butt. The boy doesn't know what it is to be black."

"I know what you mean," she said. "We should move to the projects, get him a pet rat. Ask around, see if there's a gang he can join." She wore a bandanna that brought out the green in her eyes, green like a still pond that takes in more light than it lets out. Her voice still had its Haitian lilt; when he was angry, it rolled over him like water. She took an ice cube out of his mug and rubbed it across her forehead. "You've been working too hard. What you should do is get one of those big inflatable plastic doughnuts and just float the rest of the summer away."

"Summer, hell. You looking at the same pool?"

"They'll get it done." She hooked her arm in his and led him back up the path to the house. They'd both put on weight over the years, and their hips bumped together as they walked. "Twenty years waiting for a pool," she said. "You know what? I bet we can heat it ourselves, after twenty years. Just jump in and listen to the hiss. We've stored up a lot of heat."

"What should I say to Brian?"

"Say we didn't bring him up to be a truant and a liar. Dock his allowance for a few weeks if it'll make you feel better. But stop taking it so personally."

"I don't like him spending all his free time at that store. He should be playing sports, not shopping."

"He isn't any good at sports," she said, "like me. And he doesn't like to do something if he can't be the best at it." She squeezed his triceps and saw him wince. "Like you, Terry."

"He shops," Terence Willoughby said, shaking his head. "My son shops."

"Doesn't it ever amaze you," she said, twisting the ribbon from Brian's mathematics medal around her wrist, then swinging the medal back and forth in front of her husband's eyes like a hypnotist, "that he came from us?"

"Doesn't it ever amaze you," he shot back, "after how much we've taught him, how little he knows?"

She pressed the medal to her cheek. "Knows his math."

"Last time I checked, he wasn't making out so well in his other classes. Might have something to do with the fact he doesn't go to them."

"You want him to suffer for the sake of suffering."

"I want him to remember where he came from. I want him to use his smarts and stop getting by on charm. I want him to stop talking like Bryant Gumbel."

"And start talking like who—Leon Spinks?"

"It's what he says, not how he says it. He depresses me."

"You need your pool," she said. "Your pool will make you feel better."

"I can't swim."

"What better excuse to learn?"

◆　◆　◆

RENNIE AHMAJIAN smiled at the man as he unloaded the items from his cart onto the rubber conveyor belt. She never took her foot off the conveyor pedal as the groceries paraded past her: milk, orange juice, steak, chicken, pork chops, hamburger, spaghetti sauce, dishwashing liquid, two sizes of disposable diapers, ice cream, potatoes, cabbage, onions, asparagus, three heads of lettuce, six tomatoes, four cantaloupes, and two cartons of strawberries. The conveyor belt was over ten feet long and ended at a metal platform. When the groceries reached the platform, they crowded together uncertainly like kids at a dance.

Rennie took her foot off the pedal. "Do you need bags, sir?" she asked cheerfully. The man held up the bags he'd brought with him and shook his head. Customers bagged their own at Heartland. It helped keep the prices low and the lines moving. "Well, then," she said, "that will be ninety-nine cents, please."

"Ninety-nine cents?"

"That's right, sir," she said, and held out her hand, bent with arthritis but still nimble enough to play the Schumann Piano Quintet at half tempo if the string members agreed to stop for the page turns. "We're not the best," Mr. Stibovitz, the second violinist, had told Brian one day at the nursing home where he and Rennie lived, "but we sure are the oldest. Average age of seventy-seven. Can you believe it, kid? They should call us the Three Hundred and Eighty-six Year Old Quintet." Mr. Stibovitz could be grouchy, even abusive, but no one had more visitors. Rennie never paid attention to who they were. That wasn't important. What was important was that Stibovitz always seemed to have someone around to listen to him. Stibovitz still had influence in the world. "This is no rest home," he would growl at his visitors. "Do I look like I'm resting?" He and Rennie and eight others from the home worked three mornings a week at Heartland. Of all the senior citizens, he was the fastest checkout person, and for that reason the manager's favorite, but Rennie thought it rather picky of him to insist upon working at register five. Everyone knew register five had the best view. The manager, Mr. Phan, said Stibovitz deserved it. Stibovitz agreed.

"We've got to keep an eye on Mencken," Stibovitz had confided to Rennie that morning in the bus on the way to the store, referring to their first violinist. "I think he's losing his eyesight. Maybe he and I should switch soon." Mencken played the violin like an angel. He'd lost some dexterity and vision, but he'd kept his soul, and when it soared out of his instrument everyone at the home felt younger.

"It's frightening, growing old," Rennie had replied.

"His vibrato's going, too," Stibovitz had pressed on. "Have you noticed?"

"No."

"Well, it is. I think maybe he and I should change soon. For the good of the group."

"But he's our leader."

"I could lead, too," Stibovitz had said, raising his voice. "I just need an opportunity."

Stibovitz was singing now at register five, a piece of the Hallelujah Chorus. He was in good spirits. So far, both of Brian's clients had purchased some of the flank steak he'd recommended to Brian the day before. His voice, once robust, now sounded like a breeze going through a wheat field. In his mind, though, he still heard a baritone that could bring sweat to an audience's palms.

The man in the checkout line on register eight looked suspiciously at Stibovitz, then leaned forward, dirty palms pressing against the conveyor belt. "What's going on?" he asked Rennie. "Am I the millionth customer or something? Or is this some kind of gag?"

"Ninety-nine cents, please," Rennie said slowly, confused now, and feeling slightly dizzy. Hadn't the man heard her? "Please pay at the register."

The man looked over his shoulder. "I'm at the goddamn register." No one was in line behind him. He looked up at the clear glass booth where Mr. Phan totaled receipts. The booth was empty. Outside, it had begun to rain. Mr. Phan waved a produce truck into its berth and shouted orders at the workers who'd lined up to unload it.

Carefully, smiling now at Rennie, the man reached into his pocket, pulled out a dollar bill, and handed it to her.

She put it in the register.

He packed his groceries in under a minute and started to push his cart toward the "out" door.

"Sir?" she called after him anxiously.

He swiveled his head around. Rennie was waving her hand. He left the cart and walked back toward her.

"One penny is your change," she said, holding out the coin. The man took it and hurried off.

As he did, a pregnant woman swung her cart into Rennie's checkout and began unloading her groceries. A two-year-old boy stood crying in the front of the cart, both hands red from being slapped. "You don't shut up," his mother said, reaching back for cigarettes and a *National Enquirer*, "I'm going to buy you a muzzle."

"Good day," Rennie said.

"It's a crappy day, honey," the pregnant woman said. She pointed to her son, who was now attacking the metal spokes of the shopping cart with his teeth. "Want to buy a kid for next to nothing?" Rennie held on to the register with both hands, trying to make the dizziness go away. She could hear Stibovitz's voice faintly, as if it were drifting up from the bottom of a well. "Hey," the pregnant woman said, "are you okay?"

Rennie smiled and pressed her foot down on the conveyor pedal.

"WHAT'S THE TALLY?" Mrs. Winter asked, putting a package of frozen bagels into her cart.

"Seventy-four thirty-two," Brian said. He took the bagels out of the cart and tossed them back into the freezer case. "There are real bagels in the bakery." His voice was flat. "Fresher, bigger, cheaper, and better-tasting. You want, you can still freeze them. And with what you save, you can indulge in a couple of chocolate croissants."

"Pain au chocolat," Mrs. Winter said. "Here?"

"That what they call it in Harvard Square so they can charge five times as much for it?" Brian said, frowning. Half an hour with someone who didn't know the first thing about shopping made him long for a client who would appreciate the art behind the savings: his research, his techniques, his guile. A client who would take an interest in the eight varieties of sausage ground fresh daily, in the bulk items like rice and nuts and bolt corn flour and coffee and dates that you could shovel out of the barrels in Produceland for a song. A client who would share his enthusiasm for the bracing smells in the detergent aisle. But this woman with the tanned legs and the almost certain Volvo station wagon didn't care about the mysteries of shopping. Her few attempts at conversation had centered on her fanatical dedication to tennis, which Brian found lacking in interest. They didn't have much to talk about.

Mrs. Winter, however, couldn't wait to tell her friends she'd met a strange black kid who counted the sheets of toilet paper in a roll and the calories in breakfast cereals, read the "Catch of the Day" reports in the Boston *Globe* to anticipate bargains in the seafood department, followed the commodities market, and weighed produce to within a quarter of a pound by simply holding it in his hands.

Brian loaded a flat of canned dog food into the cart. "Your dog have a name?"

"Dow Jones," Mrs. Winter said.

Brian laughed. "He your broker?" he asked. When he imagined Mrs. Winter spreading out the newspaper on the floor so Dow Jones could paw at the sure gainers, she seemed a little more human to him.

"He happens to be a champion English setter," Mrs. Winter said.

"Good for him," Brian said. "All the same, I suppose you'd trade in the ribbons for a pooch who could predict the market."

"My husband takes care of that." She checked her watch: 10:50. Dow Jones was getting groomed. She wondered if she could pick him up and still make it to the club by 12:30. She decided no. Dow Jones could wait, but if you were ten minutes late for a reserved court, they gave it to somebody else.

They picked up the bagels, half a dozen Lean Cuisines, and a flea collar, and headed for the checkout area.

"Eighty-five fifty," Brian announced. "Did I tell you?"

"You told me."

"All the day cashiers are from the Shady Grove in Newton," Brian said. "It's an old folks' home. Mr. Stibovitz says there isn't a tree anywhere in sight on the grounds and it's hot as hell in the summer because the AC always craps out and they should rename it Sunny Grove so the seniors at least know what they're getting into. Mr. Stibovitz is kind of a literal-minded guy."

"Is he one of the cashiers?"

"Yeah," Brian said, steering the cart toward the singing old man at register five. "He must be about a hundred years old, but you'll see, he's fast. Knows the business, too. I visit him sometimes. He tells me when all the shipments are due in."

There were four people waiting at register five and all of their carts were filled to overflowing. Mr. Stibovitz, a jar of silver cleaner in one hand and a box of frozen pudding pops in the other, saw Brian, smiled, raised his chin in greeting, and shrugged his shoulders. The only shopper at register eight was already loading her groceries into her cart. Brian rolled his cart into the vacant aisle, narrowly beating a fat woman with a red wig and a yellow sundress who opened a *Redbook* and pretended not to care. Brian began to unload the cart. Mrs. Winter stood waiting at the end of the conveyor belt, jingling her keys. Brian looked at the key chain out of the corner of his eye: Saab. Close enough.

"Good day," Rennie Ahmajian said.

"Hi there," Brian replied. He had seen Rennie once or twice at the home, slumped in a chair, trying to warm her legs in the bands of light that slanted through the windows. He finished unloading the groceries. While Rennie checked them through, Brian said to Mrs. Winter, "Might as well give me the money now. Save us both some time."

Mrs. Winter opened her purse and counted out eight tens, five ones, and two quarters. She handed the money to Brian. "Eighty-five fifty." Brian continued to hold out his hand. "Plus ten dollars for services rendered."

"Of course." She handed him another ten. He put it in his pocket.

"Sir?" Rennie said, smiling. Such a graceful-looking young man.

"I've got exact change," Brian said.

"That will be ninety-nine cents, please," Rennie said.

"What a bargain," Brian said, counting up the money again, making sure it was all there. It didn't occur to him until later that Rennie hadn't passed Mrs. Winter's items over the UPC reader.

"Ninety-nine cents," Rennie said.

"Excuse me, ma'am, but these groceries come to eighty-five fifty. On the nose."

"No," Rennie said, shaking her head and frowning slightly. "You owe ninety-nine cents. Please pay at the register."

Mrs. Winter left her cart and joined Brian at the register. "What's going on?"

"Lady says we owe her ninety-nine cents. Ma'am, if you don't mind my asking, what's your name?"

"Rennie. Rennie Ahmajian."

"Mrs. Ahmajian, we've got a lot of groceries here."

Rennie nodded her head. Old Stibovitz didn't have such a bad voice. A little pushy when it came to music, but how could he help being a little jealous of the sound that Mencken brought out of the violin? It made everyone else feel younger, but it made Stibovitz feel old, old, old. Poor Stibovitz.

"Why don't you pay her?" Mrs. Winter suggested.

"That's what I'm trying to do," Brian said.

"Please pay at the register," Rennie said.

The fat woman with the sundress put down her magazine. "Hey, you mind? I don't have all day." Then her face was gone again behind the cover. "LOSE WEIGHT WITH AERO-BICS!" the cover advised.

"Mrs. Ahmajian, these groceries come to eighty-five fifty." He held out the money.

Rennie looked away. Her foot was still on the conveyor belt, and the groceries bumped and skidded around on the end of the platform. "Don't . . . you . . . hear . . . me?"

"Give her a dollar," Mrs. Winter said. She had stopped jingling her keys, and there was a little bounce in her calves, as if she were waiting to return serve.

"You want to steal your groceries, go ahead and give it to her yourself."

The fat woman moved forward. Brian realized she had to approach sideways to fit through the aisle. "What the hell is the problem here? You telling each other your life stories?"

"Give it to her," Mrs. Winter said.

"No," Brian said.

"Stop giving the old lady a hard time," the fat woman said.

Mrs. Winter dug into her purse. She couldn't find a one-dollar bill. She scraped her fingers along the bottom of the purse, feeling for change.

"Move it, or I'm going to get the manager," the fat woman said, her face reddening to match her wig.

"Why don't you shut up?" Brian said.

Rennie pitched forward against the cash register. Mr. Stibovitz craned his neck from register five, and Mr. Phan came running. "Rennie," he said, taking hold of her under the arms, feeling her shallow breath through her apron.

"Ninety-nine cents," she said. "Ninety-nine cents for the groceries."

Mrs. Winter put the change she'd found back in her purse.

"I heard him," the fat woman said. "He was threatening her."

"Like hell," Brian said.

Mr. Phan waved two stock boys over. They led Rennie away. Mr. Phan came around the counter and gripped Brian's arm. "What did you say to her?"

"Nothing."

"I see you all the time. Why do you hang around here?"

Brian's neck felt rubbery. His eyes darted up the empty aisles, looking for Jill, the candlepin bowler. "Look, I was just helping this lady shop."

"He's got my money," Mrs. Winter said.

Jill had heard the commotion. She walked up to the register and asked one of the stock boys, "What's going on?"

"I think they caught a nigger trying to steal food."

"TERENCE?" CONNIE WILLOUGHBY said, bracing herself in the doorway, the green in her eyes choppy now, her voice uncertain. The way she looked made him sit straight up in his chair. "Terence, come quick."

"What is it?" he said. "What's wrong?"

"It's Brian."

What followed was the messy business at the police station, where an officer named Stingley promised Brian his first look at the inside of a cell, and Terence Willoughby, upon arriving, offered Stingley a closer look at the police department's gray-tiled floor. Brian noticed that Stingley bore a disturbing resemblance to the man his father had contracted to lay the concrete foundation of the pool—a man who would be daunted by neither heaven nor hell, provided each paid an hourly wage. Stingley had driven to Heartland

in his black-and-white. He promptly took Brian into cus-
tody, keeping Mrs. Winter's ninety-five fifty as evidence.
Mrs. Winter went home. At the police station, Mr. Phan
hugged himself in spite of the unseasonably warm weather,
and scowled at Brian, and demanded justice, and complained that he paid many taxes, and that people shouldn't
be running around stealing his food. Connie Willoughby
wrapped herself around Brian like a blanket. He felt hot and
short of breath, but he didn't try to pull away. He had always
enjoyed the pleasant chaos of Heartland, but the chaos that
surrounded him now made him want to shut down his
senses. Ringing phones that no one seemed in any hurry to
answer. Dirty mops that left trails of gloom and succeeded
only in replacing one bad smell with another. The monoto-
nous clacking of typewriters as policemen in peeling leather
jackets filed their reports. And people everywhere: shouting,
crying, sweating, complaining, apologizing, smoking, lying,
demanding. Finally, Jill arrived, propping up Mr. Stibovitz
on one of her stout arms. Stibovitz explained that Rennie
Ahmajian hadn't been quite one hundred percent lately and
tended to forget things, like where she was and how much
things cost. "You know how pianists are with figures," he
said to Stingley, who didn't know how pianists were with
anything, including groceries. Mr. Stibovitz assured the officer that Rennie's was a temporary condition, that she
wasn't flashing back to the Depression, or—God forbid—
going senile, or developing a philanthropic streak, or getting
interested in crime, or anything serious. "So you see," he
said, opening his arms wide as if he were telling them all
the end of a story, "you've made a mistake. You have no
choice but to let this enterprising young man go." Stingley
said he wasn't about to take orders from an old geezer whose
voice creaked like a rusty lawn chair, but then the Willough-

bys' lawyer showed up, and within minutes Stingley was typing out an apology and signing it, and Mr. Phan was nodding his head in agreement that the matter was closed, and Jill was rubbing her legs to increase the circulation, and Mr. Stibovitz was telling everyone how to spell his name, and Brian was gathering himself together to go home.

HE WAS BACK in the store a month later. Mr. Phan occasionally ran him off out of habit, but in general business was good.

A woman entered the store and paused just inside the door to survey the shelves of produce. A tall man in running shoes followed her. Brian would have judged him an athlete if he hadn't spotted the cigarette concealed in the man's hand. The man took a last drag at the door and stamped the butt out on the rubber bottom of his shoe. He appeared to be very interested in the woman. The woman removed a list from her purse. Then she turned and said something to the man. It was only then that Brian realized they were together.

"Good afternoon," he said.

"Hello," the woman said. Her hair was wet. She had gathered it in a thick knot on the top of her head. The man said nothing.

"Welcome to Heartland Food Warehouse," Brian said.

"Are you the official greeter?" the woman asked. She was standing under a ceiling fan. Brian could catch the faint scent of chlorine coming off her hair.

"No. Nothing official about me." Brian wasn't sure he liked the hard look the man was giving him. But the woman was simply too beautiful to pass up. "I'm a food service manager."

"What does that mean?" she asked him.

"It means I'm here to save you money." He tapped his pencil on his clipboard. Coupons bulged out of his back pocket. "Would you mind if I had a quick look at your list?"

She looked at the man, who nodded.

Brian studied the list, spotting several areas for possible savings. He then explained his service to the couple and offered to help them shop for a fee of ten dollars.

"How's the corn?" the man asked.

"Not bad. But I'd wait a week," Brian said. He found it difficult to look the man in the eye. He never blinked, and his eyes had a hazy gleam that made it difficult to tell what color they were. "It takes a little while to get into the big stores. Right now, you have to head west for the good corn. I can give you the name of a roadside stand on Route 2, if you want."

"That's all right," the man said. "I can wait."

"So," Brian asked, "can I be of service?"

"I've got another idea," the man said. "You say you can get everything on that list for eighty dollars. I don't believe you. So we'll do our own shopping. But you come along with us. When we're through, I'll pay—"

"Well, sir," Brian interrupted, looking past the man to see if any more promising customers were coming in, "it doesn't really make any sense for me to follow you around if you're going to do it yourself, does it?"

"You didn't let me finish. When we're through, you take our cart and our list. If you can get the same things for eighty dollars or less, I'll pay you that amount in cash."

"In cash?" Brian asked. "You mean, like a bet?"

"Yes."

"What do I have to put up?"

"If you can't get everything for eighty or less, you pay for the first cart of groceries."

"I don't have that much on me."

"That complicates things." The man smiled at his wife; by now, Brian had noticed that they were wearing identical rings. "But you look fairly honest. You can pay me whatever you've got now, and the rest later."

Brian thought for a moment. Then he started smiling, too. "It'll be a little tricky."

"How's that?" the woman asked.

"Well, I could bring you in for less, but seeing as how your husband wants to spend some money, it'll have to be eighty on the nose."

"Your father told me you liked a challenge," Martin Oakes said.

8

Penny

Penelope Gunn's parents divorced when she was nine. Running brought them back together four years later at a 10K race in Marblehead. Penny's mother came in seventeenth in the women's division. Penny's father, who'd pulled up after three kilometers with a bad hamstring, offered to train her if she'd give him a break on the alimony.

"You've got to be kidding," Penny said, using her thumbs to massage the stiffness out of her mother's neck. It was a soft, cloud-wrapped morning. The race had just finished. Steam rose from her mother's hair.

"Not so hard, Penny," Vivian Gunn said, hunching her shoulders. "You're hurting me." She'd been a serious smoker. When she looked at her ex-husband now, her steaming hair made it appear as if the smoke from their marriage still clung to her. "She's right, of course, Paul."

"I saw some things," he said. "I could help you."

"What did you see?"

"When did you start rinsing your hair?"

"Two years ago."

"Looks nice," he said. "Very nice."

"What did you see, Paul?"

"Are we talking about a professional relationship?"

"We're talking. At the moment, that's hard enough for me to deal with."

"Heel-toe. You've got to concentrate on going heel-toe. Right now you're running on the balls of your feet. Fine for a sprint. Terrible over distance. You're probably beating hell out of your knees and ankles. Am I right?"

"I get some lower back pain."

"Well, the rest will follow if you don't clean up your form. You've always resisted doing things the right way."

"Excuse me, Dad," said Penny, "but aren't you the one with the pulled hamstring?"

Frowning at her, he stopped rubbing the back of his leg. Vivian Gunn turned and began to walk away from him. He laughed. "Well, it's true. With her it always has to be original. Like that minefield walk." That froze her. "Look, Viv," he said loudly, knowing she hated it when he called her Viv, "you're not modeling the latest fashions from Florence, you're running a road race. Tip-toe instead of heel-toe —that's what's killing your running form."

"You know something, Paul?" she asked, turning back to face him. "I don't miss your advice. And I certainly don't miss that wicked laugh."

"You look younger, Vivian."

"Must be the rinse."

"Attitude helps. I imagine the new kid's keeping you busy."

"Seven months on a waiting list, but I finally got her

into day care." She still hadn't told anyone who the father was.

"Where?"

"Newton Highlands. A couple named Calloway. Very intense. Very conscientious. They read to the children constantly."

"And how about you, Penny?"

"I try to read as little as possible," Penny said.

"As far as Penny is concerned," Vivian Gunn said, "everything is ridiculous. Her teachers. Her studies. Her friends, of which she has precious few. Me. Especially me —right, Penny? And, of course, running. I got her to try out for the track team at school. She decided her event was the pole vault. She stuck with it a month and quit. The other kids gave her a pretty hard time."

"The pole vault?"

"Hasn't she told you?" Vivian Gunn asked. "She's officially laid claim to the women's world record, at 7 feet 6 inches. Says she's retiring until someone else breaks it."

"But women don't pole-vault."

"You know how I hate to compete," Penny said. She kept kneading her fingers in the air, even though her mother was now several feet away from her. She could have strangled them both.

"You're so athletic." He sighed. "What a waste." He turned his attention back to his ex-wife. "Ever thought about running the Marathon, Viv?"

"You know I have." She brushed back her hair with her fingers. She felt younger. It had taken roadwork, proper diet, contact lenses, blond hair rinse, and an increasing willingness to say no, but she felt younger. "This is the year I'm going to do it," she said.

"You'll need a coach."

"I won't consider any adjustment to the alimony. And I certainly won't pay to have you yell at me."

"The stopwatch doesn't yell."

"The stopwatch doesn't lie, either," she said. "Small wonder I find it such an improvement over you." It still made her giddy to think of the day she got married, standing at the back of the church looking up the center aisle. She inhaled her last cigarette as a virgin so fast and deep that the smoke gathered like incense when she lowered her veil and seeped through it in thin strands as she swayed her head back and forth, waiting for the organ to begin the voluntary. Her mother turned from the front pew, saw her daughter's white veil smoldering, and promptly fainted. By the time the smoke stopped and the organ played, her mother was revived and the veil was gray. It took only a short walk to change your whole life. A short walk that never seemed to end.

He could tell she was weakening. "We couldn't live together," he said, tuning his voice to the morning mist. "That doesn't mean we can't train together."

"I don't like this," Penny said.

"No one asked you if you did," her father said, favoring her with a smile.

THREE MONTHS LATER, in January, her parents agreed to a training schedule. "It's just temporary," Penny's mother insisted. She and Penny were in the car on their way to pick up Caitlin from day care. Newton was in the clutch of an ice storm that had torn branches from the trees and started cars sliding backward at the stoplights on Heartbreak Hill. "After the Marathon, I'll find someone else."

Penny used her finger to draw awkward stick figures on

the fogged-up passenger window. Her hand shook slightly and her eyes were rimmed with fatigue. The stick figures held hands like paper dolls.

"Penny, I'm talking to you." Despite the weather, a steady stream of runners in slickers and bicycle caps picked their way along the carriage road adjoining Commonwealth Avenue, strides shortened, spirits undaunted. Sitting in the car made Penny's mother impatient.

Penny had split a bottle of Mouton-Cadet with Melanie Bradley at lunch and felt pleasantly numb, discounting the soreness around her eyes, which never felt good, and were now even more out of focus than usual. Mouton-Cadet was a good wine for the price. Smooth. "What do you want me to say, Mom?" She and her mother always seemed to carry on two versions of the same conversation. The first was plainspoken: requests, orders, explanations, compromises —simple fuel that pushed them through the day. The second consisted of fragments, gestures, expressions, silence— slippery little exchanges that dealt with more important but less easily articulated topics. "I don't trust him, that's all," Penny said.

"We couldn't live together," her mother said tonelessly, impatient to be out with the slickers and bicycle caps. "That doesn't mean we can't train together."

"If you say so," Penny said, wiping the window clean with her palm.

"Talking is the problem," her mother said, barely controlling the car's fishtail as they took the corner on Centre Street. "We used to talk. Now we run. Running's better."

"Were you and Dad ever in love?"

"Oh, God yes. We still are."

"You can't stand each other."

"That has nothing to do with it." One hundred dollars a week was cheap for a coach with his experience.

"Is he seeing anyone?"

"I don't know." Not anyone worth mentioning. Just a fast blonde, a graduate student at Harvard he had no business trying to keep up with. Let her have him at home. She'd take him for seventy miles a week on the road any day. She happened to know that she had the blonde beaten by thirty seconds over 10K.

"Well, you can bet he is," Penny said. "He needs someone around to tell him how great he is."

"Don't talk about your father that way." The blonde was a theology student. Leave it to Paul to find religion in such an attractive package. Someday he would die in his sleep.

"Hey, I don't care what he does," Penny said. "It's his life." Selfishness with a smile. That was her father. Her ridiculous father, who combed his sparse graying hair in a swirl to cover the bald spot that sat on the top of his head like an egg in a nest.

"What a rotten day," her mother said, to change the subject. "I hope Caitlin hasn't picked up a cold from one of the other kids."

"I don't like her being there," Penny said.

"I don't either. But I have to work, right?"

"Don't you ever wish you could bring her up yourself?"

"I'm satisfied that the Calloways are responsible people." Penny could have recited the litany with her. "Their program is strict but fair," her mother said. "You've seen how much Caitlin's speech has improved. They're taught to say 'please' and 'thank you.' They're made to take naps. Toys are shared. The house has a wonderful southern exposure. You can't overestimate the positive effect sunlight has on children, Penny. And the Calloways don't serve sugar snacks."

Penny already understood one of the fundamental truths about life: no matter what you did, when you looked back on it, it would embarrass you. She had never asked her mother which of the men she'd dated was Caitlin's father. She didn't want to embarrass her. What did it matter? Caitlin would never see him. Anyway, no one was clean. When Penny found out that Abraham Lincoln sent diseased hospital blankets to the Indians, it depressed her for a week. Killing them with warmth. At the time, blankets filled with foreign germs probably seemed like a slick way to get rid of some very cold and angry people. Penny couldn't be certain that sending the blankets later embarrassed Lincoln, but it ruined him in her eyes. Ruined setting the slaves free. Ruined the Gettysburg Address. Better not to know. No one was clean. Not even Honest Abe.

"I do the best I can," her mother said as they swung into the Calloways' driveway.

"So did Abe Lincoln," Penny said.

"Please, Penny. Don't start up with Abe Lincoln and his dirty blankets again."

"Would you prefer to hear about how FDR ignored the Nazi ovens?"

"Later," her mother said, slamming the car door.

Caitlin stood damp and smiling on the Calloways' porch, the image of her mother, thick curls shooting off in every direction like jack-in-the-boxes, tights stained at the ankles with dye from her blue Nike running shoes. She was two years old. Mrs. Calloway waved goodbye from the living-room window, a book open like a fan in her hand. Caitlin bounded down the steps to her mother, who held on to the railing with one arm and caught her daughter with the other. Penny could feel the first twinges of a headache coming on. Her mother had a gallon jug of California Pinot Chardonnay open in the front hall closet. Better for marinating pork chops than drinking from a glass, but it would beat the headache, which promised to drive a spike into her temple. Her mother hugged Caitlin and spun her around on the sidewalk until the little girl's back faced Penny. "Damn it," Penny said to her mother through the windshield, unable to remember the last time she'd been hugged, let alone swung around in an ice dance, "let's get out of here. Not being able to stand each other has everything to do with it. You hear me? You don't watch out, you're going to crack her head. Read my lips, you ridiculous woman."

Her mother carried Caitlin to the car and buckled her into her car seat. "What were you saying?" she asked.

"I was just singing along with the radio," Penny said. She tousled Caitlin's hair.

"Pockalips!" Caitlin said gleefully.

"It's amazing," Penny said to her mother. "In the middle of an ice storm, she still smiles."

"It's her nature," her mother said, immediately regretting her tone of voice.

"Mommylips!" Caitlin said.

"Give me a kiss," Penny said.

"Mr. Lips is coming," Caitlin said.

"She's probably named one of the Calloways' animals," Penny's mother said.

"Or one of the Calloways," Penny said.

"Pennylips!" Caitlin wailed, pleased with herself.

That night, Penny wound up Caitlin's mechanical rabbit and tucked it into bed with her. The rabbit played the Brahms Lullaby in a continuous loop for twenty minutes, enough to put you to sleep or drive you crazy, depending. Penny returned to her own room and tried to solve the daily chess puzzle. "Leverage the queen knight," the clue suggested. An hour later, she still hadn't figured the puzzle out, and she thought she could hear moaning coming from Caitlin's room. Her mother was out taking a run. Penny crept to Caitlin's door, anxious not to wake her unless there was something wrong. She put her ear to the door. Nothing. Just when she started to walk back to her room, it started again. A low moaning. Not the moan of a child. The moan of a woman. But it was coming from Caitlin's room. Carefully, Penny pushed the door open and stepped in.

"Ooooh," someone moaned, startling Penny so much that she had difficulty locating the light switch. When she did, she turned the light on. She and Caitlin were alone. Caitlin lay on her stomach, frowning, eyes half closed, her nose poking between the slats of the crib. "Oooh," she moaned again, "my girdle is killing me."

"Your what?" Penny asked.

"*Killing* me," Caitlin said. She had the mechanical rabbit in a headlock.

"You don't even know what a girdle is," Penny said.

"Oh," Caitlin said, more in pain than agreement.

The phone rang. It was Penny's father. "Your mom home?" he asked.

"She's out running."

"I keep telling her she's going to peak too early, adding fifteen miles a week now," he said, laughing slightly, "but she doesn't listen to me. Why do you think that is?"

"Well, I could be wrong, Dad, but maybe it's because you usually don't know what the hell you're talking about. Anyway, that would be my guess."

"Look, young lady, maybe your mother lets you get away with that crap—"

"I'll tell her you called," Penny said, and hung up. The phone rang again, but she ignored it. She poured herself a glass of wine, went upstairs, sang Caitlin to sleep, solved the chess puzzle, read a Damon Runyon short story, breezed through her math homework, and began to weep without knowing why. The front door creaked open. Penny went to the top of the stairs. Her mother stood in the front hall, her hair flecked with snow, her face also streaked with tears, frozen tears that the wind had swept back from her eyes like cats' whiskers. Penny resisted the urge to run down the stairs and ask to be held. "How was the run?"

"Okay." Her mother looked at her wristwatch. "Getting there."

"Dad called. He says you're going to peak early."

"You should be in bed."

"Feel like playing a game of chess?"

"I feel like taking a bath. Besides, you always kill me."

"Maybe I need my morale boosted."

"Tomorrow. We'll play after Caity goes to bed."

But Penny knew it would never happen. Her mother hated to lose, even at chess, which she called "a game for Russians who never wash their hair."

THE WEEKS PEELED AWAY. Soon the snow and ice left the streets, and the rains came, leaving the asphalt warm and bringing the street people back like exotic flowers. Penny knew many of them. There was Sloper, who had boxed with a detached retina until virtual blindness retired him. He had practiced similar caution outside the ring, eventually guiding his taxicab through the emergency door of a school bus. Sloper didn't hack anymore, but he continued to insist that boxing, not booze, was at the root of his troubles. There was Mad Maggie, who pulled rotten feathers out of the pigeons on Cambridge Common. And there was Brody, the fabulous Mr. Brody, who danced for money on the Green Line LRVs between Riverside and Park Street in a pair of boots that stank of urine. The trains would lurch and bend around turns and jerk to sudden stops, but nothing could knock the fabulous Brody off his feet. "That's what they're waiting for," he had told Penny, smiling his black-toothed smile. "All them whiskers and skirts, they're just waiting for that train to knock ole Brody down. Now, I see a real fine gentleman with an attaché case and an umbrella and a gold tie clasp and a hanky sticking out of his fine pinstriped pocket? I will fall on him. Folks love to see someone like me fall on someone like him. It's entertaining. I make it look good, they give me dollar bills. But I'm dancing, I don't want to fall? Nothing can knock me down then. Not even wine." There was Tillie, whose son had had the hiccups for two years; nothing the doctors tried could stop them for long. The social workers came and took him away when Tillie got a little too drunk and broke his wrist. Tillie said she was trying to get him back, but everyone knew that wasn't true, that it was lucky the kid had a roof over his head.

Penny rolled a carriage to the Calloways' in the afternoons and let Caitlin ride home in it when she got tired of walking. One hot day in early March, Penny recognized Tillie's feet sticking out from the side of a bush and stopped to say hello. Tillie was wearing a coat that appeared to have been woven together from old bath mats.

"This is my sister," Penny said. Caitlin was standing in the carriage. Penny had brought along a tin of sardines in case she ran into Tillie. She handed it to her now.

"Hello, sister," Caitlin said.

"Pleased to meet you," Tillie said, rubbing her eyes.

"There's more for your life at Sears," Caitlin said.

"That's what you think," Tillie said.

One evening a week later, Penny was arguing with her mother when Caitlin appeared at the top of the stairs, clutching her rabbit. "I rule for the plaintiff," she said. She didn't say who the plaintiff was. Penny went upstairs to tuck her back into bed.

"Heal me, sister," Caitlin said.

"You're a strange kid," Penny said. "What's the matter, girdle killing you again?"

"Pockalips is coming."

"Go to sleep," Penny said.

"Praise Jesus," Caitlin said.

Patriots' Day arrived. Three Japanese were favored to win the Marathon, but one of them had been picked up by the police in the Combat Zone, unclothed and well lit, and sent home to Kyoto. Penny hoped he wouldn't be too hard on himself. Her father arrived before dawn to take her to the re-enactment of the battle on Lexington Green. The Redcoats had better uniforms than the Minutemen. After getting separated from her father in the crowd, Penny bumped into Erika Jaagstrom, whose father masqueraded as one of the Minutemen and died splendidly after several howls of defiance. There was a wonderful mingling of smells around the Green: coffee, tobacco, fog, doughnuts, gunpowder, and patriotism.

"Hello, Erika," Penny said. She had taken a small drink of peppermint schnapps before breakfast but was pretty sure it couldn't be detected on her breath. Penny and Erika sang in the youth chorus at New England Conservatory. Erika belonged to a tight group of girls that had nicknamed itself "The Top Ten." Penny had never been asked to audition. Before chorus rehearsals started, The Top Ten gathered outside on the Huntington Avenue steps and harmonized old Beatles and Motown songs. Waiting alone inside the huge glass doors to the Conservatory, Penny had scrutinized Erika up and down and found her flawless. But Erika's ability to attract other people filled Penny with a terrible envy, enough to wish that something bad would happen to Erika Jaagstrom. A minor tragedy that would show up in wrinkles around Erika's eyes and put a permanent slump in her shoulders.

It took Erika a moment to recognize Penny as the squinty-eyed girl in glasses who sat alone before rehearsals with her nose in a book and a magnetic chessboard on her lap, every now and then nudging a piece to a new position or scribbling herself a note. "The chess player," she said finally, and Penny nodded. "Where have you been?"

"I haven't felt like singing lately."

"Me neither. But my parents make me go. Look . . ." she began, but Penny's eyes anticipated the dismissal and kept her from finishing the sentence. Erika's father was still sprawled out on the ground. He wasn't accustomed to getting up this early. Concerned that he might have fallen asleep, Erika walked across the Green and lifted a corner of his tricorne hat. "Would you like a cup of coffee?"

"I'm dead," he answered, without opening his eyes. "Coffee won't help." He rolled over onto his back. His shirt was riding up over his pale, hairy stomach, and the string that bound one of his boots together was coming undone.

"Hey!" a man yelled from the crowd. "Hey, you girls! Get the hell away from there!"

Penny had followed Erika out onto the battlefield. "Excuse me," she said, pointing over her shoulder to the stocky Redcoat who was charging toward them. "I think we're about to be bayoneted."

Erika stared past Penny at the Redcoat. Her bearing suggested that if she decided to declare the battle over, it was over; anyone could see that she was the reason all these men were fighting, to begin with. The Redcoat stopped running and lowered his weapon. "Move out," he said, but to Penny it sounded more like a request than a command. Without answering him, Erika whirled and strode back toward the crowd that ringed the field.

Penny noted with interest that there was a deck of cards in the back pocket of Erika's jeans.

By the time Penny and her father returned to Newton, the temperature was in the mid-seventies, hot for running. Penny's mother ate two stacks of pancakes to pack in the carbohydrates, and washed them down with half a gallon of orange juice. "Of all the miserable luck," she said. "Who'd've known it would be this hot?" Her bare feet never stopped moving under the table, *tap tap* on the linoleum. "I don't even know where the water stations are, Paul."

"Don't worry about that," he said. He hadn't told her that his graduate student was also running. As two of several hundred unofficial runners, it was unlikely they'd spot each other. "People set up water tables every half mile or so. If anything, you'll have to resist the urge to drink too much. And for God's sake, Vivian, stay away from those people with the hoses. They mean well, and the water feels nice at first, but it'll turn your legs into tree stumps."

"Stay away from people with hoses," she repeated, the makings of a runner's trance settling across her face.

Her former husband smiled. The concentration, the focus, was there. Heat or no heat, she was ready to run. She was so ready to run he didn't think she'd even miss the child-support check this month. A deal was a deal.

Penny admired the way her mother looked in her peppermint-striped shorts and blue tank top. Her breasts in perfect proportion. Her hair spilling back across her shoulders in calculated waves. Young men along the Marathon route wouldn't just be watching her run.

"You'll be watching, won't you?" she asked Penny.

"Look for me at the intersection of Commonwealth and Centre," Penny said. "I'm meeting some friends."

"After twenty-two miles," her mother said, "I don't know if I'll recognize you."

"Maybe you'll be walking," Penny said. "After all those hills."

Her mother just glared at her.

Penny packed Caitlin into the stroller and took her to the Calloways'. An enormous American flag drooped off the Calloways' porch, its bottom corner anchored on a rosebush. In the garden, Mrs. Calloway was propping up a row of tomato plants with sticks. Mr. Calloway was on the front porch reading the Boston *Herald* and wearing his war medals.

"I thought you were supposed to wear those on Veterans Day," Penny said.

"You are," he said. "But I woke up today, and it was so sunny and fine I thought, What the heck, Calloway, put them on." His chin and neck were smudged with newsprint. "There's a new mood in America, Penny, a new spirit. There really is." A ridiculous man. She handed Caitlin over like a treaty she'd been forced to sign and hurried home.

Once there, she filled a plastic tub with Japanese potato salad, adding an extra Granny Smith apple to make it tart. She hoped her friend Heather would like it. Heather had called the night before to warn her that one of the boys she was bringing chewed tobacco. Oh well, Penny thought, just as long as he doesn't spit on the blanket. She drank a bottle of Guinness while she worked. The beer put a pleasant burn in her stomach. She cut three long loaves of French bread and filled them with turkey, roast beef, provolone cheese, lettuce, tomato, Bermuda onion, and hot grained mustard. Then she peeled and sliced a dozen kiwi fruits, and mixed them in a bowl with bananas and strawberries. After pulling out silver knives and forks and cloth napkins for four, she packed the whole picnic in a Bloomingdale's bag. The only thing missing was a beverage.

Penny decided this day called for a special wine. A wine with legs that matched her mother's. It would have to be white and slightly chilled. She decided on champagne. There were ten bottles in the cellar: three Dom Pérignons, three Mumms, two Perrier-Jouets, and two Taittingers. She ran her finger across the dusty necks of the wine bottles and finally pulled out a D.P. and a Perrier-Jouet. About a hundred and fifty dollars' worth of certain trouble. They fit comfortably in her mother's portable cooler. Penny shook three trays of ice into a dish towel, folded the towel over, crushed the ice with a hammer, and packed it into the cooler around the champagne. There were some plastic champagne glasses, with separate bowls and stems, left over from a party her mother had thrown for a local selectman. Penny assembled four glasses and put them in the Bloomingdale's bag. Before she left the house, she put in her contacts and rummaged through her mother's closet until she found a hat she liked, a straw Princess Diana job with a blue ribbon and a downturned brim. No time for makeup. She picked up the bag and the cooler, slung a beach blanket over her shoulder, and set off for the race.

The strip of grass separating Commonwealth Avenue from the carriage road was shoehorned full of people, food, beer, and radios. A block from the intersection of Commonwealth and Centre, Penny staked out a spot half the size of the beach blanket, pinned the blanket down on either side with the cooler and the picnic bag, and went off looking for Heather. They'd arranged to meet at a cul-de-sac near the Greek Orthodox church on Centre. There was no sign of Heather. Penny made three circuits around the area looking for her. After the third circuit, aware that Heather was already twenty minutes late, she started to look for a boy spitting tobacco. She could feel a knot at the back of her throat. She'd begun to sweat in the Princess Diana hat. A television crew sped up Commonwealth Avenue, followed by more advance vehicles. Policemen yelled at people to get out of the street. There were radios everywhere, providing a syncopated account of the race. Penny stopped a man and asked for an update. "Alvarez is leading the two Japanese by seven seconds in Auburndale," he said. Ten minutes away. Maybe fifteen. Penny was on the edge of panic. If she didn't leave soon, it would be too late to dodge the police and get back to her blanket on the median. She made up her mind. "Damn you, Heather Campbell," she said bitterly. "Damn your eyes."

Tillie was there waiting for her when she crossed the street. "Thought I recognized the blanket," she said. She was wearing her bath-mat coat. There was room now to spread out the whole blanket. "You okay?"

"Yeah," Penny said. Tillie handed over her paper bag, and Penny took a long pull on her wine. It was sickeningly warm and sweet, but it calmed her nerves. "Want something to eat?"

"Sure," Tillie said. Penny handed her a sandwich. Tillie took a bite and said, "Fancy. They putting the seeds back in the mustard these days?"

A van with bullhorns mounted on its roof sped up

Commonwealth Avenue. "The runners are five minutes away," one of the men inside announced. "The runners are five minutes away. Please clear the street."

"What's this?" Tillie asked, opening the tub with the Japanese potato salad.

"Potato salad," Penny said.

"With apples?" Tillie tried some with her finger. "I've never heard of that."

"There's silver in the bag," Penny said.

Brody arrived. Penny gave him a sandwich and asked him to keep his boots off the blanket.

The first wave of runners came galloping by. They had plenty of company: bicyclists, half-naked roller skaters, wheelchairs, cars with time clocks, vans with water and orange slices, fat policemen on Harley-Davidsons, even a six-seater plane trailing a banner that read MR. TELL-THE-TRUTH SAYS THE RUSSIANS TRIED TO KILL THE POPE. The sun beat down. The plane flew lazy arcs over Newton. A second group of runners arrived, then a third. Fifteen minutes later, the crowd screamed itself hoarse as the first woman passed.

Brody had never tasted kiwi fruit before, and doubted he ever would again. He pulled one of the plastic glass stems out of the bag and said, "What are these for?" Penny pointed to the cooler. Brody touched the handle. Penny nodded her head. Brody opened the cooler and nearly fainted. Tillie crawled across the blanket and let out a yelp.

"I'll pour," Penny said, pulling out the bottle of D.P.

It took them fifteen minutes to drink the first bottle of champagne. They tried to take it slow, but it was hot and they were very thirsty. By now, the street was congested with runners, and people's hands had grown sore from applauding. A man holding a pewter beer mug and a hot dog on a stick screamed hoarsely, "They're nuts! They're all certifiably nuts!"

"A picnic," Tillie said. "What a surprise."

"I was going to meet some friends," Penny said.

"Didn't you?" Brody asked, Dom Pérignon tickling the back of his throat. "Huh? Didn't you?"

"Let's open that other bottle," Penny said.

As the runners streamed by, people turned up their radios and matched the numbers on runners' shirts with their names in the sports pages. One of the Japanese had taken the lead. When he was two miles from the finish line, a group of Japanese drummers who had taken over the sidewalk outside the Hancock Building began to strike their drums. "Those mallets must weigh twenty pounds each!" the radio announcer shouted. "Look at the forearms on those guys!" Together, the drummers produced a single beat. In Newton, the drumbeat echoed along the median from radio to radio, strong and steady as their runner's heart; faster now, some of the drummers breaking off into syncopation; exultant as the winner broke the tape and staggered into the arms of his trainers.

Penny spotted her mother's peppermint-striped shorts when she was still two hundred yards away. An hour and a half had passed since the first runners sped by.

Penny's mother darted around the spray from a hose and wiped her forehead with the sweatband on her forearm. She glanced at her watch. Her pace was slow but determined. She'd never felt this much pain. Not even when Paul flew away to Florida one Palm Sunday and never flew back.

Penny shouldered her way to the front of the crowd.

Keep the arms pumping forward, her mother thought. Don't let them flail from side to side.

She'll recognize me, Penny thought. She's got to.

Finish, her mother thought, each breath like sand in her lungs. Just finish.

Penny began to wave.

I've got to pull Caitlin out of day care, her mother thought. Those people are ruining her.

"Mom!" Penny shouted, stumbling off the curb into the street. "Mom! Over here."

She turned toward the voice. Saw Penny. Squeezed out a thin smile. World record in the women's pole vault, she thought. Maybe she has something there.

Penny held up a paper cup and began jogging. "I love you, Mom," she whispered. She was smiling, too. Her face was extremely red.

Thank God, her mother thought, still twenty yards away. Her throat was so parched she wasn't even sure she could swallow. She reached out with her left hand.

Penny jogged faster to match her mother's stride.

Oh, no, her mother thought. It's all sloshing out of the glass.

Penny's brows knit together, as if she were trying to make up her mind.

I don't believe it, her mother thought. She's going to pull it away, just to punish me. But Penny handed her the glass. It was still three-quarters full. Her mother raised the glass and drained it in one swallow.

Penny stopped jogging and started to cry, leaning forward, elbows on her knees. In a moment, her knees dropped to the pavement. The road tore the skin off her palms as she pitched forward.

Her mother took ten strides, then whirled her head around, thick curls spraying sweat. Her stomach and legs begged her to stop. But her mind was still determined to finish. She continued to run, churning inside and out, on

the verge of fainting now. Tears burned out of her eyes.
Her taste buds, starved to a keen edge, screamed with
delight.

It was a little warm, and a little flat, but there was no
mistaking a glass of Perrier-Jouet.

9

Finn

Finn Collins lived a short smell away from the Cambridge city dump with his father, mother, brother, two sisters, an Irish setter, and a pack of skinny young cats that wound around the house like vines. The road separating the house from the dump was heavily trafficked and the cats seldom grew into their names. The dump bordered on a park with two baseball diamonds and a basketball court. A retarded man dribbled his scarred leather ball back and forth for hours each day, talking to himself when he shot, using the nickname Finn had given him for play-by-play. "Rebound looks, Rebound shoots. . . . Yes! What a player Rebound is!" During their games of one-on-one, Finn kept track of Rebound's baskets. Sometimes he didn't keep track of all of them. Finn hated to lose, even to the mentally retarded. "Rebound is tired," Rebound would say, sensing he could never win. When winter came, Rebound disappeared and kids began using the dump's hills for sledding. But Finn would chip away the ice on the basketball court with a blunt shovel and shoot jumpers until his toes bled and he could no longer open his right hand wide enough to grip the ball in the cold. There was just enough light from the street to see the hoop in the dark.

"Practice for three hours every day and you might actually get somewhere," said Finn's father, whose first significant move upon being picked to coach one of the Lexington junior high school teams was to import his own son as a ringer.

Finn's sister Erin, the youngest, lived in a room the size of a large closet off the front hall, her shelves cluttered with goldfish clinging to life in murky bowls of water, slugs in jars, and gerbils running a treadmill, frequently escaping their cage to leave pellets in the dust beneath her bed. Erin stashed all sorts of treasure under the bed: ribbons, marbles, bald dolls, half-eaten candy, and, one time, a bird with a broken wing. The bird had died but Erin couldn't bear to part with it.

Eileen, the cat keeper, climbed in and out of her room through a window propped open above the tomato plants that lined the southern side of the house. Using the same window, the cats woke her from time to time with rats they'd hunted down in the dump clenched in their jaws. They found the rats entertaining, and kept them alive as long as possible, playing a grim game that sometimes ended with the rats sleeping soundly in Eileen's sock drawer.

Finn's older brother, Michael, occupied the room directly above the kitchen, from which he intended to launch an unprecedented career in rock 'n' roll. Each night, the kitchen ceiling shuddered beneath the vibrations of his amplifier, a Fender Bassman, earned in ten-cent increments selling the Boston *Globe.* At half volume, the amplifier could send ripples through Erin's goldfish water and rattle the latch on the back door. "My God, I'm just trying to make dinner," Meg Collins would mutter to herself, listening to a James Taylor tape through her Sony Walkman, taking refuge in his voice, clean as a baby's tear. But her son's music still swelled up through the soles of her feet like the groan of the sump pump after a heavy rain. Michael idolized Led Zeppelin, read *Variety,* and rode with his head ducked down beneath the windows of the family car, a VW bus with no heat and bad brakes. He had nothing against the car. He just didn't want to be seen in it.

Daedalus, the Irish setter, ate, slept, and relieved himself on day-old *Globe*s in the hallway between Finn's room and the basement door. At first, ammonia removed the smell, then blended with it; finally, Finn's mother gave up applying it. The dog's urine swelled the floorboards and stripped them of varnish. Orange hair swept into Finn's room on torn pieces of newspaper.

Finn wished that his parents would stay together but never be in the house at the same time. Since they used up most of their energy fighting, Bill and Meg Collins took a creative approach toward home improvement. Wanting the interior of the house painted, Bill brought the children together one Saturday and told them they could paint their rooms whatever color they wanted. Erin was too young to paint, and no one volunteered to paint for her. Michael couldn't be bothered. Eileen chose purple. Finn chose black. Next came replacing the kitchen's dilapidated plasterboard walls. "I'll put the new ones up," Bill Collins told Finn, "if you'll knock the old ones down." Afterward, Finn remembered the feel of the crowbar in his hands on impact, the plasterboard breaking, dust filling the air, his parents' yells punctuating each silence. New plasterboard went up, but in many ways the dust never settled. Throughout the summer, Finn sat outside his parents' room on the porch roof, the road that had claimed so many cats just a good leap away; beyond it the softball field, the teams mostly Latino now, playing from noon until the lights went out at ten, staccato Spanish bursting from their mouths like rain from a sun shower, the field often shrouded in mist, the air thick with the slowly cooked smells of the city's trash.

A week after the right fielder for the Yankees killed a sea gull with a fastball during warm-ups in Toronto's Exhibition Stadium, Bill Collins took the family to see the Yankees play the Red Sox at Fenway Park. As the Yankee right fielder trotted out to right field before the bottom of the first inning, a wonderful thing happened. One by one, then in twos and threes, and finally by whole sections, the bleacherites stood and began flapping their arms. Young and old, drunk and sober, they flapped their arms, spilling popcorn and beer, ten thousand screeching sea gulls. "Yes!" Finn hollered. "Yes!" He flapped through the rest of the game, flapped in the car on the way home, flapped into bed, flapped off to school the next day. It broke his father's heart.

Finn was obsessed with flying. On his fifth birthday, Bill Collins had heard him yelling and walked outside to find him teetering on the roof of the garage. "How did you get up there?" he said, trying to sound unconcerned. "Watch me, Dad. I can fly," Finn said. "You can't fly, Finn." "Yes, I can." And down he came into the tomato plants, a look of mild surprise on his face, his nose and ankle about to be broken. Unconvinced, he jumped from the ladder to his treehouse a year later and landed on a nail sticking out of a board. The nail pierced the bottom of his sneaker, traveled through his foot, and popped out of one of the shoelace holes.

These days, Finn usually fell asleep watching TV, the light of the screen spreading out over him like a second blanket. One night, his sneakers thudded against the door as it swung open and light framed the silhouette of his father, back from his weekly bridge game. "You could knock," Finn said, without looking up from the television.

"You could stop stealing the TV. My favorite movie is on," Bill Collins said, and sat down, smelling of beer and perspiration. *"The Light at the Edge of the World.* Kirk Douglas takes on two hundred and fifty pirates."

They watched the movie together. When Yul Brynner, in an effort to flush out Kirk Douglas, ordered his pirates to row Kirk Douglas's long-lost love out to their boat in the harbor and take turns mistreating her, Bill Collins said, "Now watch what Kirk does." Kirk Douglas proceeded with stealth but without hesitation to the battery of cannons hugging the shoreline, filled them, fired them, and sank the pirate vessel, long-lost love and all. Only Yul Brynner was left now, and Kirk Douglas stalked the lighthouse. "Play the odds," Bill Collins said, staring into his palms as if looking at what life held for him, teeth bright in Finn's black room. "You've got to play the odds."

LUCK TURNED DARK the day Finn Collins decided to play the odds, and the temperature turned hot. Besides the humidity, and the Red Sox, who had wilted under it, the main topic of conversation around Boston was the Massachusetts State Lottery Megabucks Game. No one had won Megabucks in four weeks and the pot had grown to twenty million dollars, an intoxicating sum by even the most respectable standards. Garbagemen and bankers, hairdressers and lawyers, pensioners and statisticians, politicians and priests—

all waited in line to buy tickets at the local Handy Spa, sucking popsicles and wiping the sweat and mosquitoes from their foreheads, imaginations poised to test the cool swell of fortune. Finn spotted old Mrs. Tremmel laying down forty dollars on a stack of tickets, a substantial wager considering the tickets were taking the place of a week's groceries. Mrs. Tremmel threw firecrackers off her second-floor porch onto the neighborhood children every Fourth of July and seemed to derive a certain satisfaction from seeing them scatter.

Behind Mrs. Tremmel, Finn could hear the local post-man, Domenic Derosiers, known along his route as "Dead-line," arguing with Sammy Vicks over which was better, Wrigley Field or Fenway Park. Sammy Vicks sold candy for a living. "Look, Deadline," Sammy Vicks said, holding a can of soda against the back of his neck, "what the hell do you care which park is better? What you got playing on those two pretty diamonds are the Red Sox and the Cubs. Biggest chokers in the history of baseball."

"Sometimes I think they're two versions of the same plague," Deadline agreed. "When Yaz popped up for the final out in the Red Sox–Yankees play-off game, I'm telling you, Sammy, Fenway Park turned into a thirty-four-thousand-seat open coffin. My wife turned to me and said, 'Domenic, it takes heart to root for these Red Sox, but they just ripped mine out for the last time.' "

"I thought you were divorced," Sammy Vicks said.

"I am. Four years. When Marjorie's lawyer handed me the papers, I spent the weekend alone at Fenway watching the Sox drop three of four to the Orioles, wondering when she'd given up rooting for me."

"Season's tickets behind the first base dugout?" Sammy Vicks asked, scratching the rim of hair beneath the bald dome that dominated his head. "You telling me she gave up season's tickets behind the first base dugout?"

"And I didn't even scalp her ticket," Deadline said. "Do you believe it? I mean, a civil servant, you'd figure I could use the money, right? But I didn't want anyone else sitting next to me. I kept the seat empty the rest of the season."

"Waiting for her to start rooting again?"

"No," Deadline said. " 'Anyone else' includes Marjorie. I think I was just afraid if I sold the seat it would mean I'd given up rooting, too." Deadline had a talent for talking and a passion for current events that made him extremely popular in the neighborhood, even though people sometimes had to wait until after dark before he delivered their mail. Since he liked to keep up with what was going on in the world, he spent his lunch hours reading the most interesting periodicals in his bag on Sammy Vicks' front steps. His fingertips were naturally oily and left smudges on the magazines he read; the darker the smudges, the more excited Deadline had got while reading a particular article. Finn subscribed to *Sports Illustrated* and had concluded by tracking the smudges in each issue that after baseball, Deadline's favorite sports were professional hockey, college basketball, and amateur boxing. Finn wasn't the only one who used the smudges as conversational tip-offs, either. Sammy Vicks knew he could get Deadline going on the latest invention in *Popular Science*. "It'll never work," he always said, then settled back to hear Deadline explain why it would work, and how. Quite apart from the merits of the invention, Deadline's conclusion was always the same: "The world needs more inventors and fewer candy salesmen, Sammy." Mrs. Tremmel would snatch up her copy of the *American Kennel Club* and, blocking Deadline's escape, deliver a prepared speech on cruelty to animals. He approved of it. She didn't.

Waiting in line, they all had their fantasies about what they would do with the Megabucks money. Mrs. Tremmel dreamed of the slot machines in Las Vegas and a bottomless cup of quarters. A limousine and a chauffeur for getting around. A private doctor for the aches and pains. A house on the ocean where she could listen to the waves roll up on the beach. Money would make the ceaseless rhythms of life so much easier to bear. The waves would come to caress her, not to sweep her away. Sammy Vicks would build a chocolate factory and invent the perfect candy bar. He would call it The Sammy, and it would sell like TV religion. Deadline would buy a piece of the Red Sox.

"Deadline," Finn said, thumbing a wad of bills in his hand, "can I talk to you for a minute?"

Deadline saw the bills, pushed his cap back on his head, and said, "Let me guess, Finn. You want to get in on the action."

"I've got seventy-five dollars."

"But you're not old enough to bet it," Deadline said.

"Is it your money?" Sammy Vicks asked. He continued to hold the can of soda against the back of his neck, even though the soda was no longer cold and the beads of condensation on the can had run to sweat.

"It's mine to bet," Finn said, still looking at Deadline.

"Where did you get it, Finn?" Deadline asked. Mrs. Tremmel shouldered her way past them with her clutch of tickets and glared at Finn with eyes that hissed like fuses in the heat.

"Friends of mine," Finn said. He had no fantasies about what he would do with the Megabucks money, and no faith that he would win it. But he had agreed to place friends' bets for a commission of twenty-five cents on the dollar. When his older brother handed him a dollar to bet on the 7-9-27-31-32-36 combination and started to describe the recording studio he was going to build in California, Finn had said, "One shot in two million, Michael. With those odds, maybe you should plan on using Dad's tape recorder for a while longer." Craning his neck to make sure the man behind the counter wasn't looking, Finn patted the Megabucks tickets in his shirt pocket and offered the money to Deadline. "I've got all the tickets filled out."

"What do you want to waste all that money for?" Sammy Vicks asked.

"Same reason you want to waste yours," Finn said. "So I can get rich and live someplace where it doesn't smell."

Sammy Vicks leaned forward. There were little freckles on the top of his head. The freckles had turned reddish brown in the heat. He said, "Maybe you'd like to consider making a smarter investment."

"Such as?" Finn asked.

"Candy bars. I've got an extra case of Sloane Marvel Streets. Give them to you for fifty dollars."

"What am I going to do with fifty dollars' worth of candy bars?"

"Sell them."

"I'm not a salesman."

"Kid, everyone is a salesman." Sammy Vicks crossed his arms on his chest and twisted his mouth into a smile. "Besides, Marvel Street sells itself. The Marvel is pure, rich chocolate, made from an original secret Swiss recipe—"

"If they sell themselves," Finn interrupted, "how come you've got an extra case of them?"

Sammy Vicks steepled his pink fingers under his chin and looked at Finn without blinking. "Norton, the guy who manages the Convenient across from Mount Auburn Cemetery, ordered a case last week. So I take it over there yesterday, last delivery before quitting time, just in time to catch Norton pulling out of his driveway with the wife and kids. 'Where are you going, Norton?' I say. 'The Cape,' he says. 'Who's minding the store?' I say. 'Store's closed, Sammy,' he says. 'But I've got a case of Marvel Streets here. You ordered them, remember?' 'I'm sorry about that,' he says, and before I can persuade him to do the responsible thing and pay up, he's two blocks gone and I'm choking on his exhaust. Now you tell me, how am I supposed to do business with a guy just shuts up his store and drives off to the Cape when it gets a little warm out?"

Deadline said: "I wouldn't mind being on the Cape myself right now. *Fisherman's Weekly* says the blues are running so hard off Chatham all you have to do is cast and three of them'll be fighting to tie into your plug."

"What about my tickets?" Finn asked Deadline. Deadline was next in line.

"I wish you'd seriously consider my offer," Sammy Vicks said. "This bar is going to be big. Bigger than Snickers. Bigger than Milky Way. Bigger than goddamn Cadbury's."

"Doesn't sound to me like it's gotten big yet," Finn said.

Deadline flattened his ten-dollar bill on the counter and watched the storekeeper punch his tickets into the computer.

"You know what sets the Marvel Street apart?" Sammy Vicks continued, frowning as Finn stuffed the wad of bills back into his pocket. "Integrity. They don't pump it up with air. They don't stuff it full of stale nuts and gluey caramel. Marvel Street is just good, honest chocolate. You ask Sloane what they wanted to put in this bar and they'll tell you: taste with integrity."

"Buy my tickets," Finn said to Deadline, who was ready to leave the store, "and I'll pay you five dollars."

"Keep it," said Deadline. He didn't like to be hurried into delivering the mail, and he wasn't going to be hurried into buying Megabucks chances for a minor.

"Tell you what, Finn," said Sammy Vicks, steering him out of line. "You come have a look at the merchandise, listen to my offer, and if you still don't want to deal, I'll buy your tickets."

Deadline left the store. The door slapped hot air into the Handy Spa as it closed behind him.

"How many bars in a case?" Finn asked.

"Five hundred."

"At a dime apiece."

"Stores sell them for forty."

"So if I sell them to stores for twenty cents, which I probably can't—"

"You make a hundred percent profit. With no overhead."

"I'll have a look at them," Finn said, convinced that was all he would do.

They walked around the corner to Sammy Vicks' house. Finn waved a bee away from his shoulder and noticed several others buzzing lazily out from under the warped iron lid of the dumpster behind the Handy Spa. More bees hovered around the garage adjoining Sammy Vicks' house. His Cadillac idled in the driveway. "Hop in and cool off," Sammy Vicks said.

"Just show me the candy."

"It's in the car."

So was Deadline, shoes off, stretched out across the

back seat, smudging up the pictures in Mrs. Tremmel's *Life* magazine. "Too hot to read," he said. "You go shoot baskets now, Finn, your feet're liable to stick to the blacktop."

"It's not that bad," Finn said. Baked by the summer temperatures, the bottoms of his feet had become as thick and tough as a pair of moccasins.

Sammy Vicks and Finn got into the car. Finn stuck his face in front of the blast of cool air coming from the dashboard vent. In the yard, Rebound was on his hands and knees pulling up weeds and picking up after the neighborhood dogs. Finn was tempted to ask Sammy Vicks if he paid off Rebound in candy, but decided he didn't want to know the answer. It was too hot for sympathy. Rebound held a paper bag in his left hand. A plastic sandwich bag protected his right hand from the weeds and dog mess. He smiled at Sammy Vicks and held up a handful of weeds. Sammy Vicks powered down his window and tossed Rebound his warm can of soda. Rebound drained it in two swallows.

"It isn't very economical to keep your car running in the driveway," Deadline said. "Think of the gas you're burning."

Sammy Vicks pushed Deadline's feet off the cardboard box they were resting on and hoisted the box into the front seat. Then he took a penknife out of his pocket, slit the tape, and opened the flaps. His face became placid. There were twenty-five Marvel Streets packed neatly side by side in the top row. "This is a wonderful candy bar," Sammy Vicks said, pink hand tracing a path over the wrappers, voice soft as the air-conditioning. His bald dome glistened.

Finn tore the wrapper off a Marvel Street and took a bite. "Not bad." Outside, Rebound was pulling up dandelions and blowing the seeds into the air before he put the stems into his bag. Suspended in the heat, the seeds fanned out horizontally like paratroopers making an assault on Sammy Vicks' lawn. "The guys who gave me this money expect me to bet it," Finn said. "They trust me."

"Trust," Sammy Vicks said dismissively. "People who don't know how to invest their money always give it to someone else. It's got more to do with stupidity than trust."

"Then I'd be stupid if I gave our money to you."

Sammy Vicks had set him up for that one. "I'll be honest. You'd be stupid if you threw it away, all right? They gave it to you to invest. Invest it. If you feel guilty, you can always split your hundred percent profit with them." He shifted the Cadillac into reverse. "Don't tell me it never bothers you that all those kids you go to school with now have so much dough. You think they care about how good you are at dribbling and shooting a basketball?"

It made Finn nervous to have so much money on him.

"Let's take a spin," Sammy Vicks said. "We sit still here, the carbon monoxide'll get us."

"Why don't you ask Rebound along?" Deadline suggested.

"Oh, the heat doesn't bother him," Sammy Vicks said. Rebound stood up and waved to them as they pulled out of the driveway, a man with a boy's rough red eyes, accustomed to the heat, and to being abandoned. Sammy Vicks, Deadline, and Finn drove up Garden Street into Harvard Square and took the underpass onto Broadway. Sammy Vicks' constant patter faded out Finn's objections and amplified his sales pitch at the same time, as if Sammy Vicks were a disc jockey changing records. He didn't notice the precise moment when he stopped describing the Marvel Street and started describing the perfect bar: The Sammy. "I'll even give you a guarantee, Finn. Return the bars you can't sell and I'll buy them back for what you paid me."

Finn counted out fifty dollars in fives and singles and slipped the bills under the box of Marvel Streets. "I've still got twenty-five dollars," he said, "and I want Megabucks tickets."

"Deal," said Sammy Vicks. "But how do you decide which of your friends get them and which don't?"

"Easy," Finn said. "There are kids you just don't mess with." He took out a pen and a crumpled list and circled twenty-five combinations; five were his, five were Aaron Simon's, and fifteen were Jimmy V's. Besides a demonstrated preference for solving his problems with his fists, Aaron claimed to be naturally lucky, and was certain to react poorly if Finn deprived him of his opportunity to become a millionaire. Jimmy V, a known thief, and the only kid Aaron didn't push around, had recently developed the disturbing habit of coming to school in leopard-skin vests, gold chains, mirrored shades, leather pants, and studded boots. Finn and Jimmy V sometimes rode the morning bus together from Cambridge to Lexington, but most of the time Jimmy V got a lift from his brother. Everyone knew Finn had been allowed into the school because his father was the coach of the basketball team. But no one knew how Jimmy V had swung it. It was rumored that his brother Salvatore, an ex-con, had some dirt on a guidance counselor named Spriggs. One day, Finn had been waiting at the bus stop when the BMW swept by. Jimmy V had pointed out the window at Finn and said something to his brother, but the car didn't stop. "I don't want you talking to either of them," Finn's father had warned him.

Sammy Vicks pulled the Cadillac over to the curb near Kendall Square, went into a drugstore, and came out five minutes later with Finn's tickets. "I got some errands to run now, kid," he said when he climbed back into the car, "and

I got to get Deadline back. Mind if I drop you off here?"

"I don't know where the stores are," Finn said.

"Just follow Broadway to Prospect and hang a left on into Central Square. Then work your way back along Mass. Ave. to Walden. There's got to be a hundred stores between here and there. Go ahead. Make yourself some money."

Finn opened his door and dragged the box off the seat before lifting it out and setting it down on the sidewalk. "What do I tell them?"

Sammy Vicks let the car roll forward a foot. "Just tell them you're the Marvel Street man, Finn. Bar sells itself."

"But I can return the ones I don't sell."

"Right." Finn slammed the door shut. Sammy Vicks powered down the passenger-side window, slipped the car into gear, and leaned across the front seat. "Provided, of course, they're in good condition."

Finn watched the car speed away, then started walking up Broadway toward Central Square. His T-shirt stuck to his back in the time it took him to walk two blocks. His first stop was the White Hen Pantry, where he sold twenty-five bars for fifty cents each by convincing the manager that the proceeds were going toward leukemia research.

"Do you . . . that is, I mean, are you a sufferer yourself?" the manager asked.

"Yes, I'm afraid I am, sir," Finn replied. Through his shirt, his sweat defined his ribs.

He had to walk seven blocks before he found another store that sold candy. It was run by a Greek who was not interested in leukemia research or fifty-cent candy bars.

"I'll take forty bars at a dime apiece," the Greek said. His teeth were brown. A clove cigarette hung out of the corner of his mouth, and he fanned himself with a grocery bag. Every now and then, the bag came too close and knocked the ashes off the cigarette into his lap.

Finn tried a dizzy spell. Braced on the counter, coughing through the cigarette smoke, he said, "I'm sorry. I didn't want to say anything . . . well, the fact is, I'm sick."

The Greek laughed. "I had the pimples, too, young man. Don't worry. They won't kill you." His wife stuck her head out from the back room and asked what was going on. "Nothing," he said in Greek. His laugh had always been a magnet to her. "This boy here is trying to convince me he's dying so I'll buy his candy bars." She smiled at him and went away. Finn offered him the bars for twenty cents, and settled for fifteen. The Greek stubbed out his cigarette, opened a bar, and took a bite. "Very nice. I never heard of this Marvel Street."

"Neither had I," said Finn, abandoning his disease, "until today."

When he took the box off his shoulder before entering the next store, there was a patch of melted chocolate on his shirt where the box had been resting. The woman who ran the store shook her head at him vigorously while he tried to get sick again. "This is typical," she said. "I run out of ice cream. So a candy-bar salesman appears at my door. Good Lord, give a hot black woman a break."

"I'll sell you the whole box for fifteen cents a bar," Finn said.

"You aren't sick," she said, "but from what I can gather, you're deaf. My customers want ice cream, sonny, and I want beer. Go bring me one or the other and we'll talk."

The Marvel Street bars turned to liquid in their wrappers before Finn reached Central Square. The bars in the top rows retained their shape, but the bars in the bottom of the box flattened out and eventually burst beneath their weight. Chocolate dripped from the corners of the box and streaked the front and back of Finn's shirt with thin brown exclamation points.

Finn bought a bag of ice from a Chinese restaurant for three dollars and repacked the Marvel Streets around it. The ice melted, the bag leaked, and the bars slumped into the bottom of the box. Finn walked home. The sun set in his stomach, and its flames burned black behind his eyes.

Michael was home alone, locked in his room, shaking the walls with his guitar. Finn sat down on the front porch to rest. A stack of mail bound together with a rubber band propped open the screen door. Paint peeled on the steps. Daedalus appeared. Finn patted him and came away with a handful of wet orange hair. The windows in his parents' room shuddered in their frames. Finn closed his eyes. Upstairs, Michael dueled Pete Townshend, B. B. King, and "Skunk" Baxter. Michael had his favorite tracks memorized note for note and was now concentrating on mastering the artists' underlying emotions. When he did his B. B. King imitation, it sounded as if he were drawing sweat from his Telecaster.

Finn walked down the street to Sammy Vicks' house. The Cadillac was not in his driveway and he didn't answer his doorbell. Rebound was taking a nap under the porch. Finn shook him awake. "Where's Sammy?"

"Rebound is tired," Rebound said, standing up. He rubbed his eyes, then dribbled and shot an imaginary basketball. "Rebound looks, Rebound shoots. . . . Yes! What a player Rebound is!"

"Stop that," Finn said. "I've got to find Sammy."

"Sammy gone."

Finn had five hours to kill before the Megabucks drawing, and several people to avoid. He took the bus to Lexington to give Aaron Simon his tickets. The bus was hot but the ride was pleasant. Finn always liked to get out of Cambridge. There was a lot of grass in Lexington and people spent a lot of time cutting it. Men took walks in their tennis clothes and women grew tomatoes better than any you could buy in a store. The Simons had a brass door knocker shaped like a kettledrum mallet. Aaron's father answered the door and told Finn that Aaron had been confined to his room for insubordination. Finn found Aaron in a lounge chair in the backyard reading *Our Oriental Heritage* with a flashlight. Aaron closed the book, marking his place with a well-wrinkled queen of spades, and examined his tickets. Then he took Finn inside. Finn called Jimmy V. Jimmy V had Aaron read him his numbers over the phone. "It's already eight-thirty," Aaron told Finn after he hung up. "You can watch the drawing here, you want." They split two quarts of beer and a bag of goldfish crackers behind the garage. A spotted dog stood on his haunches in the kitchen, trying to paw the screen door open so he could join them. A Bach cantata soared out of the tape deck above the refrigerator; the dog's ears twitched every time the music crescendoed. "My parents are going away in a couple of weeks and I'm having a party," Aaron said. "Think you can make it?"

"Is Erika coming?"

Aaron smiled. "She asked the same question about you."

"Really?"

"No. Not really. Jesus, Finn."

They found Aaron's basketball and played a few games of one-on-one in the dark. Finn won them all handily. Finn could knock down a variety of shots from eighteen feet in, and he possessed a sinister quickness for stealing the ball on defense. Aaron kept him entertained with stories about Martin Oakes. Lexington wasn't a particularly clean town. It boasted the usual run of suburban embezzlement and marital infidelity, but this guy Oakes was something else again. Quite a bit had been made of the number of vehicles that had begun to accumulate on his property: cars, boats, pickup trucks—there was even a streamlined trailer up on blocks next to his garage. A few citizens complained that the Oakes lot reflected poorly on its exclusive neighborhood. Then a reporter from the local paper traced a late-model Audi to a member of the school committee, and established a link between the streamlined trailer and a former district judge. After his report appeared on the front page of the Middlesex *News*, people continued to go out of their way to drive by Martin Oakes's house, but they were now less worried about the neighborhood than they were curious about connecting the vehicles to the neighbors. "He can't help it if he wins them faster than he can sell them," Aaron said. Finn asked Aaron to describe the curriculum in Martin Oakes's poker class. Aaron replied that he was forbidden to discuss it. "Goddamn bugs are eating me alive," Aaron said, swatting a mosquito on his arm. With a quart of beer under his belt and the texture of Erika Jaagstrom's thick braid on his mind, Finn found Lexington sad but peaceful. "Of course," Aaron said, clapping him on the shoulder, "I shouldn't complain, Finny. Where you live, you got to worry about being bit by rats." They went back inside past the spotted dog and watched the Patriots play the Redskins in a preseason game. The Patriots were getting drubbed.

At 9:55, "Megabucks Live" interrupted the football game. A man with a tuxedo and patent-leather hair pointed to the thirty-six hard rubber balls in the spinning plexiglass globe behind him and announced, "Tonight the Megabucks jackpot stands at twenty million dollars!" The balls jumped around inside the globe like popcorn. "And here comes the first ball!" A ball popped out of the hole in the bottom of the globe and rolled to a stop in the gutter beneath it. "Twenty-seven!" the tuxedo announced.

The second ball rolled into the gutter. "Thirty-one!" Aaron ripped up his tickets and threw them at the television.

The third ball rolled down. "Nine! We're halfway there!" Finn pulled out his list and checked the numbers.

"Thirty-two!" the tuxedo announced, toupee shifting on his head.

"Oh Christ," Finn said.

"What?" Aaron said.

"Thirty-six!" the tuxedo yelled.

Finn couldn't breathe. He leaned forward, gripping his knees. An electric guitar played in his head and Michael's number formed a frightening chord in front of him: 7-9-27-31-32-36. "I don't believe it. I'm dead."

"What is it?" Aaron asked. "What the hell is going on, Finn?"

Finn stared at the screen. "Anything but seven," he said. "Anything but seven."

The last ball dropped out of the bottom of the globe and rolled into the gutter.

"Anything but seven," Finn said.

THAT SATURDAY, Martin Oakes woke from a strange dream in which the balls he used to sharpen his students' hearing jumped out of their box in the empty poker studio and began bouncing—in defiance of gravity and human intervention—on the brick platform around the potbellied wood-burning stove. To others, the dream might have been disconcerting, but Martin Oakes found it quite pleasant. Asleep in his bed, separated from the poker studio by a flight of stairs, three rooms, and the closed French doors, he couldn't see the balls and he didn't care to speculate about what they might have escaped from the box to celebrate. But he took comfort in his ability to separate out the distinct sound of each ball from the complex rhythms they produced together. As the bright red wash of the morning insinuated itself though his closed eyelids, the rhythm of his dream became more regular, until all of the random bounces had fused together into the slow, steady beat of a basketball.

Martin Oakes turned in the bed. Jennifer had already left for the club. She swam an extra mile on Saturdays before meeting him at Peking Garden for dumplings, curried meat pies, and several pots of tea. He couldn't recall hearing the doorbell ring. He got out of bed and went to the window. The balcony that had been built on top of the four front-porch pillars prevented him from seeing the person who was standing there. All he could see was a hand and a scarred leather ball. He watched the ball for a while, noting the slight delay between the time the ball slapped off the porch and the sound reached his ears. The hand belonging to the person he couldn't see controlled the ball expertly. Martin Oakes put on a robe and went downstairs to see who it was.

10

Jimmy V

Jimmy V remembered what he did by what he wore. The more articles of clothing he could recall, the more vividly etched a particular event would be in his mind. He remembered everything he'd worn the day the dog attacked his mother on Pearl Street. Tan safari shirt with a London label, pleated blue dress chinos, navy-blue ski jacket with green shoulders and collar, argyle socks, and black leather ankle boots with zippers. He'd bought the socks.

"I don't know why it happened. Usually he just barks," Jimmy V's mother said, more shaken than hurt. Her favorite produce market was on Pearl Street. She'd walked past the dog dozens of times without incident. But this time, she said, "The hair stood up on his neck. That growl of his made me so scared I couldn't move. Next thing I knew, he'd knocked me down."

Salvatore dressed the cuts the dog's claws had made on her face. "What kind of dog was it?"

For some reason, his use of the past tense frightened her. "Usually he just barks," she said.

"What kind of dog, Ma?" Salvatore said calmly.

"I don't know. A mutt, I guess. Just a big, mean mutt."

Salvatore wrote down the address on Pearl Street and warmed up his BMW. Jimmy V climbed into the passenger seat without asking if Salvatore wanted him along. Their mother watched them go. If Salvatore was angry, he didn't show it. He slipped the BMW into gear and drove slowly through Cambridge. Ten minutes later, they pulled to the curb in front of the Pearl Street house. There was a torn grocery bag on the sidewalk. Bunches of scallions, red peppers, and dried mushrooms formed a path across the lawn. The lawn was patched with dirt. Jimmy V saw the dog first. He was a solid 110-pounder, with none of it wasted. He crouched on the porch gnawing a soup bone, his snout unusually long with pronounced whiskers, his hair patchy as the lawn he had dug up in his boredom. "Jesus Christ," Salvatore said, opening his door. "It's a rat dressed up like Lassie."

"Careful, Sally," Jimmy V said. There was mud on his black leather ankle boots, but he didn't dare stamp it off inside the car. Not while Salvatore had those sleepy eyes.

"You coming?" Salvatore asked.

"I just got these pants," Jimmy V said.

The dog sprang off the porch as Salvatore approached, but there was something in Salvatore's bearing that arrested his charge. He put his snout to the ground and backed away on his haunches. Salvatore climbed the porch steps and rang the doorbell.

A fat man came to the door. He had spent twenty years bent over a jackhammer and his face had the consistency of scrambled eggs. He ran a hand over his deep jowls. He needed a shave. "What do you want?"

"That your dog?" Salvatore asked. His own stubble was even more pronounced than the fat man's; a deep blue, it sharpened the line of his cheeks and jaw and made his eyes recede into his head. He stared calmly at the fat man from a distance that was at once pleasant and disturbing. The dog sat on the sidewalk near the BMW, hackles raised, facing the door as if he were threatening to block Salvatore's escape route. Behind the fat man, some professional wrestlers were going at it on a black-and-white television.

"Who the hell wants to know?" the fat man said, trailing saliva from one corner of his huge mouth.

Salvatore closed to within six inches of his face. There was a starchy smell to the man. Salvatore's eyelids drifted down until the eyes themselves were no more than slits. "Who do you think, scumbag?"

The fat man shifted uncomfortably and braced an arm on the doorjamb. "Yeah. He's my dog."

"Buy him a leash or dig him a grave," Salvatore said.

The two men faced each other in silence. Behind the fat man, a wrestler wearing an executioner's mask shouted threats from the television. Between threats, he chewed on a turnbuckle and took deep breaths to inflate the tattoos on his chest. The fat man had the dangerous impulse to think the man at the door was also playing make-believe. "Maybe I'll just have him chew off that pretty coat of yours," he said.

Salvatore grabbed him loosely by the throat with his right hand and pushed him back into the house. "I can see we need to have a talk."

"Eastwood!" the fat man yelled. "Eastwood! Come!"

"Eastwood?" Salvatore said, without turning around. "Are you serious?"

"Come on, Eastwood!" the fat man yelled, panicking now. "Come on, boy!" The dog didn't budge on the sidewalk.

"Eastwood isn't interested," Salvatore said, closing the door behind them. "He only likes to gnaw on old ladies can't defend themselves."

"WHAT DID YOU say to him?" Jimmy V asked when Salvatore got back into the car.

"I asked him to be reasonable."

"And?"

"He seemed like a reasonable guy." Salvatore had some bills in his hand. He counted them out on the dashboard.

"He give you that?" Jimmy V asked.

"I thought he should pay Ma back for the vegetables."

"Vegetables don't cost that much."

"Some is for the vegetables. The rest is for the inconvenience." When inconvenienced, Salvatore put into practice the theory that the world owed him a living. "I've got to run over to Boston, see Carol for a couple minutes. You mind?"

"Mind?" Jimmy V clutched his heart, closed his eyes, and knit his eyebrows together. "Do I mind ecstasy? Do I mind setting my eyes on the ranking goddess of Greater Boston?" He traced an hourglass in the air with his hands. "Do I mind touching the Holy Grail?"

"I didn't say you could touch her."

"Only a matter of time, Sally, before she sees how ugly you are, runs away with me."

Salvatore looked out of the corner of his eye at Jimmy V. "Oh yeah? Where would you take her?"

Jimmy V thought for a moment. "Marseilles. Going to

get me a gold cigarette case, a manicure, and a yacht, and take Carol Banetti to Marseilles. Put her next to a sea that matches her eyes."

"What do you think she'll say when she finds out you sleep in a velvet mask?"

Jimmy V frowned. "You should try it, Sally. I'm serious. It helps you remember your dreams."

"If you were me, you wouldn't want to." Salvatore drove across the Longfellow Bridge onto Charles Street. Carol Banetti was waiting for him at the curb outside the Sevens Pub. She was wearing a miniskirt and a wide-shouldered French jacket over a white blouse. At first glimpse she seemed to be all legs, perfectly tapered legs, legs so beguiling Jimmy V couldn't take his eyes off them. But on closer examination, she became much more. She filled out improbably above the waist. Her black hair fell in gentle curls around her face. And then her mouth, with just a touch of lipstick, curved into a smile that lit up her entire body with vulnerability and innocence. If there was one thing that bothered Jimmy V about Carol Banetti, it was her smile. If you looked at her long enough, you couldn't help noticing that the rest of her had grown up, but her mouth had remained the mouth of a little girl. She walked over to the car. Salvatore rolled down his window. She kissed the air next to his cheek. "You talk to Miller about the Celts-Knicks game tonight?" Salvatore asked.

"Yes," she said. "He can't make it."

"Can't make it? I already bought the tickets."

"Sorry." She smiled at Jimmy V. "Hi, kid."

"Jimmy's going to take you to Marseilles," Salvatore said.

"That's nice."

"First I got to get a yacht," Jimmy V said.

"What are we going to do with a yacht?" she asked him.

"Have parties. Sail around."

"Goddamn Miller," Salvatore said, gripping the wheel. "I told him about this game a week ago."

"Something came up," Carol said. "His wife is dragging him to a play or something." She smiled at Jimmy V. "That's a nice shirt, Jimmy. Where'd you get it?"

"London," Jimmy V said, then corrected himself, "I mean, that's where it was made."

"I don't want to waste these tickets," Salvatore said. "Can you think of anyone else?"

Carol looked at her watch. "I've got to meet someone in half an hour. I doubt I could find anyone."

"I like the Celtics," Jimmy V said. Salvatore and Carol looked at each other and laughed. "Hey," Jimmy V complained, "what am I, a leper?"

Carol looked down at the street, waiting for Salvatore to make up his mind. Finally, he squeezed her hand, turned to Jimmy V, and said, "Sure. Why not? The three of us will go, take the night off."

SALVATORE TOOK CAROL and Jimmy V out for lobster at Legal Seafood before the game. He and Carol drank champagne. Jimmy V wore white cords, a Lotus Metro T-shirt, and a vented blue pinstriped dinner jacket he'd heisted during the Fourth of July Pops concert on the Esplanade. The men at the restaurant stared at Carol, but looked away when they saw Salvatore.

After dinner, they walked to Boston Garden. Carol caught Jimmy V trying to carry himself like Salvatore and teased him: "Just a little version of big trouble, aren't you?"

Salvatore laughed and punched Jimmy V in the shoulder—
not a hard punch, but Jimmy V's whole arm went numb.
They stopped for ice cream in the North End. Several men
came up to greet Salvatore. Salvatore introduced them all to
Jimmy V, but acted as if Carol were not there. When he saw
Salvatore treat Carol like that, Jimmy V wanted to tell her
she was a street goddess, that the world wasn't all hardness,
that she shouldn't let her mouth give in to the rest of her
body, that he loved her and wanted to steal her away from
his older brother with every fiber of his larcenous little
heart.

Their seats were directly behind the Celtics' bench.
They rose for the national anthem, but Salvatore was the
only one who could remember all the words. Jimmy V went
to get them all pizza. By the time he got back, the Celtics
had already jumped out to a ten-point lead. "Bird has been
hitting from everywhere," Salvatore told him. The Celtics'
lead grew to twenty-four at halftime. By the end of the third
quarter, victory assured, Bird came out of the game. One of
the Celtics' ball boys handed him a Coke and draped a
warm-up jacket over his shoulders. Bird put the cup on the
floor and hooked his gnarled hands behind his neck.

"I want that jacket," Jimmy V said.

"Is that all you ever think about, grabbing clothes?"
Salvatore said angrily.

Jimmy V was unfazed. "I walk into school with Bird's
warm-up jacket, Erika Jaagstrom probably just falls down
and worships me."

"It's not such a kick," Carol said, "being worshipped."

An involuntary twitch ran through Jimmy V's entire
body. He bobbed up and down in his seat, gripping the
armrests. There were ten minutes left in the game. Before
the final buzzer sounded, security guards would draw a tight

ring around the parquet floor to keep fans from streaming onto the court. Jimmy V could see some of the guards coming up the ramps from the concessions. "I get that jacket, the whole school dies."

"Well, go ahead and get it, then," Salvatore said. "I'll tell Ma where she can bail you out."

"Wouldn't be her first time," Jimmy V said.

Salvatore slapped him. "Never talk to me like that. You hear me? Never!"

Jimmy V covered his head with his hands.

"You didn't have to do that, Sal," Carol said.

"You want one, too?" he asked.

"Sure," she said. "Go ahead. Show everyone what a tough bastard you are."

Salvatore dug his fingers into Jimmy V's shoulder, the shoulder he had hit earlier. "Do you realize how much it cost me to bring you to this game?" he asked. "Show some respect."

"I'll pay you back for the ticket," Jimmy V said.

"You idiot," Salvatore said. "I'm not talking about the ticket." He stood up, put on his coat, and glared at Carol.

"Look, Sally," Jimmy V said, "I didn't mean any-thing." There were still five minutes left in the game.

"No one ever means anything," Salvatore said quietly. He had seen men die in the joint from saying things they didn't mean, and was still getting used to what he considered a lackadaisical attitude toward talking on the outside. "You should try picking your words as carefully as you pick your fights, Jimmy." He turned to Carol. "Meet me in front of Polcari's in twenty minutes." He disappeared around the corner of an exit ramp.

Jimmy V stood up. "All I said was—"

"Don't worry about it," she said, catching him by

the sleeve and pulling him back into his seat. "He'll be fine."

"We used to kid around all the time," Jimmy V said, "before."

"Yeah, well, this is after, isn't it?" Carol said. "Don't take it personal, Jimmy. It's the basketball. The basketball makes him flaky."

There were two minutes left in the game when Jimmy V spotted Salvatore making his way down the aisle to the Celtics' bench. "What the hell's he doing now?" Jimmy V asked Carol, pointing out Salvatore's location. Salvatore shouldered his way past a security guard and walked right up behind Bird. The security guard approached Salvatore, speaking into his walkie-talkie. Bird's warm-up jacket was hanging on the back of his chair. Salvatore pulled the jacket off the chair, rolled it into a ball, and stuck it under his arm. The security guard pocketed the walkie-talkie and reached out with both hands to grab him. Salvatore snapped a back fist into his solar plexus. The security guard staggered back and fell into a spectator's lap. Salvatore stepped by him and started up the aisle, breaking into an easy jog. "I don't know," Carol said. "Looks like he's cracked." The final buzzer went off as Salvatore fled down the runway toward the Celtics' locker room.

WHEN THEY HAD waited outside Polcari's for an hour, Jimmy V said, "He should be here by now."

"You want to go, go."

Another twenty minutes passed. It was Jimmy V's first chance to talk to Carol alone, but he couldn't think of any topics that seemed appropriate. They waited in silence, Carol staring straight ahead, Jimmy V admiring her. Carol was so beautiful that men in cars slowed down to look at her as they drove by. Wind blew in from the harbor, spitting a fine rain. Jimmy V went into the restaurant and bought Carol a cup of coffee. She used it to warm her hands.

"You and Sally've been together so long," Jimmy V said finally. "Think you'll ever get married?"

Her laugh parted the column of steam that rose out of her Styrofoam cup. "I wouldn't put any money on it," she said, and Jimmy V thought he could almost see her mouth hardening in the darkness.

A taxi screeched to the curb. Salvatore got out and held the door open. "Get in," he said. He was wearing the Celtics jacket and smoking a cigar. There was another man in the back seat of the cab. Jimmy V and Carol got in. "Carol, this is Angelo Lopresti," Salvatore said, pointing his cigar at the man next to her. "Remember? You met him last summer, down the Cape."

"Angie," the man said, holding out his hand. He was thin and well dressed, with silver hair and a leathery, sun-creased face. His cologne was almost as potent as Salvatore's cigar.

"Nice to see you again," Carol said, but she did not take his hand. After a moment, he withdrew it.

"It's an accident I run into Salvatore," Angelo Lopresti said. "I am driving down Hanover when this crazy man runs into the street. Doesn't look or nothing. Just runs right out. It's Salvatore. He doesn't see us. But we almost hit him. From the way he's running, I expect to see someone behind him with a gun. So I have my driver pick him up, and I give him a cigar, and he is most kind to tell me about his adventure, and now here we are." When he smiled at Carol, his lips pulled back and stretched tight across his gums. He had four gold teeth.

"It's a nice cigar," Salvatore said slowly, his head enveloped in smoke. He shifted in his seat. The Celtics warm-up jacket clung to him. He took it off and handed it to Jimmy V. "You owe me," he said. Jimmy V ran his hands over the jacket, then rubbed it against his cheek. "Go ahead," Salvatore said. "Try it on." Jimmy V slipped into the jacket and pushed the sleeves up to his elbows. "There's just one thing," Salvatore said. "Look at the back."

Jimmy V took off the jacket and turned it over. The name stitched into the back of the jacket was Kite, not Bird. "Kite?" Jimmy V said. "Greg Goddamn Kite? Jesus, Sally, you grabbed the wrong jacket!"

"Bird was wearing it, wasn't he?"

"It isn't the same," Jimmy V said.

"I can always take it back, you don't want it."

They drove past the Boston Common and turned up Beacon toward Kenmore Square. Streetlights flickered like candles above the rain-slicked blacktop. There wasn't a downpour big enough to clean the city of Boston; all the rain ever did was move the dirt around. "Tell me, Carol," Angelo Lopresti said, "you ever think of becoming an actress? You got the looks for it."

"No," Carol said, hands folded in her lap, staring straight ahead. "No, I never have."

Jimmy V leaned over to Salvatore and whispered, "Who is this slime?"

Turning sideways so Angelo and Carol couldn't see his face, Salvatore exhaled a mouthful of smoke, raised his thumb and forefinger to his lips, and slowly zipped them shut. Then he patted Jimmy V on the shoulder. "The jacket looks good," he said. "Maybe take a little growing into, you know?"

"I don't think I'm ever going to be six nine," said Jimmy V.

Salvatore's eyelids fluttered down. "Jimmy, you don't have to be big to be bad."

THE COUCH THAT killed Jimmy V's grandfather was intoxicatingly comfortable. No one was prepared for what happened, least of all Jimmy V. Giorgio Petrocelli was eighty-three years old and Jimmy V had got used to the idea of him being around forever. His death whittled the Vitaglianos down to a family of three and raised some serious questions about what to do with the couch. "The day he bought that couch was the first day I ever saw him relax," Mary Vitagliano told Salvatore and Jimmy V. Giorgio Petrocelli had left Palermo for America with two daughters, five hundred dollars, a guitar, a trunk full of clothes, and a reasonable feel for produce. His wife hadn't survived the birth of Mary's younger sister, Theresa, and Theresa didn't survive the Atlantic crossing. Giorgio brought Mary north to Boston, opened a pushcart in the Haymarket, and did his work and minded his own business. He paid the people he had to pay for protection. When his daughter married Johnny, the oldest Vitagliano boy, he didn't have to pay anymore. But he and the Vitaglianos never got beyond formally tolerating each other, and when the Vitagliano family lost its clout and Johnny disappeared for good one day, he refused to let his daughter wear black. "Not for him, Mary. Not for me. Not for anyone. Listen, there's already too little light in the world. The world doesn't need beautiful young women walking around shrouded in black." But he was curiously traditional in other ways. He wore two watches: Palermo time on his right hand, Boston time on his left. Whenever his Italian customers asked him what time it was, he always smiled and responded, "Where?"

The one thing missing in Giorgio Petrocelli's life was

a decent meal. Before she discovered northern Chinese food, Mary Vitagliano had managed to stay out of the kitchen for over forty years. "This fear of the stove isn't natural, Mary," Giorgio complained. "And I'll tell you something else. It isn't healthy." Little by little he wore her down, until one day he came home from his walk to a house filled with unfamiliar smells: sesame oil, coriander, ginger, wood ears, lily blossoms, brown vinegar, burnt Szechuan peppers, Chinese cabbage. Even the cooking wine smelled Oriental. "What in God's name is going on?" he asked.

"Dinner," Mary Vitagliano replied. "Have a seat." Salvatore and Jimmy V were already at the table. Jimmy V's starched Brooks Brothers shirt and black bow tie attested to the solemnity of the occasion. Mary brought out a platter of pan-fried dumplings, and served them with hot oil and slivers of fresh ginger.

"What are those?" Giorgio asked.

"Raviolis."

"Those aren't raviolis."

"For your information," Mary Vitagliano said, "the Chinese were eating raviolis before the Italians learned how to mix dough." Next came hot and sour soup, then shrimp with black bean sauce, then two-sided yellow noodles. Giorgio felt as if his stomach were being invaded. But the meal settled nicely, and so did the meals that followed, and in time Giorgio began to look forward to the surprises that arrived from the kitchen in steamer baskets and lacquered bowls and wonton wrappers. Dinner became a time for adventure and discovery. They all had to adjust. Jimmy V started to look around for Chinese clothes. Salvatore frequently burned his throat by grinding espresso beans in the coffee mill the night after his mother had used the mill to shred hot dried Szechuan peppers. He eventually learned to check the mill for telltale flecks of red. Giorgio, meanwhile, put on fifteen pounds and secretly vowed to curb his cravings for two-sided yellow noodles.

Salvatore always shaved at six o'clock, just before dinner. He liked his pillow to feel smooth on his face at night. But his barbed-wire whiskers grew in fast and threateningly while he slept. By the time he woke up in the morning, his face already lay in shadow, and his appearance would continue to darken throughout the day. Mary Vitagliano liked him clean-shaven, but had difficulty understanding his motives. At first, she mistook his habit as a sign of reverence. Forced by the weight of the evidence to rule out reverence, she settled on believing that for all his misdeeds Salvatore was at least capable of common courtesy. While he fumbled with his chopsticks at dinner, she would pinch his chin between her thumb and forefinger and say softly, "A terror during the day. But still my little boy at night."

THEN THERE WAS the matter of the couch. Giorgio claimed the couch was upholstered in corduroy but stuffed with tranquility. Its deep cushions were just soft enough to sap away tension, just stiff enough to provide support where it was required. "This couch knows anatomy better than any doctor I've ever been to," Giorgio told Jimmy V one day between naps. When Giorgio was out strolling the neighborhood, Mary Vitagliano would sit down on the couch fully intending to read a book, but after a few minutes she would decide to lie down and put her feet up; then she would close the book; then she would fall asleep. Salvatore watched football games leaning on one of the couch armrests. He was the only one who fell asleep sitting up. Jimmy V was forbidden to do his homework on the couch after he tried to implicate it as an accomplice in his poor performance at school. But if he had a problem, he always went to the couch before he went to his family. Jimmy V could sleep off almost anything.

Giorgio Petrocelli smelled garlic and Parmesan the morning he stretched out on the couch to read the Sunday paper for the last time. But the smell was coming from his memory, not the kitchen. Coming from the couch. He checked his watch. It was dinnertime in Palermo, and a teenaged breeze was blowing in his mind. His wife appeared before him, slim and pretty in a white dress tied at the waist with a pink ribbon. "It's time," she said, and she held her hand out to him. But he was afraid. "What are you making?" he asked. "You know I'm not talking about dinner," she said. There was a little tightness in his chest. "I feel fine," he told his young bride. "The garlic here, though, it doesn't taste the same. Maybe it's because Mary will only cook Chinese. Well, at least she's finally cooking." His wife took hold of his right hand and smiled at him. Him so old, her so young. After all these years, their hands still fit together perfectly. "Come on, Giorgio," she said. "Come back to Palermo."

AT FIRST, Mary Vitagliano wanted to get rid of the couch. She thought she would always see her father there as she had discovered him that Sunday, slumped embarrassingly over the want ads—had he actually been looking for a job? —eyes open, his body still knotted with energy but emptied of spirit. There was only one thing to do, and that was to throw the couch out. No one would buy it. It was too old, too worn. It was comfortable, too, so comfortable, but you couldn't put a price on that kind of comfort, comfort that had nothing to do with how the thing looked. She asked Jimmy V to see to its removal. He nodded, but two weeks after they buried her father it was still in the house. They didn't sit on it. They didn't even talk about it. Another month went by. The couch became a sort of shrine. One night while all three of them were watching the evening news, Salvatore, who was sitting on the floor, backed up until he was just barely leaning against the front of the couch. The next day, while she was dusting, Mary Vitagliano reached down and pushed her hand into one of its cushions. Jimmy V came home from school that Friday and, without thinking, dropped his books on it. His mother saw the books and screamed at him. Salvatore put an arm around her and held her face against his shoulder so Jimmy V wouldn't see her crying. "It's okay, Ma," he said calmly. "He said you shouldn't wear black. He didn't say you couldn't sit on the couch." Time passed. They missed Giorgio. They also missed sitting on the couch. No one wanted to be first, though. Mary Vitagliano thought they should all join hands and jump in together, as if the couch were a May ocean. But the proper moment never presented itself. One day, Jimmy V came home after flunking an exam and just collapsed on the couch in his Celtics jacket. When his mother found him, she fell to the floor, propped her elbows on his heaving chest, and thanked God for the memory of her father. The house had finally begun to breathe again.

THE VITAGLIANO BROTHERS heard about Martin Oakes's poker class from Claude Rivoli of Saugus. Rivoli had lost a customized fishing vessel to Oakes in a game of seven-card hold 'em. "I don't know why he bothers to teach the game," Rivoli told them. "He's the best I've seen. With what he can make off the sucker trade, not to mention the legitimate sharps, I just can't figure the kid angle. No money in it." The prize tuna Rivoli had boated off Nantucket in the annual summer tournament was mounted above the living-room mantelpiece of his two-story Cape in Saugus, but lately he had been skipping some of his mortgage payments and it looked as if he and the tuna might have to find another place to live. With his wife's lawyer calling him several times a week about delinquent alimony payments, he'd borrowed money from Salvatore and now did most of his fishing off a pier in South Boston, where the flounder were plentiful, if somewhat bloated and tumorous. Jimmy V felt sorry for Claude Rivoli. In his present circumstances, it was doubtful that he would ever be able to touch the principal on his loan, but he was a well-meaner, and he might come in handy sometime if Salvatore decided not to hurt him.

"May I help you?" Martin Oakes asked when Jimmy V and Salvatore showed up at his door without an appointment. His tone of voice suggested he doubted it.

"We hear you teach poker," Salvatore said.

"Not to adults," Martin Oakes said. He didn't invite them into the house. He was getting ready to go out. Jimmy V noticed the ghostly quality to his face, something that looked through them even as they were looking through it. A cashmere scarf hung from a peg by the door. Martin Oakes flicked it free, snapped it over his head, then pulled it with each hand several times, left and right, left and right, as if he were shining the back of his neck.

"Why not?" Salvatore asked.

"Because before I could teach an adult anything, he would have to unlearn too much of what he already knows."

Jimmy V thought it was a little warm for the scarf. Reaching the same conclusion, Martin Oakes took off the scarf and wrapped it around the inside doorknob.

"We're friends of Claude Rivoli," Salvatore said.

From the expression on his face, Martin Oakes looked as if he'd been watching at the pier when Salvatore had thrown Claude Rivoli's fishing equipment into Boston Harbor and dumped his bucket of fish onto the pavement and pushed his face nose-deep in the rank water and called him a shiftless little bottom feeder in an effort to get him interested in maybe making some money. Jimmy V could have told Martin Oakes that Salvatore didn't really expect Rivoli to pay off—not with money, anyway. But it was bad PR to have one of your accounts whistling on a pier all day, dangling his toes in the water as if he had no more cares than Huck Finn floating down the Mississippi. People weren't stupid. With what Rivoli owed Salvatore, he would need a trawler to pay it off in fish. Rivoli cried while he watched his fishing gear sink. He didn't make any noise, but the tears streamed down his pinched little face. Jimmy V didn't understand how Rivoli could get so worked up over not being able to catch inedible flounder, but seeing the gear sink seemed to take all the hope out of him.

"How old are you?" Martin Oakes asked.

"Fourteen," Jimmy V replied.

"I don't have an opening right now. If you'd like to be put on the waiting list, I'll let you know if a place opens up."

Jimmy V squared his shoulders, suddenly conscious of his posture. Martin Oakes's eyes were too bright to admit to a color. Maybe it was just the way they were picking up the sun.

Salvatore had taken a step back on the porch. He offered Martin Oakes a business card.

"And what is it you do, Mr. Vitagliano?" Martin Oakes asked, pocketing the card without seeming to move his hands.

"I'm in real estate." Salvatore threw his head back and

peered at the house with the skepticism of a tax assessor. Martin Oakes nodded his head at the performance, but his eyes said he didn't believe it. "Investments," Salvatore continued. "That sort of thing. What do you do?"

Martin Oakes smiled without warmth. "I'll call if a place opens up," he said, and shut the door. The phone rang but he decided to ignore it. It was getting cooler outside. He finished putting on his jacket and reached for his scarf. It wasn't on the doorknob. He glanced at the empty peg, scanned the floor, and checked inside the sleeves of his jacket.

By the time he reached the end of the footpath, the BMW was just making the turn from Estabrook onto Massachusetts Avenue. The passenger window was open. As the car accelerated up the hill, Martin Oakes's cashmere scarf fluttered out of the window as if it were waving good-bye.

THE SECOND TIME the dog attacked Mary Vitagliano, she needed fifteen stitches in her calf, and the doctor decided to keep her overnight in the hospital to make sure the wound wasn't infected. When visiting hours were over, Salvatore and Jimmy V drove to the supermarket. They both went inside. Jimmy V bought shoe polish. Salvatore bought a thick slab of prime rib. Then they drove home. Salvatore unwrapped the prime rib and laid it on the dining-room table. Jimmy V put a tape into his cassette player and searched through his drawers for a rag and a buffing brush. Salvatore rummaged through the kitchen cupboards until he found a cleaver and a tin of rat poison. Jimmy V found a rag and the buffing brush and began shining his black ankle boots. Salvatore returned to the dining room, opened the tin of rat poison, and poured three teaspoons of pellet onto the prime rib. He used the flat of the cleaver to press the poison into the meat.

Jimmy V had finished one boot and started the other when Salvatore came into his room, holding the cleaver loosely by his side. "Let's go take a ride," Salvatore said, his throat constricted. "Something I want you to help me with."

Jimmy V held up the boot on his left hand. "I'm almost finished."

"Wear sneakers." Jimmy V suddenly connected with the sleepy look in Salvatore's eyes. He put the half-polished boot down immediately. "Okay. Just give me a minute."

They drove to the house on Pearl Street. Salvatore didn't talk, so Jimmy V didn't know where they were going until they got there. The house was dark except for the unsteady glow of the fat man's television. There was no sign of the dog. Salvatore drove past the house to a corner three blocks away. He parked the car and handed Jimmy V a plastic bag.

"I don't get it," Jimmy V said, feeling the prime rib through the plastic.

"With any luck," Salvatore said, "neither will the dog."

"You put something in the meat?"

"Rat poison. Dog looks like a rat. I figure he should die like a rat."

Jimmy V looked down at the floor of the car. "Sally, all we got to do to get the dog destroyed is call the police."

"The police will want sworn testimony, and twenty-five forms signed, and after we go through all that crap, maybe —just maybe—in three or four months they'll give old Eastwood a lethal injection, which will allow him to die painlessly." Salvatore barely opened his mouth as he spoke. "I don't want him to die painlessly. I want him to suffer."

"Christ, Sally, he's just a dog. A dog can't help it if he doesn't have a leash. It's his owner's fault."

"I want him to suffer, too," Salvatore said.

"I still think we should call the police," Jimmy V said.

"I went and got the Celtics jacket for you," Salvatore said. "You're going to do this for me, Jimmy."

Jimmy V got out of the car. Some of the blood had dripped out of the plastic bag onto his pants: green chinos with pleats and an elastic waistband. He walked slowly up the street, legs feeling strangely disconnected from his body. It was a clear, cool night. Jimmy V couldn't stand to see his mother in pain. Salvatore was right. The dog really did deserve to die. Jimmy V swung the plastic bag as he walked, and thought of his mother in the hospital, and wondered if he would ever understand honor. The poisoned meat sloshed back and forth in the bag. Jimmy V came to the house, and started up the path to the front door. Tires peeled out and guns went off on the television inside the house; the fat man's jackhammer had ruined his hearing. Jimmy V whistled, short and high. The dog didn't come. Jimmy V took the meat out of the bag and waved it around in the air. He was almost at the front door when he heard the first growl. He turned around quickly, expecting to be charged. But he didn't see the dog. Another growl. He turned back to the door. Scratching. "Jesus Christ, he's inside." Jimmy V walked to the door and, standing on his tiptoes, peered through one of the narrow windowpanes at Eastwood. Eastwood looked hungry. Eastwood also appeared to have at least a dozen skin diseases. Jimmy V held the meat up to the window. Cars collided on the television. Ring the doorbell, Jimmy V thought, and ask the fat man if Eastwood can come out to die. "Eastwood," the fat man yelled—there was a commercial on now—"you mangy mutt, get the hell in here!" Eastwood backed away from the door on his haunches. Jimmy V went quietly over to the living-room window and peeked inside. The fat man was watching television with his feet propped up on an ottoman and his back to the window. The TV reception was poor, and the screen was filled with ghosts. There was a quart bottle of tequila and some 7-Up and potato chips on the table next to the television. The tequila bottle was about three-quarters empty. Eastwood padded into the room and took up what looked like a habitual position to the right of his owner. The fat man reached down and scratched him behind the neck. "What's the matter with you? I thought this was your favorite show." Eastwood shifted his head from side to side to get the full benefit of the scratching. The fat man's hands were so arthritic the joints looked as if they had been soldered together. "Good dog," he said, and reached for the tequila. Jimmy V backed away from the window. Blood dripped from the meat onto the porch. Jimmy V noticed the blood, knelt down, and wiped it up with his shirt sleeve.

BEFORE SALVATORE could ask Jimmy V why he had run home instead of to the car, he saw the Celtics jacket, what was left of it. There were pieces of the jacket everywhere: on the floor, on the couch, hanging off lampshades, wound around the dining-room chairs. Jimmy V heard the door shut and walked out of his room, holding the cleaver. Salvatore saw him coming. Jimmy V's mouth quivered. Salvatore's face showed nothing. Jimmy V walked over and put the cleaver down gently on the couch. "Your meat's in the freezer," he said. "I didn't kill the dog."

Salvatore held his hands out, palms up. "Jimmy."

Jimmy V took a step back. "I'm all right, Sally. There's just one thing you've got to understand." He looked around the room sadly at the remnants of the best piece of clothing he had ever owned. "You're not going to do to me what you did to Carol Banetti."

11

The Test

All of you have been cheated," Martin Oakes said, realizing as he spoke the words that they had been true even before any of his current students had joined the class. He had chosen Aaron, Erika, Carl, Brian, Penny, Finn, and Jimmy V with the conviction that among all his applicants they were the seven who needed the lessons most. "Betrayal is a weakness which one of you has unfortunately spent the last several weeks practicing as a skill. I assert it now. If the rest of you will just calm down, and try to be orderly, we can proceed."

An orange band of sunlight cut through the west window of the poker studio and mingled with the smoke from his cigarette. He was chaining the Camels together now, using the stubs to punctuate his sentences. Outside, leaves swirled and fell on the porch. Martin Oakes had never liked autumn. To him, it was all dwindling light and dissipated energy, students rushing off to the first day of school with sharpened pencils to learn the wrong things over and over again until the lessons became so dull they barely left an impression. With the kind of education children received at the schools that Martin Oakes drew his students from, it was no wonder so many parents mistook brittleness for discipline. "Teach your child to squirrel away facts in a file drawer," Martin Oakes had warned one proud parent, "taking proper care to label the facts so that she can pull out and present them upon request, and you will succeed in making her a squirrel." Not in my class, he thought now, squinting into the orange light. In my class, they must squirrel away victory and acknowledge defeat. Organization without guile is nothing. Facts will never do them any good until they learn how to manipulate them.

His students stared intently at everything except each other. From across the street, they could all hear the sound of a neighbor's rake scraping against the flagstones on his front walk. Their senses were so keen that the faintest sound popped in their ears, the autumn light hurt their eyes, and the poker table felt cold and slick as marble. Pine sap hissed in the fireplace, a crisp sweet smell telling of the end of summer, a draining away of greens to gray. Martin Oakes visualized the pillow-shaped smoke hovering above his house, spreading out beneath the cold weight of the air come south from Canada.

Waiting had turned the accused student's face a brilliant red. "Proof," the student demanded. "You need proof. What have I done to deserve a Test?"

"I think you can guess. For starters, you currently enjoy the distinction of having the lowest cumulative point total in the class."

"People go up and down the points ladder all the time."

"And some simply stay at or around the bottom of the ladder, as you have done for the past four months."

"Are you saying I haven't been trying?"

"I do not measure trying in this class. I measure results. You know that. You must act upon that. In the last five exams, you have scored no higher than fifth. Your grasp of the game's mathematics is fair—not, I suspect, because you are incapable of grasping them, but because you simply don't believe in them. Your chip management is consistently poor, your card memory and analysis skills are almost nonexistent, and your attitude toward learning the subtle refinements of the game is, to be generous, questionable at best. Your patience, meanwhile—"Martin Oakes held up a supple, resigned hand and said, "But then, patience is not the point. You stand accused of being a cheater. How do you plead?"

"I won't stand," the student said, "and I don't plead."

"Well put," Martin Oakes said. He stared at his remaining six students and allowed himself a smile. Even when a student failed, it was a pleasure to see courage, however futile. A poster on the wall reminded the class KNOW WHEN TO QUIT BUT NEVER SURRENDER! When he had brought his smile under control, Martin Oakes folded his hands, leaned over, and rested his elbows on the table. "But there's really no point in being stubborn, Finn."

"I'm not being stubborn, Mr. Oakes," Finn said. No longer Mr. Collins. Just Finn. Calling his victims by their first names was the first way Martin Oakes began to separate them from their classmates. Finn said evenly, "I'm just waiting."

"Waiting," Martin Oakes repeated, thinking back to the morning Finn had stood bouncing his scarred leather basketball on the porch without ringing the bell. "Would you care to tell us what for?"

"Well," Finn said, "take one of your examples. You say I cheated Erika and Willow by looking at discards and peeking at their hands. But that particular game was two weeks ago, and you didn't stop it then. What were you waiting for? And how could you know what I was looking at unless you were using my eyes?" It was a fear all of Martin Oakes's students shared: that he could use their eyes. He couldn't possibly see all the things he saw and play all the angles he played with his own no-color pair. The slightest glance from him could influence a decision to bet or fold up. Finn continued, "You've admitted that all of your evidence is circumstantial."

"Not all," Martin Oakes replied. "Actually, I had a reason for collecting the cards when I did. Isn't there something you'd like to show us, Finn?"

"No."

"Oh, I think there is. I think there's something very interesting that you need to show us." He took the deck of cards that Finn, Aaron, Penny, and Jimmy V had been playing with and handed it to Erika. "Would you count these, please, Miss Jaagstrom?"

Erika dealt the cards, slapping them down on the table in five piles of ten cards each. Having a deck of cards in her hand made her feel older. After she finished counting the cards, she held the last card in her hand for a moment, then flipped it face up across the table toward Martin Oakes. She hoped he was impressed. "Fifty-one," she announced quietly, eyes drifting up to Finn at the end of the table. "There are only fifty-one cards in this deck. One card is missing."

"Not exactly missing," Martin Oakes said, steering the card Erika had flipped him back toward the rest of the deck. "Misplaced, I think, would be the more accurate word." He nodded to Jimmy V. "Separate the cards by rank."

Jimmy V combined the five piles Erika had made and flattened the cards face up on the table with a practiced sweep of his hand. The movement reminded Martin Oakes of a glissando on the piano: just as wide, just as false. Martin Oakes watched Jimmy V's arms swim out of his Hawaiian shirt as he spread the cards, and chuckled inwardly at the thought of him in an oversized sequinned jumpsuit with epaulets, mashing cards on a bar table or notes on a bar piano beneath the chintzy glow of a candelabra, playing more for the smiles than the dollars. Though his fashion sense would fluctuate, it seemed entirely within the realm of probability that Jimmy V's clothes would someday outweigh Jimmy V himself.

Jimmy V tapped the spread deck with the tips of his perfectly trimmed fingernails until the corner of each card was visible. Instead of separating the cards by rank as Martin Oakes had ordered, he simply ran his eyes across them three times, and said, "Ace of hearts."

"Are you sure?" Martin Oakes asked.

"Positive," Jimmy V answered. He turned to Finn. "Cough it up."

"I don't have it," Finn said.

Brian, when he weighed the deck in his hand, didn't trust Jimmy V's quick appraisal. The heft seemed right, but with only one card missing he couldn't be certain. He checked the deck one card at a time, relegating the cards to their proper suits as Martin Oakes had commanded, and verified that the deck contained only three aces. "Nice trick, Jimmy," he said. "Quick."

"He doesn't look for what's there, Willow," Penny said, rubbing her eyes. "He looks for what isn't there."

Aaron got out of his seat and took two steps toward Finn. "I suppose the first place to check is up his sleeve."

"Sit down, Mr. Simon," Martin Oakes said.

Aaron remained standing. "I say we search him."

Carl steepled his fingers under his chin. "Don't be an ass."

"Who's an ass," Aaron said, whirling to face him. Carl Rice would never survive in feudal Japan, Aaron thought. In feudal Japan, Carl Rice would whisper lies into a warlord's ear and eventually have his head handed to him on a samurai sword, wise mouth and all. End of discussion. There wasn't a mouth in the world that would look wise at the end of a samurai sword. In fact, if Carl's head were forced to look back objectively upon Carl's body, it would probably even cease to mourn the separation.

"He says he doesn't have it," Carl said, thin voice making it clear that Aaron irritated rather than intimidated him. Carl wondered how Martin Oakes planned to draw the card out of Finn. Seated calmly in his chair, Carl studied Finn with a pleasant feeling of detachment, concentrating to make sure he would spot any movements that might prove useful in future games. It was always fascinating to see a student unravel during a Test. It usually started with the hands. They would twitch involuntarily. Then the shoulders would roll forward. Breathing would become constricted. Finally, the head would begin to bob up and down at a very rapid rate, erratically, until the subject's mouth was gulch dry and his eyes could no longer focus or blink. Carl had seen all these symptoms before, and it surprised him that Finn was showing none of them. Finn simply looked petrified. Perhaps he would begin falling apart at the feet, just suddenly crumble from the bottom up. Carl rubbed his calves together under the table, pleased with how strong they had become since he had started bicycling twenty miles a day. His thighs had grown, too; the only problem was that they were separated from his calves by his under-lubricated knees. But Carl wasn't complaining. When class was over, he would hop on his ten-speed and race down the Massachusetts Avenue hill, crouched low over the handlebars, defying the brittleness in his knees and his elbows and the back of his neck, parting the wind and putting an invisible crease in autumn.

"Take it easy, Aaron," Brian said. "No sense in heating up." Brian had always felt sorry for Aaron without knowing precisely why. When he joined the class, Brian immediately recognized Aaron as the enthusiastic marauder he had met by accident the previous Halloween near the Lexington-Arlington border on his way home from a soccer game. Aaron, who had long since passed middle age as a trick-or-treater, was wearing a samurai costume. As Brian approached, Aaron darted back and forth across Massachusetts Avenue, slashing bags in half with his wooden sword, preaching discipline and sacrifice to the uncomprehending ghouls and goblins who wept as their candy spilled into the gutter and nearby puddles. "Be glad that I don't split you in half with a nashi-wara," Brian heard Aaron warn a boy who could not have been more than nine years old, at which point he intervened for fear that Aaron had misinterpreted the somewhat flexible rules of Bushido.

Still staring fiercely at Carl, Aaron nodded to Brian, went back to his chair, and sat down.

"Finn," said Martin Oakes, extending his hand, "this may come as a surprise to you, but it offends me when people remove cards from the deck. For one thing, it is discourteous to honest players, who depend on fifty-two cards to calculate the odds. For another, by the time the hidden card finds its way back into the game, it is usually crimped or damaged in some way and thereafter sticks out in the deck. So at the same time the card that is held out robs honest players, it also tempts them into planning their own robberies. The crimp, or tear, is a piece of information, and poker players must not ignore a single piece of information that confronts them during the course of a game. I certainly wouldn't expect it to escape the notice of your classmates." His hand was close enough to grab Finn now. His fingers flexed white at the joints, then curled back toward his palm, asking for the card. "With limited insight into this matter, I am assuming the others didn't see the ace on its way out, Finn. I would at least like to make sure that they learn how to spot such a card on its way back in. Come on." Flex. "Be reasonable." Curl. "I bet you couldn't help putting a crimp or two in the ace, could you?"

"I don't have it," Finn said evenly. "You want to search me, go ahead."

"There's another way," Martin Oakes said mildly. "Stand up, all of you." When the students were all standing, all but Finn, he continued, "Since Finn insists on being uncooperative, I'm afraid we'll have to do this by process of elimination. Search the room."

Penny looked at her jacket hanging by the door and mentally unscrewed the cap from the pint bottle of Jim Beam stashed in the inside pocket. "Why don't you just take out the card and get it over with, Finn?" she suggested, swiveling her head back and forth in a general appeal to her classmates, imagining the sweet burn of liquor sliding down her throat.

Finn presented a curious spectacle, sitting with his chair pushed away from the table, back straight, eyes unblinking, hands cupped on his knees, almost as if he were anticipating a surge of electricity at any moment. Erika and Penny maneuvered around him, looking under chairs, opening books over the floor and shaking them up and down to see if he'd wedged the ace into one of the bindings. Aaron checked the throw rug.

Carl studied Finn's face as Finn watched the whirl of activity. "Willow," Carl said finally, "why don't you try the fireplace?" When Finn snapped his head around, Carl silently congratulated himself.

Brian removed the grate from the fireplace and scattered the ashes with the cast-iron poker. "I don't see anything."

"Look for what isn't there," Jimmy V said.

"What the hell do you mean by that?" Brian asked.

Jimmy V stepped up to the fire and breathed in a lungful of the smoke Brian had raised. "All you're doing is mixing it up. Let me have a look." The fire made Jimmy V's Hawaiian shirt transparent over his slight frame. He peered for several moments into the fire, brown irises dancing red, before exclaiming, "Got it!" He snaked an arm into the fireplace and drew out a scrap of charred paper no more than a half inch around.

"I knew it," Carl said.

Jimmy V handed the scrap of paper to Martin Oakes. Martin Oakes laid it on the table while Aaron, Penny, Erika, Carl, Brian, and Jimmy V huddled around.

"What is it?" Penny said. "Looks like a little red blob to me."

Brian traced the part of the shape that was missing. "It's a heart."

"Finn?" Martin Oakes asked.

Finn stared at the floor.

"You can see by the shape of the corner that this had to be an ace," Erika pointed out.

"I'm running out of what little patience I was born with," Martin Oakes said. "Let's get on with it."

Finn closed his eyes.

"Do you refuse to defend yourself, Finn?" Martin Oakes asked.

Again, Finn said nothing.

"Show nothing," Aaron said.

"Know nothing," said Jimmy V blandly, checking his fingernails for dirt.

"What's the point?" Brian said uncomfortably. "No one's ever passed a Test before."

"Just tell him to go," Penny said.

"Finn?" Martin Oakes repeated.

"I think he's in a coma," Carl said.

Finn stood suddenly and swayed forward, as if his legs were locking up on him.

"That's enough out of all of you," said Martin Oakes. "If you're going to show anything, show some class. Otherwise, I would recommend that you keep your mouths shut." He leaned back in his chair, head tilted sideways, arm fully extended, and poured the rest of his tea into a small spider plant hanging forlornly in the window. If the plant managed to survive on a steady diet of cigarette smoke and cold camomile tea, there was always a chance that Jennifer might rescue it to the lush life of the kitchen.

"Last chance, Finn," Martin Oakes said. No response. He surveyed the room. "Very well, then. Prepare to vote." His students leaned forward, eyes closed and pressed against their forearms on the table. "All those in favor of expulsion, raise your hands." Six hands shot up immediately and refused to come down, hanging in the air with the certainty of kites above a park on a clear day with an even breeze. Only Jimmy V peeked. The fire spit embers through the metal grate of the potbellied stove onto the brick hearth. Martin Oakes snapped the lid of the Coffin shut. Lower on the horizon now, the orange band of sunlight had filled out into a thick column, its impression on the poker studio interrupted only by the green legs of the spider plant and the shadows of six arms that fell across Finn like prison bars. The neighbor's rake continued to scrape across the flagstones as if it were keeping time for the dry melody of autumn: dead leaves and hungry birds. "All those against," Martin Oakes said, for Finn's sake.

12

Smooth Jake

When Martin Oakes got the word that Smooth Jake Warner had finally agreed to play him, he tried to sleep, but he couldn't, so he got in the car and drove all night to Virginia. It was summer, a year since the Sam Kim bet; another year would pass before he started the poker class.

Smooth Jake was a legend. Ace Roldan, one of the men Martin Oakes had beaten, called Smooth Jake "the meanest, roughest, hardest-bitten cardplaying snake east of Vegas," and Roldan had seen enough gambling pits to be reliable about identifying the reptiles that managed to crawl out of them.

Smooth Jake's face and hands were red and dry as Arizona clay, and it was said about him that he could work his eyelids like Venetian blinds. Some even went so far as to say that his concentration made it possible for him to see his opponent's cards. It wasn't clear whether he accomplished this by looking through the backs of the cards or by actually peering into the opponent's mind, but the result was the same.

Smooth Jake lived in Middleburg on an estate called The Little Boltons that was anything but: the front door was exactly 1.4 miles from the front gate. He employed a full-time staff of thirteen. The youngest employee did nothing but cut grass. The oldest, a former jockey named Johnny March who had retired to raise Smooth Jake's horses, did nothing but collect the paper every morning. A stroke had fixed a permanent smile of bewilderment on his face, and getting the paper had become the focus of his entire life. The plastic *Washington Post* box was next to the front gate, and Smooth Jake thought the walk was good for him. Smooth Jake also thought that 1.4 miles was too far to go and get the paper himself. Johnny's daughter Martha was Smooth Jake's cook. Seeing her father set off on his journey each day made her sad, but seeing him return made her proud. Sad because it was all he had left. Proud because he could still find his way. And Smooth Jake made a point of looking genuinely pleased when he took the paper. "There's a lot happening in the world, Johnny," he would say, shaking his head. "I'm damned if I can make any sense out of it." The two qualities Smooth Jake looked for in his remaining ten employees were loyalty and a willingness to be flexible. Between the cars, the carriage houses, the guests, the tennis courts, the pool, the greenhouse, the parties, the cooking, the silver, the horses, the topiary, and Smooth Jake's reputation, there was enough work to go around.

Martin Oakes pulled into Middleburg before dawn, slept for three hours next to the *Washington Post* box at the end of Smooth Jake's driveway, and awoke when Johnny March hobbled down to get the paper at eight o'clock. Johnny March paid no attention to him. An engine sputtered to life in the distance. Too small for a car, not loud enough for a motorcycle. A lawn mower or a go-cart, Martin Oakes decided. Johnny March carefully folded the paper under his arm. His smile looked as if it had been dried in place by the sun. Martin Oakes rolled down his window. "My name is Oakes. Mr. Warner is expecting me." Johnny March didn't answer him or even look at him. Instead, he turned and started walking back toward the main house. An enormous lawn mower appeared in the distance, chewing up grass and spitting its smell into the humid air. Martin Oakes nodded to himself, lit a cigarette, and instinctively reached for the deck of cards inside his coat pocket. Ten minutes later, a chocolate-brown Mercedes sped up the road and turned in to Smooth Jake's driveway: chauffeur in front, a man and a woman in back. Johnny March was still visible in the distance. The woman turned to look at Martin Oakes as the Mercedes drove past. He kept his face passive, his eyes unblinking. The coffee in his thermos was cold. He drank it anyway. Between sips, he shuffled the cards on the dashboard. Middleburg, Virginia, seemed much too serene for poker. Too quiet. Too still. A good place for a Civil War battle. Screams and Confederate picnics and the smell of gunpowder would provide the balance that was missing here. Somewhere in the main house that was too far away to see, Smooth Jake was taking his coffee hot and black, smoking the day's first cigar, calling his brokers and real-estate agents, working those Venetian-blind eyes, buying friends and marking victims and warming to the day's gambles.

The word was Smooth Jake Warner had a mean streak where everyone else had a spine. Just as calm and courteous as could be, he would take you apart, and you would never be able to put yourself back together again. Representative

Bedford, the conservative Republican from Michigan, had visited Smooth Jake at The Little Boltons for a weekend the previous December. The following Monday, he called a press conference to announce that he would not be seeking re-election, even though his campaign war chest was full to brimming and the polltakers had made him a prohibitive favorite to return to Washington for a fifth term. Asked to comment on what had compelled Bedford to pull out, Smooth Jake would say only, "Perhaps he's had enough of politics," but anyone who had known Frank Bedford for any length of time knew that without politics he did not have a life at all. Ivan Smid, the pianist, had visited The Little Boltons for three days one spring. He hadn't played a concert since. He had also reneged on his recording contract with RCA. By all accounts, he no longer practiced, and didn't even keep a piano in his Manhattan townhouse. No one knew for sure why he had quit. Smid wasn't playing. Smid wasn't talking, either. Neither was Malcolm Frederick, who had his bantamweight crown stripped by the World Boxing Council after he spent two weeks at The Little Boltons and subsequently declined to fight the number one contender—or, for that matter, anyone. Frederick would have received nearly two hundred thousand dollars for the title defense. Unfortunately, what he had lost in aggressiveness he had apparently gained in appetite; at a soft one hundred and eighty pounds, it was a reasonable bet he'd bid adieu to his bantamweight days forever.

Smooth Jake believed that people had a marvelous capacity to adjust.

Martin Oakes lit another cigarette. The Blue Ridge Mountains really did look blue. Smooth Jake's guests seemed to experience a certain career paralysis after they visited The Little Boltons. Everyone who had come up against him was apparently willing to endure the harshest sacrifices with the utmost discretion. Mosquitoes hovered aimlessly around Martin Oakes's car. Up north, mosquitoes made the most of their two-week life spans, biting anything that moved. Down here they seemed to think mealtime was an obligation. He swatted three of them flat on his arm before they got around to biting him. He had fifteen thousand dollars in a duffel bag in the trunk of the car.

At nine sharp, shirt wrinkled, hair combed, face dry-shaved, he steered his Torino up the path to the main house. White and low to the ground with no sharp edges, the Torino looked as if it had been designed to clean the inside of a fish tank. But its 302-cubic-inch engine could blast down the highway and blur most of his cosmetic objections. Martin Oakes held the engine to Smooth Jake's ten-mile-per-hour speed limit. Half a mile up the path, the fourth floor of the house peeked out over the steep pitch of the lawn, then the third.

The house got wider as it got lower. Outside, there was a satellite dish; Smooth Jake monitored his stock quotes and sports bets in real time. Inside, according to what Martin Oakes had read, there were thirty-three rooms, including five baths, two kitchens, a seventy-by-twenty-five-foot dining hall, two elevators, a sauna, a library, and a greenhouse. None of this particularly impressed Martin Oakes. What impressed him were the Doric columns that dominated the front of the house and proved Middleburg was a place to play poker after all. There were six of them, in alternating latex colors: two white, two red, and two blue. Six giant stacks of poker chips. Architecturally speaking, Scarlet O'Hara had moved in with Jimmy the Greek. Martin Oakes was so transfixed by the columns that he nearly flattened the birdbath at the bottom of Smooth Jake's oval driveway. When he pulled to a stop, he counted the horizontal lines across one of the columns. There were twenty-five chips in each stack. The kid on the lawn mower waved. There was grass to cut in every direction for as far as the eye could see. By the time the kid cut it all, it would be time for him to start cutting it again.

A woman came out of the house. Not the one he had seen in the car. This one looked as if she worked on her exits as hard as she worked on her entrances, and was always doing one or the other—Martin Oakes wasn't certain which now. Once she descended the stairs from the porch, she turned and made her way toward him. With ten feet to go, she held out her hand and said, "Mr. Oakes? I'm Meghan Warner. *Welcome* to The Little Boltons." She said it as if he had won the trip. She had the height and grace of a model, but there was a vibrancy in her thick auburn hair and a focus in her eyes that Martin Oakes guessed couldn't be captured on film. "Jake's a little busy just now," she said, her voice projecting out across the lawn. "He asked me to come and meet you."

"It's a pleasure to make your acquaintance, Mrs. Warner." She was an extremely attractive woman, but he couldn't stop staring at the columns.

"Like them?" she asked.

"Well," he said, "I've never seen anything like them."

She laughed and ran her hand through the air; if the columns were strings, she might have been strumming a chord. "Yes. Well. They've given half the town heart attacks."

"I can imagine."

The Mercedes was parked in the shade of a rhododendron bush. It had diplomatic license plates. Meghan Warner gestured toward the house. "Won't you come inside and have a drink?"

"If it's coffee," he said.

"It can be anything you want it to be," she said. "You take it black, don't you?" He nodded. "Like Jake," she said. She was either perceptive or well informed. They went inside. In the kitchen, Martha the cook was serving coffee and apple pie to the chauffeur of the Mercedes. There was a large wheel of cheddar cheese on a cutting board in the middle of the table. The chauffeur carved off a wedge of cheese to put on his pie and glanced suspiciously at Martin Oakes.

"What's the matter with him?" Martin Oakes asked. "Is he mean or just hungry?"

"Oh," Meghan Warner said, one hand to her mouth as if she were asking the chauffeur if he liked the pie, "you know these people who're paid to break heads. They're always looking for heads to break." When the chauffeur stared at them blankly, Martin Oakes realized he didn't understand English. Martin Oakes was already beginning to like Meghan Warner. She steered him through a side door and out onto a patio overlooking the pool. A brass frog spit water into the shallow end. The surface of the pool rippled with liquid clouds and the odd band of sunlight. The patio was shielded from the sky by a hydraulic tent top. Smooth Jake sat facing the pool with his back to his wife and Martin Oakes. He was wearing a pink polo shirt and Bermuda shorts and rubbing some sort of lotion into his bare feet. The feet were propped on a glass table crowded with empty orange-juice glasses, a silver coffeepot, and three plates smeared with egg yolks, syrup, and uneaten scraps of French toast. The man and woman from the Mercedes, dressed in business suits, sat together on an all-weather couch at an angle from Smooth Jake, drinking coffee. From the man's appearance, along with the strong aroma of the coffee, Martin Oakes guessed he could have grown the beans —or, to be more specific, owned the land the beans were grown on. His female companion, by contrast, looked Nordic. She was tall, blonde-haired and cream-skinned. Meghan Warner's entrance seemed to fall across the blonde like a shadow.

The Latin was leaning forward, one hand on each knee of his immaculate trousers. Martin Oakes glided quietly onto the patio. He could see that the Latin had mistaken his unobtrusiveness for the skill of a servant come to inquire if Mr. Warner and his guests required a fresh pot of coffee or perhaps some cigarettes. Smooth Jake was concentrating on lubricating his feet. "I'm afraid I still don't see how poker players are really any different than, say, horseplayers," the Latin said to Smooth Jake.

"For one thing," Smooth Jake said, "poker players do their own running. I know this guy, The Needle, serious poker player. We're sitting in a nice restaurant one day after a session and there's this party of four on the other side of the place drinking champagne and eating lobster. It soon becomes clear from their boisterous conversation that they have just been at the track, where they have won a large amount of money. The Needle thinks horseplayers are dim, and he doesn't change his mind when he finds out that one of the guys happens to own the horse that has won them all this money, which they are now investing in champagne and lobster. The horse's name is Lotus Position, which for some reason further irritates The Needle. After introducing himself, he says to Lotus Position's owner, 'I'd be willing to bet you that I can beat your horse in a fair race over six hundred yards.' The owner takes a look at The Needle, who looks like a race to the death between food and smoking, and says, 'You're not serious, man.' 'Sure I am,' The Needle replies. An argument ensues, during which The Needle, who is exceedingly well oiled, makes disparaging remarks about higher-quality horses not being fit for much besides higher-quality glue. Lotus Position's owner, meanwhile, speculates that The Needle will drop dead halfway through the race, making it tough for him to collect on his bet. In no time, eight of us are on our way out to the track. Lotus Position's owner offers us a ride in his limo, but The Needle insists on taking a cab. 'Get your money down before it's too late, Jake,' he says. 'This one's a cinch.' "

Martin Oakes listened to the story. He knew The Needle. He wondered when Smooth Jake would look up from his feet and say hello. The Latin caught Martin Oakes's eye and nodded casually toward the silver coffeepot. Martin Oakes smiled and held out his hand for the Latin's cup and saucer. The cup rattled unsteadily during the exchange because the Latin wasn't looking. Martin Oakes steadied the cup and saucer on the glass table, lifted the coffeepot, and filled the cup. The coffee smelled strong. He lifted the saucer, inclined the steaming cup toward his mouth, and took several rapid sips. It was good coffee. Much better than the cold stuff he had drunk in the car. The Latin scowled. The icehouse blonde sucked in her cheeks in what struck Martin Oakes as an unusual expression of mirth. He drank more coffee.

Smooth Jake continued: "We get to the track. The Needle hands the cabbie a fifty and tells him to wait for us. The limo arrives. Two of the owner's friends head back to the stables to grab a jockey and get Lotus Position limbered up. The owner instructs the track attendants to open the gates and let us in. The Needle removes his hat and coat and starts stretching, a painful sight that all assembled find quite amusing. He can't touch his toes, but he can almost touch his knees. The horse crowd is passing around a bottle of Southern Comfort. The Needle asks for the bottle. When he gets it, he pours out about three jiggers' worth into his palm and rubs the liquor into his calves. In trots the jockey on top of Lotus Position. Lotus Position is a fine horse; you can tell he spends all his time working out and eating wholesome grains. The Needle suggests that they take their marks. The owner nods to the jockey, and the jockey starts to bring the horse around. Meanwhile, The Needle turns and waves the cab in through the open gates. The cabbie drives right across the manicured grass infield onto the track. The Needle climbs into the back seat, and says, 'Would you mind dropping a handkerchief or something to get us started, Jake?' Lotus Position's owner, of course, registers his displeasure in no uncertain terms, but The Needle is unmoved. 'Our bet is that I can beat Old Glue Pot in a fair race over six hundred yards,' he says. 'I never said anything about running.' "

The Latin smiled hollowly at him. "But I thought you said poker players did their own running."

"Yeah," Smooth Jake replied, clay-red hand gesturing with the tube of moisturizing lotion. "But we never run when we can drive."

"Don't you own horses yourself?" the blonde asked.

"Yes. Eight of them. I won them playing cards." Following the Latin's gaze, he turned and looked up at his wife. She introduced Martin Oakes with an impressive sweep of her hand. "Martin Oakes," she said, "Jake Warner."

"Well," Smooth Jake said, "I'm damned if the man doesn't look like a poker player." He held out his hand. He had black hair and a wide forehead, thin slats for eyes, and a brow ridged with uneven deposits of cartilage. He was sixty-three years old, and he'd been gambling seriously for fifty of them. It was clear to Martin Oakes that the cartilage had built up beneath an accumulation of blows. What struck him as curious was that Smooth Jake's craggy brow somehow harmonized the rest of his face; experience had beaten him like a drum, but he seemed to have weathered the blows and come out the winner. His smile was wide but his lips were thin; the corners of his mouth seemed to jut out directly from his cheekbones. The skin on his neck and arms and hands was as dry and snug as scales on a desert dweller.

"It's an honor to meet you, sir," Martin Oakes said, shaking Jake's hand.

"You know, it really wasn't necessary for you to sleep at the end of the driveway," Smooth Jake said. "We've got a spare room or two up here at the house." No amount of moisturizer would saturate that arid skin, thought Martin Oakes. He might as well rub sweat into the Sahara.

"I pulled in late."

"Mr. Oakes, what's late for most people is morning for you and me." He put the tube of lotion down next to the breakfast plates and rose. "I'd like you to meet Mr. Hernández, and his companion, Miss Stecker."

"We've heard all about you," Hernández said, without extending his hand. The woman nodded from the couch.

"Are you here to play cards?" Martin Oakes asked.

Hernández sighed as if it were an effort to answer him. "Nothing so exciting, I'm afraid. I'm just looking for a place to live."

Smooth Jake said, "Mr. Hernández is from Central America. He's got a good shot at becoming his country's next President if the military decides to let people vote."

"A decision," Hernández added in a more serious tone, "that at the moment seems too remote for serious consideration."

"I'm trying to convince him to buy The Little Boltons and make it his country's capital," Smooth Jake explained to Martin Oakes, the wrinkled corners of his mouth making it difficult to tell if he was smiling or not. "That way, if the people ever get the vote, he can run the country from up here."

"Where it's safe," Meghan Warner said.

"Unless I am mistaken," Miss Stecker said quietly from the couch, "one of Nicholas's grandsons is still living in a house outside Paris, waiting for the Russian people to ask him to be their czar." Hernández frowned at her. There was a thin film of sweat on his brow, but her voice was cool. "He's still living outside Paris," she said. "An old man now. Drinking wine. Reading newspapers. Tending his garden. Keeping the line pure."

Meghan Warner said, "Well, I'm sure he has a very nice life."

"That is rather beside the point, isn't it, Mrs. Warner?" said Miss Stecker.

"There's so much to do in France," Meghan Warner said breezily to Hernández. "I'm always after Jake to take me to Paris, but he never will." She turned to Smooth Jake. "If you don't mind, I think I'll show our guest to his room."

"I was rather hoping you would," Smooth Jake said.

As they were leaving, Meghan Warner's whispered words to Martin Oakes contradicted the smile she had displayed to the rest of them: "An hour of that woman is more than anyone should have to bear."

They climbed two flights of stairs and walked down a narrow hallway. She stopped and opened the door to a room with a huge four-poster bed, ornate lamps, a chest of drawers, a raised bathtub on cast-iron eagle's claws, a matching cast-iron sink, and an antique desk and chair. "This is where we put Jake's guests," Meghan Warner said pleasantly. "I do hope you enjoy your stay." She pointed out soap, towels, and a small refrigerator and bar above the sink. The chest of drawers gave off a scent of lemon-verbena sachet. "If there's anything you need, just let us know."

Martin Oakes sat down and spread his arms out across the desk. "Maybe a quill pen."

"Try to enjoy yourself while you're here," she said. "You can always write about it later."

"Has your husband mentioned when he wants to start our game?"

"How could he?" she asked, in the doorway now, braced for one of her exits. "He's not even sure if you'll play yet."

MARTIN OAKES took a bath and a nap. During the nap, he dreamed about lemon trees. When he woke up, he considered unpacking his clothes into the chest of drawers, knowing that if he did he would have to wear the lemon scent for as long as he stayed at The Little Boltons. He decided he would dress out of his bag. He went out into the hallway and traced his steps back to the phone he had seen on the staircase landing. He picked up the phone.

"Yes, hello," a voice said brightly on the other end of the line before he could dial. It was Martha the cook. "What'll it be?"

"I could use something to eat," Martin Oakes said.

"See what we can do," Martha said, and rang off before he could ask her what time it was.

Fifteen minutes later, there was a knock at his door. "Come on in," said Martin Oakes.

Smooth Jake opened the door and entered the room holding a tray. He was dressed in tennis whites, and his sneakers were streaked with clay dust. The dust matched the color of his skin. He put the tray down on the desk, stood up on the antique chair, and poked at a spot in the ceiling. "Damned leak," he said. "I thought I'd fixed it." Small brown rings of dampness had expanded outward from the spot he was pointing at, like the rings in the trunk of a tree. The tray held two bottles of Mexican beer, a pair of cut-glass tumblers, and a plate with steak, a baked potato, and creamed peas on it. Martin Oakes let the smell of the steak take hold of his stomach. "Go ahead," Smooth Jake said, "dig in." Martin Oakes took the tray over to the bed and started eating. "You own a house?" Smooth Jake asked.

"Yes."

"Does it bother you?"

"The house?"

"No. Owning it."

Martin Oakes poured beer into one of the tumblers and took a sip. "I haven't thought about it much," he said. It was living in it that worried him.

"I have," Smooth Jake said. "I remember the first house I owned. Little ranch job in Chevy Chase. Pamela, my first wife, was all worried about the social scene: who to invite to her parties, whose parties to go to, whose parties to avoid. Me, I was worried about the faucets, the oil, the storm windows, the termites in the beams, the five layers of wallpaper that had to be peeled off. I had always thought it would be difficult for me to adjust to being married. But marriage was nothing compared to owning a house."

"A house is easier to get rid of," Martin Oakes said.

Smooth Jake's laugh was a quiet hiss. "You've met Pamela, then?" Martin Oakes shook his head. "All the same," Smooth Jake said. "It got to the point where I would win someone's boat and the first thing I would think of was leaks. Leaks and pitted chrome and bad gas mileage." He shook his head at the ceiling and stepped down off the chair.

"I ran a credit check on you. As far as I can tell, you're free of debt."

"I brought the fifteen thousand."

"Good. I'll send someone around to get it, put it in the safe." Smooth Jake picked up the second bottle of beer from the tray and opened it. Then he walked over to the window and looked down.

Outside, Martin Oakes could hear the steady chewing of the lawn mower in the distance and, nearer, the bounce and *thwock* of a tennis rally. "Who's playing?" he asked.

"Meg and the Stecker woman. Really going at each other. Meg has her by a set, but I think she'd prefer to have her by the throat." Smooth Jake drank from the bottle. "Perhaps you'd care to join us for doubles later on?"

"I'm not a tennis player."

"Neither was I, until recently. With all the money I sink into the court, I figured I might as well learn. I just hired a landscaper who has a terrific serve. Used to be nationally ranked." He looked out the window at Miss Stecker thumping forehands from the baseline. "The grounds are going to hell, and I've got a two-ton pile of flagstones waiting to be laid. But my service return is improving. Do you know what the key to returning serve is? Anticipation."

"Anticipation's the key to a lot of things," Martin Oakes said. He didn't ask Smooth Jake why a nationally ranked tennis player had taken a sudden interest in landscaping. "That was an interesting story you told Hernández. Is it true?"

"True enough. The car won. No money changed hands. A good memory, though. Tell me, do you think you could have given Hernández a haircut before he noticed you were there?"

"Maybe."

"I hope Hernández doesn't manage to get himself killed. He doesn't really pay attention, does he?"

"I spoke with The Needle the last time I was in Vegas. He says to tell you he misses the action."

"What's The Needle doing now?"

"Drinking, mostly." Martin Oakes chewed a mouthful of steak and listened to the tennis ball go back and forth. "Why did you finally agree to play me, Mr. Warner?"

"Your name's been getting around."

"I've been trying to get a game with you for four years."

"Everyone has to pay their dues. You're no different." Smooth Jake sat down in the chair and propped his feet up on the desk. Some of the dust from his sneakers settled on the desk blotter. "I heard about your game in New York with Roldan and Constantine. Picking those two guys clean in the same night is quite an accomplishment."

"I had some cards."

"Constantine won't talk to me about it, which I take as a point in your favor. Constantine has always been very handy with excuses when he loses, so he must not have any. Roldan says you're still a little rough around the edges, but you know how to bet them up. Did I hear correctly that Roldan paid you off with one of his Jaguars?"

Martin Oakes nodded his head. "He was shaking when he handed me the keys and the title." From the look Smooth Jake gave him, Martin Oakes guessed that he, too, had seen the once-great Roldan crumble.

Smooth Jake peered out the window. "I had Hernández's chauffeur take your Torino down to the garage by the stables. I hope you don't mind. We like to keep the driveway clear." Miss Stecker had come over to Meghan

Warner's side of the net to argue a call. She pointed to the
spot where she believed the ball had landed and circled it
with her racket head. Her opponent refused to give her the
benefit of an audience. While Miss Stecker continued to
search for clues in the clay, Meghan Warner turned and
stalked back to the service line, racket under her arm, palms
to the sky.

"I don't remember leaving my keys in the car," Martin
Oakes said.

"You were asleep, so I had him hot-wire it. I didn't
want to disturb you."

"You speak Spanish?"

"No. Once I pulled a twenty-dollar bill out of my
pocket, he seemed to catch on."

Martin Oakes took a last sip of beer and wiped his
mouth with the damask napkin on the tray. "Well, if you
plan to send him up to take a similar approach to this room,
I'll save him some time. That's where I put the fifteen
grand," he said, pointing with the empty bottle to the sad-
dlebag he'd hung over the antique chair. "After I check my
car to make sure he didn't maul the ignition, I'd like to take
a swim before we begin our game."

Smooth Jake let the blinds down on his eyes. Martin
Oakes wasn't sure if he was keeping light out or in. "You
may have heard that I no longer play for money," Smooth
Jake said.

"I've heard it. Since you told me to bring fifteen thousand dollars, I didn't believe it."

"That's your incentive."

Martin Oakes said, "What's yours?"

"I play for what interests me."

"Do politics interest you?"

"Occasionally."

"Enough to try to influence the outcome of a congressional race?"

Smooth Jake let another hiss laugh escape from his inscrutable mouth. "When you reach the point I've reached, it's no longer so much a matter of what you stand to gain as what your opponent stands to lose."

Both men stood at the window, watching the tennis match. Meghan Warner was running Miss Stecker all over the court. Miss Stecker looked ready to collapse in the heat. "You know," Martin Oakes said, "I really enjoy Ivan Smid's playing. I have his recording of the Chopin Nocturnes. His touch is haunting. Unique, really, in the way it wakes up the dynamic possibilities of the piano."

"Classical music is one of my greatest passions," Smooth Jake said. "I hear you play the piano yourself."

"I'm no Ivan Smid."

"It might comfort you to know that when it comes to poker, he is no Martin Oakes."

"I didn't come here for comfort."

"Neither did he. I hope you prove to be better competition. In fact, I'm counting on it. People like Roldan and Constantine are spreading the word that you're good enough to become the next Smooth Jake Warner."

"If you have some other stake in mind, why don't you state it explicitly? I assume you don't want me to stop playing the piano."

"I match your fifteen thousand. We play until one of us has the whole thirty. If I win, you stop playing poker."

"For how long?"

"Permanently."

Martin Oakes could feel the color starting in his cheeks, and concentrated on controlling his breathing. The beer didn't help. "I don't understand. Even if I said I would stop, what's to keep me from playing?"

"Your honor."

"I never said I was honorable."

"You don't have to. If you make the bet, you'll stick to it."

"Then I won't make the bet."

"Fine. Then you can go home." Light slanted in the window. The tennis game was over. Miss Stecker sat on the grass next to the court, massaging a cramp out of her calf muscle. Meghan Warner had filled a wire basket with tennis balls and was practicing her spin serve into the deuce court. Smooth Jake looked at the widening leak in the ceiling and said, "Damned place is going to hell." He walked to the door. "You're welcome to stay for dinner."

The door was half closed when Martin Oakes said, "Maybe the stakes are too high."

"For whom?" Smooth Jake said, turning.

"I make my living playing poker."

"In my opinion, Mr. Oakes," Smooth Jake said, "nothing could be nobler. I'm afraid, however, I didn't make myself clear. The odds may be against you, but the stakes are the same."

"I don't see how."

"Because," Smooth Jake said, "if I lose, I'm going to stop playing, too."

MARTIN OAKES SWAM a mile in the pool. At first, he tried to imagine Jennifer swimming beside him, stroke for stroke, breath for breath, but he finally gave up. He couldn't synchronize her swimming with his. When he finished the mile, he floated on his back listening to the water slap against the pool gutters and watching the dusk spring out over the hills in the near distance. For Martin Oakes, night didn't fall; it blossomed. As he floated on his back, recalling the details of Jennifer's face, a face that had once showed nothing and now showed everything, the air fell like petals on his chest. Twilight in summertime Virginia could be as benign as the humid afternoons were oppressive. Martin Oakes remembered how the bales of just-cut grass had reeked during the day. Mingled now with chlorine and budding darkness, the same grass smelled almost aromatic.

"I'm afraid we've been ignoring you," Meghan Warner said, appearing at the edge of the pool. Martin Oakes hadn't heard her approach and didn't know which direction she had come from.

"I don't mind being alone," Martin Oakes said.

"If you say so," she said, looking back toward the house. "Jake wasn't sure if you would be staying for dinner."

"I guess it depends on what's for dinner."

She had on a light blue dress and high heels. There was no wind, but she gathered the dress discreetly at her knees before climbing the three-step ladder to the diving board. "We will begin with cream of asparagus and morel soup," she said, pacing back and forth on the diving board. "Then on to the main course: baked redfish en papillote. Martha's creole sauce is first rate." Her heels were at least three inches high. Martin Oakes hoped she wouldn't fall into the pool. "I just had an argument with Jake," she said, one of her heels buckling slightly as she pirouetted at the end of the board. "He wanted to uncork a Soave, but I held out for a California Sauvignon Blanc. The wine should go with the food."

"Sounds reasonable to me," Martin Oakes said. Meghan Warner strode purposefully to the end of the diving board and began bouncing, still holding her dress with one hand. "Are you sure you want to be doing that?" he asked.

"This day has had a very high degree of difficulty," she said, landing neatly on the balls of her feet after each jump. "I wish Jake wouldn't sell The Little Boltons."

Martin Oakes heard a little plop in the pool. "What was that?"

"Probably one of my barrettes. No big deal." It had, in fact, been a gold brooch that was roughly ten times more valuable than Martin Oakes's car: she would send someone out in the morning to pick it up. Her arms moved in time to her jumping. Her hand movements were balletic. "You swam a long way."

"I drove a long way."

"I hate the city. How do you stand it?"

"By living in the suburbs."

"Think you can beat Jake?"

"I've been waiting four years to try."

"Well," she said, "at least stay for dinner." Without warning, she turned a hundred and eighty degrees in the air, but instead of diving backward into the pool, she struck the board at an angle that sprung her back toward the ladder. She caught the aluminum tubing on either side of the ladder, letting go of her dress, and climbed down. There was still no wind, but now the gesture of letting go seemed a bit immodest. "When did you know you wanted to become a poker player?" she asked.

He ducked under the water and swam the length of the pool holding his breath. When he surfaced, she was standing by the shallow end waiting for him. One underwater lap had failed to wash away his notion that being a poker player was a question not of choosing but of being chosen. "I got on the subway one day," he said, "and I felt so uncomfortable I could hardly breathe. There were ten other people in my car." He ran his arm across the surface of the water. "I realized I knew what they were all thinking. All I had to do was look at one of them and it was as if I were listening to a radio station. There was an old guy who smelled like the cat food he could barely afford to eat. He scratched his plastic subway seat with both hands and twitched his head from side to side. His diet had done as much damage to his mind as it had to his body. One look and I could tell he measured his spirit in ounces." Martin Oakes dunked his head again. He had a frightening talent that couldn't be washed away but, being in a pool, it was difficult to resist the impulse to try. "There was a woman who was getting ready to cheat on her husband, I could tell by the way she stood. For five stops, she stood next to the doors, spinning her wedding ring with her thumb. Then the sixth stop came. The doors opened. Two passengers got out. Four passengers got in. The doors began to close. At the last second, she jumped between them: she'd decided to cheat after all. There was an old lady who lived by herself. Hadn't had a visitor in years. Riding the subway was the only time she ever came into contact with other human beings. She wasn't going anywhere. The subway was her fountain of youth. The heat and jostling that annoyed everyone else renewed her." Meghan Warner eyed him skeptically. "Some people find peace in pandemonium," he said calmly.

Meghan Warner took hold of her dress and climbed up the ladder to the diving board. Despite her heels, she maneuvered back and forth on the board with uncanny assurance. But Martin Oakes failed to appreciate the full extent of her elegance until she sat down at the end of the board, dangled her feet above the water, and leaned her head back toward the stars. It was as if Miss America had sat down at the end of the winner's ramp in Atlantic City and tossed her crown back to the judges. "You couldn't have known all that," she said.

"Maybe not," he said. "Anyway, you asked me why I play cards."

"Jake doesn't show anything."

"Everyone shows something."

"Even you."

"As little as possible."

"Are you going to play?"

"I haven't made up my mind yet."

"He'll spot your weaknesses before you spot his."

"That's what I'm afraid of." He floated on his back from one end of the pool to the other. She left the diving board and strolled along the side, billowing hair blending nicely with the purple sky. Her hair was complete, Martin Oakes thought. A crown could only interfere with it.

"I suppose if you leave now, though, he'll tell everyone else you're a quitter." She could see his smile in the light from the windows of the house. "What's so funny about that?"

"Quitting's just part of the game," he said. "Find me a poker player who doesn't quit, and I'd be willing to bet you he's either broke or in debt."

Meghan Warner opened her arms expansively, as if the emerging constellations fell within the boundaries of The Little Boltons. "Jake never quits."

"On the contrary," Martin Oakes replied. "He quits all the time. The biggest intangible in gambling is knowing when to quit, and your husband is a master at it."

"Why is it an intangible?"

"Because you can never say, 'I quit at exactly the right time.' How could you possibly know?"

She waited until he stopped floating and held on to the side of the pool. "Miss Stecker has been trying to convince Jake that, deep down, every gambler wants to lose."

"I saw some of your tennis."

Meghan Warner's arms and legs were still warm from the sun. Looking down on Martin Oakes clinging to the edge of the pool, she said, "You're a gambler. Do you believe that?"

"Well," Martin Oakes said, shrugging under the water, thinking of the look on Sam Kim's face when his son Tom had raked in the last of his ten thousand dollars in Monopoly money, "it gets back to what I was saying about quitting. Most people don't think they've lost until they run out of money."

Back up on the diving board, she let her left leg dangle until two inches of the shoe's heel were submerged in the water. She traced a spiral with the heel. "Or hope."

"Sometimes they amount to the same thing," he said. "Tell me. Have you ever been in a beauty pageant?"

She shivered in the heat. "You make me feel as if I'm riding the subway."

"Have you?" he asked again.

"I went from beauty pageants to soap operas to game shows," she said. Looking up at the stars, the information bubbled out of her. "To Jake," she concluded.

Martin Oakes had gone underwater again. "Win any of the pageants?" he asked after he had surfaced.

"I was runner-up for Miss Butler County," she said. "I lost out to a girl who parallel-parked for the talent competition." Now it was his turn to look skeptical. "They held the pageant outdoors," she said. "It was part of that year's county fair. When they got through judging the steers, the 4-H riders, the pigs, the chili, and the cheesecake, they judged the girls. The girl who won—I'll never forget her name: Mirna—with an 'i'—Dodge; have you ever heard of a beauty queen named Mirna Dodge? Old Mirna, who's probably toothless knitting a sweater someplace now and balancing a beer mug on her belly, drove a '56 T-Bird convertible. Drove it right onto the stage."

"Why are you telling me about the one you lost?" he asked.

"Because that's the one I remember." She peered into the now inky water and tried to imagine her brooch twinkling gold on the pool's blue bottom. "First they wheeled the T-Bird onto the stage. Mirna had popcorn-blond hair and a very pronounced chest and a thick red sash strangling her waist, and, of course, about two jars of Vaseline in her mouth so the judges could see the sun glint off her teeth as she backed up. It was like a magic act. One guy drove in from the left in a Packard. Another drove in from the right in a Buick Wildcat. For a moment, everyone thought the two cars were going to collide, but then they both stopped, leaving just enough room for the T-Bird to squeeze in between. I was sure the stage was going to collapse under the weight of all those cars. The crowd was howling. Needless to say, I was suspicious about parallel-parking being considered a talent, but the way Mirna breezed into that tiny space, smiling like all joy to the world—well, she changed my mind. She zipped in and out four times without a hitch and the judges could hardly wait to pin the crown on her head."

From the angle Martin Oakes was looking at Meghan Warner, the stars above her head formed a much more imposing crown. "Do you and your husband often swim at night?" he asked.

"No," she said. "Why?"

"Because warm water just started coming into the pool."

They heard the diesel engine of the Mercedes turn over. "There is a God," Meghan Warner said. She scrambled down from the diving board, removed her shoes, and ran barefoot to the patio. A fan of light opened and closed across the pool as she disappeared through the door to the main house. Martin Oakes got out of the pool, toweled off, and walked around to the front of the house. Smooth Jake stood on the gravel driveway with Hernández and Miss Stecker. He had installed spotlights on the poker-chip columns to keep the colors distinct twenty-four hours a day. Miss Stecker seemed to have acquired a limp. The driver's door of the Mercedes was open. Hernández's chauffeur sat in the back seat, polishing glasses. There was a television console built into the space between the two front seats. The car phone was buzzing, but no one paid any attention to it. Miss Stecker slumped next to the chauffeur and poured herself three fingers of vodka. Martin Oakes thought of The Needle and wondered if he had really rubbed the Southern Comfort into his legs. It sounded like something The Needle would do. Maybe Miss Stecker would try it. The chauffeur kept polishing. The phone kept buzzing.

"I'm sorry we can't stay for dinner," Hernández told Smooth Jake.

"I think you have a call," Martin Oakes said.

"I always have a call," Hernández said.

The front door opened and Meghan Warner swept out onto the porch. "Don't tell me you're going already," she said to Hernández. She looked genuinely sad.

"Lana wants to get back to Washington," Hernández said. "I must admit I would like to stay and watch these two gunfighters battle it out."

"Gunfighters are extinct," Smooth Jake said. "Poker players are only endangered."

"There are plenty of gunfighters in my country," Hernández said, wearily cheerful, "but they tend to fire indiscriminately into crowds." Miss Stecker had already drained her glass of vodka. "Maybe she's still depressed about Russia," Hernández theorized, seeing that Smooth Jake and Martin Oakes were looking at her. "Or the tennis. In any case, we must go."

The Mercedes wound down the path to the front gate. The car's taillights blinked shut after the first rise in the driveway, but the drone of its diesel engine took a full two minutes to die away.

Smooth Jake, Meghan Warner, and Martin Oakes stood together between a red column and a blue column.

"Lana forgot to say goodbye," Meghan Warner said wickedly.

Smooth Jake turned to Martin Oakes. "Was the pool warm enough for you?"

"Just right, thanks."

"You'd probably like to get dressed."

"Martin's agreed to join us for dinner," Meghan Warner said, careful not to look at him. "He claims redfish en papillote is one of his favorites."

"You'll find that Martha's creole sauce is one of the very best," Smooth Jake said without sounding excited about it himself. Then to his wife: "Call me when it's time." With that, he vanished into the house.

"Where's he going?" Martin Oakes asked.

"It's a compliment to you," she said. "He doesn't want to give you the chance to study him."

Martin Oakes opened the front door. The hall was empty. "So where does he go when he doesn't want to be studied?"

"It's a big house," she said happily. "He could be anywhere."

"Give me a hint."

That seemed to make her even happier. "If I had to guess," she said, "I would say he's listening to his quartet."

"Which one?"

"Beethoven. Opus 127. E-flat Major."

"Is that the only one he listens to?"

"Lately. I can't really latch on to it, but Jake swears it's a masterpiece." She bounded into the grass.

"Did you meet Ivan Smid?" Martin Oakes asked.

She ran as gracefully as she walked.

"Ivan Smid!" he called after her.

"I've got to check the grass!" she yelled back.

Martin Oakes stood alone in the doorway, empty light in one direction, empty darkness in the other. His fingers and toes were puckered from his soak in the pool. He wondered how much of Smooth Jake's skin was floating around in the pool gutters. Probably about the same amount as in the maid's vacuum-cleaner bag. That was why the grass grew so well—he passed on his success to the land as it peeled off. A man who didn't waste money wouldn't waste skin. Martin Oakes could hear Meghan Warner's erratic whistling in the yard. (The *yard:* Smooth Jake would enjoy that. Some yard.) Nothing from inside the house. He could always grab his suitcase, walk down to the stables, fire up the 302, and head on home.

But there was no challenge in that. Even though it would be tempting to try and catch the Mercedes, just to see the look on the chauffeur's face. If he wanted to flush Smooth Jake out of his hiding place, on the other hand, he could let the Warners' eight horses loose and wait for all hell to follow. No. Not that either.

He decided he would find Smooth Jake and express his thanks. Or his regrets. He wasn't sure which. Maybe both. He suddenly had one of his uncontrollable urges to see

Jennifer. He always had them when she was out of reach. He looked at his puckered hands and knew that being in the water had caused his longing. Jennifer practically lived in the water. If he tried hard enough, perhaps he could learn to live there with her.

He continued to search through the house. Sometimes he would see Meghan Warner two or three rooms away, not looking for anything in particular herself, just entering and exiting as if her gracefulness depended on constant motion. In her bare feet, she didn't so much walk as float. When by accident he passed his own room, he went in and dressed himself perfunctorily, determined to interrupt his search only for the time it took him to find a shirt and pants.

The entire house was silent. No talking. No footfalls. No singing. No playing. No pots. No pans. No Beethoven.

Martin Oakes searched for a music room. It was difficult to find because he couldn't hear any music. He remembered seeing a grand piano in one of the sitting rooms. He went to the room and found it empty. The piano, a shiny Bosendorfer, stood out black-etched in the night. If there was any sheet music in the room, it was hidden. Martin Oakes sat down and played a Chopin Nocturne from memory. At one point he was convinced he heard Smooth Jake's laughter, rising up through the radiators like a hiss in the hot night. When he left the room, he caught a faint whiff of redfish baking, heard the tinkle of glasses. Meghan Warner floated by at the opposite end of a long corridor. "Where does he usually listen to his quartet?" Martin Oakes called out to her.

"In his head," she answered. "I just saw Martha. Dinner is still at least half an hour away. If you find him before I do, will you tell him?"

Martin Oakes listened to her softly ascend a flight of

stairs to the third floor. He didn't know what she was really looking for, but he was certain it wasn't Smooth Jake. He returned to the front hall and began opening doors one by one, without knocking. The third door he tried opened into a dark hall, at the end of which there was another door, so small in its frame that light emanating from the room behind formed a perfect square of light around it. He walked the length of the hall and knocked on the small door.

"Come in, Martin," Smooth Jake said.

Martin Oakes turned the doorknob and went inside. The room was sparse: no windows, low ceiling, off-white walls, hardwood floor, card table, two chairs, a phone on the floor, and a long mahogany bar. There were glasses and mirrored shelves behind the bar, but no liquor. On the ceiling there were two rows of lights, with three lights on each track. All of the lights were trained on the card table. The card table held two decks of cards and two piles of chips, each totaling fifteen thousand dollars.

Smooth Jake sat in one of the chairs, leaning slightly back. The score to Beethoven's String Quartet in E-flat Major, Opus 127, lay open in his lap, but he wasn't looking at it. His eyes were open, but the pupils seemed to have rolled back into his head. Slowly, his head came forward; its movement restored his eyes to their normal position. "Will you deal or shall I?"

Martin Oakes remained standing. "Looks like you were meditating."

"In a way, I suppose, yes, I was."

"Dinner will be ready in about half an hour."

"Food is overrated. You want real nourishment, listen to Beethoven."

"I don't see anything here to listen to him with."

Smooth Jake held up the score; he had been studying

the recapitulation in the first movement. "By 1826, when Beethoven wrote the Opus 127, he was completely deaf. Had been for nearly four years. The only way he could perceive sound was to imagine it." He held the score out in front of him. Martin Oakes could see that the margins were full of scribbled notes. A thick flap of red skin seemed about to fall off Smooth Jake's thumb. "It is impossible to express Beethoven's accomplishment, his vision, in human terms," Smooth Jake went on. "Could a baseball player who had hit for average all his life suddenly go blind, then step up to the plate and start knocking one home run after another out of the park? How would he see the ball? How could he possibly sense it? And where would he get the strength he had never had before when he could see perfectly? Could a master chef lose all taste in his mouth, all smelling in his nose, and continue to create masterful flavors in his dishes? How could he possibly know which ingredients to add? You see, Martin, these late quartets are inexplicable. Particularly the Opus 127. It has a perfection that alternately moves me to ecstasy and despair."

"Why ecstasy?"

"Because it is so perfectly formed. Despair because it is full of maddening contradictions, and can only be truly appreciated if one listens to it with one's mind, as opposed to one's ears. Some days I can hear it. Some days I can't."

"How about today?"

"Today I am having trouble." He rose from his chair. "There's a stereo in one of the dens. I have eight recordings of it: the Guarneri, the Juilliard, the Quartetto Italiano—you name it. I've grown to hate them all. They all share the distinction of being full of interpretation rather than understanding." They went to the den and put on one of the recordings. The stereo system's fidelity was so accurate and overwhelming that Martin Oakes could almost feel the play-ers' chests heaving as they breathed through each phrase. But good speakers, compact disks, a powerful amplifier, and some of the finest musicians in the world weren't enough for Smooth Jake. "Do you hear that?" he kept asking. "Blasted second fiddle scoops every time he shifts into third position. Those lines must be crisp, precise. Instead, he slides around." During the second movement, he complained, "Now they're fudging the dynamics. You fudge the dynam-ics in 127 and you ruin the damn quartet." He didn't like their tempos: "Does that sound like *scherzando vivace* to you, Martin? It certainly doesn't sound like *scherzando vi-vace* to me." He couldn't tolerate the first violinist's vibrato: "All width and no feeling." He ridiculed the cellist's ensem-ble playing. "A recording that would truly make Beethoven roll over," he concluded, blinds down on his eyes as the performers ripped through the final coda in the fourth move-ment. He slapped his thigh with the score when the piece was over and said, "Let them stick to Brahms and Schubert. Let them saw through some Mozart. The Opus 127 is beyond them."

AT DINNER, Meghan Warner picked at her redfish but took an active interest in the wine. The candles she had lit left much of the huge dining room in darkness. The three of them sat at one end of the main table, Smooth Jake at its head, his wife and his guest on either side of him. Revolu-tionary War paintings decorated the walls. In one of the paintings, a regiment of English soldiers stacked their weap-ons in a pile while an equal number of triumphant but ill-clad Americans watched. The Americans all had enor-mous chests, the result, Martin Oakes thought, of holding their breath. The Redcoats' weapons could have been poker chips.

"Do you realize that we are all in bare feet?" Meghan Warner said while uncorking a third bottle of Sauvignon Blanc.

"*In* bare feet?" Smooth Jake repeated, holding out his glass and scratching one of his feet with the other under the table. "That's an interesting way of looking at it, Meg." The *andante con moto* segment of the Opus 127 second movement ran through his head, the first and second violins delicately intertwined, the underpinning sixteenths of viola and cello precisely synchronized. Hearing the music activated several different parts of his consciousness. It had been a pleasant surprise to find out that different parts of his brain played different instruments. He had always expected one part to play them all.

Martin Oakes, watching him, tried to guess which movement he was on. "First variation of the adagio?" he asked finally.

"Right movement, wrong variation," Smooth Jake answered, feeling the music recede as his eyes rolled down and took in his opponent. "But not bad. Not bad at all."

"I don't know about you two," Meghan Warner said.

"I'm glad you talked him out of the Soave," Martin Oakes told her. "The wine you chose goes splendidly with the fish."

She gave him an absentminded wave of her hand, then pulled her feet up and sat cross-legged on her chair. "I let Martha go early," she informed Smooth Jake. "I feel horrid. Do you realize Emily died a year ago today? Martha had to remind me. After I'd kept her in the kitchen all day making redfish and creole sauce. Entertaining that leering chauffeur."

"Poor Emily," Smooth Jake said, and for a moment the angles in his face defined genuine sadness and regret. "A year already?"

"Martha's mother," Meghan Warner explained to Martin Oakes. "And Johnny's wife, of course, although for the last couple of years he barely recognized her. Poor Martha, I say."

"How did she die?" Martin Oakes asked.

"Very quickly, once she got started," Smooth Jake said, the planes of his face even again.

"Nothing dramatic," Meghan Warner said, and frowned at her husband. "She was netting leaves out of the pool. When she was through netting all the leaves, she put down the net, stretched out on one of the lounge chairs, and just stopped breathing." She looked at her husband as if his testimony would verify her account.

"Taking care of Johnny got to be too much for her," Smooth Jake said, with an almost imperceptible shrug.

"No one could clean a house like that woman," Meghan Warner said. "We have three people doing now what Emily used to do by herself, and in less time." She joined her bare feet in the middle of her chair and began to rock her supple legs up and down like butterflies' wings. The light from the candles cast an exaggerated shadow of the rocking on the wall behind her. Martin Oakes still thought Jennifer's legs were unsurpassed, but it was possible Meghan Warner's would win greater popular acclaim. "I came home from shopping in Washington early one day," she said, "and almost tripped over the mop pail in the kitchen. It surprised me because Emily never left things like that lying around. There was no sign of her anywhere. I heard some noise out in the hall and pushed through the door that comes out behind the main staircase. As I pushed through the door, I saw one of my shoes come bouncing down the stairs. So I stopped and hid behind the staircase. A moment later, another shoe came bouncing down. Then another. This went on for about five minutes. I had about thirty pairs of shoes—I give them away when I stop wearing them—and all but the pair I was wearing came bouncing down the stairs. Jake's shoes were mixed in. It was literally raining shoes. Some of them got caught in the bannister railing on the way down. Some bounced all the way over to the door. When the shoes finally stopped falling, Emily came down the stairs, holding a big laundry basket and humming a song to herself. Very carefully, she put all the shoes into the laundry basket and walked back up the stairs. When she reached the top, she started throwing them down again. Once, I thought I could hear her giggling. Some shoes she just threw. Others she aimed." Meghan Warner took a sip of her wine. "This went on for half an hour. Throwing the shoes down the stairs. Picking them up in the laundry basket. Throwing them down again. After a while, her humming got so thick it sounded like gargling, as if the notes had gotten stuck in her throat. I still remember that sound. I didn't like it the least bit. Finally, when she was halfway up the stairs with all the shoes in the laundry basket, I closed the kitchen door loudly and called her name. From where she was, she couldn't see me. Without answering, she rushed up the rest of the stairs and disappeared into our room. I walked up the stairs. When I reached our room, the sliding door to the closet was open. All my shoes were arranged neatly on the closet floor. All of Jake's shoes were back on his shoe tree. Emily was folding laundry on the bed. Nothing was the slightest bit out of place."

"Fast," Smooth Jake said. "The woman was always very fast."

"Did any of your shoes just disappear?" Martin Oakes asked.

"I lost a pair of heels once," Meghan Warner replied. "They probably fell apart clattering down the stairs. And Jake lost some tennis sneakers. We think Emily burned them in one of the autumn bonfires."

Smooth Jake wiped his mouth. "If you sent Martha away early, I suppose that means we don't get dessert." His mouth was a straight line with hidden corners as he spoke to his wife. She nodded. He turned to Martin Oakes. "Have you made your decision?"

Martin Oakes got up from the table. "I noticed that the paint on the columns out front is peeling," he said. "Especially the red."

"It's the humidity," Smooth Jake said. "Will you be going or staying, Martin?"

"Oh," Martin Oakes said, "I really don't see how I can walk away from the perfect bet."

THEY WALKED side by side down the narrow hallway to the windowless room. An invisible servant had put two pitchers of ice water on the table. Already switched on, the track lights hung low over the table, catching the swirling ice at different angles. Martin Oakes watched the unpredictable patterns of light circle slowly round the tabletop. The fingers on Smooth Jake's dealing hand flexed slowly. Martin Oakes was aware of Smooth Jake's reputation as an unrivaled card mechanic, but he wasn't worried about which cards the man would deal him. Smooth Jake would play it square. If the cards themselves were transparent to his probing mind— well, that could hardly be called cheating. The walls stretched just seven feet from floor to ceiling; a pale band of wainscoting seemed to divide the room in half. Air rose from a wrought-iron grate in the floor under the table, but the low ceiling gave the room the cramped feeling of a cell.

Martin Oakes stood across the table from Smooth Jake, waiting for a signal to sit down. He noted with gratitude that their simple, straight-backed chairs were identical. When he had played Roldan and Constantine, Roldan had insisted on sitting in a velvet-upholstered, U-shaped throne, providing Martin Oakes with a rickety excuse for a seat that was uncomfortably lopsided and several inches lower. Martin Oakes recalled with pleasure sinking into the front seat of the Jaguar after he'd taken the keys from Roldan. He'd gone from stool to luxury car in a matter of hours. The Jag was more fun to win than it was to own, and he had unloaded it for cash soon afterward—too much of Roldan's personality had rubbed off on it—but yes, oh yes, that had been a nice one to drive away.

"Please sit down," Smooth Jake said.

A soft, turning feeling crept into Martin Oakes's stomach, a tiny ball of fear, nervous and darting. "Are you sure you wouldn't rather just play for the money?" he asked.

"The money is insignificant," Smooth Jake replied. "One of us must be eliminated for it to be the perfect bet." They settled into their chairs. "I'm happy to wait for a few minutes if you would like the time to recover your breath." When Martin Oakes shook his head, Smooth Jake snapped the seal on a package of cards and offered his opponent the deck for inspection. "Playing for the right to play again," he said cordially. "I can't think of a purer motive, can you, Martin?"

Smooth Jake cut the high card and they began. The games were dealer's choice. "These days the sharps insist on seven stud and seven hold 'em," Smooth Jake complained, "but a good player should be able to win any fair game. I know too many professional gamblers who have forgotten how to play a simple hand of five-card draw. Let's see if you remember. Jacks or better." He began dealing. "Openers?" Martin Oakes shook his head. Smooth Jake pushed fifty dollars into the middle of the table. "Being a good poker player is like being a good musician. You must build up a repertoire."

"But you only listen to one quartet," Martin Oakes said, matching the bet. He had once played seven stud high-low for forty-eight hours straight with nothing but coffee and his cards to fuel him.

"Is that what Meg told you?" Smooth Jake asked, chuckling dryly. They drew cards.

"So far, that's what I've observed," Martin Oakes said. He pushed a raise into the pot. He felt sharp.

"Call," Smooth Jake said.

"Tens and fours."

"Three sevens."

Martin Oakes held out the second deck. "Cut?"

They played well into the night. Smooth Jake barely paid any attention to his cards, but by two o'clock he was already up eight hundred and fifty dollars. Martin Oakes spoke only when it was his turn to bet or call the next game. Sharp as he felt, the game refused to come into focus for him. Smooth Jake's hands were as difficult to judge as the ice shadows on the surface of the table. What did he have? How many cards had he drawn? Somehow, Smooth Jake managed to blur the betting intervals to the point where Martin Oakes didn't know who was following and who was leading. There was an almost hospitable pattern to the way Smooth Jake played—*This is where we put Jake's guests*—but as buoyant as Martin Oakes felt about the evening in gen-

eral, he couldn't help noticing that the individual games
were continuing to slip away from him. At three o'clock,
Smooth Jake spread a jack-high straight on the table, gathered in the pot, and said benignly, "If you don't mind, I'd
like to retire for the evening after a few more hands."

"Certainly," Martin Oakes said. He estimated he was
down about thirteen hundred dollars and he wasn't sure
why, or how, he'd lost it. He had studied Smooth Jake
intently for more than five hours without gaining a glimmer
into his true strategy. From the way Smooth Jake peered
back with his Venetian-blind eyes, however, Martin Oakes
worried that he was showing something. But he couldn't
stop showing it until he could figure out what it was. Perhaps
he was just thinking too loud.

Smooth Jake dealt out the last hand of the evening.
"Seven-card draw. Twos and threes wild."

"Twos and threes wild?" Martin Oakes repeated, in-
credulous.

"You heard me."

"The *National Enquirer* would pay twice what I've lost
tonight for this story."

"I appreciate discretion," Smooth Jake said, in a serious tone. "I also practice it."

"Oh, all right. No one would believe me, anyway."

They bet and drew and bet again. "Five kings,"
Smooth Jake announced.

"You mean two kings, two threes, and a two."

"Wild's wild."

"I'll say." Martin Oakes slipped his cards back into the
deck without divulging that he had four sevens by virtue of
the other pair of threes. "You call that poker?"

"No," Smooth Jake said, stacking his chips. "I call it
about three hundred dollars." He got up from the table.
"Good night, Martin. Better luck tomorrow."

"No more wild cards."

"Agreed."

The second night, Martin Oakes won back five hundred dollars after a grueling but inconclusive seven-hour session in which Smooth Jake frequently looked ready to fall asleep. "You have a lot to learn," Smooth Jake said after the game, yawning before he climbed the stairs to his room. "There may be time. But I'm not optimistic."

THEY STAYED EVEN for another day, until Smooth Jake rode a streak of good cards and better judgment to pull ahead by another five thousand dollars. Smooth Jake seemed to have learned to play cards the way Beethoven had learned to write music. He anticipated all of Martin Oakes's good hands. He invariably called Martin Oakes's bluffs. And since Smooth Jake never dealt the same game twice in a row, Martin Oakes could detect no rhythm in his thinking, no cadence in his betting. Smooth Jake sat straight and still in his chair while Martin Oakes mentally reeled in his, off balance and uncertain, hearing the wrought-iron grate beneath the table hiss to life to whisper his cards, perhaps his exact thoughts, into Smooth Jake's ear. But the hiss was just Smooth Jake's laugh, a disembodied expression of world-weariness that marked the beginning of their games as often as it did the end of them. The laugh was all the more annoying because it left no trail. Martin Oakes was not a superstitious man, but as the pressure continued to bunch up between his shoulder blades and the creaks in the floor-boards made it increasingly difficult for him to concentrate, he struggled to the conclusion that he wasn't just playing Smooth Jake; he was playing the house and lawn and legend, too.

Smooth Jake slid a hundred and fifty dollars into the

pot after dealing the last card in a game of seven stud. Martin Oakes hesitated for a moment, then said, "Fold."

Smooth Jake allowed himself a sigh as he slipped his three down cards back into the deck. "I'm going to tell you something," he said, breaking the unwritten rule that poker players should never offer advice or criticism to each other during a session. "Never hesitate to pay a fair amount of money to find out how your opponent thinks. When you think you stand to gain an important insight, put in whatever it takes to call him. That investment will return to you ten times over, provided you know how to analyze what you're about to see." Smooth Jake raised his glass to his lips. He drank so much water that Martin Oakes was surprised he didn't float away. But his riverbed voice remained dry: "Now, you knew you were going to lose that hand, Martin. Fine. An accurate deduction. But for a measly hundred fifty, you missed the opportunity to see some very interesting cards. For fifty bucks a card, I can tell you, it would have been worth it." He used the deck to whisk flecks of his dried skin off the table.

"Each player has his own style," Martin Oakes said defensively.

"I'm not talking about style. I'm talking about substance."

Martin Oakes shuffled his deck. "Talk is a weapon, too."

"Tell me," Smooth Jake said, his voice not just dry, but cold. "Do you want to play cards or be a cardplayer?"

DURING A BREAK in play, Martin Oakes called Jennifer. "Help."

"Nice of you to call, Martin. It's only been—what, four days?"

"They have a pool."

"Their pool is four hundred miles away. Our club is just down the street. What's the matter? You've never wanted me at one of your games before."

"I'm getting killed."

"You knew he was good."

"Not this good." He told her about their bet.

"Well, you can always re-enlist."

"Thanks for the sympathy."

"Sympathy has never done anything for you. Do you really want me to come down?"

"Yes. I don't know why, but I think having you here would turn things around for me."

"Long way to go for a swim. You don't usually play hunches."

"Well, I'd better do something quick before he grinds me into dust."

"I wonder if you still fit into your old uniform."

"I'd rather live in poverty than die in dress whites any day."

"If you're losing so badly," she said, "why is it you sound so excited?"

"Because I'm going to figure the old bastard out, that's why."

"I'll catch the morning shuttle to Washington tomorrow. Then what? A bus?"

He told her where to pick up the bus, then said, "There's something I'd like you to bring."

"What?"

"My chips."

"Martin, where am I going to put that clunky old box?"

"I'm playing in his house, at his table, with his cards, and his chips. With my money in his safe. I want to feel something familiar."

"I hope that applies to me as much as it applies to the chips," she said.

"I love you, Jen."

"My God," she said. "You must really be in trouble."

Martin Oakes's game continued to fall apart as he waited for Jennifer to arrive with the Coffin. There were no further outbursts from Smooth Jake. If anything, he looked ready to fall asleep again. But when Martin Oakes stopped looking at his face and instead projected its reflection onto the poker table, he no longer saw fatigue but an implacable resolve. Smooth Jake's play became more aggressive, his betting more vigorous. He stopped drinking water. His laugh changed from a hiss in his throat to a hollow rattle under his rib cage. He barely seemed to move in his chair. For the first time since he had arrived at The Little Boltons, Martin Oakes could imagine venom dripping from the invisible corners of Smooth Jake's reptilian mouth. Ten thousand dollars ahead and sensing the almost complete paralysis in his victim, Smooth Jake was coiled for the kill.

They ate separate dinners and began their evening session promptly at ten. When Smooth Jake took his seat, Martin Oakes felt fear pull tight across his chest. The cause of the fear was Smooth Jake's complexion. It had cleared up. The underlying dryness of Smooth Jake's skin was still apparent. But something softer had filled the cracks beneath his brow and erased the creases around his eyes. It was as if, unable to lubricate his skin with creams from without, he had somehow done it with concentration from within. A look at his hands confirmed the transformation. Manipulating the cards, they were for the moment no longer a claylike red but a burgundy-colored velvet; no longer arthritic, but supple, poised. The hands he had won from Ivan Smid.

"Martin," he said pleasantly, after winning a game of seven-card hold 'em, "you have a tic." Martin Oakes had stopped objecting to his sly advice, but had an image of himself in the window of a burning building while Smooth Jake stood, stories below, trying to toss him up a life preserver. "It's almost imperceptible," Smooth Jake went on, "and it's not really a tic but a reaction which you share with the human race in general, and fair-skinned, blue- or green-eyed people in particular. So far, it has cost you about four thousand dollars." Smooth Jake let the word "dollars" slip ever so gently off his tongue; after all, it wasn't tasting money that counted; it was smelling it, and right now he had a noseful. "Chinese opium dealers used to look for the same tic in the British explorers with whom they traded. You see, Martin, when you get a particularly good hand—on limited observation, I would say three of a kind or better—your pupils dilate. The Chinese used to watch the British, waiting for their eyes to dilate, knowing that once they did, the British were ready to deal. The British would continue to talk tough, but again and again their eyes would betray them, and the Chinese would wait patiently and finally get their price. For the British, it was a certain quantity of opium. For you, it's three of a kind or better. I haven't determined the exact cutoff point." His tone was cordial, but the current that ran beneath it was mocking. Martin Oakes could feel the track lights on Smooth Jake's side of the table boring into each of his eyes. "The fact is, Martin, you are already on your way to curing this problem. Your facial muscles are under complete control, your breathing is relaxed and even, and you move your hands with admirable confidence and economy." Smooth Jake massaged his eyelids and continued: "For most people, the effect is temporary—lasting, I should think, not more than three or four seconds. You might try lowering your eyelids a bit when you first get your cards, then once again when you draw."

"Thank you," Martin Oakes said quietly.

"It could save you a lot of money," Smooth Jake said. "Provided you have a future in this game, which I'm afraid at the moment doesn't appear likely."

After playing five more hands and winning only one, Martin Oakes asked for an adjournment until the following afternoon.

"No problem," Smooth Jake said, only three thousand dollars away from retiring Martin Oakes forever. "We have plenty of time."

Something in that simple remark bolstered Martin Oakes's spirits more than advice about his telltale pupils, but he couldn't yet attach an explanation to it. "Anyone else ever walk out of The Little Boltons a winner?" he asked.

"Not yet," Smooth Jake said blandly.

"So this will be the first time," Martin Oakes said. It was dawn before he fell asleep. When he woke up, his sweat formed a bond between his skin and the bedsheets. He went for a swim. This time he could feel Jennifer swimming beside him, swimming south to him, bringing him the Coffin of chips to bury Smooth Jake in, if he could only solve the riddle he was sure had been inadvertently posed to him.

"How's the game going?" Meghan Warner asked from the side of the pool. She was wearing cutoff jeans and a halter top. Her hair was tied back in a ponytail.

"One of us is having fun."

"Jake says it's almost over."

"It's far from over."

"You know, Martin, you were wrong about Jake's being a master at quitting. He doesn't know how to quit."

"Then I suppose I'll just have to make him."

A truck came up the path to the house. Its chassis was too wide for the path, and nine of its eighteen wheels chewed up the adjacent grass as it approached. Meghan Warner glanced at her watch. "Only three hours late."

"What are they here for?" Martin Oakes asked.

"New pool furniture, computer equipment for Jake, and a higher fence for the tennis court," she said. "Some other things. I can't remember."

"Well, whatever they've got, I'm sure you can find a place to put it."

"We give it away as fast as we take it in."

Martin Oakes saw a bright object glimmering at the bottom of the pool. He dived down and retrieved it. When he surfaced, he reached out and handed the object to Meghan Warner.

"Oh," she said. "My brooch. I'd forgotten all about it."

"It's a nice brooch."

"Yes," she agreed. "It's almost ridiculous, how much it's worth." She considered for a moment, then held it out to him. "I heard your wife is expected down. Perhaps you'd like to give it to her?"

"No, thanks," he said. "Might raise her expectations too high for the future."

"What will you do?" Embarrassed, she shoved the brooch into her pocket. "I mean, if you lose?"

"I'll worry about that if I lose. At the moment, I'm still planning to win."

"What will you do if you win?"

He laughed. He liked Meghan Warner very much. "You've got me there," he said.

The truck honked in the driveway. "Well," she said, gesturing toward the plume of diesel fuel rising above the house, "time to go supervise while they unload. They aren't very careful. It's just boxes to them."

Martin Oakes picked up Jennifer at the bus depot that

afternoon. He took her in his arms without speaking, and for several minutes they just hugged, new together again, bathed by an invisible thousand-foot waterfall in Lauterbrunnen, their love for each other cool and constant. "So tell me about it," she finally said.

"Later," he said. "After we swim and eat and sleep."

"You're forgetting something."

"No, I'm not."

SMOOTH JAKE WAITED for Martin Oakes in the hot, windowless room, the Beethoven score in his lap. Most people take journeys to see, but Smooth Jake had taken his to listen. Sitting in his chair now, he realized he had never heard the Opus 127 better. Every phrase seemed perfectly formed, every trill neatly turned. The *pizzicato* in his mind was firm and round as fresh-plucked apples. Soon he would no longer simply hear; he would understand. Beethoven would transport his mind to a level of consciousness that the laws of probability could not reveal, or even acknowledge. A place where the pianissimos were ear-shattering and time crescendoed to a single moment, the same quiet moment from which the crescendo had begun. A man who had never believed in spirits, Smooth Jake felt an almost indescribable elation at the prospect of finally reaching a spiritual destination. He wasn't certain what he would do or how he would change once he got there. Arriving was the important thing. The only other thing he was sure of was that he would never want to come back.

He was dimly aware of Martin Oakes entering the room, a foreign sound, a shadowy figure with a cracked wooden box under his arm. The box was caked with coal dust and gun grease. Martin Oakes put the box down on the table. When he looked at Smooth Jake, he saw a man in a trance. "If you don't have any objections, I was wondering if we could play for a while with my chips."

Smooth Jake waved his hand over the table. "Just as long as we play with my cards." His own voice seemed to come from a body he no longer occupied. The shadowy figure across the table from him appeared small and vulnerable, crouched miles away. A mouse skittering blindly across a wheat field while Smooth Jake, a hawk, soared effortlessly above, drawing a bead on him. For Smooth Jake, flapping his wings took only as much effort as closing his eyes. The mouse ran back and forth from a canvas bag filled with silver coins, pulling the coins out of the bag one at a time and hiding them in the wheat. High above, the hawk peered down and the hidden coins twinkled up at him like rhinestones. Smooth Jake rubbed his eyelids and felt his heart quicken.

"Is something wrong?" Martin Oakes asked, opening the Coffin and removing the chips. Once he had removed the chips, he began separating and stacking them.

"No. Just give me a minute." The Beethoven had conjured up a hot Arizona sun inside his mind. If he turned his eyes on Martin Oakes before the music completely died away, he would burn him to a cinder. Martin Oakes shuffled the cards and offered them to Smooth Jake for the cut. Again, face betraying none of his splendid dizziness, Smooth Jake waved his hand over the table. "Deal them." The cards were transparent as glass. Martin Oakes dealt a hand of seven-card stud. Smooth Jake glanced at his two down cards. A pair of aces. His up card was a jack. He pushed a hundred dollars into the pot. Martin Oakes's chips had an unpleasant, greasy feel to them. Again, the voice of the snake at the table, not the hawk in the sky: "Where did you get these, Martin, at a gas station?" Martin Oakes didn't respond. Instead, he sat quietly in his chair. Ten minutes later, Smooth Jake's hundred-dollar bet was still sitting in the middle of the table and Martin Oakes was still sitting quietly in his chair. A musical sun set behind Smooth Jake's eyes. Slowly, he let his eyes drift up to his opponent. "Well?"

"Well what?" Martin Oakes asked.

"Are you going to see the bet?"

"I'm not sure. I'm thinking about it."

"So think."

Martin Oakes waited another five minutes and folded. Smooth Jake rubbed his pair of aces together once before replacing them in the deck. A good hand wasted. Not to mention fifteen minutes. It didn't matter. The cards were made of glass. He shuffled the deck and the glass melted in his hands.

The next six hands took two hours to play. Smooth Jake won another thousand dollars. Martin Oakes carefully analyzed every card, every bet. Sometimes his mind would wander and he would imagine Jennifer floating around in the pool and Meghan Warner floating around in the house. On the seventh hand, he lifted half a stack of white chips and let them fall one at a time back onto the table. He liked the clicking sound and repeated the movement several times while he tried to decide whether or not he should see a two-hundred-dollar bet.

Smooth Jake glared at him. "Do you really think there's anything to be gained in putting things off for another day, or another week?"

"When you've been playing as badly as I have, it's a good idea to question your decisions," Martin Oakes said, "then question them again."

"Only answers are going to help you."

"Then I must ask for your patience while I search for

them." He could only think of one possible answer, and he was already acting on it. Holding a stack of alternating red and white chips in his hand, he let them fall one at a time onto the table, creating an uneven striped tower.

"Count it as many times as you wish," Smooth Jake said, "and it will still come out to two thousand dollars."

"I'll see your two hundred and raise it another three."

"Call."

Martin Oakes held cards in one hand, chips in the other. "Look at my pupils, Jake."

"I don't have to look at your pupils."

"Then," Martin Oakes said, spreading a full house on the table, "look at my cards."

Though he felt mildly annoyed, Smooth Jake showed nothing as Martin Oakes raked in the pot. "Your confidence must be dwindling, Martin," he said, "if it takes you that long to bet up a full boat."

"We have plenty of time," Martin Oakes said, knowing that time was the one thing Smooth Jake did not have plenty of, shuffling the cards so slowly that he could hear each one tick into place. "I'm through losing. It may take me a while, but I'm going to beat you, Jake."

"Anything's possible," Smooth Jake said, still feeling strong and focused, "but not in poker."

Martin Oakes won another five hundred dollars before they adjourned for the day. When he returned to his room, Martha the cook was waiting for him.

"Mr. Warner says to tell you there won't be any sit-down dinner tonight," she said. "I'll tell you what we've got, you tell me what you and the missus want, and I'll send it up on a tray."

A knock on the door announced the arrival of their food at exactly eight o'clock. Jennifer opened the door.

There was no one in the hall. She picked up the tray and brought it over to the bed. "Well, I'll be damned," Martin Oakes said, lifting up a cloth napkin. There was a bill under the napkin:

5 nights @ $100 per	*$500*
7 breakfasts @ $5 per	*$ 35*
7 lunches @ $10 per	*$ 70*
8 dinners @ $20 per	*$160*
TOTAL	*$765*

Please note: charge for double occupancy = $150

"At least he's not charging us for swimming," Jennifer said, looking over Martin Oakes's shoulder.

Martin Oakes tore out a blank check from his checkbook and put it on the tray.

"Mind if I eat mine in the tub?" Jennifer asked.

"I'll join you." He propped the tray next to the bathtub on the antique chair and turned on the water. They took off their clothes and climbed in. The tub was huge.

"When we get home, let's put one of these in the middle of our bedroom," Jennifer said, taking a bite of curried chicken with apples. "It's so practical to have everything in one place."

His eyes were closed. He wasn't eating. She flicked some water at him.

"Breathe, you ghost," she said. "It scares me when you get like this."

He opened one eye without curiosity. "You don't look scared."

"It's your influence. You're so all-or-nothing. Will life be completely intolerable if you lose?"

"I'm glad you're here," he said, sinking lower in the water.

"Careful, Martin," she said. "I think the steam's loosening you up."

When they were finished, Jennifer added water to the tub until she was submerged up to her neck. Martin Oakes pulled on a pair of pants, carried the tray to the staircase landing, and picked up the phone to speak to Martha.

"How was the food?" she asked, as if she were expecting his call.

"Wonderful," he said. "And very reasonably priced." He returned to the room and practiced mental-agility drills, rattling off strings of complicated odds, solving hypothetical problems he hadn't encountered yet. After Jennifer climbed into bed and fell asleep, he went downstairs to the den and put on the Opus 127. It was the only sound in the house. No one came. He turned up the volume. The second movement, marked *adagio ma non troppo e molto cantabile,* sang out through the house and spilled out the open windows onto the lawn.

Meghan Warner flung open the door to the den. "What do you think you're doing?"

"Listening to some music."

"You're as ruthless as he is."

"It's just a game."

"The poker or the music?" she asked him accusingly.

"The poker."

"Not to you and Jake it isn't," she said. "To you and Jake it's everything."

She had an amber-colored drink in her hand. Martin Oakes ruled out wine. "Sometimes," he told her, "poker is the only thing that makes sense to me."

"Jake says you're stalling."

"Tell Jake I've learned to appreciate the second movement," Martin Oakes said. "Tell him I'm going to play slow, but not too slow, and *molto cantabile*. Tell him I'm going to do what it takes to win."

"Turn it down," she said, and some of the amber liquid splashed out of her glass. "Jake doesn't like other people touching his records."

He turned off the stereo. "It's all right. I've heard what I need to hear. I don't think even Beethoven can help old Jake now."

The next day, Martin Oakes won two thousand dollars playing only twelve hands. Smooth Jake directed his remarks to Martin Oakes just once, reminding him that they were playing poker, not chess, but both of them knew that in many ways chess was what their game had become. Chess without time clocks. Five days later, Martin Oakes won back his original fifteen thousand and took a four-thousand-dollar bite out of Smooth Jake's initial stake. Meghan Warner no longer floated through the house. She ricocheted. Martin Oakes spotted her careening down the main staircase at one in the morning and caught her by the shoulders.

"Are you all right?" he asked.

She wriggled free and smiled up at him wickedly. "No, Martin," she said. "I'm a shoe." The focus in her eyes was gone. Her hair sagged around her face. If her breath stumbled across a match, the flame would be tall and blue. She began to stagger back up the stairs.

He grabbed her wrist before she could get away. "Have you taken something?"

"Taken something?" she asked, leaning forward, neck rubbery, laugh skittering across the room like a speedboat over a lake. "Why, Martin, isn't it obvious? I never had to take anything. It was all given to me."

"Not all," Martin Oakes said.

"If you could be any kind of shoe, what kind of shoe would you be?"

"Come on," he said gently, slipping his arm under hers and pressing his hand against her back. "I'll help you to your room."

"Follow me," she said, slipping free again, "and I will show you wonders beyond your richest imagination." She flung open a door to the cellar and scurried down the stairs, holding her skirt. The hall at the bottom of the stairs was black. Martin Oakes waited there until she threw on the light in an adjacent room. He followed the light and found her holding a bowling ball. "A brand-new bowling alley!" she announced. The room was three times as long as it was wide. "Two lanes," she continued, with professional enthusiasm in her voice. "Automatic pin reset. Overhead electronic scoring. Genuine plastic chairs. Shoes to fit absolutely every size. Care to roll a string or two?"

"No, thanks."

"No one ever does," she said, rolling her ball into the gutter. The ball skidded on the lane before it left her hand, and the nail on her ring finger broke. By the time the ball had fallen off the edge of the lane, she had disappeared back up the stairs. When he walked out to the foyer, she waved him down to another room he had never been in. "Behind these doors," she said, swinging them open, "Virginia's most state-of-the-art video arcade!" Martin Oakes peered into the room. Cars sped up imaginary highways and tumbled off imaginary cliffs. Pinball marquees flashed invitingly in the darkness. The other games all required the player to run away from his pursuers, or shoot them down. The pursuers were invariably bigger and faster, with better arsenals; they also tended to travel in groups. "Jake installed this arcade for our staff," Meghan Warner said. "Isn't it something?" She walked to the back of the arcade. "And just around this corner," she said, with a graceful sweep of her hand, "a new pool table." No one played pool at The Little Boltons except the grass cutter, and after logging several miles on the John Deere, he was usually too beat to bother. Dust clung to the table's felt surface. "I think of you as a black football shoe, Martin," Meghan Warner said. "Ankle high, with big metal cleats. Like the ones Johnny Unitas used to wear."

"You're too young to know about Johnny Unitas."

"Jake was a big Colts fan until they sneaked off to Indianapolis. Can you imagine anyone sneaking off to Indianapolis? In the middle of the night? I can't."

"Maybe from Baltimore. I think you had better get to bed."

"Stop the game. Please stop it."

"It's too late to stop it." He took her arm. She felt as stiff as a mannequin. "Jake wouldn't want to, anyway."

"How dare you touch me," she said savagely. He released her arm. "You're taking this house away from us as if it meant nothing more to you than Hernández's coffee cup."

"I'm not after your house."

"I don't want to leave The Little Boltons," she said. "But Jake will make me."

A WEEK LATER, Martin Oakes had Smooth Jake down to three thousand dollars, and the room had a fine dusting of dried skin. Remorse crept slowly into Martin Oakes's consciousness, and it was only with great difficulty that he managed to keep it from taking a firm hold there. They hadn't reached the end yet, the two of them, but the end had become so palpable it was as if they were already watching themselves replay the last few hands in slow motion.

"No one's ever taken his time playing me before," Smooth Jake said tonelessly. "Everyone else has always been in a hurry. Usually in a hurry to lose."

"Outlasting you was the only thing I could think of that might work," Martin Oakes replied without looking up from his cards, almost ashamed that such a simple strategy could have produced such brilliant results. His hand forced more chips into the middle of the table.

"I wasn't expecting it," Smooth Jake said, voice still without inflection. "Why would you lay siege? You were already inside the fort." He matched Martin Oakes's bet. "Of course, I should have seen it coming. Anyone who can wait four years to get a game will have the patience to play them tight for a month until things start going his way."

"I suppose as victories go," Martin Oakes said, "it's a little tainted."

"Everything's tainted," Smooth Jake said. His face was placid, even though his resolve had long since surrendered to fatigue, and his concentration had stretched out over time until, tight and brittle, it, too, had finally burst. But his calm remained. Like Martin Oakes, he had never fully pondered what life would be like without poker to sustain it. Tennis, however physically rewarding, would always be an unsatisfactory substitute, and playing the stock market full-time would be only as lucrative as it was boring. Perhaps it wasn't a question of what to play, but whether to play at all. Poised to lose the one thing he couldn't possibly do without, Smooth Jake had made a startling discovery.

He could still hear the Beethoven.

Tired as he was, the *pizzicato* no longer sounded firm

and round, but rather more indistinct, like gravel crunching under car tires. The dynamics in the phrases that ran through his head, meanwhile, were watery and almost without sound: one minute boiling, the next changing to ice (what did water sound like when it froze?); then boiling again; then vanishing to air. It was a new Opus 127 he was hearing, unlike any he had ever imagined. The instruments in his mind—the two violins in one part, the viola and cello in another—demonstrated much less grasp and far more reach in their playing. But it was what they were reaching for that planted his calm bone-deep. He had studied Beethoven's score as if it were a map, only to discover that there was no direct way to his destination. The notes themselves couldn't point the way. But the calm he felt now assured him that though he had never been there, he finally knew the way. "Fold," he said, feeling weight lift not from his shoulders but from his hands. The cards were glass keys that could set him free.

"You never told me what instrument you play," Martin Oakes said, eyes counting Smooth Jake's last chips on the other side of the table. He hoped he could win them before Smooth Jake fell into another trance.

"No," Smooth Jake said, "I never did." The hawk's wings had turned to wax and melted away, but the hawk kept flying. As if he had heard Martin Oakes's silent wish, Smooth Jake slid the rest of his chips into the pot. "I'll cut you for the rest."

"Is that really the way you want to end it?"

"I'm beginning to think that luck is underrated."

"There's a grand piano in one of the sitting rooms."

"Yes. A wonderful instrument. It used to belong to Ivan Smid. He had it shipped here after our game. At the time, I thought it was rather petulant of him." Smooth Jake brushed the table with his cards, even though there was no skin to whisk away. "If you must know, Martin, I play the violin. Not well, and not often. I once failed to take adequate precautions for my safety before a game in New Jersey, was falsely accused of cheating, and got the fingers on my left hand broken as a consequence. It has always been a mystery to me how they knew which hand to break. In any case, I couldn't play very well anymore, but I still had enough dexterity to deal."

"Did you win the game?"

"Well, I suppose that depends on how you look at it, doesn't it, Martin?" He put his deck of cards on the table in front of Martin Oakes. "Pick a card."

Martin Oakes fanned out the deck and let his fingertips trace a path over all the cards before finally removing one from the pack. He flipped the card over. It was the ten of spades.

Smooth Jake found the card he wanted and parted the fan on either side of it until it was the only card left in the middle of the table. He glanced quickly at the card before flipping it over. "Seven of hearts," he said. "So much for luck."

Martin Oakes picked up his ten. "I'd like to keep this if you don't mind." Smooth Jake waved his gnarled left hand. Martin Oakes put the card in his pocket and stood. "I'd be happy to settle the bill for our room and meals in cash."

"Forget that," Smooth Jake said. "Please don't leave, however, until you've said goodbye to Meg."

"Any idea where I might find her?"

"Yes. I think she talked your wife into a game of tennis."

13

The Game

Cheater! Cheater!"

They were all saying it now, shouting it, whispering it, laughing it, chanting it—a nice controlled little frenzy. Finn Collins stood staring at Martin Oakes, feeling the word swing through his stomach like the clapper of a large church bell. Mrs. Tremmel, the old lady who threw firecrackers off her balcony and gambled away her grocery money on Megabucks tickets, had informed Finn that she read the police log every week and looked forward to seeing his name appear in it sometime soon. "What's it going to be?" she would call out to him from her balcony, recognizing the beat of his basketball on the sidewalk. She'd clutch the local newspaper to her breast, newsprint blue on her bent fingers. The creak of her red metal rocking chair blended with her voice. "Stolen car? Breaking and entering? Assault? I've got confidence in you."

Finn never actually saw Mrs. Tremmel during these tirades. Her voice, flecked with rust but infinitely nimbler than her body, crept over the cracked wooden slats of her balcony railing and slid down into the street to hurry him home. "Drugs, maybe? I catch you walking by this house with pipes and needles and plastic bags, Finn Collins, and as the Lord God guards little children I'll turn you in myself." When Mrs. Tremmel was in the street, she wrapped her blue hair and wrinkled face in a scarf so thick that if she ever muttered a word chances were no one would hear it. If teenagers were going to be allowed to run wild, she had suggested to Deadline, the authorities should set up some sort of game preserve for them. "Fence it in," she rasped, safe on her balcony again, rocking her metal chair, "and let people drive through in their cars with the windows up, taking pictures."

Standing before his classmates, Finn considered climbing quietly up the gutter pipe to Mrs. Tremmel's balcony to tell her that he had been run out of poker class for cheating and sentenced to a lifetime of shame. Nothing short of incarceration would satisfy her completely, but she would be pleased to know that he was finally being punished for something. She might even light off a few firecrackers in celebration.

"Cheater." Instead of tightening Finn up, it hollowed him out.

"I really think you should go home now, Finn," Martin Oakes said, the low register of his voice cutting through his students' high-pitched commotion.

Finn gave Martin Oakes an answer, but he spoke so quietly that no one could make out what he was saying.

Martin Oakes inclined his head to hear better. "What's that you said?"

Finn straightened his shoulders and mumbled something at the floor.

"You what?"

"I challenge you." Finn pulled a rumpled ten-dollar bill out of his pocket and flattened it on the table.

"Oh, right," Jimmy V said.

Martin Oakes smiled. "I don't think so."

"Really, Finn," Erika Jaagstrom said mildly from her seat next to Martin Oakes. "What sort of challenge do you think you would be?" Finn had tied a bouquet of fourteen balloons filled with helium to Erika's locker on her fourteenth birthday. When she found the bouquet, she crumpled up the attached card—which Finn had been too afraid to sign—untied the string, and, pulling the balloons along after her, walked outside. The balloons were so full of helium that five of them burst against the cinder-block walls along the way. Erika could draw attention without balloons. With them, she attracted an instant flock. The students who followed her outside jumped each time a balloon burst against the wall, but the sudden pops didn't startle Erika. Upon reaching the playing field, she let go of the nine remaining balloons and promptly walked back inside. She had wonderful posture. Looking out from a window on the third floor of the school, having abandoned quadratic equations to trace the erratic path of the balloons up into a dull spring drizzle, Finn was not saddened by Erika's aloofness or curious about why she had let the balloons go. The thing he couldn't understand was why she didn't stick around to watch them float up and out of sight. She had come out with twenty students trailing, but she walked back inside alone. The students who had followed her didn't even see her leave. Once they reached the playing field, they followed the balloons, which rose slowly, fighting the drizzle. Erika didn't look up. "For God's sake, Finn," she urged him now, "put your money away."

Finn's shadow bothered her. There was something familiar about it that had nothing to do with the person it was attached to, but she couldn't remember where she might have seen it before.

"Erika's right," Brian Willoughby said, resting his hands palms up on the poker table as if he were waiting for someone to put something besides evidence in them. "Ten dollars isn't going to change anything, Finn." Earlier, when Brian had suggested that Jimmy V's discovering the charred ace of hearts in the fireplace didn't necessarily prove that Finn had put it there, Erika had smiled and pointed to the residue of black ash on Finn's fingertips. "If you take a look, Willow," Erika had said, "you'll see that his hands have been near a fire." Confronted with Finn's apparent guilt, Brian's hands sank knuckles down against the poker table, feeling the thickness of the air, empty but not empty, certain that nothing ever really came out to what it weighed. Brian had discovered the only discernible weakness in Carl Rice's game by theorizing that the cards got heavier as the hands got better. When dealt sure winners, Carl's hands dipped slightly, a quarter of an inch at most, but enough to give away his windfall. Since Carl was the best player in the class, Brian took this as conclusive proof that good cards weighed more than bad cards.

Brian was the only student who had got into the class by taking money from the teacher. He had returned to Heartland several times after the incident with the ninety-nine-cent groceries and his subsequent encounter with Martin Oakes. There were other supermarkets, of course, but none with the kind of bargains Brian was looking for. Brian no longer shopped for hire. He was on his own now. He practiced shopping five times a week, tracking down the bargains, timing each session with a stopwatch, using every possible coupon from the Sunday paper, and imposing a one-cart limit on himself; on his more ambitious days the groceries were taller than he was. When Jill, the candlepin bowler, spotted him prowling the aisles, she would call out, "What are you today?" and Brian would answer, "I'm a single parent with seven mouths to feed" or, "I'm a retiree on a fixed income" or, "I'm page 138 of *I Hear America Cooking.*" Brian called it situation shopping. Several of the clerks had complained that he should be banned from Heartland for life. It didn't concern them that Brian never paid for his groceries. They were simply tired of having to wheel his abandoned carts back through the store, replacing items on the shelves. One day, Mr. Phan, the store manager, spotted Brian poking bran muffins for freshness in the bakery section and chased him toward the door. A butcher, his apron covered with fresh blood, saw Mr. Phan streak by and also took up the pursuit. Brian calmly put the muffins on top of his groceries, pushed his cart for about twenty feet as he made his final calculation, and called back to his pursuers, "Sixty-three fifty-nine!" He then let go of the cart, which careened into a frozen-food counter. The force of the collision pressed a package of hamburger through the spokes of the cart, the meat popping out of its plastic wrapper into little squares. "Sixty-three fifty-nine!" Brian shouted with joy as he sped out into the parking lot, smiling back at the determined face of Mr. Phan. "Now that's shopping!"

Palms up on the poker table, Brian was angry with Finn for the black ash. But he was equally infuriated with Erika for smiling. He didn't know that Erika couldn't control her mouth. She was doing her best to appear impartial, but her mouth just wasn't cooperating. When she moved her jaw up and down, the muscles that allowed the mouth corners to relax seemed to have shortened at the temple, even aged, transforming what was by habit a placid line into a splintered expression that resembled a smile but hinted at considerable strain. Martin Oakes said the trick to strain was letting the good stay put and the bad seep through. So Erika smiled the smile of a television reporter paid to deliver bad news, all the while working her jaw and wondering how she could get her temples to loosen up.

Carl Rice felt winter coming in his knees. Cold he could take. Snow he could do without. Snow would keep him off his ten-speed, and the prospect of having to get around on his feet depressed him. Since his parents had bought him a top-of-the-line Peugeot, Carl had discovered that biking was as useful for exercising his powers of observation as it was for building up his legs. Aided by the lights and traffic in downtown Boston, he had little trouble keeping up with the taxicabs his father took to a barbershop near Quincy Market every Tuesday afternoon. A girl Carl didn't know met his father in the barbershop. She couldn't have been more than twenty. When there was a free chair, Carl's father climbed into it and one of the old bald barbers gave him a shave. While the barber lathered him up, he closed his eyes and the girl paced back and forth with her face in the day's newspaper, saying things that made him laugh, laugh so hard that the barber would be forced to stand idle with his straight razor for long moments at a time. As the weeks passed, the barber started laughing, too, the girl took to applying hot towels to her face, and the shaves took longer and longer. Carl sat in a coffee shop across the street, feeling his jaw for signs of stubble, thinking how strange it was finally to see his father's laugh and not be able to hear it. Spying brought you to the edge of what you didn't want to know. He considered tailing the girl, but she took the subway, and he was afraid to leave his bike locked downtown.

Though he gathered information on all of the students,

Carl enjoyed spying on Erika the most. Erika did some interesting things when her parents weren't home. One afternoon, Carl peeked into the Jaagstroms' living room and discovered Erika wildly shaking her head from side to side and stamping her feet on the floor. Carl thought she was having some kind of fit. But just as he was about to break a window to rush in and rescue her, she stopped shaking and sat down on the couch, legs crossed, hands folded, perfectly composed except for a line of perspiration along her brow, a touch of red on either cheek. That was an exciting day. Watching people through windows when they didn't know he was looking struck Carl as a good way to hone his poker skills. People showed the same things in public that they showed in private. The public displays were just a bit subtler; as Jimmy V would say, you had to know how to look for what wasn't there. Carl wondered if he could fly down Massachusetts Avenue through Arlington Heights and turn up Fresh Pond Parkway in time to see Finn arrive home. It all depended on how long it took Finn to catch his bus. Certain that he had heard rain, Carl rose from his chair and walked to the window to find it was only leaves falling on his bike.

Meanwhile, Penelope Gunn's desire for a belt of whiskey had subsided somewhat owing to the keen embarrassment she felt from having to witness Finn's expulsion. The scene grew more distressing as Finn insisted on prolonging it. Penny couldn't look at Erika without thinking of her father; he'd been struggling with a similar expression for nearly forty years. He even ran races with it. Those were the two constants about her father: he was always running, and he was always smiling. Smiling through things instead of at them, no more efficient at covering distance with his twenty-year-old legs than the thin swirl of hair on his head was at covering his forty-year-old scalp. Somehow, Penny thought, her father and mother had the kind of endurance that didn't count all mixed up with the kind that did. She frowned at what Erika was smiling through now.

"Go, Finn," Penny said. "Please, please go." But Finn just stood there, implacable as alabaster. A statue in blue jeans. She wanted to shake him.

"Don't touch him," Jimmy V said, absentmindedly smoothing the creases from the flowers and coconuts on his Hawaiian shirt. "He thinks he's art."

Finn let his eyes travel down the waterfall on Jimmy V's right sleeve, and laughed abruptly.

"He breathes," Aaron announced, feigning reverence.

"There's really nothing to laugh about," Erika said.

"No reason to stay," Penny said.

"I'm not sure if he belongs in a museum or a cornfield," Jimmy V said.

Aaron, Erika, Penny, and Jimmy V chanted through this cadence several times together, with slight variations— a children's choir performing a dirge. Penny sang her part reluctantly, loyalties divided between the class and the bottle of Jim Beam hidden in her jacket. If she could just get a couple of sips from that bottle, she knew she would sympathize with Finn more. One or two slick hits of whiskey might persuade her that being embarrassed was only slightly worse than being alone. The neighbor's rake scraped across the flagstones on the other side of the street. Purple light, bordering on black, washed across the sliding glass door of the studio, transforming the glass into a mirror that reflected the polished wooden surface of the poker table. Outside, it was almost certainly too dark for the neighbor to see his leaves, and the wind was picking up, threatening to scatter the piles he hadn't bagged yet.

Penny stared at her jacket. Jim Beam was getting impatient. Truth was, Jim Beam really didn't give a wink about Finn Collins and his penny-ante troubles. It was quite clear to Jim Beam, as it must have been to Penny, that Finn no longer belonged in the class. "You know, of course, Finn, that there's nothing left to do but leave," Penny proposed, trying another variation, but Finn had other ideas.

Penny's trouser pockets bulged with travel brochures. She was planning to leave home soon, but she hadn't picked a destination yet. There were the obvious domestic choices: New York, San Francisco, Los Angeles, Miami. But lately she had been thinking foreign. The dollar was strong, and her father was weak. Penny couldn't decide between France, Greece, and Germany. On the days that were too good for school, she would smuggle a bottle of Bordeaux into the library and march east with Napoleon, paint the flower of the Moulin Rouge with Toulouse-Lautrec, observe the splendid rhetoric of the guillotine with Robespierre, drink and tan and despair with the Fitzgeralds in Antibes. The Greek library trips featured ouzo with retsina chasers, a combination that made Penny cry and Homer sing, even through the British translations. Judging from their liquor, the Greeks were an odd race. Penny found it difficult to imagine that anyone could get philosophical under the influence of anise and resin. Germany, however, was the most difficult study topic, logistically speaking, because Germany required beer, lots of beer. Penny stole her mother's seal coat on the beer days, clipping a plastic half-gallon jug under each huge lapel. All the librarians would nod deferentially as Penny strode across the lobby to the World War II section, dusting the pink marble diamond-shaped tiles with the bottom edge of her mother's fur. No matter how many times the Third Reich fell, Penny could always open a book of Luftwaffe photographs and watch it fall again, watch transfixed as the Spitfires buzzed like glory and the Messerschmitts with broken propellers and shattered cowlings tumbled from the sky in flames. She frequently ran into Aaron at the library and was disappointed to learn that he didn't share her historical perspective. He was interested in her beer but not in her war. He asked Penny if she knew that the seals stitched together to form her coat had been beaten to death with clubs. "It's my mother's," she answered. He told her that didn't do the seals any good. They had a fine time in the library together, sitting on the floor between the huge metal stacks of books. They agreed that the smell of great masses of books was one of the best smells there was, almost as significant as the words between the hard covers. But Aaron warned Penny about too much formal book learning. "A samurai only needs two things," he would confide to her on the beer days. "A sword and something to cut." Wanting to please him, she would respond that it was a good thing she didn't have a sword. But he never asked her to elaborate.

One night, Penny fell asleep on her back on the library floor, wrapped in the seal coat, empty plastic beer jug dangling outside the coat's lapels as if awaiting a refill, a book on the Dresden fire-bombing shielding her eyes from the fluorescent light. It took three librarians to wake her up and carry her to the door. She thanked them, wandered across the street to the Lexington Green, and wrapped herself up in the seal for another hour, after which two boys on motorcycles shook her awake and asked her if she had any drugs. She responded no, she was from Newton, and they, seeming to understand, drove her there. The house was dark, and her mother was asleep. Running clothes dripped dry in the front hall. Scuffing her bare feet across the front hall carpet, Penny could have sworn she had caught a whiff of her father's distinctive pipe tobacco. Of course he had quit smoking, and quit living there, long ago. But when she got a certain kind of drunk, her feet scuffed up memories of the days when he had taken her with him to Harvard Square on Saturday mornings to have his tobacco specially mixed. "Nothing like a good smoke after a long run," she mumbled to herself in the hall, wondering why people ever got together in the first place. She went upstairs and looked in on Caitlin, found her sleeping in a tangle of toys on the floor, picked her up, and gently lowered her into her crib, covering her with the seal coat.

Aaron caught Penny staring at him across the poker table and made a silent vow never again to look for cards in her Coke-bottle lenses. The risk was too great, and the information he gained by taking it was too unreliable. It had only recently occurred to him that Penny showed him precisely what she wanted him to see. Turning, what Aaron saw now in Finn gave him the same uncomfortable pleasure he'd once got from torturing his family's late dog, Itzhak. Poor Itzhak. Aaron's mother, Jane Simon, had tried to expose the beast to culture. Itzhak lived in the kitchen. He was mostly Dalmatian but a little bit of something else, too, since tufts of brown hair grew on his hind legs and his snout took a slightly wolfish turn at the nostrils. As part of Itzhak's education, Jane Simon kept the radio above the refrigerator tuned to one of the commercial-free classical music stations twenty-four hours a day. It drove Aaron crazy. Jane Simon knew that dogs could hear better than they could see, and had concluded that Bach stood a better chance of making an impression on Itzhak than the painters who had made her year as an au pair in France so memorable. Just to be on the safe side, though, she wallpapered the kitchen with the works of her favorite French masters. The Degas print made her feel younger, but left Itzhak unimpressed. He couldn't distinguish the generous red in the ballerina's hair or the subtle thistles in her teacher's brush. He seemed to have a bit better grasp of pointillism; he would sometimes paw at the Seurat of the picnickers along the Seine, threatened in the near distance by lumbering blue smokestacks. But music: that was where Itzhak distinguished himself from the food-and-shelter preoccupations of the average Dalmation. Bach's "Brandenburg" Concertos ran across his wiry coat like a wicker brush, starting a sound in his belly not unlike a cat's purr. With Bach on the radio, Itzhak became the most contented member of the Simon household, which was why, when Aaron was left in charge of the house, the first thing he did was go into the kitchen and change the radio station from classical to country. "Say goodbye to Johann Sebastian," he told Itzhak. "Say hello to your friend and mine, Merle Haggard." It was a perfect form of torture. No marks. As soon as the baroque instruments gave way to steel guitars and hillbilly hollers, Itzhak would slink into a corner, the room that was usually soothed by the Boston Symphony and the Academy of St. Martin's-in-the-Fields now filled with cheating wives, prison breaks, illegal immigrants, and intermittent battles with the bottle. Poor Itzhak. Poor Finn. Country music would have been preferable to the burial hymn Aaron and the other students were singing now, some cheerfully, others by rote. No marks. Just words. Just notes that entered through the ear.

Jane Simon had never been the same since Itzhak committed suicide by jumping over the rail of a cruise ship and belly-flopping to his death some fifty feet below. The water was so clear that after he hit, he just seemed to keep on falling.

Jane had been after tightfisted old Stanley to take her

on a cruise for years, but when he finally surprised her on her birthday with tickets for a two-week Caribbean junket, the first thing she had insisted upon was that they take Itzhak with them, cost be damned. Itzhak was a glum dog, and she didn't think he could adjust to being in a kennel. "He's not nasty, and he doesn't have airs about him," she reminded Stanley. "He just needs his peace and quiet." Itzhak had lain across her feet in the kitchen as she said this, flaring his nostrils impressively at Aaron. Jane gestured toward the radio and said, "Itzhak has never liked Ravel." Aaron observed that Itzhak didn't seem to like Johnny Cash much, either, but as he spoke, he realized Itzhak was the only one paying attention to him.

They called Aaron from Nassau with the news: Itzhak was dead. No one knew why he had interrupted the senior citizens' shuffleboard tournament to leap over the rail, and few were sympathetic with Jane Simon's attempts to have the ship turned around to retrieve him. The general feeling among the passengers was that a properly bred and cared for dog would not willingly offer himself up as shark bait. "Itzhak never had anything but the best," Jane protested, leaving her tears in the ship's wake, still hopeful that Itzhak would somehow fight the foam and propellers and appear wet but repentant along the port bow. But the dog was gone forever. For the rest of the cruise, whether they were shopping in St. Thomas or sunbathing by the pool, the Simons could feel the stares at their backs and hear the quiet voices speculating about what they had done to persuade Itzhak that living was no longer worthwhile. Months later, in the middle of the pasty New England winter, Stanley would catch Jane studying him, and each time he would swear that he had no new information on the hound. Stanley's position was that dogs didn't leap to their deaths; dogs did, however, leap over fences. Itzhak had simply mistaken the ship's rail for a fence. "Not a chance," Jane countered. "Itzhak had the keenest eyesight of any dog I have ever known. Something was troubling him, Stanley. Something terrible." Denying complicity in Itzhak's leap to eventual peace and quiet made Stanley so ill-tempered he began to wish aloud that the dog would come alive so he could kill him again. In front of Jane. Maybe run the mutt over with his car. Jane, who always sought out Aaron for comfort, warned Stanley not to mock the dead.

Martin Oakes shimmered in front of his students like a mirror, moved among them like a breeze.

"I challenge you, Mr. Oakes," Finn said again, trying to bring the teacher back into focus. Finn's shadow, cast across the poker table by the lights above, was as supple as his body was stiff. Pieces of thread dangled from his blue jeans and flannel shirt.

"You don't have anything to challenge him with," Erika said.

"Get out," Jimmy V said, waving his hand at Finn. "The crows are eating your corn." Jimmy V was partial to clothes that had been lived in a little while, but when they were falling apart, it was time to get rid of them.

Jimmy V had recently begun to follow a policy that required him to give up one piece of clothing for every new piece he acquired. He was more concerned with balancing his wardrobe than he was with keeping his conscience clean, and he didn't extend the policy to shoes. He would never be able to get enough shoes. But he no longer stole an article of clothing unless he was prepared to give one away.

Jimmy V's policy had been put to its greatest test the night Salvatore woke him up from a velvet-masked slumber and told him to get dressed, they were going to take a ride.

Jimmy V climbed into his green chinos and pulled on his London safari shirt. Angelo Lopresti was waiting at the curb in Salvatore's BMW. Jimmy V asked Salvatore what was going on. Salvatore said, "It's a surprise. Just get in the car." Jimmy V was groggy. He had tightened the band on his sleeping mask before going to bed and the mask's outline was still visible on his face. "Any dreams slip out tonight, Jimmy?" Salvatore asked. When Jimmy V didn't answer him, he said: "You know something, Jimmy, that mask makes you look like a goddamned raccoon." Angelo Lopresti filled the car with cigar smoke. They drove to a mall. The mall was closed. Salvatore parked the car. All of the storefronts were dark. A security car drove by them as they walked across the parking lot to the side door of a department store. There were two security guards in the car. The man who was driving the car waved. Angelo Lopresti waved back and smiled, half his teeth flashing gold under the parking-lot lights, the other half brown with tobacco stains. "Rent-a-Cops," Salvatore said, frowning. "God bless them." Jimmy V asked Salvatore where they were going. Salvatore said nowhere, they had arrived. Angelo Lopresti produced a key and used it to unlock the side entrance to the department store. They went inside. It was dark. Angelo Lopresti disappeared for five minutes. The night-lights clicked on and the escalators whirred to life. Angelo Lopresti returned. "Salvatore tells me you like clothes," he said to Jimmy V. "Please. Have a look around. Let me know if you see anything you like." Jimmy V stared at him with wonder and asked, "Is this your store?" "No, Jimmy," Angelo Lopresti replied, exhaling smoke from his Cuban cigar, puffs punctuating his laughter. "Tonight it is *your* store." The smoke dulled the glint of his gold teeth. Salvatore was beaming. "Anything you want, Jimmy, is yours,"

he said. It sounded like a terrific opportunity. Jimmy V rode
the escalator up to the second floor. There was fresh wax on
the floors, and everywhere a smell of newness. Jimmy V
walked past a column of designer jeans and came to a
mannequin wearing a sports jacket. He took the jacket off
the mannequin and tried it on. The sleeves were too long,
the shoulders too narrow. He decided it really wasn't his
style, anyway. He slung the jacket over the mannequin's
outstretched arm and rode up to the third floor. Rows of
shoes awaited him. The variety was overwhelming. Jimmy
V measured his feet in one of the metal slides on the floor
next to the fitting chairs. Then he went back into the stock-
room and chose seven different pairs of shoes to try on. In
style, the shoes were all quite different. In fit, they were
uniformly uncomfortable. Jimmy V could hardly wait to get
back into his black ankle boots. He continued his tour,
strolling past dress shirts and tie wheels and bedroom linen
displays. A cardboard commuter train on the fourth floor
was full of mannequins in pinstriped suits. Some of the
mannequins held briefcases and checked their watches, all
synchronized to the correct time, but the train wasn't getting
anywhere fast. Jimmy V tried on a straw Panama hat with
a smartly downturned brim. When he caught his profile in
one of the tall mirrors, he noted that the brim emphasized
the length of his nose, and he tossed the hat into an under-
wear bin. Beneath the wax on the floor, black marks traced
the paths people took through the store during the day.
Jimmy V ran his hand along an aisle of trench coats and
listened to the hangers clatter on their aluminum pole. Finally, he picked out a pair of socks and rode the escalators
down. "You look through the whole store and all you find
is a pair of socks?" Angelo Lopresti asked, smiling. "I like
what I have," Jimmy V answered; "thanks all the same."

"What the hell's the matter with you?" Salvatore demanded. Jimmy V ignored him. Salvatore didn't understand that style had to be woven together with imagination before it could be stitched into fabrics. Too many push-ups in prison was Salvatore's problem. Something had just popped in his head. "Do you really own this store, Mr. Lopresti?" Jimmy V asked. Angelo Lopresti smiled again at the pair of socks, and said, "I have an interest in it." Jimmy V said, "I'd like to come back sometime when there are some people around." Salvatore just glared at him.

"Scarecrow," Jimmy V said to Finn now, arms flapping beneath his Hawaiian shirt.

"I'm not going until he plays," Finn said.

"I'll play you," Carl offered.

"If you would all just stop picking on him," Penny muttered, "maybe he would go."

Finn waved his ten-dollar bill at Martin Oakes. Jimmy V continued to flap his arms like some exotic bird. "Ten dollars," Finn said. "Don't you think you can take ten dollars from me, Mr. Oakes?"

"Who do you think you are now—Billy Riordon?" Aaron said, mocking Finn without enthusiasm.

But Finn's challenge was an entirely different matter from that of Martin Oakes's last Test victim and his Playboy Bunny boasting. No student had ever dared put Martin Oakes up to a real game for real money before. Playing for money was against the rules.

Martin Oakes cut his deck with one hand. No one noticed. His six remaining students were all looking at Finn's ten-dollar bill as if they had never seen money before. The evidence sat on the poker table, smaller than a thumbprint. Martin Oakes pressed his forefinger on top of the charred red half-heart of the ace, and held it up to the class.

"What makes you think you have the right to challenge me, Finn?"

"I figured you might want to give me a real test."

"You had your chance. You passed on it."

"I don't think you can beat me," Finn insisted.

Carl Rice turned his palms up at Martin Oakes. "So take his money."

Martin Oakes knew it wasn't as simple as that. He scratched his temple and considered Finn's motives. Winning didn't seem to be one of them. Finn could beat him at poker only if a lightning bolt interceded or if Martin Oakes decided to lose on purpose. Nature did not produce lightning bolts on clear days, and Martin Oakes's nature would never allow him to lose intentionally. So that was settled. He would certainly win the game. But there was no reason to play it. Martin Oakes flicked the charred half-heart toward the fireplace. It caught a draft and veered wide to the right. Penny reached down and picked it up. "No," Martin Oakes said.

Penny's hand shook. She dropped the heart on the floor.

"Why?" Finn demanded.

"Because you haven't earned it. And because ten dollars isn't worth wasting my time on."

"Maybe you don't really believe what you teach."

"Finn, there's no point in trying to bait me."

"I'm just asking a question. I get kicked out because I won't take your Test. But you won't take mine. Why do you get to stay in class if you refuse to play the game you're supposed to be teaching?"

"Finn," said Martin Oakes, "as you go through this life you will never stop marveling at how little fairness there is in it."

"Poker's fair."

"Not if you and I are playing." The deck of cards rose and fell in his hand, a single continuous wave. Erika couldn't stop smiling. Carl stared at her thick braid as if it were a mystery that was about to unwind at any moment. Martin Oakes said to Finn: "The reason I won't play you is simple. I have nothing to win. You have nothing more to lose."

Finn shook the ten-dollar bill. "You've got this to win. This is real. And you've got something to prove, too. Poker consists of chance, probability, and character. What about *your* character? You talk a lot about discipline, but all I've ever seen you do is smoke cigarettes and drink tea." Finn tried to fit a sneer on his face to match the mixture of anger, pity, and contempt he saw in Martin Oakes's eyes, soon realizing that he did not require one sneer but several. Martin Oakes's eyes presented a moving target that was difficult to interpret and virtually impossible to reflect. By the time Finn's frown adjusted itself to anger, Martin Oakes's eyes twinkled with disdain. From disdain the eyes lapsed into pity, widening imperceptibly from pity to a brief flicker of compassion, then—just as suddenly—emptying of all emotion into a look that pierced Finn more than any of the others because it already took his eventual departure for granted. Struggling to assert itself against this barrage of stares, Finn's mouth could only quiver with various degrees of uncertainty. It didn't help that Erika's mouth remained uncompromisingly cheerful. "When the cards are dealt," Finn said, looking away from Erika and Martin Oakes, trying to establish a rhythm in his mind, putting his thoughts together as deliberately as he would dribble a basketball on a pitted asphalt court, "poker is purely a game of chance. But once you pick up your cards, it becomes a game of skill. Knowing when you're beaten. Knowing when what you have isn't good enough. Figuring out how to make the best of what you get dealt."

"It's gratifying to know you took your eyes off the birds long enough to pay attention from time to time," Martin Oakes said. "I hope you'll remember to apply those principles whenever you play. Assuming someone will give you a game."

Finn stuck his hands in his pockets to prevent them from balling into fists. "Why don't you apply them, Mr. Oakes? All you ever do is talk about skill. You never show any. Is that what the sign really means? 'Show Nothing'? Absolutely nothing?"

Finn's remark produced silence, a sudden, exquisite silence, after which Finn felt the other students' eyes leave him and focus on Martin Oakes, waiting for a reply. It was amazing how much pressure those eyes could apply. Finn wondered if Martin Oakes could feel it.

"No," Martin Oakes said.

"Show nothing," Finn said again, sensing that the words would keep the students' eyes off him. "We all say it, but until now I never knew what it meant."

"He has a point," Carl observed. He had tried to spy on Martin Oakes several times, with discouraging results. The drapes in Martin Oakes's house fit the windows perfectly. Carl couldn't even see shadows through them. Hoping to gain some insight into Martin Oakes's character, Carl would wait in the woods next to the poker studio until his car came up over the lip of the Massachusetts Avenue hill by the stone store. Martin Oakes drove deliberately, signaling the turn into his half-moon driveway two houses in advance. After he parked the car, he walked up the path to the front door, confident but unhurried, and disappeared inside. His wife, whose hair always seemed to be wet, had a more expressive face, but she walked fast, then closed the door just as firmly behind her. The only two rooms not shrouded by drapes were the kitchen and the poker studio, and they were protected by the wooden fence that wound around the backyard. It was a house that showed nothing.

"You have to admit, it might be interesting," Erika said. She was the only one who had ever seen Martin Oakes play poker, and that had been in a smoke-filled dream.

Having already weighed the consequences of playing the game, Martin Oakes acted decisively. "Fine." Nothing to win. Nothing to lose. Just get it done. Finn was a clever nuisance. No one else had ever come up with such a scheme. Sometimes, poker was the only thing that made sense. "You know, Finn, though your performance in my class has been singularly lacking in distinction, I must commend you for ingenuity. I had assumed you wouldn't need to be shown—sitting here in front of us with ashes on your fingertips, a cheater—shown why you do not belong in this class." Martin Oakes wiped off the finger he'd used to pick up the charred ace, leaving a thin black stripe on his pants. "I suspect once I do show you, you will wish you had left while you had the opportunity." Cutting the cards now: "Right. Miss Jaagstrom, if you would be so kind as to divide the chips." Martin Oakes stared briefly into the Coffin, a small wooden box that could bury an infinite amount of hope, and saw the pillars of poker chips that had held up Smooth Jake's Virginia castle. Hernández lived there now. He hadn't been elected, but The Little Boltons probably made him feel important, anyway. It was a good location for killing time. Martin Oakes wondered if by now Hernández had painted the poker-chip columns a uniform sun-baked white. "You needn't stay," he said to the rest of the class, resigned to his chore. "I don't think you're likely to learn anything of value."

They weren't going anywhere.

Penny reached down and picked up the charred piece of the ace of hearts off the floor.

"Terms," Finn said.

"You're in no position to bargain," Martin Oakes said.

"Just asking."

"If you win, you keep your place in the class. If I win, you pick up your books and leave immediately. And you do not extend your challenge to any of the other members of this class. Agreed?"

"What if I don't want my place in class?"

"Then we're wasting our time, because you'll be leaving one way or the other, and you might as well leave now." Martin Oakes's face had already begun to fade into a mask of blandness. Distinctly featureless. A plain pink-white face, smooth as a rim of clouds above a sunset. Not a face you would notice, and certainly not a face you could read. Just a covering for skull and brains. His eyes had locked in the neutral look. Only his hands conveyed menace, manipulating the deck so expertly that all fifty-two cards seemed connected together like the bellows of an accordion. Finn recognized in Martin Oakes's hands the song the others had been singing, heard it ripple through the cards.

A polite but toneless tune: Go home, go home, just go home; home to a black room filled with electric guitars, to a shedding dog and feuding parents; home to trucks dumping the steaming trash that would make for steeper sledding this coming winter; home to hard rubber balls spinning in a plexiglass globe, each ball a seven.

Fortunately for Finn, the seven had stayed in the globe that night at Aaron Simon's house and a three had popped out and rolled into the gutter instead. No one had ever saved twenty million dollars faster. A five-number winning ticket was still worth four hundred dollars, however—"Enough for a used Gibson!" his brother Michael had shouted, when Finn returned home, holding out his callused fingers to receive the lucky ticket that Finn had never bought. Michael's face was happier than Finn had ever seen it, and his fingers were already forming chords in the air, anticipating the smooth action of his new guitar. That was what killed Finn: seeing Michael playing the invisible guitar. The tears rushed out of him then, and Michael, who knew nothing about Sammy Vicks' chocolate swindle but could see that Finn was melting, let go of his anger almost immediately and told Finn it was no big deal; but of course it was a very big deal, Michael's eyes stung, too, and before they knew it they were sitting together on the porch with their arms clumsily around each other, watching the softball game across the street through the mist in their eyes, two tough boys whose luck was rotten even when it was good. Finn was determined to pay Michael back. So far, he had scraped together nearly two hundred dollars.

"I'll stay," Finn said.

"That remains to be seen." Martin Oakes arranged himself in the chair opposite Finn. The tension drained away from his temples. A feeling of calm ran through him now, as it did whenever he sat down to play. He had once got excited during games. Now he only got excited after them. Lately, he had been smoking more cigarettes when his games were finally over, playing more Chopin, squinting into more hot-wired dawns. Jennifer warned him that he couldn't really be feeling calm if he was always holding back so much excitement. But Martin Oakes remained more interested in action than analysis. No longer in need of aspirin, he lit a cigarette and looked clear through Finn. "Dealer's choice," he said, and put the deck down in front of Finn. They were beautiful cards. The kings, queens, and jacks all had separate medieval identities, and had been painted and reduced with great care. Discreet stripes ran through the numbered cards, connecting their thin black borders. The numbers themselves were written in an ornate hand. Martin Oakes had brought the deck back from Europe. "Cut," he said. Finn cut. "Five draw," Martin Oakes said, dealing the cards. "Jacks or better. Ante and redeal if neither of us has openers. Three raises. Pot limit." As he spoke, his students fanned out behind him in a tight semicircle, suggesting the path of a single, orbiting body, as if he exerted the same gravitational pull on each of them.

"How about making it no limit?" Finn said, sitting alone on the other side of the table. He picked up his cards: ten, seven, four, three, two. Nothing. He could hear the bird feeder rattling on its hinges outside. From his seated position, the students' individual smiles were less distinct than the frown they formed by standing together.

Martin Oakes suppressed a yawn. "I'm afraid I can't agree to that," he said, counting his chips. No limit was Finn's only chance: betting it all on one good hand. "But nice try." He spread his cards and saw three eights. "Your bet."

"Check," Finn said. Martin Oakes tossed a red chip into the middle of the table. "Fold," Finn said, before the chip even had a chance to stop spinning.

"Are you planning to make me win it a dime at a time?" Martin Oakes asked.

"When you have nothing, get out," Finn said.

Erika smiled at Finn from above Martin Oakes's shoulder. "You've already broken that rule, haven't you, Finn?"

Finn put his ante into the pot and announced the next game: "Hurricane. No openers." He hoped that by choosing one of the more obscure variations of poker he could camouflage some of his bad decisions and keep Martin Oakes off balance. He dealt two cards to Martin Oakes and two to himself. "Bet?"

"Ten."

"Raise twenty-five."

"Call."

"Cards?"

"One," Martin Oakes said. In Hurricane, to get one, Martin Oakes had to give one.

Finn stood pat.

"Twenty-five," Martin Oakes said.

Finn counted out a stack totaling fifty cents and slid it into the middle. "Raise."

Martin Oakes called again.

"Pair of jacks," Finn said, showing the third highest hand in Hurricane.

Martin Oakes held a pair of sixes. Without showing them to Finn, he slipped them back into the deck. "Seven stud," he said.

Finn pulled in his chips. There was a thin film of hundred-year-old oil on them. The white chips were really gray. The red chips had smeared to a dirty pink. The blue chips were almost rainbow-colored, swirling to the touch like puddles next to a heavily trafficked road. You could rub those chips forever and the grease would never come off. "This isn't going to be as easy as you think," Finn said.

"The only thing you're taking is my time," Martin Oakes said. It annoyed him to see hope building behind Finn's eyes. First, because the hope was misguided. Second, because it so easily seeped through. Hadn't Finn learned

anything? The game was a formality. Martin Oakes shuffled
the deck. All of the chips eventually would come back to
him. They were his chips. At the end of the game, he would
collect them and slot them back into their cracked wooden
box. There were 2,598,960 different five-card poker hands
—more than three times the number of hands a serious
poker player could hope to draw in a forty-year career, even
if he stuck to the simplest game—but there was only one
possible result when it came to playing Martin Oakes. He
was the best of the best. Poker was his game, the only thing
he had ever considered worth owning. Martin Oakes didn't
just calculate the odds. He embraced them. Each poker hand
was a fresh blade of grass, a worn pebble in the driveway,
a nail in the roof beam with proud stacks of chips to support
it. Together they formed his property.

Penny broke away from the other students. She
thought she was going to walk over to her jacket. Instead,
she walked over to Finn's side of the table and took up a
position just off his right shoulder. Her throat burned and
her legs shook. Behind Martin Oakes, Aaron first frowned
at her, then dismissed her with a shake of his head.

"It would appear, Finn," Martin Oakes said serenely,
"that one of your classmates thinks you actually stand a
chance of winning."

Finn didn't look back.

"I don't care who wins," Penny said, eyes level with
Aaron's. "I don't even care who cheats." She still had the
charred ace. "Everyone cheats. I take any edge I can get.
I thought that was the point." Without taking her eyes from
Aaron, she slowly removed her glasses, folded them, and put
them in her pocket.

"Why are you taking off your glasses?" Aaron chal-
lenged her.

"Because my eyes are tired, Aaron," Penny said, frowning at him. Two weeks earlier, she had looked at one of Carl's hands while pretending to shuffle for her deal. Carl had just won a big pot in which all the other players had eventually folded. Not needing to show his cards, Carl placed them face down in the discard pile to await reshuffling. Just as Penny picked them up, however, Martin Oakes interrupted the game to remind the class that a good bluff must be directed at a single player rather than the table at large. No one was looking at her. It took only a half second, a casual flip of the cards, a shutter click of the eyes, for Penny to find out that Carl did not have the flush she had feared but an even more imposing full house. Curiosity and competitiveness formed a dangerous combination. Penny felt the urge to confess now, but decided she needed forgiveness less than she needed whiskey. Whiskey and a new pair of eyes.

"There's a big difference between cheating and taking an edge, Penny," Carl said, certain there was information in her face but unable to read it.

"Apparently not for her," Aaron said.

"Certainly not for Finn," Erika said.

Martin Oakes dealt the cards.

Penny felt miserable. If it appeared to the others that she had thrown her support to Finn, it felt to Penny as if she had assured his defeat. Tillie, the bag lady who had broken her son's wrist, could be quite cruel when she had to drink bad liquor—or, worse yet, when she ran out altogether. "You're drawn to losers," she accused Penny on one of the dry days, refusing to accept the dented cans of vegetable soup Penny had brought her. "I feel like a success when I'm around winos who can't keep their food down. You feel like a success when you're around me. That's what success is. Finding someone who's worse off." In the present circumstances, Penny had to admit that Tillie was right. Thirsty, squinting, she felt about as useful to Finn as Abe Lincoln's hospital blankets must have been to the consumptive Indians. Dying warm was still dying; maybe his feeling bad would make her feel good.

Finn turned to her and said, "I'm winning now."

"That's true," she agreed. "But he'll probably be winning later." Finn held his cards low to the table so Penny couldn't look at the hand he was holding. "Don't bother," she said, two fingers making a V under her eyes. "I can't see them, anyway." But he kept them low, not trusting her.

Martin Oakes looked at Finn and Penny. It was a shame he could only shape character, only work with what was already there. In some cases, it just wasn't enough. "Fifty," he said, pushing a blue chip into the pot.

"Call," Finn said.

They drew two cards each. Martin Oakes bet a dollar. Finn called him again.

"Three nines," Martin Oakes said, spreading them.

"Three tens," Finn said evenly. The way he gathered in his winnings—hand poised over the table with fingers spread far enough apart to reach all the chips, but close enough together to keep any of them from slipping through —blended nicely with the noise from across the street. For a moment, the hard wood table became a flagstone walk, Finn's fingernails the prongs of the neighbor's rake, the smooth, flat chips crisp as leaves.

"You're winning now," Penny said. She wasn't optimistic.

Finn lost the next three hands. He had good cards. Martin Oakes had better ones. The pots were small.

Brian walked over to Finn's side of the table, leaned

down, and whispered in Finn's ear: "Good cards weigh more than bad cards. You're letting your hands dip when you get dealt winners, and he's picking up on it."

Martin Oakes, who could hear Brian perfectly, had in fact not been picking up on it, but took note of it as an interesting concept. Good cards weighed more than bad cards. Leave it to Willow. "Finn," Martin Oakes said, eyes flashing at Brian before reverting to the liquid brightness that prevented anything from penetrating their colorless surface, "as I'm sure you are aware, it is considered somewhat outside the rules to accept advice during the course of a game."

"I didn't ask for it," Finn said, glancing quickly at Brian, who was behind him now. "I can play my own cards."

"Hold them up," Brian advised, facing Martin Oakes, neck straight, dark eyes absorbing rather than reflecting the track lights. "Prop your elbows on the table if you have to, but don't let them dip."

"I'm doing fine by myself," Finn said, eyes focused on the table. There was no sixth sense. There were only five. Combining them provided the winning margin. Finn opened his eyes wide and tried to concentrate on what Martin Oakes was feeling. Martin Oakes didn't seem to be feeling anything.

Penny stood next to Brian. "Do you mean to tell me, Willow," she said, "that if I blindfold you and put an ace in your left hand and a deuce in your right hand, you'll be able to tell me which is the higher card?"

"Sure," Jimmy V said. "About half the time. Some swami. He might as well flip a coin."

"It doesn't work that way, Penny," Brian said. "You've got to be looking at the cards. You don't weigh them with your hands. You weigh them with your mind."

Martin Oakes looked across the table. Finn, Penny,

and Brian formed an odd three of a kind. He dealt a hand
of Shotgun: three cards at the start with an obligatory draw
of two. Just to let Finn know that the strange games were
no refuge.

"Keep your elbows up, Finn," Brian said.

"Why?" Finn asked. "So you can see my cards?"

Carl, behind Martin Oakes, folded his arms and said:
"While you're holding your cards up, Finn, you might want
to remind Willow not to hold his breath. When he's weighing good cards with his mind, he tends to light up like the
Citgo sign above Fenway Park. I'd hate to see him give away
your best hands."

Aaron dug his fingers hard into Carl's shoulder. "I
want you to do something for me, Mr. Tour de France," he
said cheerfully. "I want you to watch what the hell you say
about Willow. Okay? Think you can do that for me?"

Jimmy V said, "Come on, Aaron, knock it off."

Martin Oakes didn't turn around.

Carl felt his whole upper arm go numb.

Jimmy V touched Aaron's wrist very gently. "Let go,"
he said. He was shorter than Aaron by at least two inches,
but when he spoke, he raised only his eyes, not his chin.
Aaron released Carl's shoulder. Aaron and Jimmy V had
fought once, privately, on a soccer field. Aaron picked the
fight and Jimmy V finished it, putting Aaron in such a
fearsome headlock that he almost lost consciousness and an
hour later was still sitting on the soccer field, rubbing his
jaw and dreading the next day at school. Yet Jimmy V never
mentioned the incident to anyone. Aaron had no idea why.

"Really, Aaron," Erika said, authority in her voice.
"Behave yourself."

"He's always on Willow," Aaron said. His voice was
a little squeezed.

"Carl's a creep," Jimmy V said. "Ignore him."

Carl's arm hurt so much he was afraid he would cry.

"Thank you, Mr. Vitagliano," Martin Oakes said, but he still didn't turn around.

"No problem," Jimmy V said.

Aaron said to Martin Oakes: "You shouldn't let Carl get away with talking like that. *You* should be sticking up for Willow, not me."

"Stand still and keep quiet, Mr. Simon," Martin Oakes said. If he ordered them to leave, would they obey? "Mr. Willoughby is capable of sticking up for himself."

"He's right, Aaron," Brian said from the other side of the table. "You don't have to worry about Carl making fun of me. But Carl has something to worry about. Carl dips his hands."

"I do like hell," Carl said, almost weeping.

"Watch him sometime," Brian said to Martin Oakes. Behind Martin Oakes, Erika, Aaron, and Jimmy V were paying very close attention. This was the first time in their experience that one of the students had shared information. They weren't supposed to share. "You'll see," Brian said. "He gets good cards, his hands dip."

"You can't share victory and you can't share defeat," Martin Oakes began, "so—"

"So why share information?" Brian finished for him, reading the handwritten poster on the wall. "Because Carl is a pain in the ass, that's why." They were all out for themselves, but in Carl's case Brian was willing to gang up.

"How good would these cards have to be," Jimmy V asked, trying not to sound too interested, "before Carl gave them away?"

"Offhand?" Brian said. "Straight. Maybe a flush. But when his hands twitch, get out fast."

"I'm going to ruin you, Willow," Carl promised.

"I don't think so," Brian said. "Not with what you've got."

"With what I *know*," Carl said. Brian's father was learning how to swim. He hadn't really got the hang of it yet. He thrashed from one end of his new pool to the other with a technique that appeared to Carl to be half sidestroke, half crawl. In the middle of autumn, with the temperatures in the low forties and the sun going down earlier every day, Brian's father continued to swim his laps, swim right through the leaves that swept across the surface of the pool.

"You don't know nearly enough," Brian said.

Finn didn't care whose hands dipped and whose hands didn't; he just wanted to win. He slid a bet into the pot and looked on impassively as Martin Oakes matched and raised it. "Call," Finn said. His elbows had crept up onto the table.

"Tens and sevens," Martin Oakes said.

Finn tossed his cards face down toward the deck.

Erika watched Finn's shadow as he leaned over the table, and wondered why she connected it in her mind to her grandmother's dignified slouch.

No one was prepared for what happened next, Finn least of all. What happened next was luck, pure luck. No one knew why it came, and no one could predict how long it would last.

Finn started to receive exceptional cards with each cold deal. The students in class had come up with different names for this phenomenon. Jimmy V called it the "dancing deck." Erika called it "card quilting." They had all seen it happen to them, but no one would have guessed it was about to happen to Finn against Martin Oakes.

Oblivious of everything but his cards and Martin Oakes's chips, Finn pulled one good hand after another: straights, flushes, full houses; high cards when they were

playing high, low cards when they were playing low; good
cards by any two-hand probability table, but, more important, good enough cards to win. Even Martin Oakes was
surprised, although of course he didn't show it. For five
hands, Finn beat him by the slimmest possible margins,
winning by a higher flush suit, a lower seven-six-four, a
superior two pair, a jack-high straight that edged a ten-high
straight, and finally, improbably, four deuces to beat Martin
Oakes's three sevens and two kings.

Carried along by his initial decision to play, Martin
Oakes was now the cool surfer fallen into the gully of a wave,
still confident, still nimble enough to maneuver, but knowing he had misjudged the way the wave would break. Too
late to change his mind: he had to keep going now, had to
use his skill to make sure the wave didn't break above him.

"Feeling nervous yet, Mr. Oakes?" Penny asked.

"Not at all," he replied truthfully, but the question
itself was rather unnerving. Without her glasses, what could
she possibly have seen?

The good cards kept coming to Finn. It was an impressive run, hampered only by Finn's reluctance to bet up his
cards to their fullest potential. They would have been worth
considerably more money had Finn manipulated them properly but, riding his luck, he was content to see each of his
promising hands through to the showdown, letting Martin
Oakes take the lead in the betting. After fourteen hands,
Finn was up five dollars.

Finn had forgotten the third rule: When you have the
best hand, make them pay. His luck only lasted until he
picked up his cards. After that, Martin Oakes's superior
betting skills prevented Finn from cashing in.

Jimmy V did not walk over to Finn's side of the table.
He slipped. He feinted. A tropical storm of movement,

Jimmy V suddenly appeared on Finn's side of the table as if he had been there all along. "What are you waiting for, Finn," he asked upon his arrival, "divine intervention? Or is it you figure maybe you're going to nickel and dime him to death?"

Finn didn't even look up. His skills were limited, but his concentration was total.

"Tell me what you think you're doing," Jimmy V insisted. "I really want to know."

Finn barely heard him.

Jimmy V had always suspected that Finn possessed little fashion sense. The question now was whether he possessed any sense at all. Martin Oakes glimpsed the pattern of Jimmy V's Hawaiian shirt as its coconut trees swayed above Finn's head. "The cards aren't going to keep dancing forever, you know," Jimmy V warned. "You don't bet them up, he's going to beat you, guaranteed."

"Betting them up isn't going to do him any good," Carl observed from the other side of the table.

"You know what, Carl?" Brian asked. "I have a feeling Finn's going to surprise you."

"I'm never surprised, Willow. When you're surprised, you forget to breathe."

"That's your problem, Carl," Jimmy V said. "You're never surprised and you have a big mouth."

"At least I wear my own clothes," Carl said.

"Too bad you wear them in other people's yards," Finn said, looking up from his cards. Finn appeared relaxed, but his stare sent a shudder through Carl.

"I don't know what you're talking about," Carl said. The first time he had peeked into Finn's black room, it had taken him nearly a minute to realize that the bedside lamp was turned on.

Erika had known the shape of Finn's shadow for a long time, but his remark to Carl had finally connected it to his feet. It was the shadow she had seen through Aaron Simon's garage window the night she'd been crying. A shadow bent toward the sound of her weeping like a divining rod toward water. So it belonged to Finn. "Who are you," she asked, "to accuse Carl of being a sneak?"

"Someone he's sneaked on," Finn said. Even Mrs. Tremmel was good for something.

The irony to Carl was that of all the people he had spied on, he had actually planned to pay a regular visit to Finn. But Finn's brother, Michael, was playing his guitar upstairs, each chord rocking the porch, and as a consequence, no one had heard Carl ring the doorbell. After ringing several times, he did what came naturally to him: he went around the side of the house and peeked in. All of a sudden an old lady with a sandpapery voice had begun to scream at him from a nearby balcony. Between the sound of her screaming and Michael's angry guitar, Carl would not have considered it odd to discover that he had stumbled upon a nursing home with a punk-rock group. Old people certainly had more to complain about than any of the punks Carl had met. Before he could figure out what to do, the old lady started throwing firecrackers off her balcony. The crazy bitch was trying to blow him up. "I deny it," Carl said. "I deny everything." When Finn shut the door to his black room, Carl thought, he might as well have been shutting himself in the trunk of a car. At least Finn's parents screamed out in the open. Carl's parents went in for costly analysis and secret shaves.

It all came down to one game of five-card draw. Martin Oakes dealt. Finn picked up his cards and slowly fanned them open: jack, four, ten, jack, jack. The first jack was holding a scroll. The second jack was strumming a harp. The third jack, the jack of spades, a palace guard, was holding a wooden staff with a knife blade tethered to either end. "Thirty," Finn said.

Martin Oakes matched the bet and offered a fifty-cent raise.

Jimmy V saw Finn's cards and silently begged him to bet them up. Only the jack of clubs was missing from Finn's hand. Finn already had the scholar, the minstrel, and the foot soldier. The jack of clubs was a knight. Jimmy V stared at the deck and wondered if the last jack was preparing to gallop out of it into Finn's hand. The jack of clubs was the best-dressed card in the deck. He held a red-and-white-striped lance in one hand, a two-horned jousting helmet in the other. Metal gauntlets extended to his elbows, and chain mail rose from his breastplate to the bottom of his chin. The jack of clubs' horse, mane braided neatly along his strong neck, had hard, battle-soaked eyes with lashes that appeared to have been singed by fire.

Jimmy V thought that if he had to be a card, he would want to be the jack of clubs.

"Call and raise," Finn said, putting another fifty cents into the pot.

More, Jimmy V pleaded silently behind Finn. Bet more.

"Up another fifty," Martin Oakes said.

"Call," Finn said.

Jimmy V squeezed his hands together behind his back. Finn should have raised again. Martin Oakes had approximately four dollars left. Three jacks gave Finn the opportunity to clean him out in one reckless hand. The jack of hearts would open his scroll and proclaim the rules of poker null and void. Finn would rise from his seat, victorious, and walk to the piano, where he would press down the pedal, releasing the felt-covered hammers, and pull the jack of diamonds across the piano strings. The jack of diamonds would turn the piano into a harp and fill the quiet poker studio with medieval sounds. The diamond minstrel's song would be peaceful, soothing. But when Finn substituted the jack of spades and his double-bladed staff, the piano strings would snap apart and spill over the piano's polished body, the music cut out of them. Without strings above it, the piano's pin block of hard rock maple would be just another piece of wood. Jimmy V could see all of this happening in his mind as clearly as he could see the boat that he and Carol Banetti were going to throw parties on in the Mediterranean.

"Come *on*, Finn," Jimmy V said.

Martin Oakes looked up at him in amazement. Aaron, Erika, and Carl stared across the table at him as if they were unsure they'd heard the exhortation.

"Shut up, Jimmy," Finn said. "All right? Do me a favor and shut up."

"I didn't say anything," Jimmy V protested, his upper body a tropical paradise.

"He wants to do it by himself, Jimmy," Brian said.

Penny knew that Finn was holding three face cards, but without her glasses, she couldn't tell if any of them matched. Without her glasses, the jacket Jim Beam was hiding in was just a blur against the far wall. Finn's chair vibrated with his desire to win, but Penny, her hand resting against the back of the chair, suddenly felt a tremendous and inexplicable lack of need. Her legs stopped shaking. The studio's stark colors softened. The poker chips clicked together politely like cups and saucers at a lawn party. The feeling lasted only a moment, but during that moment, Penny didn't need drink, didn't need family, didn't need sight, didn't need explanations, didn't need tears. She thought of the house in Martin Oakes's breathing exercises: curtains pulled back, doors and windows open, a clean breeze blowing through. She had always been able to imagine the house, but she had never been able to put herself in it. Even when she'd had a few drinks, it was difficult for Penny to believe that there was any consolation in emptiness.

Brian felt a burning sensation starting in his cheeks and looked away from Finn's hand. When he performed Martin Oakes's breathing exercises, he imagined a supermarket surrounded by automatic glass doors that whooshed open as his thoughts approached them. Like Jimmy V, Brian sensed that this was Finn's chance to do the impossible. He concentrated on pulling each breath down as far as he could, trying to make the supermarket doors whoosh open, afraid that he might instead please Carl by letting the small spots of color in his cheeks ripple outward until his face resembled the neon Citgo sign above Fenway Park. He wondered how Martin Oakes would behave if Finn cleaned him out. Ten dollars was not a great amount of money. But Martin Oakes's ten dollars was a fortune. Brian wasn't even sure Finn would be able to lift it.

Carl looked at Martin Oakes's cards, then took a side step to get a glimpse at what Jimmy V's hands were doing. Jimmy V turned, but not before Carl saw that his hands were clutched together. Jimmy V was praying behind his own back.

"Cards," Martin Oakes said.

"Two," Finn said, discarding his four and ten and resting his three jacks face down on the table. Martin Oakes flipped him two cards. Finn added them to the top of his jacks, so that his new cards would be the last he would see when he picked his hand up again.

"Dealer takes one," Martin Oakes said. He picked up his new card and slipped it into the middle of his hand. "Your bet, Finn."

Finn picked up his cards.

Jimmy V peered over his shoulder.

Brian continued to take deep breaths. His feet were solidly anchored to the floor. But his neck and arms and torso felt weightless. Brian recognized the feeling as the same giddy loss of gravity he had experienced several times after the first long climb up the rickety tracks of the roller coaster at Canobie Lake Park, poised at the crest of the first steep drop, sandwiched in the front car between his shrieking mother and grim-faced father, determined not to hold on when the car plummeted downward, but always changing his mind and grabbing on to the crossbar. Other people enjoyed the ride itself, but for Brian the most special moment was that feeling of weightlessness at the top.

Penny felt her thirst returning. But she didn't want Jim Beam. She needed a drink that would wash away the taste of warm champagne in the back of her throat. A potion that would make her beautiful.

Finn ticked the jack of spades aside with his thumb, revealing the jack of diamonds. He nudged the cards again, and the jack of hearts came into view. The second and third jacks were hidden except for the suit and the J in their upper left-hand corners. Finn paused for a moment, then gently pushed the jack of hearts aside. The first thing he saw was a club, and the pastel border that indicated he'd drawn a face card. But the letter under the club was a Q, not a J. Exhaling evenly, Finn slid the queen over. Again, a club, and the pastel border of a face card.

And under the club, a J.

It was the jack of clubs.

"How much is there in the pot?" Finn asked.

"Two twenty," Martin Oakes said.

"Two twenty to you," Finn said, pushing a stack of eight blue chips and two red chips toward the middle of the table.

In Finn's haste to make the maximum bet, his stack of chips toppled over. Penny thought of teacups breaking.

Erika and Aaron and Carl stood motionless behind Martin Oakes.

"See your two twenty," Martin Oakes said, voice without inflection, pushing the rest of his chips into the pot, "and raise you another two."

It was a moment the students never thought they would see. Martin Oakes without chips. Martin Oakes vulnerable.

Jimmy V looked into Martin Oakes's eyes and saw that they were green. A brilliant green, certainly, but finally identifiable as a color.

Penny put her glasses back on. Martin Oakes's face had always washed past her notice, elusive as driftwood. A smooth, weathered face without any recognizable origins. A face that might have spent a lot of time submerged. No discernible edges. No attachments. She knew it was there, but it was always what was around it that drew her attention. Under normal circumstances, he could mesmerize her with the continuous waterfall of cards in his left hand. But today was different. During his game with Finn, certain of his features had gradually become more distinct to her: the thick, dark hair, the strong definition of cheekbones, the slightly cruel mouth, and the uneven growth of stubble along his jawline. The cards he never stopped shuffling were no longer a fluid extension of his hand. Instead, they looked as if they were stuck to him. He could shake his hand and they wouldn't come off. With her glasses on, Penny saw him in clearer focus. He was someone she had never seen before, and it frightened her.

Meeting Penny's gaze from his chair on the other side of the table, it frightened him, too.

Finn counted out two dollars. "We can play for more if you want to, Mr. Oakes."

Martin Oakes said, "I appreciate the offer, Finn, but we probably shouldn't change the rules in the middle of the game." Penny stared hard at him and his eyes fixed on the warped reflection of himself in her glasses. He took in her slightly hunched shoulders, and the cruel expression she had formed with her mouth. She could have been his daughter.

"This is the end of the game," Finn said, calling the two-dollar bet.

"If you say so," Martin Oakes said, laying down four kings.

Finn did not spread his cards. The four jacks simply dropped out of his hand. The jack of hearts' scroll didn't open, the jack of diamonds' harp didn't play, and the jack of spades' double-bladed staff didn't cut.

Martin Oakes was still looking at Penny, and feeling a surge of pain at having lost her.

Jimmy V stared at the jack of clubs, the best-dressed card in the deck, and his horse with the battle-soaked eyes. Lying prone before the four monarchs that Martin Oakes had assembled, the jack of clubs looked as if he had decided to pick his fights more carefully than Finn did. The kings all had crowns and scepters. As the jack of clubs bowed before them, his mustache looked rather straggly, his chain-mail turtleneck and two-horned helmet seemed almost comical, and his red-and-white-striped lance stood like a barbershop pole next to his hair, which, when Jimmy V looked at it now, seemed in need of immediate maintenance.

Finn continued to hold his empty hands in front of his face. He could see Martin Oakes through them. He closed his fingers, reached down, and began to pull the deck together.

"Finn," Martin Oakes said, measuring his words carefully, keeping his voice neutral, "I would hope that if I've taught you anything, I've taught you not to show your cards unless you absolutely have to."

"Goddamn," Jimmy V said, Hawaiian shirt storming. "Goddamn it all to hell."

Finn couldn't speak.

Martin Oakes, eyes too bright to be seen again, composed himself and extended both arms to collect the pot.

Finn was certain he could identify which chips had been his as Martin Oakes pulled them away. His thumbprint still swirled across the rainbow-blue chips he had lost. Sixteen blues: too bad marking them didn't mean you could keep them. Martin Oakes never touched the tops or bottoms of the chips. He only touched the sides. Finn watched Martin Oakes stack his winnings—carefully, one chip at a time, filing the edges of each stack with his fingernail—and wondered if he was afraid to leave an impression on the surface of the chips. Perhaps he considered it bad luck.

Behind Martin Oakes, Carl closed his eyes and painted the walls of the poker studio black. "He almost had you."

Martin Oakes didn't turn around. "There are only forty-one possible hands that can beat four kings in a fifty-two-card deck, Mr. Rice. Forty-one hands out of over two and a half million."

"Who cares," Carl said.

"You don't have to care," Erika said, the sound of her own voice strange to her. "You just have to know the odds. The odds don't care, either."

"He almost took you, Mr. Oakes," Carl said. "We know it and you know it."

"His jacks might as well have been a pair of twos, Carl," Martin Oakes pointed out, "for all the good they did him."

Carl started toward Finn's side of the table.

"Don't you come over here," Jimmy V warned him.

Carl stood off to the side of the table by himself, oddly exposed, knees brittle, wispy yellow hair looking as though the slightest breeze could scatter it like dandelion seeds. Carl was used to being alone, but under normal circumstances the people he was watching couldn't watch him back.

"Let him," Brian said to Jimmy V.

"Finn?" Jimmy V asked.

"I don't care where he stands," Finn said.

"Don't worry about me," Carl said, but he had already taken another hopeful side step toward Finn.

"Suit yourself, Carl," Brian said.

"Five stud," Finn said, slapping the deck in front of Martin Oakes for the cut. "Deuces up are kill cards."

Martin Oakes tapped the top of the deck. "Deal them." He removed a handkerchief from his pocket and dabbed at his forehead.

Carl took another step. It was a long way to walk for such a short distance.

Penny hooked one of her arms in his and guided him the last few steps to the other side of the table. There was a little hitch in his walk. Brian smiled at him and said, "You do dip your hands, you know."

"Maybe I do," Carl admitted.

"You've still got enough left to make a game of it, Finn," Penny said, trying to encourage him.

Finn ignored her. On his third up card, he dealt himself a two and killed his hand. Carl shook his arm loose from Penny's and worked his way around to a position near Finn's shoulder. Jimmy V glared at him, but he kept coming. He couldn't stop.

Martin Oakes looked up and caught Brian smiling broadly at him. "Is there something you would like to say, Mr. Willoughby?" he asked.

"No," Brian said, trying to work his face into a scowl, feeling the scales tipping. Brian had a curious image of Martin Oakes, strong and placid above the table but light as air beneath it. Under the table, Martin Oakes's feet were rising. He was suspended in his chair at the top of a seesaw, thrashing his legs in the air but unable to bring his side back down to the ground—too light, somehow, to change the seesaw's direction, even though his chips were heavy as lead.

Martin Oakes said: "Even if you're not playing, Mr. Willoughby, you should practice staying under control."

"I know, sir," Brian said politely, but his smile continued to widen on its own, like a rip in a favorite old piece of clothing. There was nothing Brian could do about it. The harder he tried to frown, the faster the corners of his mouth twitched upward. Brian wondered if he'd caught something from Erika. Now that she'd stopped, he'd started.

But she hadn't stopped. "You neglected to point out," she said to Martin Oakes, a smile flickering across her face, "that there are only forty-three hands that can beat four jacks."

Aaron had a little dance step going. Finn looked up and wondered what Aaron was doing. Aaron wondered himself.

"We almost had you," Brian said, letting his smile go. If Finn had turned around to see the smile, he might have been reminded of one of the balloons Erika had set free over the playing field.

"What are you talking about, Willow?" Jimmy V asked him, pointing to Finn's slim pile of chips. "He's ruining us."

Finn heard the people behind him, but he didn't see them. He was too busy losing.

Martin Oakes saw that he had trained Finn well.

Finn saw nothing but the cards.

Martin Oakes saw the smiles breaking like waves behind Finn. The palm trees swayed on Jimmy V's shirt.

Finn felt nothing but the chips.

Don't you ever worry about what you're teaching them?

Finn tried to block out the strange song in his ears.

Aaron spun over to Finn's side of the table. He was breathing very hard and there were patches of sweat under his arms. He danced silently. Brian and Jimmy V nodded their heads as if they knew the beat.

"If you find you cannot restrain yourself, Mr. Simon," Martin Oakes said, "I'm afraid I'll have to ask that you wait for the others outside."

"Yes, sir," Aaron said solemnly. He didn't want to stop moving. He didn't want to think about being disloyal. A true samurai would kill himself before he would consider changing sides in the middle of a battle. Especially from the winning to the losing side.

Looking through the sliding glass door, Carl saw Jennifer Oakes appear in the kitchen window. A magnificent woman with perpetually wet hair. When he hadn't succeeded in discovering anything about Martin Oakes from the outside in, Carl tried spying on the house from the inside out. He considered it an experiment, but thus far it hadn't yielded any satisfactory results. Martin Oakes slept soundly and his wife wouldn't talk to Carl on the phone anymore.

Since he always called at precisely three in the morning, she didn't even have to say hello. Carl couldn't fathom why she still picked up the phone when she could just take it off the hook. He kept calling, listening for clues in her breathing, being careful not to breathe himself. No one else knew why Jennifer Oakes lurked in the kitchen window during poker class, pruning plants and rinsing dishes that were already clean in steaming water. But Carl assumed she was trying to figure out which one of them was placing the calls. He felt sorry for her, almost sorry enough to stop calling. What she saw when she looked out the kitchen window must have discouraged her: seven faces shaped into implacable masks by her husband, seven faces that showed nothing.

The masks were gone now.

Something terrible is happening, Jennifer thought. They're turning on him.

Carl stared at her.

Across the dark gulf of the backyard, Jennifer's eyes accused him. It's you, isn't it?

Carl nodded his head very slowly. It felt good to admit it.

Martin Oakes's eyes were waiting for Carl when he turned back to the table. Empty, three-o'clock-in-the-morning eyes, with perhaps just a touch of green in the almost transparent irises.

"Deal," Finn said.

It took Martin Oakes three more hands to win the rest of Finn's chips. Erika stood behind him, wanting to put her hand on his shoulder, wondering if he would recognize the curves her body hadn't developed yet when she walked over to the other side of the table. Martin Oakes's winning seemed as sad to her as Finn's losing. Better not to feel anything. Happiness and sorrow were equally unreliable.

Erika was starting to lose confidence in secrets. Better not to know them. After the Boston Celtics' most recent championship, her father had appeared at her door with gin on his breath and a briefcase in his hand, tie knotted three inches below the unbuttoned collar of his shirt. "Let's celebrate," he had said. They'd never rooted for the Celtics until Erika's grandmother had moved in and died on them; it was one of the legacies she'd left. Erika followed her father up to the cupola. He set the briefcase down and wrinkled his nose. As hard as Erika's mother scrubbed, she couldn't get the pigeon smell out of the room. Her father opened the briefcase. There was confetti inside. The individual twists of confetti expanded, slowly at first, then exploding like popcorn. Erika remembered thinking there was no way that much paper could fit into so small a briefcase. The confetti spilled over the sides of the case. Erika's father grabbed a handful, snaked his arm through one of the broken cupola windows, and gingerly tossed the confetti into the air. "Go, Celts," he said, eyes a bit glassy: too much fluorescent light at work, he claimed. The confetti fluttered down into the side yard, little twists of paper catching in the trees, the pigeons watching quietly from the rain gutters on the house next door. They seemed to know right away that the confetti wasn't edible. Only one of them even flew over to inspect it. "Do you miss her?" Erika asked. "Who?" he asked, but he knew whom she meant. Martin Oakes had once instructed Finn to tell his Megabucks story to the class, and Erika had calmly responded to it by informing them all that her grandmother—with the numbers 1-2-7-6 stamped as incontrovertible evidence on her arm—had participated in a lottery where the odds for being chosen were much more favorable, and much more frightening. "I hope they can't read," her father said. Erika frowned. "The pigeons," he explained. He pointed to the confetti and chuckled to himself. For someone who was supposed to be celebrating, he sounded rather wistful. "These documents are top secret. I took them out of the paper shredder at work." He grabbed some more confetti from the pile. "Strictly confidential, Erika." Out the window it went. "Think of it as our secret celebration." Erika put her hand on his shoulder. "Oh, Daddy." "Don't *oh Daddy* me," he said. He threw confetti out the window. His arm caught a shard of glass when he threw it. A ribbon of blood popped up on his arm. He rolled up his sleeve. The wound was shallow and the blood didn't spread. "It's your mother's influence," he told Erika, holding her head to his shoulder, his free hand still kneading the pile of confetti. "I even bleed neat."

Finn lost interest in his cards as soon as he saw her coming.

Erika walked over to Finn's side of the table. There may have been a secret in the game Finn and Martin Oakes had played, but as far as she was concerned, it had already been shredded.

Finn had trouble bringing her into focus. Set next to Erika and her snowy braid, the queens in Martin Oakes's medieval deck of cards were nothing but pathetic handmaidens. As she approached, his concentration unwound like a spell he had cast over himself. A touch from her could cure him.

She had magnificent posture. But she walked uncertainly, reluctant to leave Martin Oakes and unfamiliar with the feeling that she belonged with the others, that somehow they all belonged together. It was a wonderful feeling, but very strange.

Sometimes even the sad things were worth celebrating.

Penny, the first to throw her support to Finn, saw in

Erika's joining them the opportunity to form a new group. They could call it "The Top Seven." It was unlikely they would be able to harmonize together worth a damn, but they could play some mean hands of poker.

Erika met Penny's appraising glance and had the sudden, ridiculous notion of embracing her. Instead, she turned and stood next to Finn. Right in front, where she was used to singing in the youth chorus. Aaron danced behind her.

Martin Oakes was on his own now. He stared at the combination of the six students behind Finn: Penny – Brian – Jimmy V – Carl – Aaron – Erika.

With ten dollars, Finn had finally bought himself a winning ticket. Martin Oakes hunched forward in his chair, the creases beneath his cheekbones deepening, his skin chalky, his mouth dry and inflexible, his eyes admitting to a stark and sudden green.

"Your bet," Finn said quietly.

Martin Oakes faced them. They really were a splendid pack of misfits. He was almost certain he hadn't meant to keep them that way. He lifted his chin in wonder at their coming together. A smiling jury, assembled not to prove his guilt but to confirm their own innocence. It all seemed mathematical somehow. Finn had hit upon a simple proof, as elegant in its way as Martin Oakes's decision to wait out Smooth Jake. An instinct that had helped him see through to the one habit that stamped Martin Oakes as an unmistakable adult. Martin Oakes had fallen into the habit of playing it safe, keeping his lost suppleness a secret to himself by getting fat on the cinch games. What had he risked since playing Smooth Jake? He couldn't think of the last time he had really tested himself. Testing himself hadn't even occurred to him. His students formed the upper half of a circle around Finn, stretching once again into a collective frown, but their eyes were bright and their mood was merry.

"Twenty to you, Finn," Martin Oakes said, betting the exact amount Finn had left.

"Call."

"Three tens."

Finn pitched his cards toward the deck. "You win. I won't come back."

Erika put her hand on Finn's shoulder.

Martin Oakes left the last chips in the middle of the table. He didn't really want the game to end, but as soon as he touched the chips it would be over. So he left them alone. By now, they had been handled by gunfighters and rough-necks and prairie marshals and liquored-up brokers and stone-fingered surgeons and cheating teenagers and even Smooth Jake himself. Perhaps they had been handled enough. Martin Oakes glanced up from the table and felt the energy his students created by standing together. Thanks to him, they possessed hardly any of the acquired caution and nervousness of their parents. At least not yet. They were sharks. Now it was his turn to be tested. It was a natural consequence of their coming together. Someone had to face them. The prospect didn't frighten him. He expected it to happen.

But when he stood up, they looked through him, if they looked at him at all.

He couldn't find the slightest reflection of himself in Finn's smile.

Penny, glasses down at the tip of her nose, was whispering something in Aaron's ear. Aaron's legs still hadn't stopped moving. Jimmy V was laughing and combing his hair and looking as if he might be planning his next clothing heist. Carl was in the middle of the pack, letting his shoulders bump against the others as they swirled around him, obviously amazed to be one of them. Brian's eyes were closed, but his neck was proud and straight, and there was a faraway, contented look on his face.

No one looked at Martin Oakes.

He was just another adult now.

He was invisible.

Finally, Erika drew a breath—a deep, practiced, poker-playing breath—and stepped forward. For a moment, Martin Oakes thought she was actually going to cut loose with a song. But she spoke instead: "I don't think I will be coming back, either." Her tone of voice was friendly. There was a warmth in it that he hadn't detected before. Her smile refused to judge him.

Finn, still feeling the imprint of Erika's hand on his shoulder, rose from the table and put on his jacket, then picked up his books and opened the door to leave. When he flew down the steps, he pulled them along after him. Carl, Jimmy V, Brian, Erika, and Aaron rose up behind him with the certainty of kites above a park on a clear day with an even breeze.

"One hand!" Jimmy V said, laughing cordially and shaking his head, wishing he could conjure up the end of the game again behind his velvet sleeping mask and fix it for Finn. "One hand goes the other way and he beats you!"

Only Penny stayed behind. She didn't look as happy as the others.

Martin Oakes felt the tightness building in his temples.

Penny turned back halfway down the steps. Martin Oakes was standing on the porch. He could see that she was resisting the urge to run and join the rest of the group. She took the charred half-heart out of her pocket. "Here," she said, holding it out to him. "Something for the trophy case."

He smiled at her, but he didn't take the heart. The cap of her whiskey bottle was visible above the zipper on her inside jacket pocket. "You keep it," he said.

"I wish he'd really beaten you," she said. The heart disappeared into her palm.

Martin Oakes wanted to reach out and hug her, even if her bottle came between them. But instead of moving toward her, he backed up a step. "You saw what happened."

Penny peered up the walk toward Finn. Finn moved gracefully, stride confident and measured, arms swinging relaxed at his side. The other students followed him. Aaron ran in elliptical orbits around the group. Brian was patting Carl on the back. Carl's head nodded up and down. Erika walked next to Finn, thick braid slapping proudly against her back. Jimmy V was waving his arms so hard Penny thought the coconuts might fall off his shirt. "You mean *that?*" she asked Martin Oakes.

Martin Oakes nodded.

"Won't last," Penny said.

"What does?" Martin Oakes asked.

She took off after them.

Martin Oakes walked down to the last step of the porch. It was completely dark. He could smell wood burning and hear the sound of laughter as his class swept down the hill toward Lexington Center. Then the sound of glass breaking. Penny's bottle had fallen out of her jacket. She just kept running. Streetlights marked her progress until she disappeared around a banked turn. She ran gracefully. The neighbor across the street was trimming his hedges. Some people were always raking their leaves or trimming their hedges or slapping a new coat of paint on their garages. Martin Oakes wondered where they got the energy.

He ran his hand along the side of the house. His eyes knew the surface but it was unfamiliar to his hands. His gait was stiff-legged and gangly, the way he imagined a colt must feel when it first struggles to its feet: old enough to know what it's supposed to do, but lacking the facility to do it yet. What, Martin Oakes wondered, could be left for him to explore? He tested the soft earth with the heel of his shoe and paused to hook a loose window shutter back into place. Clumps of leaves had formed against the sides of the porch. The pine trees behind the studio blended together in the darkness, defining a gentle polygraph across the sky. He remarked to himself how strange it was to think of a simple batch of trees that way. The only story they could tell was a chronological one: which had been planted sooner and which later, which had caught the light, which had been forced to struggle in the shadows. Maybe there was such a thing as chance. It was easier to think so outside. He could hear something moving on the matted needles beneath the trees: a large cat, or perhaps a raccoon. Staring at the jagged tree line, he had a vague desire to step out of himself, to shed all at once what had taken Smooth Jake years to grow out of layer by layer, to leave the dried, brittle shell of the reputation he'd built behind him, to sharpen himself into a sleeker package, to navigate in the darkness, to take Jennifer dancing, to form something new.

He lit a cigarette and mounted the steps to the poker studio, the emptiest room in the house, its door open, a chill autumn wind blowing through. He entered the studio and pulled the door shut after him. Warm air gently lifted the posters on the walls. Martin Oakes looked at the cards and chips scattered on the table, thought about putting them away, and decided he wouldn't bother. He walked over to the piano and played the first few bars of a Chopin Nocturne without sitting down, just enough to confirm the lack of coordination he felt in his fingers.

There was a pile of unopened letters on his desk in the corner of the room. Four of the letters were from parents who had enclosed their children's résumés. He put them aside. Two were requests for interviews. Martin Oakes had done one interview. That was enough. He opened a letter that contained a check and a photocopied bill of sale for a Porsche. He knew he could have got more for the car, but he hadn't really expected the man he'd won it from to be any better at negotiating a sales transaction than he was at playing poker. The last letter, postmarked Reno, was from a player named Caswell whom Martin Oakes had just begun to hear about. Caswell, in formal but unmistakably aggressive language, proposed a game. Martin Oakes found a pin and stuck the letter to the wall. He felt an odd sort of smile poking up at the corners of his mouth. Oh, yes, some interesting possibilities lay ahead of him. *You are going to have four aces on every hand.* Caswell probably wouldn't be willing to play for his stakes. But he'd never know unless he asked.

There was another letter Martin Oakes wanted to read. He poked through the desk drawers until he found it. It was more than four years old now. It had come from Sam Kim with a check for ten thousand dollars and a promise to devote less time to his business and more time to his son Tom:

When I spoke with Tom's karate instructor, he told me a story about one of the men he studied with on Okinawa. The foundation of the Goju-ryu style is a form called sanchin, in which the student's breathing must be carefully synchronized with a series of slow-motion hand strikes. To strengthen their legs, some Okinawans walk around with cinder blocks on their feet. They also make their own dumbbells by inserting steel pipes into thick cardboard tubes and filling the tubes with cement. Once the cement hardens, they can hold the steel pipes during sanchin to strengthen their arms and shoulders while they practice the form.

Well, Martin, for this particular student, cinder-block shoes and cement-filled arm weights were not enough. His goal was to make the tips of his fingers so strong that his shuto could penetrate an opponent like a knife. So he got a bucket and filled it with buckshot. When he had nothing else to do, he would sit in a chair with the bucket between his legs and thrust each hand into the buckshot, rigid fingers pointing downward, each strike crunching into the lead pellets. His fingers got stronger and stronger, until he could sink his whole forearm into the bucket with the force of each blow. What he didn't know was that the lead in the buckshot had entered his bloodstream through his fingertips, and was slowly poisoning him. Eventually, he went blind. His hands were like knives, but they were no stronger than yours or mine because without his sight, all he could strike was the air, and air is easy to cut.

It is with the deepest sorrow and the deepest shame that I must admit to having taken a similar approach to business.

In Oriental cultures, it would be considered somewhat unusual for a father to learn an important lesson from his son, especially at a cost of ten thousand dollars. But I must face what Tom has taught me.

Thank you for what you have taught him.

Martin Oakes folded Sam Kim's letter, put it back in its envelope, and rose from his desk. There were four switches for the track lights. When he had turned them off, he walked over to the sliding glass door. He held a deck of cards in his left hand, but he didn't shuffle it. The glass door needed cleaning. It was nice to be in the dark. He could move around in the dark and it wasn't really like hiding. Embers crackled in the potbellied stove. A slant of light danced out and he caught the reflection of Finn's crumpled ten-dollar bill on the table behind him. Across the yard, in the kitchen window, Jennifer was rinsing dishes. Steam billowed up from the sink. Jennifer's hair was damp. Her face was calm and blank, but it looked as if there were tears in her eyes. Martin Oakes wasn't sure. It could have been the steam. He was suddenly very tired. He leaned forward, palms pressed against the glass, and waited in the dark for her to look up at him.

A NOTE ABOUT THE AUTHOR

Conall Ryan, born in 1958, is the author of *Black Gravity*, a mystery nominated for the Edgar Allan Poe Award in 1985. Mr. Ryan works for a computer firm in California and lives in Palo Alto with his wife and two daughters.

A NOTE ON THE TYPE

This book was set in a digitized version of Bodoni Book, which was named after Giambattista Bodoni (1740–1813), son of a printer of Piedmont. After gaining experience and fame as superintendent of the Press of the Propaganda in Rome, in 1768 Bodoni became the head of the ducal printing house at Parma, which he soon made the foremost of its kind in Europe. His *Manuale Tipografico,* completed by his widow in 1818, contains 279 pages of type specimens, including alphabets of about thirty languages. His editions of Greek, Latin, Italian, and French classics are celebrated for their typography. In type designing he was an innovator, making his new faces rounder, wider, and lighter, with greater openness and delicacy, and with sharper contrast between the thick and thin lines.

Composed by ComCom, a Division of The Haddon Craftsmen, Inc., Allentown, Pennsylvania. Printed and bound by R. R. Donnelley & Sons, Harrisonburg, Virginia. Designed by Julie Duquet.